The Firefighter's Heartwish

Heartwishes, Volume 3

Daisy Dexter Dobbs

Published by Department of Daydreams, LLC, 2022.

THE FIREFIGHTER'S HEARTWISH

First edition. July 26, 2022.

Copyright © 2022 Daisy Dexter Dobbs.

ISBN: 978-1587850851

Written by Daisy Dexter Dobbs.

Dedication

This book is earnestly dedicated to victims of child abuse, those who survived (and hopefully thrived), as well as those who didn't. As a survivor myself, this tender subject matter is especially close to my heart. While I wholeheartedly long for adults to stop abusing innocent children, as an optimistic realist I know that's not feasible. Alternately, I wish for all abused children to be able to connect with kind, caring individuals who can offer help and protection; and for those kids to learn coping mechanisms to help them reach adulthood with as few lasting emotional scars as possible. The Firefighter's Heartwish, just like all of my books, concludes with a satisfying happily ever after. Combined with the inevitable pain that comes with abuse, this story is lavish with soul-deep love, joy, hope, and the wondrous, healing power of humor. I so enjoyed adding some special heavenly intervention in the form of little Harold's angel as I crafted the rewarding ending. My greatest wish is for happy endings to be the case in real life for all those whose lives have been touched by physical and emotional abuse.

ABOUT THIS BOOK

~<>~

Isolated for months in Antarctica, amid icebergs, glaciers, and his own dark thoughts, glaciologist and part-time firefighter Gard Malone returns home, grumpy and craving more solitude.

Gutted by the tragic accident that took the life of his best friend, Gard blames himself for failing to save him. Surrounded by well-intentioned friends and family determined to brighten his spirits, he just wants to be left alone.

Brooding over coffee at the café, he hears a young boy singing a Christmas carol about "Hark," his special angel. Little Harold's mistaken song lyrics force a smile from the stoic Gard, expanding as he spots his server, a stunning redhead with the same big blue eyes as Harry.

Thankful she found the courage to leave her sadistic husband and move across the country, back to her hometown, Sabrina Hanklen feels confident she and Harry are safe. Harry's stuttering and developmental delay are the direct result of his father's cruelty.

Working as a server in her sister's café, she's distracted by the ruggedly handsome customer responding to her son in a kind, patient manner. Sabrina can't help wondering what life would be like with a good man like Gard in their lives.

Unfortunately, her idyllic daydreams are shattered by the sudden arrival of the one person she never wants to see again.

Heartwishes, Book 3: A grumpy knight in shining armor, fiercely brave heroine mom, precious little boy, beloved dog, heavenly angel, drama, humor, and an incredible Christmas miracle. This guaranteed HEA contemporary romance can be read as a standalone but is better appreciated when read in order.

Content Warning: contains scenes of child and domestic abuse.

Chapter 1

~<>~

"HANG ON, TIM. I've got you. I won't let go." Coiling the rope around one hand and arm, Gard Malone held the cord tight with both hands, determined not to let his closest friend fall to his death. "Wally's getting an extra rope so you can prusik up the second line."

"Can't do it, Gard. Feels like both legs and one of my arms are broken. Can't really move... back might be broken too. I'm hanging here like a damn, useless rag doll."

Hearing the extent of Tim's injuries, Gard shuddered. Tim was so far down the yawning crevasse Gard couldn't see him. He could barely even hear him.

"Can you see a ledge?"

"Nothing," Tim answered. "There's no support. Just a straight drop."

As experienced glaciologists, Gard and his crew knew the importance of avoiding falls. More importantly, they knew it was easier to stay out of Antarctica's crevasses than to rescue someone from one of the icy, yawning chasms.

Nonetheless, Tim McKevitt had plummeted deep into a crevasse. Hidden beneath a thin bridge of blown snow only a few inches thick, the fissure had been invisible and the bridge wouldn't support the weight of a man.

"Stay with me, buddy. We'll get you out of there," Gard promised. "Jack and Tom are on the way with more rescue gear."

Gard felt a hand on his shoulder. "Gard, the lip of the crevasse looks ready to collapse at any moment," their fellow glaciologist,

1

Wally, warned him in a subdued voice not loud enough for Tim to hear. "Tim's too far down. It's too dangerous. We'll lose both of you."

"Damn it, Wally, I've got to save him. If we don't get him out of there soon hypothermia's going to set in." They'd radioed the other two members of the crew at the research station, apprising them of the dire situation. Gard prayed they got there in time to help haul Tim out because he didn't know how much longer he could hold Tim's weight.

"Jesus, look at your hands," Wally noted.

Friction from the rope had torn through Gard's two pairs of gloves, leaving him with bloodied hands. Gard could tell his shoulder was dislocated and he had other injuries, but tending to his own wounds would have to wait. If he eased up on his hold he'd lose Tim.

They'd all worn proper safety equipment, including crash helmets and full body harnesses, tied to heavy ropes as well as to each member of the trekking team which, in this case, amounted to only Gard and Tim. With a broken arm and rib due to an equipment accident, Wally wasn't able to assist in holding Tim's weight.

Tim's fall was stopped by the ropes before he reached the bottom of the crevasse. The problem with this cavity was its boundless depth and lack of ledges or footholds of any kind. Without Tim having a foothold, Gard held Tim's full dead weight as the man hung suspended.

There was only one thing Gard thought of that might help at this point. "Wally, you think you can help me build an anchor so I can transfer Tim's weight and rappel down?"

"Yeah, I think so. But you can't—"

"I'm going to anchor and rappel down, Tim," Gard called down the chasm.

"No!" Tim hollered. "Too dangerous. Listen, Gard, I'm—"

The horrific sound of Tim shouting out as he slid further down the icy crevasse, along with the snapping sound of cracking ice, chilled Gard to his marrow. Tim's deep cry of anguish grew more distant as he fell.

"Tim?" Dead silence. "Tim! Don't give up, man, I'm not going to let you die, you hear me? I'm going to get you out of there."

"It's no use. I'm done, Gard," Tim called from what seemed like miles away. "The rope was sliced on the last fall...not going to hold. Love you, buddy. Don't blame yourself. Tell Laila I love her and—"

The sound of Tim McKevitt falling deep into the abyss was bloodcurdling.

"Tim! Tim, hold on, I've got you!"

But Gard didn't have him. All he held in his torn hands now was a weightless length of rope...with no one attached at the other end.

"I've got you, Tim, I've got you!" Gard yelled, abruptly sitting, snapping to attention from his deep sleep and the same nightmare he'd had frequently for the last three years. Drenched in sweat, he raised his knees, resting his elbows on them as he cradled his head in his hands.

His mind still gauzy from sleep, he growled his anguish from the depth of his soul, blaming himself for being unable to save the life of his best friend and his sister's fiancé.

"Home...Glassfloat Bay..." Gard muttered to himself as a reminder. "I'm here...I'm here..."

Plowing his fingers through his hair, he expelled a deep breath, glancing at the pills on his nightstand, one bottle to control anxiety and the other for pain. He kept them there just in case. There were times he was tempted to pop a couple of pills, but he hated resorting to them. They didn't do much to ease his pain or anxiety anyway, unless he took the maximum dosage at least. He'd learned early on that the more he took, the more he needed to get the same effect.

For a guy who disliked polluting his body with something as innocuous as aspirin or ibuprofen, Gard knew prescription meds weren't the answer. Developing a dependency on pills would only create more problems.

His best buddy chose that moment to leap onto the bed, eagerly nuzzling Gard with his wet nose.

"Hey, Tundra, how's my boy? Happy to be back home and out of that bone chilling cold, I'll bet, huh?" He mussed the dog's short black and tan fur and patted his flanks. Tundra went everywhere with Gard, even on his assignments to Antarctica. This last job was a four month stint. They'd been home for a week now. Having Tundra at his side while he was healing from his injuries three years ago and climbing out of the depths of despair, had helped Gard every bit as much as the medication the hospital docs had pumped into him.

Gard's gaze slid to the digital alarm clock. It was five thirty. "Looks like you've decided it's a good time for our morning run." Tundra answered with a long lick up the side of Gard's face. The sizeable canine came from a long line of oversized mutts. It was the family joke that their dogs were part German Shephard, part donkey.

Catching a glimpse of himself in the bathroom mirror as he brushed his teeth, Gard made note of his shaggy appearance. His blond hair was well overdue for a cut and the scruffy stubble across his cheeks and chin made him look like a bum. If it were up to him he'd just let the hair and beard grow wild but then he'd be hounded by his mother who'd be convinced he looked like a bum because he was depressed. Maybe she was right. But the last thing he wanted was to do anything that might trigger her motherly scrutiny.

Once outside Bekka House, the family home, Gard jogged the half-mile to the ocean, his faithful dog keeping pace beside him. Along the way he noticed Bekka House was the only place without holiday lights twinkling against the pre-dawn indigo sky. He smiled, recalling how the people in town wasted no time getting fully into the holiday spirit. There was no escaping Christmas in Glassfloat Bay.

It was two days after Thanksgiving. In the past, the day after Thanksgiving marked the annual Malone family Christmas decorating frenzy. He and his entire family would pull out all stops to decorate every nook and cranny, inside and out, of the main family home as well as the homes of everyone else in the family. But yesterday he skipped it. All he'd wanted to do was hole up and pretend it was just like any other day of the year. He used to love Christmas but the holiday had lost its luster for him.

His sister, Laila, told him decorations started popping up at the mall right after Halloween this year. Santa had arrived the first week of November, complete with an elaborate setup including pricey photos with Santa as well as T-shirts and other products for sale.

"That's crazy," he said as he ran. "Next thing you know Santa will be sharing space with the Easter Bunny." The money-grubbing aggrandizement of what used to be a joyous, family-oriented time of year disgusted him.

Even so, he knew he needed to get some damn lights strung before his parents and siblings arrived en masse, wearing their godawful Christmas sweaters knitted by his yarn-happy sister Maureen, and gleefully encouraging him to get into the Christmas spirit. He could picture them all singing carols as his brother-in-law, Varik, strummed his guitar.

His mom, Astrid, would have her trusty, decades-old Kodak Instamatic camera in hand, snapping away to memorialize the family gathering just as she did each holiday...and pretty much any other time the opportunity for picture-taking arose. She vastly preferred *real photographs* you could touch and put in a photo album, to those from a phone.

They'd pass cups of eggnog, spiked cocoa, and hot mulled wine while making merry, threading popcorn, baking ginger cookies, and decorating the family house from top to bottom.

And every one of them would be focused on making Gard feel better.

God how he hated that.

As much as he loved his family, being around them all for Thanksgiving dinner two nights ago was tough. So many questions, so much concern, endless hugs and kisses and positive, encouraging words.

It felt overwhelming, smothering, invasive.

And then there was all the well-intentioned nudging about Gard finding a good woman for himself, along with a full roster of suggestions of all the single prospects in Glassfloat Bay as well as neighboring Wisdom Harbor. He wasn't interested. Not only was getting involved in another relationship not at the top of his list of priorities, it didn't even make the list. He was perfectly happy being a bachelor. Good old loyal Tundra was the only companion he needed.

The best part of Thanksgiving was seeing Laila so happy with her husband, Zak, and their baby twins, his niece and nephew, Abby and Gus. For the past three years it had been damned hard looking her in the face after he'd failed to save her fiancé. Of course, Laila would never blame him for what happened. Neither did anyone else he knew...but that didn't make it any easier for Gard, who still shouldered a weighty sense of responsibility and guilt for the loss of Tim's life.

Fortunately his sister, Kady, was supposed to be arriving from her overseas backpacking trip soon. That should help take the focus off Gard. His globetrotting little sister had left on her latest trip shortly after moving from Chicago to Glassfloat Bay so the family would be scrambling to show her the town. She'd be staying in one of the bedrooms at Bekka House but Kady usually kept pretty much to herself so Gard wouldn't have to worry too much about endless chitchat.

With each footfall, he watched the gentle morning waves roll in and out. Relaxing. Hypnotic. Meditative. A helluva lot better than trudging through the snow in his hometown of Chicago, or freezing his ass off in Antarctica.

"I've got to get my shit together and stop being the poster boy for the anguished," he decided.

Gard remembered a time when he was fully on board with all the Christmas jollity. He bought into the magic of it all, loved seeing the awed looks on kids' faces waiting in line to sit on Santa's lap. Heck, he was even Glassfloat Bay Mall's Santa the year before the Antarctica tragedy. Sure it was hot as hell under all the padding necessary to puff out his lean muscled frame but how could he mind when he saw the kids' joy and excitement?

Back then, the Christmas spirit boldly had Gard in its grip as he enjoyed being in charge of spicing and spiking the anticipated wassail and eggnog.

But now? Now he'd much rather escape into a good first-person shooter videogame than be bothered by all the frivolity.

"Jeez...I've turned into Scrooge. Or is it the Grinch? Probably both. Yeah, no doubt about it, I've become the Scrinch."

Focus...he needed to focus on the moment. It was one of the tips he'd learned from his sessions with the therapist. He'd resisted therapy, convinced it was for weaklings and losers who were looking for excuses; for somewhere or someone to place blame rather than accept responsibility for their own decisions. Once it became clear he wouldn't be able to get his well-meaning mother and stepfather off his back, Gard finally agreed to see a psychologist who worked as a counselor at Wisdom Harbor University.

He could admit today, albeit grudgingly, that his mom and stepdad were right. The twice a month therapy sessions, which were unlike anything he'd expected, had made a positive difference. He only wished he'd started them earlier.

Just let the anxiety go, like sand sifting through your fingers until it's all adrift in the wind, Dr. Rikard Svenningsen told him. Gard did just that, paying attention to the birth of a new day. There was nothing as majestic as dawn, when the sun climbed over the horizon, painting the sky with swashes of pink, gold and purple as it rose to greet the day...unless it was the magic of a Northwest Pacific coastline sunset.

Ever vigilant and well-trained by his mom and sisters, Gard kept his eyes open for glass floats, agates, and sand dollars as he leapt over driftwood logs on the way to the shore. He'd been lucky to find a host of objects for their collections on his early morning runs.

A moment later Tundra took off, happily chasing a pack of cawing seagulls cruising and diving in search of breakfast. Breathing the salty air as he watched his dog romp in the wet sand, Gard felt the last vestiges of his nightmare dissipate.

"Home...Glassfloat Bay. I'm here...I'm here..." Gard again muttered his helpful mantra, designed to help keep him in the here and now.

Running in the sand with the early morning breeze in his hair and the waves softly crashing along the shore made him feel alive. Cleansed. Even hopeful. Dwarfed by the rising sun, he smiled, remembering to give thanks for being alive and able to experience the magnificence of dawn.

"Yeah, this is far better medicine than any damn pills."

Ever his loyal pal, the returning Tundra agreed with a companionable bark.

~<>~

"You haven't heard a thing I've said."

"That's nice, dear."

"Varik!" Delaney Jenssen rapped her knuckles on the table, rattling the vintage Santa and Mrs. Claus ceramic salt and pepper shakers she'd recently found at a church rummage sale.

Her husband blinked, almost looking surprised that his wife sat across the kitchen table from him. "I'm sorry, hon, I guess I was distracted. Did you say something?"

"I was asking why you've been sitting there staring into space while twisting that ring on your finger for the last twenty minutes. Your poached eggs must be ice cold by now. Sweetheart, is something wrong?"

"No. No, it's just that..." Varik gazed up at Delaney who was sipping her coffee. "Gard's been on my mind lately."

"My brother?" Delaney's shoulders slumped as she lowered her mug. "Me too." She worried her bottom lip while twisting her napkin. "I'm afraid he'll never be the same. All this time and he still blames himself for Tim's death."

"I know." Varik nodded, expelling a lengthy breath. "I worry about him too. He's been working so hard without a break for too long, no doubt to help keep his mind off the accident."

"If he's not out there in that frozen wasteland," Delaney said, "freezing his butt off for humanity, doing whatever the heck it is that's apparently so damned important for global warming, Gard's here risking his life as a firefighter, picking up anyone's shift who asks."

She looked up from wringing her hands. "I-I'm almost afraid my brother has a death wish the way he takes on one dangerous duty after another."

"Don't think like that, Delaney." Varik reached across the table, patting his wife's hand. "Your brother has problems but he's not that screwed up."

Delaney wasn't so sure. After failing to save the life of Laila's fiancé, Gard had been plagued with nightmares. That is, when he could sleep at all. The doctors said he was suffering from PTSD. During the treacherous rescue attempt, Gard nearly died himself, sustaining serious injuries in the process that kept him hospitalized for a small eternity.

"He'd probably be a lot further along if he hadn't been so stubborn about seeing a therapist," Delaney said.

"True, but at least he finally agreed to see Dr. Svenningsen. I think his appointments have made a big difference, don't you?"

"I do. Laila and Reen think so too." Delaney nodded. "Rikard's given Gard some excellent advice. I'm glad Tore recommended him—and thankful as all hell that Gard finally agreed to start seeing him. Seriously, that brother of mine can be so stubborn!"

"Just like his sister." Varik snickered while Delaney lifted an eyebrow. "When Tore told me Svenningsen counsels the professors as well as the students at WHU," Varik gave a thumbs up, "I knew he was the one. The fact that my colleague is a fellow Norwegian didn't hurt either."

"Naturally." Delaney gave him a knowing smile. She was thankful Gard thought the world of Tore Thorkelson, Varik's cousin and their mom's second husband.

Absently watching her vintage black cat wall clock with its moving eyes and swinging tail, her thoughts returned to that awful time more than three years ago.

To no one's surprise, Gard had gone above and beyond in his attempt to save Laila's fiancé. He came home with badly torn hands, a broken arm, dislocated shoulder, three broken ribs and injuries to his spine and legs. At least he'd made it home alive. It was during his hospitalization, when Gard was still in critical condition, that his fiancée, Joanne—just the thought of her made Delaney bristle—left him for another man, claiming she didn't feel strong enough to cope with Gard's multitude of physical or emotional wounds.

"You're thinking about Joanne again," Varik said, taking Delaney by surprise.

"How did you know?"

"You get that certain narrow-eyed look when she's on your mind." He chuckled. "It was three years ago. You need to let go, Delaney. How can you expect Gard to get over what happened if you can't?"

"I know, I know." Delaney sighed. "It's just that every time I think about how she was cheating on my brother when he was working so hard in Antarctica to make money for that monstrously expensive wedding she wanted..." She growled her annoyance. "And then that lame excuse she gave about being unfaithful because she hated being alone," she said, imitating Joanne's sorrowful voice, "ugh! I swear, Varik, I want to punch her lights out." Delaney's eyes narrowed again as she folded her arms across her chest. "Selfish little bitch."

"You won't get any argument from me." Varik rubbed his wife's arm. "Just remember it was far better for Gard to find out Joanne was a self-centered two-timer, *before* rather than after they were married."

"Amen. Talk about a nightmare." Delaney shuddered. "Can you imagine having her as our sister-in-law? The thought makes my skin crawl."

Varik rose from the table to dump out his cold coffee and pour himself and Delaney a fresh cup. "I've heard around town that Joanne's got her sights set on Hudson Griffin."

"What?" Delaney bristled. "Well I'm just going to have to have a talk with Hud to let him know what—"

"You'll do no such thing my little Vengeance Queen." Standing behind Delaney, Varik enveloped her in his arms, kissing the top of her head. "Hud and Gard are good friends. He knows what Joanne did. He's not about to forget what she put your brother through."

"Yes but men don't always think with their brains," she pointed out. "And don't bother denying it because we both know it's true."

"I wouldn't dream of denying it." He leaned further to give Delaney a kiss on the cheek while snaking his hand down the front of his wife's nightshirt. "In fact my second brain is contemplating the two of us going back to bed and—"

"There, you see?" Delaney slapped Varik's hand away. "Typical man." She tsked while pointing a chastising finger. "How you can shift from discussing poor Gard's PTSD to us making whoopee just like that," she snapped her fingers, "is beyond me. Women's brains don't work that way, so you can just forget about it, Romeo."

"What can I say? Guilty as charged." Varik's gentle laughter filled the kitchen's eating area. "Trust me," he gave her another kiss on the cheek as he whisked away Delaney's breakfast plate, "Joanne won't be getting her hooks into Hudson."

"I hope not."

"And your *poor brother*," he hung quotes around the phrase, "is a grown man who can take care of himself just fine without all his sisters incessantly mollycoddling him. Now finish your coffee and get dressed," Varik went on, ignoring his wife's indignant gasp. "We promised Laila we'd get over to her bakery this morning to help get the place decorated for Christmas."

"Christmas..." Delaney was silent for a long moment. "You know, we've barely seen Gard since he's been home. Did you see how quickly he snuck out after Thanksgiving dinner the other night? And he didn't participate in the annual family decorating festivities yesterday either. I think he's avoiding us." Varik muttered something beneath his breath. "What was that?"

"Nothing, dear."

"Gard can't keep this pace up, Varik. He needs some downtime...preferably with his family, to remind him of the closeness we share, the love we all have for him. Otherwise I worry something will happen to him, being as overtired as he must be. It's like he's daring the universe to stop him." Used to being optimistic and positive, Delaney hated hearing herself sound so fragile and negative.

"I promise, everything's going to be okay." Varik's voice brimmed with assurance.

"You're just saying that to make me feel better. I know you're just as worried as I am." Filled with hope mixed with melancholy, Delaney sighed.

"I wasn't just trying to placate you." Varik's smile was broad and genuine. "I meant it. Things are about to change for Gard."

Delaney slanted her head in question.

The sound of their baby girl's cry distracted them both.

"I'll get her," Varik said. He was back in a few minutes, cradling little Rebekka Anders Jenssen while gently nudging her chubby cheeks and making baby talk colored by his Norwegian accent.

Delaney smiled. Her husband adored their child and definitely had a way with the baby. He knew just what to do to calm her and stop her fussing. They'd named their daughter after Delaney's grandma, Bekka, and Varik's grandpa, Anders.

"What did you mean about things changing for Gard?" she asked. "You mean because Kady's due back from her trip and will be staying at Bekka House with him?"

"No..." After placing Rebekka in her bouncy seat, Varik sat at the table again, holding his hand aloft. Delaney saw it—the gentle radiance of the heartwish ring on her husband's finger.

"It-it's glowing. For Gard?" she asked.

Varik nodded. "I've known Gard was destined to be the next in line for a while now. I just didn't know when. When I woke up this morning I realized it's time. The knowing was there," he clutched his abdomen, "just like it happened for you when it was time to pass your ring to Laila."

"It's not going to be easy convincing him." Delaney screwed her expression. "He thinks the heartwish rings are...what was it he called it?"

"Supernatural woo-woo nonsense." Varik laughed.

"If he'd been home instead of Antarctica when Laila found her genie in that old perfume bottle, Gard would have—"

"Honey, listen to yourself." Varik gave Delaney's hand a gentle squeeze. "We lived through it, know it's a fact, and it even sounds preposterous to me. How the hell can we expect your level-headed facts and figures glaciologist brother to believe one of his sisters is married to a former genie? As far as Gard's concerned, we all just got carried away with the idea and romanticized a bunch of coincidences, accepting them as fact."

"But that's not true. Gard met Zak for himself, Varik. He heard all about his genie experience directly from Zak, not just from us. Plus he's seen that exquisite Victorian building Laila lives in now. How can his sister owning that place possibly be explained other than by magic? By Laila making one of her three wishes for the house?"

"Your brother is convinced Zak's an eccentric billionaire, that's how."

With her gaze solidly fixed on her husband's expression, Delaney finally broke into a smile, which expanded into a laugh. "Okay, yeah, I guess it does sound pretty farfetched. If only Gard had been here when it happened. If only he could have seen the magic for himself. If only—"

"Shoulda, woulda, coulda," Varik said. "It didn't work out that way. Once the ring works its magic for Gard, he'll be a believer too."

"You're right." Rising from the table, Delaney nodded, a thrill of anticipation coursing through her veins. "We'll invite him for dinner one night this week. I'll ask Mom and Tore to come too. Then you can pass the ring on to Gard. Oh I feel so much better already."

She grabbed her phone from the kitchen counter. "Want me to text him?"

"Sure. Just make sure you don't mention anything about the magic heartwish ring, because I guarantee your brother will make an excuse not to come."

Chapter 2

~<>~

AFTER HIS EARLY RUN, Gard stopped home to shower, shave and change before heading to Griffin's Café on Ocean Charm Boulevard for coffee and breakfast before checking in at the fire station. He took a seat at the counter, eager for a strong cup of coffee to help get his brain connected.

The place was all decked out for Christmas...even smelled like Christmas. All spicy and cinnamony. The aroma of holiday baked goods made his mouth water, especially the intense smell of fruitcake. Man, he was a sucker for a well-made fruitcake.

"Morning, Gard," Annalise Griffin greeted in a singsong voice as she poured him a cup of coffee and set a full-sized, plastic-wrapped loaf of fruitcake before him, tied with red ribbon and decorated with some sort of glittery Christmas trinket sitting atop a card with his name on it. "Merry Christmas." She gave him a buddy hug.

"A whole loaf?" He stared at the prized treat, inadvertently licking his lips. "All for me?"

"Yup. Best welcome home from Antarctica I could think of. I made this one extra potent so make sure you don't eat any while driving."

"Thanks. I think you already know how happy this makes me," Gard told her, feeling his *Scrinch* mood begin to fade. She'd known about his affinity for fruitcake since he'd moved to Glassfloat Bay from Chicago several years ago. "I could eat this stuff every day, all year round, especially when it comes out of your kitchen."

Fruitcake lovers for miles around knew that Annalise, owner of the café, made the best damn fruitcake on the planet. It was dense, dark, heavy, loaded with candied fruits and nuts, and saturated with brandy and rum. Annalise cured the cakes for months before they were ready to eat at Christmas, soaking them with spirits twice a month. Her special cakes had become renowned. No matter how many she made each year she always ran out.

Detesting the weighty "brick" of fruits and nuts had become a holiday joke, and Gard got teased plenty for holding it in high esteem. Some people shunned fruitcake, hating it the way he loathed canned asparagus. It didn't bother Gard. It just left all the more for him to eat.

Annalise walked behind the counter, pulled out a paper bag and handed it to him. "Here. You better keep it covered up or else you'll have everybody wheeling and dealing to take it off your hands." Resting her elbows on the counter, she gave him a thoughtful look. "I thought you'd be in here every day after getting back home. We've missed you around here. Where've you been hiding?" She reached over and fluffed his hair. "Not at the barber, I see."

"Hey, at least I shaved before I came in." Gard laughed. "I've just been getting acclimated after spending the last four months in the deep freeze." He couldn't very well tell her he'd needed some time to himself before facing all the kind-hearted well-wishers in his hometown. He knew they meant well but sometimes he found all their pampering suffocating. He found it necessary to ease into Glassfloat Bay's sea of nurturing earth mothers, like Annalise, little by little.

The fruitcake definitely helped.

"We're all so happy to have you home safe and sound. You doing okay?" Her hand rested atop his arm. He didn't have to lift his gaze from the fruitcake to know she had a concerned expression across her face.

"Yeah, I'm good, thanks." Fighting the urge to growl in frustration, he forced a smile instead. Annalise was good people.

She didn't deserve to be subjected to his reclusive mood—especially when there was no damn good reason for it. After spending months cloistered away with not much more than icebergs, glaciers and his own dark thoughts for companions, he'd have to adjust to being around cheery, chatty people again.

This time he made sure to look into Annalise's eyes when he smiled. "I'm just glad to be home and looking forward to a plate of—"

"Two eggs over easy with my signature hash browns, homemade sourdough toast with orange-ginger marmalade, a side of thick bacon, and a short stack of chocolate chip pancakes."

He watched Annalise as her bright smile took hold, bracketed by two rosy cheeks.

"I've been looking forward to that for the last four months," he told her.

"Good. That's just what I like to hear." She gave his back a brisk rub. "A few good strong cups of my coffee, and a big comfort food breakfast should have you bright-eyed and bushytailed in no time." She gave the order to the kitchen, telling Gard it would take about ten minutes.

"Those chocolate chip pancakes of yours are the stuff dreams are made of," he told her before sipping his coffee. This was a woman who instinctively knew how to make great comfort food. It was one of the things he missed most while working in the frozen tundra.

"Thanks. That's what your sisters, Laila and Reen, say about my Dutch baby pancakes." Her smile blazed with pride. "That's what I enjoy most."

"Dutch babies?"

"No." Her smile became softer and she patted his hand. "Making people happy with my cooking."

"Nobody does it better," he assured her.

Annalise was off to help other customers. Once his breakfast arrived he wasted no time sinking his teeth into a generous forkful of those pancakes, murmuring his satisfaction.

She was one of the first locals his sister, Delaney, met when she moved to Glassfloat Bay from Chicago after their grandmother, Bekka, passed away, leaving the house to her family. The house, now the main Malone family residence, had since become known as Bekka House.

For Gard, his siblings, and their mom, renovating Bekka House was an ongoing project as different members of the family moved in and out.

In between bites he caught Annalise glancing at the large old schoolhouse-style wall clock with its faded advertising banner for some food Gard had never heard of...probably because they stopped making it before he was born. That was part of the café's charm. It was a contradictory mix of outdated 1950s kitsch, and contemporary decor that somehow worked together, creating a warm, welcoming atmosphere.

"You're usually in here earlier," Annalise noted.

"I'm heading over to the fire station after breakfast." He took another sip of coffee and *ahhhhed*. "Figured there wasn't any need to pop in there at the crack of dawn since I'm not on the schedule until next week. I thought I'd see if anybody's got any shifts they need covered before then."

Annalise got the pot and refilled his cup. With one fist planted at her waist, she studied him. "You're tackling that breakfast like it'll be your last. I think you need another stack of pancakes. You're getting too skinny."

"Believe me, Annalise, one stack along with everything else is plenty, thanks." If she had her way he'd be unable to fit into his jeans in no time.

"Don't they feed you guys up there at the North Pole?"

He chuckled inwardly at her North Pole reference. Gard wasn't about to correct her. He already had a couple times in the past. He suspected Annalise, like many people he knew, preferred to think of him working at the North Pole. He'd learned nobody other than glaciologists really cared much about Antarctica being the southernmost continent, or that it contained the geographic South Pole. Nope, they'd rather envision Gard working alongside Santa and the elves at the opposite end of the world.

If it made them smile, it was fine with him. Heck, he was a scientist who studied glaciers, not some fussy teacher whose job it was to correct people's mistaken assumptions.

"We eat a lot when we're working there, actually," Gard said. "With all that snow trekking, we need to eat plenty of high calorie food to help keep us sustained in the polar conditions." He grinned at Annalise, anticipating her reaction to what he was about to tell her. "That means we get to eat a lot of chocolate bars."

"I'm in! How do I book a ticket to Antarctica?" she teased.

"Believe it or not, all that chocolate gets old after a while."

"Oh puhleez." She offered a sideways glance telling him she thought he must be crazy. "I guess that's one of the differences between men and women. No female chocoholic worth her salt is going to get tired of an endless supply of chocolate." She folded her arms across her chest. "What do you eat besides all that chocolate?"

"It depends on the time of year and who's manning the galley. Pemmican, sardines, canned meat, tons of crackers, and some really godawful pizza and dishwater coffee. All we have up at the research station is weak grocery store coffee that comes in one of those industrial sized cans," Gard made an exaggerated gesture, "that'll feed an army. I swear, we've probably been dipping into that same damn can for the last two years."

Wrinkling her nose in mutual distaste, Annalise said, "There's nothing like weak, stale coffee when you're freezing your butt off at the North Pole. What foods do you miss most after spending a few months up there?"

"Besides your delicious massive breakfasts? Probably fresh fruit. Getting fresh produce there is tough."

As Annalise took care of other customers at the counter, the sound of singing and humming, so faint it was nearly imperceptible, caught his ear. Cocking his head, Gard paid attention, then followed the sound until he spotted a little boy sitting by himself at one of the small booths for two away from the center of the café.

He had a notebook and crayons and was coloring as he sang. The kid couldn't have been more than five.

"Hey Annalise," Gard crooked his finger, "who's the kid?" He nodded toward the little boy.

"Cute as a button, isn't he? He's my nephew, Harry, the son of my sister and newest hire, Sabrina Hanklen." She thumbed in the direction of the rear of the café. "She's back in the storeroom getting some supplies. She just moved back to Glassfloat Bay a short time ago. Since she was in a bind with nobody to watch Harry before daycare, which starts at seven, I told her I didn't mind if she brought him in here until it's time for her to drop him off."

Gard wasn't surprised. Annalise would nurture the world if she could, and she had a definite soft spot for children. She'd make a great mom one day.

"Harry's no trouble at all." Annalise gazed at her nephew with a loving expression. "He's so quiet and mannerly." She glanced up at Gard. "Has a terrible stuttering problem though. He stays after class to see a speech therapist."

"I stuttered too when I was about that age." Gard remembered being taunted by classmates for those few years he stuttered. "The speech therapist really helped. I think I'll introduce myself. Hey, stow this behind the counter for me until I leave, okay?" After handing her the bag containing his more-precious-than-gold fruitcake, he polished off the rest of his coffee before walking over to the booth. As he approached, he could hear the boy alternately singing and humming a Christmas carol Gard remembered hearing but its title escaped him.

"Hey there. Looks like you're hard at work on your drawing," Gard said, bending forward with his hands on his knees.

Startled out of his reverie, the kid looked up at him.

"Sorry, I didn't mean to scare you. I just saw you coloring and I thought I'd come over to take a look. I'm a friend of your aunt, Annalise." He pointed in her direction. Gard stuck out his hand and after a long moment where the youngster seemed to be mentally debating, he took it. "My name's Gard Malone." He gave the boy's hand a gentle shake. "Your aunt tells me your name is Harry." He hoped his introduction made the kid feel better...safer.

The boy opened his mouth, clearly attempting to speak. It took him a while but he finally managed, "N-n-nice to m-meet you, M-m-mister M-m-malone." A bright smile lit his face and his cheeks dimpled. Annalise was right, he was cute as a button, with a full mop of blond hair and wide blue eyes.

Although the kid had one hell of a stuttering problem, Gard hadn't noticed any trace of it when he was singing. It was the same for Gard as a child. The speech therapist taught him to sing words rather than speak them whenever he got into trouble getting the words out. Apparently there was something about the ease of singing that enabled most stutterers to do it without any stutter or stammer.

"Mind if I sit down and join you?" Harry studied him before shaking his head from side to side. "So what's that you're drawing?"

"M-my a-angel." He picked up his paper, displaying it for Gard. "H-her n-name's Hark." The boy went back to coloring and humming and that's when Gard remembered the name of the carol. It was "Hark! The Herald Angels Sing."

Gard had a hunch. "So Hark is your Harold angel, hmm? Just like in the Christmas carol."

"Yup." Harry bobbed his head and smiled. "The s-song's about m-me and Hark."

It was about the cutest damned occurrence of mistaken song lyrics Gard had ever come across. Harry told Gard he talked to Hark a lot, and sometimes she talked back. He explained Hark was his Christmas angel because Harold was born on Christmas day. The kid clearly had a vivid imagination.

Gard watched the boy give Hark a long flowing mane of bright yellow hair with subtle orange streaks. Long eyelashes topped her blue eyes, and an extra wide red smile branched out from her pink cheek circles. Instead of the typical white gown, his angel wore a long, colorful patchwork coat. Something about Harry's rendition of the angel's garment seemed to evoke a distant memory for Gard but he couldn't place the reference.

"That's the most original angel drawing I've ever seen." The pleased, surprised look Harry gave him warmed Gard's heart.

"Y-you really l-like it?" he asked as if he couldn't believe it.

"On my honor," Gard assured, raising his hand and curling his fingers in the scout hand sign. "Your angel's coat looks familiar..." he squinted at the drawing, "but I can't recall why."

"Hark l-likes c-colorful things. She said her c-coat is cro..." His eyebrows scrunched down as he thought. "Crochet," he remembered.

"Ah, I see."

"It's time to go, honey. Gather up all your crayons and paper."

Gard looked up into the face of an angel, a striking redhead with the same big blue eyes as her son.

"Harry and I were just getting to know each other. He was telling me about his special angel." Gard winked and her smile spread.

"Ah yes, Hark. That's a very nice picture, Harry." She gave her son a hug. "We'll put it on the refrigerator when we get home."

Gard offered his hand. "I'm Gard Malone. Annalise told me you're sisters."

After a fleeting moment of hesitation, she accepted it. "Sabrina Hanklen. Otherwise known as the baby of the family." Her eyes crinkled at the corners.

From what he could tell she had a nice shape under the retro fifties-style pink waitress uniform Annalise had her servers wear, although she bordered on being too thin. She looked like she could benefit from one of Annalise's colossal breakfasts. Her dark reddish hair, tied back in a ponytail, was topped with one of those silly little waitress hats seen in old TV shows and movies.

"I understand you just moved back to Glassfloat Bay. Where were you living?"

"A few weeks ago." Sabrina nodded. "We moved from Pennsylvania."

"Whoa, that's a long haul. What area, Pittsburgh? Philadelphia?"

"Horntik."

"That's a new one on me."

"You're not the only one." Sabrina's smile lit up her beautiful face. "It's a sleepy little town about an hour from Pittsburgh."

He'd been trying to place her, sure that he'd met her before. He thought at first it was just her resemblance to Annalise and Hud but he finally realized Sabrina reminded him of one of the antique dolls his mother kept on display. But along with the impression of porcelain fragility, Sabrina also possessed a definite air of resilience.

"So what brought you back? Homesick?"

"Well...that and," her gaze jerked to Harry and back, "and some family issues." A little crease formed between her eyebrows. "Glassfloat Bay's a wonderful place for a child to grow up," she went on with a smile. "I lived here all my life until I got married and I really missed it. My husband, Stuart, was from Pennsylvania so we moved there. That was..." she gazed up as if mentally counting, "almost six years ago. How long have you lived here?"

"I moved from Chicago a few years ago. The Malones have been trickling over this way for the last ten years, starting with my grandmother, Bekka Eriksen."

"Bekka was your grandma?" Sabrina's smile brightened the way most people's did when Bekka's name came into the conversation. "Oh I loved her. She was such a dear, sweet woman. Her Norwegian accent always made me smile. It broke my heart when she passed away a couple of years ago. She taught me and Annalise to make pepperkaker."

With an enthusiastic nod, Gard said, "Still my favorite cookies. The more ginger the better."

"If you're Bekka's grandson, that means you're one of *those* Malones." Sabrina chuckled when Gard angled his head. "Oh I'm sorry, that came out wrong. I meant it in the nicest way, really. I'm getting to know your sisters, Delaney, Laila and Reen, as well as your mom and her husband. And I live on the third floor of the building where your brother, Nevan's, pub is.

"Yeah, Nevan owns the building. Have you tried his Irish pork pie yet? Seriously, best food on the planet. It's similar to the one my Grandma Malone used to make when I was a kid."

"No, but that's what I hear. I'll have to try it some time. So you're the brother everyone has been excited about coming home from...where is it? The North Pole, right?"

Gard smiled. "Antarctica."

"Laila said you're a glacier expert or something."

"Yup. I'm a glaciologist."

With her expression scrunched, Sabrina admitted, "I'm sorry but I have no idea what that is."

"No problem. Few people do." Some people wondered if he chopped up icebergs to help prevent them from tearing the hulls of ships, others thought maybe he was an athlete who skied down glaciers, and he'd even been asked if glaciologists built igloos. "We study glaciers, global warming and the melting icebergs in Antarctica."

"Oh..." Sabrina had that sort of vacant look most people got when he explained what he did for a living. But she was kind enough to say, "Well that sounds really interesting, Gard."

She squatted to pick something up from the floor. "You dropped this one, sweetie," she said to Harry, giving him a green crayon. "Make sure to check the booth seat for any crayons. We don't want any of Aunt Annalise's customers sitting on a crayon." She made a sort of O-face and Harry laughed as he checked the seat.

"We d-don't want anybody to g-get a g-green b-butt," he said, mirroring his mom's silly expression.

"I've probably seen your husband at Nevan's," Gard said.

"Stuart?" Sabrina looked left, right, then down as she smoothed her apron. "No, he's not...no." She kept her eyes averted.

The odd statement seemed to make her uncomfortable. Gard wasn't sure what to say, so he rambled on about the pork pie. "Well, make sure to give Nevan's pork pie a try. I think you and Harry will love it. It's tall, made in one of those tube pans." He gestured with his hands. "Nevan makes his from ground pork and pork sausage, wrapped in a lard pastry crust and served cold in thick slices with strong mustard or mayo on the side. Of course, a nice pint of Guinness doesn't hurt to round out the meal."

Gard had to swallow a laugh. Going on about the pub food made him sound like his mother and sisters waxing poetic over their cookie and scone recipes for chrissakes. For a guy who wasn't feeling chatty when he came into the café, he'd been yacking up a storm.

Amazing how conversation with a beautiful woman can snap a man out of the doldrums.

"I have a g-girlfriend," Harry happily announced.

"You do, huh? What's her name?" Gard asked.

"L-lilly. She's b-beautiful. S-she has y-yellow hair and g-greenish eyes."

Folding his arms across his chest, Gard thought for a moment. "Well I know one little girl named Lilly who's just about your age and fits that description. Her dad's a good friend, Professor Drake Slattery."

"Yup." Harry nodded. "L-lilly S-s-slattery."

Resting a hand on Harry's shoulder, Sabrina told her son, "Time to put on your jacket, honey." Harry placed his packed art supplies on the table and shrugged into his jacket.

Gard's phone pealed with the damn "Jingle Bells" ringtone Delaney insisted on programming for her calls. Since she was calling rather than texting he thought it might be important. "Excuse me," he told Sabrina. "Hi Delaney, what's up? Dinner tonight?" His sister had caught him off guard and he didn't have a believable excuse prepared. "Uh, yeah, sure. Okay, see you at seven. Well you tell little Rebekka that her uncle misses her too." He knew he'd be in for a night of his sister's rah-rah positive rhetoric designed to cheer him up.

"Sorry about that," he told Sabrina after ending the call. "My sister claims my baby niece is lonesome for her uncle." He rolled his eyes. "Anyway, welcome back to Glassfloat Bay. Harry's going to love Christmastime here the way the townspeople pull out all stops."

"Oh I remember. Sleigh rides, house decorating contests, gingerbread house contests. And if we get any snow, which isn't often, there's the snowman contest."

"Depending on the amount of snow, sometimes it's a tiny snowman contest." Holding his thumb and forefinger a few inches apart, Gard laughed and Sabrina joined in.

"It's all very festive," Sabrina said, and Gard noticed her eyes sparkled as she spoke. "Christmas is my favorite time of year."

"M-me t-too. I'm g-going to be J-joseph," Harry announced.

"In the nativity play at the community church," Sabrina clarified, "where all the kids play the roles."

"Joseph, huh? Very impressive," Gard said and Harry beamed a proud smile.

Sabrina glanced at the clock and sank her teeth into her bottom lip. "I'm sorry, I don't mean to cut you off, Gard, but I've got to walk Harry to daycare and get back here in time for the breakfast rush." In response to her crooking finger, Harry scooted out of the booth, gathering his supplies. Sabrina finger-combed his hair and partially zipped his jacket.

"You don't drive?" Gard asked.

"I do but my old Saturn gave up the ghost as soon as we made it to Glassfloat Bay. I'm just thankful it made it this far. It broke down several times along the way. So until I can afford another car, we walk. That's one of the nice things about living in a small town—nothing is too far away."

"Why don't you let me take Harry?" Gard offered. "I've got some time to kill this morning before heading to the firehouse. As long as it's okay with you, Harry." Gard gave him a questioning look and Harry responded with an enthusiastic nod.

"Are y-you a f-fireman?" Harry's eyes lit up.

"I am. When I'm not away working at my regular job, I work here at the fire department."

"W-wow!"

"I'll tell you all about it when I drive you to school."

"Oh no, I couldn't possibly impose on you like that, Gard."

"It's no imposition at all. Which daycare? The one at Maythorne Elementary School?"

"Yes, same place he goes to kindergarten but—"

"Sabrina," Annalise said, after coming through the kitchen's swing door with a tray of fragrant cinnamon rolls, "you may as well let Gard have his way because he won't let up until you do." Annalise elbowed Gard and they shared a laugh. "You don't have to worry, I can vouch for him. He'll take good care of Harry. Now why don't you hop on over to table seven. We just had a party of eleven come in."

"Eleven?" Turning to see the people being seated, Sabrina let out a whoosh of breath. "I'm on my way, Annalise." She gave Harry a kiss, told him to be a good boy, then said, "Thank you so much, Gard. I really appreciate it."

"I've gotta run, Gard," Annalise said. "Table two's waiting on their pigs in a blanket. Don't forget your fruitcake. See you tomorrow?"

"You bet." Gard looked down at Harry who stood knee-high, gazing up at him with a big grin.

"All r-ready."

"Great. Hey, do you like dogs, Harry?"

The kid's face lit up. "Oh yeah! I l-love them!"

"Good, because I've got my best buddy, Tundra, waiting outside. You can see him lapping up water in the fenced area your aunt made for her customers' dogs." He pointed and Harry craned his neck to look. "Tundra's the one twice the size of the other dogs. He's big but he's gentle and loves kids."

Gard had the oddest feeling, deep down in his gut, when he looked at the excited kid...the same feeling he'd had talking to Sabrina. It was something Gard had never experienced before. And it wasn't a good feeling. Nope, there was nothing positive at all when a single guy found himself covetous of another man's wife and child.

~<>~

"No, I haven't detected the smell of fresh-baked ginger cookies anywhere in the house, Mom. Or any of the pipe tobacco Varik's grandfather used to smoke, Delaney." Gard chuckled as he stabbed another pork chop, adding it to his plate.

They'd ganged up on him. He should have expected it. When she called to invite him to dinner, Delaney never mentioned that she'd also invited their mom and stepdad. From the food spread it looked like his mom and sister had cooked up all of Gard's favorites.

The small house his sister and brother-in-law had bought after moving out of Bekka House was covered with all of his sister's familiar decorating touches and her collections of whatnots. Even though she and her professor husband, Varik, were doing well financially, Delaney still favored shopping the thrift stores and garage sales, usually arm-in-arm with their mom and sisters. The Malone women thrived on collecting kitschy things from days gone by because, they claimed, it made a house feel comfy and inviting. He actually couldn't argue with that.

"I told you before," Gard went on, "there are no such things as ghosts and certainly not cookie-baking or pipe-smoking ghosts." He struggled not to roll his eyes at his sister. "Honestly, Delaney, you and your fanciful ghost stories."

"It's not just Delaney," his mother pointed out. "Laila smelled Grandma Bekka's *pepperkaker* when she was living at Bekka House before she married Zakkar. Zak smelled the cookies and tobacco too. More potatoes?" Astrid held the bowl of mashed potatoes out to Gard who couldn't help making a pig of himself when it came to his mom's cooking.

"Come on, Mom." Gard's chuckle evolved into full-blown laughter. "I like Zak. He's a great guy. But if he believes all this woo-woo stuff then he's just as screwy as the rest of my family." He ignored his mother's righteous gasp of indignation and continued. "Or maybe the poor guy didn't want to ruffle anyone's feathers, especially with his new in-laws breathing down his neck, insisting

Bekka House is haunted." He ladled on fresh mushroom gravy and dug in.

"It *is* haunted! Zak actually talked to Grandma Bekka's ghost." After Gard's giant eye roll, Delaney added, "Oh dear...I was hoping you'd be in a more receptive mood tonight."

And there it was. He knew it. They were finally getting around to the real reason he'd been invited to a big comfort-food dinner.

Gard's eyebrow lifted. "Receptive for what?"

"Your mom and sister are right, Gard," Varik said. "Bekka House is home to three friendly ghosts."

"See, now that's another thing."

"Don't point with your fork, dear," Astrid chastised her son.

Gard placed his fork on the plate. "Before I left for my last stint in Antarctica it was two ghosts, Grandma Bekka and Varik's Grandpa Anders. Since I got back home it's suddenly three ghosts." He gave them dubious looks. "Really?"

"Your brother-in-law discovered the ghost of Grandpa Jamie when he was still a genie," his stepfather, Tore said.

"Since when was Grandpa Jamie a genie?"

"Stop trying to be funny." Astrid gave her son's hand a playful slap. "He meant when Zak was still a genie."

"Oh brother." Resting his elbows on the table, Gard shielded his eyes with his hands. "Not the genie stuff again. Ghosts, genies, magic rings, angels..." he counted on his fingers, "I swear, sometimes I feel like I've fallen down the rabbit hole."

"Granted," Tore began, "it might sound strange to someone who's never experienced any of those things but—"

"Gee, ya think?" Gard rolled his eyes again—if he kept doing that he worried they might come unglued from their sockets.

Astrid's eyebrow arrowed as she stared down her son. Like many women, Gard's mom was proficient in The Look, something no man wanted to be on the receiving end of. When his mother nailed him with a steely glare, Gard was reduced to guilt-ridden naughty little boy status, just like that.

He could believe his mother and sisters might buy into this hocus-pocus but it surprised him that two logical-minded professors bought into it too. They'd all got caught up in wishful thinking. Maybe it was the holidays...

Gard scooped a forkful of food, sighing his pleasure as he chewed. "I haven't had your homemade creamed corn in ages, Mom," he said, hoping to change the subject. "I almost forgot how good it is. Nothing like the stuff in the can, that's for sure. And, Delaney, those candied sweet potatoes are fantastic. And the—"

"Thank you, honey," Astrid cut him off. "You know the only reason you haven't smelled the *pepperkaker* or pipe tobacco is because you've become a skeptic."

"Mom's right," Delaney said. "I've read that ghosts rarely visit skeptics. You have to allow yourself to become more open, more receptive."

His shoulders slumping in resignation, Gard laughed. "Come on, fess up, did you invite me for dinner just to gang up on me about the friendly ghosts of Bekka House?"

"Of course not, sweetheart. By the way, I made your all-time favorite dessert." Astrid broadcast a bright smile. "Just for you."

"You made bread pudding with whiskey sauce?" Gard's eyes went wide as recollections of his mom's custardy bread dessert topped with butter-toasted pecans and whiskey-spiked topping filled his head. He hadn't tasted it in a few years.

"And I made your favorite espresso fudge brownies," Delaney added.

Salivating aside, Gard put his fork down and studied his mother and sister's too chipper expressions.

"Okay, so...how come I rate?"

"Because you're my sweetie pie, my firstborn son, and I love you."

"And because your baby niece, Rebekka, loves her Uncle Gard and missed him when he was away."

"Right...so if my niece misses me so much, how come I haven't seen Rebekka all night?"

Delaney and Astrid exchanged pensive looks. "Well because it's late and she was tired," Delaney claimed, shifting her gaze to the tabletop.

Gard turned to his stepfather who'd suddenly become fascinated by something on his phone. "Tore?"

"Hmm?"

Gard turned to his brother-in-law. "Varik? Come on, something's up. What's going on?"

"Did you want coffee with dessert, Gard?" his sister asked, rising from the table and whisking dishes away.

"Delaney, I—"

"Maybe decaf would be better at this hour," Astrid chimed in, "so it doesn't interfere with his sleep. Speaking of sleep, have you been sleeping any better lately? I certainly hope so. It must be just awful having those nightmares all the—"

"Astrid..." Tore grabbed his wife's arm as she picked up his dinner plate. He said nothing more, just gave her a long, meaningful look that gave Gard a knot deep in his belly. Without another word, Astrid took the plates to the sink, then came back to sit at the table, her hands folded neatly in front of her as she stared at her lap.

"Delaney," Varik called to the kitchen. She was back in a flash, mirroring Astrid's meek position.

"What is it? Has something happened? Are one of you sick? Is the baby okay?" The horrific thought had Gard's insides clutching.

"No, no, nothing like that." Tore clasped Gard's forearm and smiled. "We're all fine. And," he added as Gard's mouth popped open in question, "so is everyone else in the family."

Gard let out the breath he'd been holding. "Then what's going on? Am I here for some sort of intervention or something? I told you all at Thanksgiving that I'm doing a lot better. Dr. Svenningsen's been a big help. And you don't have to worry about me getting hooked on pain pills because I rarely take one."

His mother grasped his other arm. "We love you and we worry about you, and that's something that will never change. But we asked you here tonight for another reason." She turned her attention to her son-in-law, nodding. "Go ahead, Varik, tell him—but wait just a minute until I get my camera."

As Astrid fished through her cavernous purse, Gard mumbled, "It's another one of Mom's Kodak moments, I see." His eyes closed in a long blink. Whatever it was, the way they were drawing it out was sheer agony.

"Okay, I'm ready. You can tell him now, Varik," his mom said, camera in position and ready to click.

"Tell me what?"

"Give me your hand." Varik held his hand open. Gard hesitated. Astrid snapped a photo. There was something weird going on. He and his brother-in-law occasionally exchanged buddy hugs but holding hands was a different matter. Finally he slipped his hand into Varik's, almost afraid to look into his eyes to see that ocean-blue gaze of his.

Click. His mom took another picture.

Varik clasped Gard's hand tight, then slowly slipped his away, leaving something in Gard's hand as he did. When Gard looked at his hand he saw Varik's heartwish ring resting there.

Click...click...click...

"What's this?" Gard studied it as if it were some alien relic he'd never seen before, rather than the ring with the lustrous stone that had been on his brother-in-law's finger since they'd first met.

"You know what it is," Delaney answered as their mom took yet another shot.

Yeah, he did. Or at least he knew what they *thought* it was. He'd heard about the legend of Odin's enchanted heartwish stones often enough from his mom and sisters, not to mention Grandma Bekka. By the age of ten he'd dismissed his grandmother's stories, along with other silly fantasies meant for wide-eyed impressionable children.

"I knew that one day," Varik said, "when the time was right, the ring would come off on its own so I could pass it on to its next rightful owner."

Gard huffed a humorless laugh. "And I suppose that would be me?" He tossed the ring in his palm a few times. Astrid snapped another photo. "Enough with the photos, okay, Mom?"

"Exactly." Varik gave a slow nod. "The magic heartwish ring is meant for you, Gard."

"So I'm supposed to make some big magical wish and, poof, everything in my life is going to be perfect, is that it?" Gard felt the heat of anger rising to the surface as he spoke. "Where the hell was this ring when I needed it, Varik? If it was really meant for me, shouldn't your special ring have known I could have used it three years ago?"

"I wish I could answer that, Gard, but I can't." Varik shook his head back and forth. "We don't know the whys or hows of the heartwish rings, all we know is that when the time is right, the ring works."

"It does incredible, magical things," Tore confirmed. "Delaney and Varik know firsthand. Ask your sister, Laila, about it too."

Gard couldn't believe what he was hearing. He'd always thought of Tore and Varik as being intelligent and rational, and here they were spouting bizarre gibberish. Varik was sounding more like Delaney all the time, naïve, trusting, gullible. And Tore—studying his stepdad as he spoke Gard was chilled by the thought that perhaps

Tore and Gard's mother were suffering from a form of dementia. It was the only thing that might explain their irrational ramblings about all this supernatural drivel.

"You'll know the right wish to make when the time is right," his sister explained, patting his arm. "As long as you let your heart guide you...as long as the wish comes from your heart, you can't go wrong."

"Uh-huh. One wish and, voila, no more worries. No more grief. No more nightmares. You seriously think this trinket," he held the ring between his thumb and forefinger, "is going to change things? You think it's going to somehow magically erase the memories I have of clutching on to my best friend only to lose him and hear him fall to his death in that icy chasm?" Gard pounded the table, "You think a wish is going to obliterate the guilt I carry for not being able to save Tim's life? How about bringing Laila's fiancé back—maybe I can wish for that, huh?" He swallowed back the bile rising in his throat.

"Gard...I wish to hell we could turn back the clock and somehow save Tim, but that's not possible," Varik said. "What you suffered is immeasurable and I know there's no easy fix. Believe me, I know the pain of losing someone close to you. I understand what you're going through."

Gard turned an incredulous gaze on his brother-in-law. "Do you? Do you really, Varik? Have you ever held the fate of someone's life in your hands?" Gard lifted a hand, turning it back and forth as he gazed at it. "I'm an adult, closing in on forty. You honestly think I'm going to buy the ridiculous story about magic and angels and ghosts and genies and all the rest of the fairytale glitter you and the family so casually accept as reality?" He bounced the ring in his open palm again, gazing at it hard.

"You want to know what I think about your *magic*," Gard hung air quotes, "ring? Here, let me show you." He leapt from the table and headed for the kitchen. When he reached the sink he ran the water and turned on the garbage disposal. "Here's what I think about Odin and his magic stone."

"Gard, no!" the four chorused, jumping up from their seats and watching in horror as Gard dropped the heartwish ring down the disposal.

"Oh, Gard..." Delaney cried. "You don't know what you've done." She sat down again, dropping her head into her hands. Varik went to her side, comforting her, just as Tore did for Astrid.

"Look, I'm sorry, but I couldn't take it anymore." Gard hated to see the unhappiness he'd just caused the people he loved but he was unwilling to listen to any more crap about mystical garbage. "I'm gonna head out now." Leaving the kitchen, he turned to walk from the dining room to the living room's front door. The instant his hand connected with the doorknob, the area lit up with a glow so bright it seemed as though every light in the house had just switched on.

"What the...?"

He and the others joined in a mutual gasp as they watched the intense radiance funneling to a pinpoint of light almost like a laser beam, zeroing in on Gard's hand that was still clutching the door handle.

"Holy shit!" Staring in utter disbelief at the intact ring that had just seated itself on his finger, he released the handle as if it were red hot, and plopped himself down into a living room chair, staring at his hand. "That did *not* just happen. It-it's impossible. I heard it being mangled in the garbage disposal." He looked at them. "You all did." The ring grew warm around his finger and the glimmer in the room dissipated as the ring's stone absorbed it. He tried to pull it off but it was stuck, almost as if it was fused with his flesh.

"Look, it's shimmering. It's just like..." Gard paused, gazing up at his family.

"Just like the heartwish stories you've always heard." Astrid nodded. "The ring is exactly where it belongs now. Last one, I promise," she said, taking a final photo.

"We've got a lot of talking to do," Delaney said with a relieved smile. "I'll put on the coffee and serve the bread pudding."

It had finally happened. No doubt about it. Gard Malone had fallen, head first, down the rabbit hole.

Chapter 3

~<>~

A COUPLE WEEKS after Thanksgiving, Annalise asked Sabrina if she'd paint a Christmas scene on the windows of Griffin's Café. An artist at heart, Sabrina readily agreed. Her sister knew she wouldn't be able to turn down a task involving artwork. This would give Sabrina a chance to repay her sister for all her help and understanding since Sabrina and Harry arrived back home.

She decided to paint on the inside of the windows rather than the outside since it rained so much in the Pacific Northwest this time of year. Sabrina could imagine the painted scene sluicing off the glass with the first advent of rain.

She'd wondered if she'd ever have any practical use for the reverse glass painting technique she learned from an art class in college. Since everything was painted exactly the opposite of normal painting, it was a challenge, but she found the concentration it took to create the backwards artwork relaxing and therapeutic. She'd used the technique to decorate the insides of glass jars which she sold at craft fairs.

She worked on the windows between serving customers during the rush times. Barring anything unforeseen, she'd have the windows complete in another day or two.

The project gave Sabrina plenty of time to reflect on the recent changes in her life. She felt bad that she still hadn't fully explained to Harry that she and his father were getting a divorce. It wasn't easy explaining to an idealistic child that his parents no longer wanted to live together as a family.

"You're just where I thought I'd find you, Sabrina. I told Annalise she didn't have to worry about getting the café's windows all spiffed up for Christmas with you back in town."

Chuckling, Sabrina turned at the sound of her brother, Hudson's, voice. "She said she's hoping to win the best retail window display this year. I told her I was happy to do whatever I can to help."

"Hi, Uncle Hud! I-I'm making a n-new C-christmas drawing," Harry announced. "I'm p-putting the H-hulk in the p-picture t-too."

Hud turned, cocking his head as Harry held up his paper. "The Hulk, hmm? Well that's an interesting idea. How come he's there with Santa?"

"B-because I've g-got a lot of g-green crayons," he answered matter-of-factly.

"Good reason," Hud said. "Your drawing looks terrific so far."

"Thanks. M-mommy's d-does too."

"It sure does, sport." Hud ruffled his nephew's hair. "Hey, Sabrina, got a minute?"

"Sure. What's up?"

Hud's gaze shifted to Harry. "Can we talk over there?" He inclined his head, motioning to a booth several feet away. Once they were seated, Hud asked, "So have you told him yet?"

Sighing, Sabrina shook her head. "How do you tell your almost five-year-old son that his father is an abusive alcoholic who doesn't give a damn about his child or his wife? That he's been fired from more than one job for his drinking...and that he's cheated on his wife several times at least." Sabrina shrugged. "I don't even know where to begin."

She'd hoped that the long cross-country drive would provide ample opportunity for her to have a heart to heart discussion with Harry. It did...but she'd chickened out.

"It's not as if Harry doesn't realize Stuart has issues," Hud pointed out. "You told me that the son of a bitch is always barking at him and ridiculing the kid."

"True but your nephew is a very loving and forgiving little boy...even though he's been the target of Stuart's mockery. I don't want to poison Harry's mind against his father, but I don't want to canonize the man either. There has to be a happy medium. I just haven't found it yet."

Hud reached for his sister's hand, clasping it. "I'm sorry things have been so rough on you, Sabrina. Stuart had us all fooled. He came across like a good guy." Hud's fingers raked through his hair. "I don't know, maybe it's that salesman's personality of his."

Nodding, Sabrina agreed, "Stuart can talk anybody into believing almost anything...at least when he's sober."

Before she and Stuart were married, his mother confided to Sabrina that he'd been diagnosed as bipolar. The diagnosis didn't mean much to Sabrina at the time since she'd only witnessed Stuart's upbeat, positive side. After they were married, when his moods radically switched between ecstatically cheerful to depressed, angry and paranoid, Sabrina finally understood.

"It was like being married to Dr. Jekyll and Mr. Hyde," Sabrina told her brother. "Stuart changed so much during our six years of marriage, I barely knew him anymore. I was at a loss as to how to help because he refused to see a therapist."

Gazing out the window onto Ocean Charm Boulevard's morning traffic, she continued, "Debt collectors were breathing down our necks as Stuart kept charging things and ignoring the bills. He likes to impress people by picking up the tab for everyone when he and his coworkers go out for drinks after work."

"And now you're dead broke," Hud surmised.

"Pretty much. Stuart went through all our savings...except for the small amount I was able to squirrel away."

She heard Hud grumble something under his breath. "How much do you need?" he asked, taking out his wallet. "I'll have more transferred into your account this morning."

Stilling Hud's hand, Sabrina gave him a warm smile. "Thanks, but I'm doing okay. It's important to me to make it on my own. I don't want to have to depend on anyone else financially. But I promise," she added when her brother's mouth popped open to protest, "to let you know if I run into trouble."

At the sound of someone knocking on the café's window, Sabrina and Hud looked up to see their sister's grin as Annalise stood in the soft rainfall appraising the Santa and Mrs. Claus painting in progress, giving two enthusiastic thumbs up.

Annalise scurried inside, rubbing the chill from her arms as she came to their booth. "It looks fabulous! You've captured the magic of Christmas right there on the café's windows. Santa, Mrs. Claus, elves, Frosty the Snowman, heck, you even managed to get Rudolph in there." With her hands on Sabrina's shoulders, Annalise bent, touching her cheek to her sister's. "Thank you, Sabrina. The customers are going to love this. And Griffin's Café is going to win that contest for best windows this year!" Clapping her hands, Annalise hopped in place.

"I'm so glad you like it." Basking for a moment in her sister's praise and enjoying her excitement, Sabrina smiled. "I'll do my best not to let you down."

"You could never do that," Annalise assured her.

"Now we know where Harry gets his talent," Hud said loud enough for the boy to hear.

At the sound of his name, Harry proudly held up his paper with his own sprightly version of Santa and Mrs. Claus.

"Great job, sweetie," Annalise said. "I like the way you have Mr. and Mrs. Easter Bunny and the Jolly Green Giant in there with Santa too."

"The jolly who?" Harry asked, studying his drawing.

Cupping a hand over her mouth, Sabrina whispered, "That's supposed to be the Hulk."

"Oh...I mean the Hulk," Annalise amended.

"Th-they're all g-good f-friends," Harry explained. "And see? H-here's the t-tooth fairy." He pointed to a small winged figure in pink and blue.

"Well isn't that just wonderful," Annalise said with enthusiasm. "You draw so well that I'll bet you want to be an artist when you grow up."

"A-and a f-fireman, l-like M-mr. M-malone!"

"Is that so?" Annalise bubbled with that wonderful laughter of hers while ruffling the loose blond curls on top of Harry's head.

"Gard's a great guy," Hud said. "Did you meet his dog, Tundra yet?"

"Y-yes. I l-like T-tundra a lot."

"You really think the windows look okay?" Sabrina asked, lost in thought. Slanting her head, she considered the painted glass again. "You don't think it looks too amateurish or childish? This is a business, after all, and it should look professional." Stuarts constant criticism had struck a blow to her self-confidence.

Both Annalise and Hud looked at Sabrina like she was crazy. "Are we looking at the same painting?" With the three of them studying the window, Annalise insisted, "Your work is every bit as good as what I've seen at the Glimmer Hope Art Gallery."

"Oh puhleez, now you're just teasing." Sabrina felt a flush of warmth rise to her cheeks.

Standing arms akimbo, Annalise gave her sister a no-nonsense look. "I can't believe you have absolutely no clue how talented you are."

"Maybe she's just fishing for compliments," Hud teased and Sabrina took the bait.

"No I'm not," she insisted. "I've seen the work at the gallery and mine simply isn't the same caliber, that's all."

"Baloney." Annalise gave a flippant wave. "I know the gallery's owner, Hugo Calloway. We went to school together, remember? Great guy, savvy, with a good eye for talent. He's always on the lookout for local artists for Glassfloat Bay's branch gallery as well as his main downtown Portland gallery. I hear he's opening another branch in Rainspring Grove too."

"Right in the heart of wine country, hmm?" Sabrina said, recalling the charming, picturesque college town. "Good reason to visit."

"Trust me, Hugo would love to see your work, especially when he hears you're my little sister." Annalise smiled. "I could call and set up an introduction."

"I really appreciate the offer. But..."

"Yeah?" Hud said. "But what?"

"But I no longer show any of my artwork." Sabrina moved back to where Harry sat and the area where she had her painting supplies set up. She started adding highlights to the back of Santa's hair and beard.

Annalise offered a pouty expression. "Why not?"

"Oh, I..." Sabrina didn't know how to answer. She didn't want to admit how weak she'd been with Stuart. She didn't understand it herself. She looked everywhere but at Annalise's inquisitive expression.

"Yeah, w-why not? You're a g-great artist, M-mommy."

"Thank you, sweetie." Sabrina managed a little laugh.

It had been forever since she'd had the chance to do something artistic. In Pennsylvania she'd called her fledgling line of cards, pictures and painted jars SabrinArt, selling them locally. Her work became popular and she soon found herself with plenty of orders for her whimsical creations. While not substantial, the added income helped pay the past due bills that kept piling up, and provided a little money for Sabrina to save.

Her SabrinArt soon attracted media attention. She'd been contacted for interviews by the local press, bloggers, and by TV's public broadcasting channel. It was all so exciting and unexpected. Having people enjoy her artwork as much as she enjoyed creating it was a dream come true.

She was floating on cloud nine until Stuart wrenched her back down to earth, objecting to the time she spent on her art, claiming it encroached on her duties as a housewife and mother.

He insisted her skill level was amateurish at best, certainly not good enough to stand up to public scrutiny. Rather than fight with him about it, risking one of his frequent rages, Annalise simply stopped her creative pursuits. She'd been away from her art for so long she'd lost much of her confidence.

"Hello there, anybody home?" Waving spread fingers before Sabrina's face, Annalise laughed. "Seems like you were a million miles away."

"More like twenty-eight hundred." Sabrina shook herself out of her pensive mood. "Sorry. I just got to thinking about everything back in Pennsylvania."

Annalise and Hud exchanged concerned looks.

"Hey, you guys, quit worrying about me." Sabrina managed a bright grin. "Really. I'm fine. I just need some time to adjust."

The bell on the door jingled, snagging their attention as four people came into the café. "Time for me to quit jabbering and get back to work," Annalise said. "I've got a full staff onboard all day, Sabrina, so be sure to get your breaks in today. You've been so busy between painting and serving customers you rarely even stop for lunch. If you get any skinnier," she elbowed Sabrina, "customers will think you don't like your own sister's food, and we can't have that now, can we?"

Sabrina loved the sound of Annalise's boisterous laugh. "No ma'am," she answered with a mock salute. She enjoyed everything she'd tasted from the café's menu. Her sister had a knack for making delicious, satisfying comfort food that transported people's memories back to grandma's kitchen. It's just that Sabrina didn't have much of an appetite when she was nervous or edgy, the way she'd been feeling lately about the situation with Stuart.

"Thanks again for all of this." Annalise gestured to the festive windows. "I'll be tucking a little extra something into your pay this week."

"Don't be silly, Annalise. I told you that's not necessary. I love doing this. Really. I don't want any special treatment just because I'm your sister."

"Shut up and let her pay you for your work," Hud said. "You already look too much like a starving artist."

"Hud's right. Besides," Annalise added with a devilish smile, "I'm getting you for less than a professional window painter." Her grin was ear to ear. "Now no more talking back to the boss." Waving a chastising finger, she went on her way to greet customers.

"Aunt Annalise is a n-nice l-lady," Harry said.

"The best," Sabrina agreed, reminded again how much she'd missed her big sister when they were so many miles apart. She had a great way with people, making each of her employees and customers feel special. Annalise Griffin was like a combination of everyone's favorite teacher and apple-pie-making mom.

"Time for me to take off." Hud gave Harry a hug. "My crew will think I've disappeared." His gaze turned serious when he looked at Sabrina. "Don't forget. If there's anything you need, anything at all, you come to me, okay?"

"Okay." She pulled her big brother into a hug, so grateful for having him and Annalise in her life. They were just what she and Harry needed.

"M-maybe you c-could p-put Hark on the w-window," Harry suggested after Hud left.

"Your angel? That's a terrific idea, Harry," Sabrina agreed, painting the last toy into Santa's bag. "I'll start on Hark as soon as I finish Santa and Mrs. Claus."

"O-okay." He looked up at her, giving his mom a killer smile. "M-make sure she's wearing her c-coat with all the c-colorful s-squares. She l-likes that a lot."

"Absolutely. You can describe everything for me so I use the right colors."

Harry had a vivid imagination. With the tense home environment they'd had back in Pennsylvania she imagined he needed to inject a little fantasy into his life. Some kids had imaginary friends. Her son had an imaginary angel. So what? As far as she was concerned, it was a harmless bit of escapism that made her little boy happy, and she wasn't about to spoil it for him. He'd grow up and have to face the harsh realities of the world all too soon.

Catching a glimpse of the time on the wall clock, Sabrina told him, "It's almost time for you to head off to daycare."

"M-mister G-gard said h-he's t-taking me again t-today." His dimples appeared with his smile.

Focused on creating shading beneath Santa's bulging bag, Sabrina was surprised when someone knocked on the window again. She looked up to see the man who'd given Harry a ride to school the past two weeks, standing there the way her sister had, with both thumbs up, saying something she couldn't hear. She watched as he walked around to the door and came inside, trying hard not to notice how handsome he was.

The first thing Gard Malone did was wave to Harry. "Hey, Harry, how ya doing?"

Harry's face lit up. "G-good, M-m-mister G-gard! H-how are y-you doing?"

"Couldn't be better. I already told you, you don't have to call me mister." Cupping his hand over his mouth in a conspirator's manner, he added, "It makes me feel old." He cringed. "Just call me Gard."

Harry looked relieved. Sabrina knew it was a lot easier for him stutter-wise to leave off the M-words. She suspected Gard knew that too.

"Thanks, Gard. M-my dad t-told me to always c-call adults m-mister or m-miss unless they g-give m-me p-p-permission to c-call them by their f-first n-name."

"Well then, permission granted." Gard gave Harry a kindly smile which was quickly returned.

"I've never heard the name Gard before," Sabrina told him. "Is it a family name?"

Gard nodded, "I'm named for my Norwegian great-grandfather, Gerhard Johannesen. He was Bekka's father. Gard's a nickname for Gerhard."

"Is Gerhard your actual name?"

"Unfortunately." As one eyebrow quirked, his laughter was quick and genuine. "I'm familiar with that pitying look, Sabrina."

"Oh no," she protested, "I—"

"Sorry," his smile still in place, Gard gave a dismissive wave, "I didn't mean to put you on the spot. Rollcall in grade school was murder. That was back in the days when teachers insisted on using a kid's full name. On top of me being a pipsqueak, all the other boys were Jimmys, Bobbys, Mikes and Jacks."

"I can't picture you short." Gard was such a tall, powerful-looking man it was next to impossible imagining him as a pipsqueak.

"I was the shortest boy in class. Even shorter than most of the girls. My mom still has all the class pictures to prove it...and she's more than happy to whip them out to tell people all about poor little Gerhard." He rolled his eyes.

Sabrina couldn't help chuckling at that."

"I got razzed until my sophomore year of high school. Over the summer I shot up to over six feet from five-foot-nine. And *that*," Gard brushed his hands together, his expression clearly confident, "was the end of their taunting."

"D-do you think m-maybe I'll get b-big and t-tall like you one day, G-gard?"

"Absolutely, Harry, no doubt about it. Eat healthy and get plenty of exercise and in a few years it'll happen." He messed the boy's hair. Taking in all the work Sabrina had done on the windows, he noted, "Sabrina, that looks fantastic. I can't believe the progress you've made the last few days. The glow on Rudolph's nose looks so real, and I like the mischievous looks you gave the elves."

"Thank you." Her cheeks warming at the compliment, she continued to focus on her painting. Glimpsing him out of the corner of her eye, she said, "I enjoy doing this almost as much as I enjoy serving pancakes." She loved the rich, full sound of his laughter.

"Did you major in art?"

"No, I'm mostly self-taught." She scooped up more paint on her brush. "I've always loved to draw and paint." All the compliments she'd received about her work this morning were refreshing and a real confidence booster. Stuart gave her praise too the first year they were together. The thought brought back bittersweet memories.

"Is that a necessary part of the painting process?" Gard asked.

Confused, she looked up at him. "What do you mean?"

"The frown." He gestured at her expression. "Is that needed for concentration?"

Not even realizing she'd been frowning, Sabrina laughed. "Mmm-hmm. Sometimes it helps."

Gard stepped closer to Harry, watching as he colored with his crayons. "I like all the happy smiles on everyone, including the sun and moon faces."

"I l-like for everyone to b-be happy," Harry explained. "B-being happy is g-good."

Her dear little optimist. Harry was always trying to make his dad feel better. He'd make his father drawings and would tell him about fun things that happened at daycare and kindergarten. He'd even give Stuart massages after he complained about his long, tiring days at work.

Stuart couldn't be bothered to respond to his son with any warmth, but Harry never gave up, convinced the next time he'd succeed in making his dad smile.

"Whoa, and who's that, the Hulk? Very cool, Harry!"

"You r-recognized him?" Obviously pleased, Harry grinned.

"You bet I did."

Sabrina was pleasantly surprised. Props to Gard for recognizing the distorted green blob on her son's drawing.

"Y-you r-really think I d-did a good j-job?"

"Harry, it's so good I want you to draw a picture like this for me with all the happy faces, your angel, and the Hulk so I can put it on my refrigerator and everybody who comes to Bekka House can see it. Would you do that for me?"

Harry grinned from ear to ear. "S-sure! This one is f-for school but I'll m-make a s-special one j-just for you when I-I'm done."

"That's a deal." Gard squatted, getting eye level with her son. "I'd be honored to display such a fine work of art in my kitchen." He took Harry's hand in his, shaking it in a gentlemen's agreement.

It made Sabrina's heart glad to see her little boy soak up the praise.

Harry turned to the back of his notebook, slipping out a smaller sheet of paper from a pocket in the vinyl. His smiling, colorful angel took up the entire page.

"I d-drew this p-picture of Hark yesterday," Harry told Gard. "You c-can p-put this on your f-fridge until I get the other one r-ready for you."

"Hey, thanks." Gard accepted the drawing, clapping Harry on the back. "That's great. You did a real good job on this." Harry beamed in response.

Sabrina allowed her thoughts to wander briefly, wondering what it would be like for her son to have a father like Gard...a man who seemed to effortlessly like and understand children. Surreptitiously eyeing the handsome firefighter, she shut off her meandering thoughts. She'd just managed to finally extricate herself from her failed marriage—the last thing she needed was to start thinking about another man.

Before her son and Gard released hands, Sabrina saw Harold smoothing a finger over Gard's ring, examining it. She hadn't noticed the unusual, eye-catching piece of jewelry before. It had an ancient look about it.

"I l-like your r-ring," Harry said, turning Gard's hand over to inspect the band and stone.

"Thanks. My brother-in-law, Varik, gave it to me. Kind of an early Christmas present."

Harry gazed up at Gard. "It's m-magic." His small hand covered the ring's stone and Sabrina could swear she saw a soft glow briefly emitting from their joined hands. She blinked a couple of times, sure her eyes were playing tricks on her after all the detailed painting she'd been doing that morning. By Gard's stunned look, she wondered if he'd seen the glow too. But that was impossible. Rings aren't magic and they don't glow, except in the lively minds of children. Or artists with eyestrain.

"What makes you say that, Harry?" Gard looked confounded.

The boy shrugged. "Hark told me." Offering a contented smile, he went back to his drawing.

Gard's fingers clasped over the ring. A moment later, he and Sabrina exchanged a quick glance. She was surprised at his somewhat dazed expression.

When Gard rose to his feet, she leaned over to whisper in his ear. "Harold just has a vivid imagination. He's convinced he and his angel communicate with each other." She punctuated her words with a little chuckle, to which Gard merely nodded, without any degree of levity in his expression.

Strange, after sharing brief conversations with him daily for the last two weeks, she hadn't imagined Gard as a guy who put any credence in supernatural stuff. He came across as pretty levelheaded. But you just never know about people.

"I almost forgot." Gard reached into his pants pocket, pulling out an envelope. "My mother wanted to make sure I give you this. It's an invitation for you and Harry to the Malone family holiday open house this Sunday."

He handed Sabrina the envelope. She put her brush in the water jar and wiped her hands on the cloth she kept near the tubes of paint before taking the card.

"How nice. Thank you." She loved holiday gatherings. It had been so long since she'd attended one. Stuart disliked socializing, especially during the holidays. He said he saw enough people all week at work and wanted to be left alone on the weekends and holidays. While she wasn't a party animal by any stretch of the imagination, Sabrina did enjoy getting together with friends and had really missed that festive interaction the past few years.

"It's a joint affair Mom and my sisters host each year," Gard explained. "Annalise is a big part of it too. You'll enjoy it. Lots of great food and activities for the kids."

"C-can we g-go, M-mom?"

"Yes, it sounds wonderful." She glanced again at the invitation and smiled up at Gard. "I'll call your mom to see what I can bring."

"Trust me," Gard held up his hand, "there'll be enough food there for an army."

As Harry started packing up his coloring supplies and getting ready for Gard to drive him to daycare, Gard took Sabrina by the elbow, walking them a few steps away. Out of Harry's earshot he said, "I heard about you and Stuart getting a divorce. I'm sorry. Annalise said Harry doesn't know yet."

"I-I'm going to tell him soon." Her tone came out sharper than she'd intended.

"I wasn't criticizing, I just wanted to make sure I didn't say anything in front of him if I shouldn't."

"I appreciate that. And I know you weren't criticizing." Sabrina smiled at him. "Sorry. I'm a little touchy because I feel guilty for not telling him about the divorce yet." She breathed a sigh. "Is the open house at your parents' condo?" Opening the envelope, she slipped out the invitation.

"No, their place is too small. It's going to be at Bekka House. That's our family home, the place I've been staying since I returned from Antarctica."

"It must be pretty big."

"It is. It was a good sized house when my grandmother bought it and after she passed away the Malones have been busy making it even bigger, adding more bedrooms and bathrooms, updating and enlarging the kitchen, and even adding a second family room so there's plenty of room for entertaining, which my family enjoys doing. They added more living space outside too with a gazebo and a deck that wraps around most of the house." He gestured with his hands.

"Wow, it sounds like a mansion."

"Hardly." Breaking into casual laughter, Gard gave an offhand wave. "It's just a big old cozy, comfortable family house filled with love and great memories." Leaning toward Sabrina, he nudged her elbow with his own. "There's even talk of a few ghosts hanging around."

"I've heard a few stories," Sabrina said, trying to conceal a smirk. "Sounds like the Malones have vivid imaginations."

"Ghosts?" Harry's eyes grew wide. "Scary ones?"

"Not at all, Harry. You have my personal guarantee that Bekka House has friendly ghosts only. They're probably good friends with your angel, Hark."

"Cool!"

Sabrina gazed at Gard, amazed at how different his philosophy was from Stuart's, who bellowed at Harry whenever the boy mentioned his angel. She picked up her brush and started painting again, focusing on the pointed spikes and veins of three holly leaves as she painted them emerald green.

Chapter 4

~<>~

"THERE ARE SO m-many rooms in this house I c-can't even c-count that high!" Harry said, laughing as he explored the upstairs of Bekka House with his mom, Gard, Astrid, and Tundra.

"I saved the best for last," Astrid told Harry as she ushered him and Sabrina into the room at the end of the hall. "This is Gard's room. He uses that corner of the room for his office." She motioned to the area where a desk and chair stood.

Sabrina noted with surprise that it was a typical young boy's room, with posters of music groups, some photos of Gard as a boy with a dog, sports paraphernalia, a few trophies, a superhero-themed lamp on his nightstand and a matching superhero bedspread. She couldn't help smiling as she looked around. It was adorable but it certainly didn't look like something an adult man would select for himself.

"I thought you said you grew up in Chicago and moved out here several years ago," Sabrina said, noting the childish décor.

"Uh-huh." With a big old smirk across his face, Gard folded his arms over his chest, shooting his mother an accusatory glance. "You'd never know it by the looks of this room, would you?" he asked, still eyeing his mother, who'd adopted a purely innocent stance.

Leaning against the doorjamb, arms still crossed, he told Sabrina, "Early this morning while I was out picking up supplies for the open house, my mother and my sisters, Delaney, Laila, and Reen decided to take it upon themselves to *spruce* up my room." His fingers drew hanging quotes.

"So out came the boxes of all my kid stuff...because my mother, who's a packrat and never throws anything away, hauled all this," he spread his hands, "from Chicago when she and Tore moved to Glassfloat Bay. Mom and my sisters decided it would be funny." His eyes squinted as he folded his arms across his chest and look at Astrid. "I'm still not laughing."

Unable to keep from laughing herself, Sabrina couldn't help but notice the affectionate way Gard looked at his mother. He wasn't angry in the least. The Malones were clearly a family who loved each other...and knew how to share in good natured fun.

"I think your r-room l-looks g-great," Harry said, enthusiasm sparking from his gaze as he scanned the space. He'd never had a real little boy's bedroom of his own. Stuart believed it would spoil Harry. "Where are all your t-toys?"

"Downstairs. We all worked on finishing the basement in our spare time. Half the space is a big playroom filled with toys now." Gard turned to Sabrina. "Mom and Tore are clearly anticipating a ton of grandkids."

"There's nothing wrong with that," Astrid said, a genuine grin splitting her face.

"How many grandchildren are there so far?" Sabrina asked.

"Three," Astrid said, "Delaney and Varik's little girl, Rebekka Anders, and Laila and Zak's twins, Abby and Gus. Tore and I are hoping to have Bekka House crawling with at least a dozen grandchildren within the next ten years."

Gard made a raspberry sound.

"What?" Astrid asked. "It's a reasonable goal. After all, there are six of you Malone siblings."

"Four of whom aren't married," Gard reminded his mom.

"Yet." Tapping her wrist where a watch would be, Astrid said, "You all need to step it up before Tore and I are too old and decrepit to enjoy those grandkids."

Sabrina loved listening to their easy banter. It reminded her of her own parents, sister and brother when she was growing up. After turning over their café to Annalise, the only sibling interested in keeping it up, her retired parents moved to San Diego and she really missed them.

"C-can I see the p-playroom?"

The three adults smiled at Harry's understandable anticipation. "Professor Slattery will be here with Lilly in a while," Astrid told him. "When they get here I'll take you two down there to play, okay?"

Harry gave a big thumbs up. "G-great! Can T-tundra come too?"

"Absolutely," Astrid said. "He's a member of the family too."

Harry and Tundra had bonded. The sizeable, patient dog stayed close to Harry's side. Sabrina had no doubt her son, who'd always wanted a dog of his own, was in seventh heaven.

"While you're here," Astrid said, "I have something to show you. I'll be back in a minute." She ruffled Harry's hair.

"Aw, Mom, not the photo albums...please," Gard said in what sounded close to a whine, making Sabrina laugh. "Yeah, you think it's funny now," Gard told her, "but just wait until your eyes glaze over and you're begging to be put out of your misery thirty minutes from now."

"Oh hush up, Gard," Astrid said. "I'm sure Sabrina and Harry would love seeing pictures of my cute little Gerhard when he was just a little pipsqueak."

"See?" he said to Sabrina. "What did I tell you?"

"In fact," Astrid turned to Harry, "Gard looked a lot like you when he was your age."

"We'd love to see the pictures," Sabrina assured her, and Harry nodded.

Clearly happy to have a captive audience for her photo albums, Astrid scooted from the room, returning ten minutes later.

"Sorry." Astrid placed three albums on the bed. "It took me a while to go through the albums to find the right ones."

"Because she has hundreds of photo albums," Gard teased.

"Don't exaggerate, Gard." Shifting her attention to Sabrina, Astrid admitted, "Dozens, maybe, but not hundreds. One of these days I'll get them all scanned into the computer."

Gard choked on laughter. "They don't make home computers with that many terabytes of storage capacity."

Ignoring him, Astrid patted the mattress, telling Sabrina and Harry, "Come sit here on the bed with me. It'll be easier."

Sabrina and Harry sat on either side of Astrid and Gard pulled over the ladder-back chair next to his desk, straddling it so he faced them. Tundra leapt up on the bed, making himself comfortable at Harry's side.

"Hey, Tundra," Gard said, "that invitation to sit on the bed wasn't intended for you. You know you're not supposed to be up there."

As if he fully understood Gard's reprimand, Tundra offered a guilty look. Rather than get off the bed though, he planted his muzzle in Harry's lap.

"Dog one," Gard said, marking the air with his forefinger, "master zero."

"He's fine here." Astrid patted Tundra's flanks. She picked up a thick photo album that looked older than the others, setting it on her lap. "This album has old photos of me, my grandparents, Helga and Gerhard, my mother Bekka and my late father, James." She turned to Sabrina. "I never knew my dad. He died in the war before I was born. He was the light of my mother's life."

The sound of Harry's audible gasp caught Sabrina's attention. "What is it, sweetie?"

Her son stared at the photos for a long moment before looking up at Astrid. "How d-did you get a p-picture of Hark?"

Astrid's head cocked. "Of who?"

"Hark." Harry's fingertip rested beneath one of the old black and white photos. Sabrina eyed it curiously. He'd never claimed to see a photo of his angel before.

"Oh, that's my grandmother, Helga Johannesen," Astrid said. "Bekka's mother. We were very close. This was taken when she was about twenty five. Her long hair flowed in flaxen waves down her back, almost to her waist. She looked just like an angel here, didn't she?"

"She is! She's m-my a-angel!" Harry insisted.

"Harold, honey," Sabrina put her arm around him, speaking gently, "this woman is Gard's great-grandmother. She only looks like Hark."

"Who is Hark?" Astrid asked. "One of your relatives?"

"No..." Sabrina took in a deep breath, gazing directly into Astrid's eyes, hoping she wouldn't think this was too weird. "Harry has...an imaginary friend. An angel named Hark."

"As in "Hark, the Herald Angels Sing"," Gard offered, further clarifying for his mother.

After some thought, understanding dawned in Astrid's expression. "Ahhh, I see." With a warm smile and a hug, she said, "So Hark is your special Harold angel."

"Yes," he nodded, still excited about the photo. "She had l-light b-blue eyes, right?"

Surprised by the question, Astrid answered, "Yes...yes, she did."

"And she t-talked with an accent, r-right?"

Astrid glanced from Harry to Sabrina to Gard.

"S-sometimes she s-says *ja* instead of yes. And s-some other l-language w-words I don't understand."

Sabrina watched as Astrid swallowed hard. "What other language, Harry?"

"Hark t-told me she w-was *weejun*."

"Weejun?" After a long contemplative blink, Astrid asked, "Do you mean Norwegian?"

"Y-yes, that's it." His head bobbed and Harry gave a triumphant smile.

Her eyes wide, Astrid muttered, "How could he possibly know that?" It seemed she was asking herself more than anyone else. Looking at Sabrina, she repeated, "How?"

"I have no idea," Sabrina admitted, startled by the details Harry had given. He hadn't mentioned any of it to her before, or maybe Sabrina hadn't really listened. He was always jabbering about his angel and she was afraid she sometimes tuned him out. She felt her cheeks warm with the flush of guilt.

"Whoa..." Gard raised both hands. "Am I the only one who thinks this is more than a little eerie?"

"Well, Grandma Helga's been up in heaven for many years. Since shortly after Gard was born." Astrid looked happy though unsettled. "So, who knows? Maybe she *is* Harold's angel." She shrugged. "Of all the people I could imagine as an angel, Helga would be at the top of the list." She seemed lost in thought before breaking into a smile. "And I suppose angels can have more than just one name. Why not? What do you think, Harry?"

"S-sure. Angels c-can do anything." Harry spread his arms wide, beaming a smile.

"Well, young man," Astrid gave him a hug, "I want to hear all about your talks with Hark." She turned to Sabrina. "We'll make a date for you and Harry to come over to my place for some hot cocoa, my fresh-baked *pepperkaker*, and some good conversation. We can look at more photos too. How does that sound?"

"Very enjoyable." Sabrina thought it was wonderful the way Gard's mother validated Harry's belief, rather than ridicule him the way Stuart did. As Harry looked at the album, Sabrina mouthed a silent thank you to Astrid, who smiled, nodding in reply.

Astrid pointed out another photograph in the album. In this one, Helga looked to be about fifty. "Here's another favorite. How about that wild and crazy patchwork coat, hmm? Only someone with a lot of panache could pull off a garment like this and, believe me, Grandma Helga's middle name was panache." Astrid laughed softly.

"What's p-panache?"

"It means she was spirited and had her own unique sense of style," Astrid explained. "Here, take a look."

As he spotted the picture, Harry's jaw dropped. "L-look, G-gard, she's w-wearing her c-crocheted c-coat with all the c-colored squares."

Gard looked up after eyeing the photo, his face blanched of color. Turning to Sabrina, he asked, "Did you see this? It's just like Harry's drawings."

One glance had Sabrina feeling the same way Gard looked, stunned and bewildered. Each time her son drew his angel, she was wearing that garment. "No...that's not possible," Sabrina said on a whisper.

"My great-grandmother, Helga's mom, crocheted that coat especially for Helga," Astrid explained, seemingly unaware of Gard's and Sabrina's reactions as she gazed at the photo. "Grandma Helga wore it all the time."

"Don't anyone move." Gard lifted his hands, catching Astrid's attention.

"What is it? Gard, what's wrong? You look like you've seen a ghost."

"You'll understand in a minute, Mom. I'll be right back." Gard hurried out of the bedroom and down the stairs, returning a few minutes later with a sheet of paper in hand.

"Take a look." He thrust the paper at Astrid. It was the angel drawing Harry had given Gard at the café.

"Harry?" Now it was Astrid's turn to look dumbfounded. "How in the world did you know about my grandmother's crocheted coat?"

"Hark w-wears it all the t-time when I see her," Harry answered. He was the only one in the room who was cool, calm and collected, taking it all in stride.

"That's incredible. Too specific to be coincidental," Astrid said, clearly flustered. She turned to Gard. "Remember when you were in the hospital after that fire at your grade school? You insisted an angel wearing a patchwork coat helped to save you."

"No, I..." A pair of creases formed between Gard's eyebrows. "I-I don't know. Maybe. When I first looked at Harry's angel drawing it reminded me of something from a long time ago. But I don't remember much about what happened that day...I think I blocked a lot of it out."

"I thought you were just incoherent from the trauma. I never for a moment imagined," Astrid rested her hand on Gard's knee, "that you actually saw an angel." She locked gazes with Gard, looking at her son with so much love it brought tears to Sabrina's eyes. "Much less that the angel was your great-grandmother. I assumed you were probably hallucinating and had been influenced by those old photos of Helga in her coat."

"How frightening that must have been," Sabrina said. "Was it a big fire?"

"Very." There was a distant look in Astrid's eyes. "Gard's dad, my husband, Sean, was one of the firefighters there. He heroically lost his life in the line of duty that fateful day, saving many children, including his own son." She sucked in a deep breath, letting it out on a protracted sigh. "I wonder if Sean saw the angel too..."

"The last time I saw Dad, he was running back into the burning building," Gard said. "I remember wanting to go in after him...someone, or something, stopped me."

"I had no idea." Sabrina covered Astrid's hand with her own. "I'm so sorry." Her gaze moved to Gard, as well. It was difficult to understand why he'd chosen to be a firefighter himself after what happened to his father.

"Thank you," Astrid said, plucking a tissue from her pocket and dabbing her eyes. "It was a long time ago that sometimes feels like it was just yesterday." They sat in silence for a moment before Astrid smiled at them and said, "There's something I need to show you. I'll just be a minute." She left and they could hear her rifling around in the next bedroom. She returned shortly, carrying a shirt-sized box. When she opened it and moved back the tissue, there was a hushed awe.

Astrid gently lifted the long-sleeved garment from the box, holding it up for them to see. The delicate garment was yellowed with age and long enough to reach mid-calf on an average-sized woman.

"That's it," Harry confirmed with an excited smile. "The c-coat Hark wears. B-but hers l-looks n-newer."

"It's lightweight cotton crochet. It was my grandmother's favorite article of clothing because it was the last thing her mother made for her before she died. Grandma Helga wore it everywhere." Astrid smiled at the memory. "She loved snuggling up in it while she sat knitting or reading." She ran her fingertip along a couple of patches. "You can see where it's been repaired here and there but, all in all, it's still in good condition. Amazing it's lasted this long considering how often she wore it."

Constructed of patches of various shapes and sizes, some pieces were granny squares while some had solid backgrounds and detailed floral designs. No two patches were alike. The vibrant crocheted pieces were joined together with fanciful stitches in different colors. Sabrina had no doubt the intricate garment was made with love, probably over a long period of time by an expert needleworker.

Astrid smiled at Sabrina. "Your son's imaginary friend may not be quite as imaginary as you thought."

"It seems that way, doesn't it? But..." She left the word hanging, not knowing what to make of all this. Harry's frequent mentions of his angel were elaborate and amusing but she'd never even remotely considered the possibility that any of his ramblings were factual.

Harry's head popped up as he sniffed the air. Sabrina found herself inhaling too as a sudden spicy fragrance wafted overhead. It wasn't just them; Tundra was sniffing the air too and licking his chops.

"It s-smells l-like somebody's b-baking c-cookies in your b-bedroom, Gard."

"It's the *pepperkaker*," Astrid explained. "Gard, have you told Harry and Sabrina about our friendly ghosts yet?"

"He did," Sabrina answered, "but I thought he was joking."

"I thought I was too." Looking as dazed as Sabrina felt, Gard whipped his head toward his mother. "That's the first time I smelled it. I-I didn't believe it."

"Ahh, ye of little faith," Astrid wagged a finger at Gard. "We tried to tell you so. The ghosts are as real as Harry's angel," she claimed. "Our ghosts are *very* friendly, Harry. That cookie aroma is Gard's grandma's way of letting us know she's here and thinking about us...watching over us as we talk about her mother, Helga."

"Well..." Dumbfounded, Sabrina carefully measured her words. "I'd say cookie-baking ghosts, or angels, are probably the best kind to have."

In the next instant, the heavenly *pepperkaker* fragrance ceased—gone, as if it had never been there.

"Time for me to show you those pictures of Gard when he was little." Astrid slipped the old album from her lap, selecting another. She flipped to a page and sat back with a loving smile. "There's my baby boy. Wasn't he a cutie pie? And he still is." Astrid reached over to give Gard's cheek a fond pinch.

"Aw, Mom, seriously?" He rubbed the spot where she'd pinched.

"Shush," Astrid said. "Here are all his class photos. My little Gerhard got to sit in front because he was the shortest child in his class...poor thing."

Gard shot another *I told you so* glance at Sabrina and she muffled a chuckle.

"Here he is in first grade," Astrid said, her fingernail tapping the top of Gard's blond hair in the picture. "See what I mean about Harry resembling Gard?" She tilted the album in Sabrina's direction, skimming her finger over several pictures.

Sabrina was surprised at the resemblance. "You're right."

"Let m-me see!" Harry positioned himself to get a good look. "Hey it does k-kinda l-look l-like me!"

Obviously intrigued, Gard leaned in to have a look, turning the album toward him. Sabrina watched his eyebrows lift in surprise. "Well look at us, Harry. A couple of little towheads." He reached over, tousling Harry's blond hair, which was a few shades lighter than Gard's.

"I never noticed it before. We look enough alike to be brothers, or father and son."

"You do." Sabrina felt a lump form in her throat at Gard's words as she admitted to herself how much she wished she and Harry really were a part of this loving family. It pained her to think how much better off her son would be if he had a dad like Gard instead of a father who made a point of avoiding or ridiculing him.

She wondered what it might be like being married to Gard. While he was blessed with good looks, it was his character that made a lasting impression. He made the effort to make her feel valued, while Stuart excelled in making her doubt herself.

She stole a quick glance at Gard and Astrid. No, there was nothing productive or positive in making comparisons, nothing fruitful in wishful thinking or daydreaming about a family life that wasn't hers...or Harry's.

"Sabrina, dear, are you feeling all right?" Astrid clasped Sabrina's forearm. "You're all flushed."

"Am I?" Her hands flew to her cheeks. "I feel fine. I-I must have gotten a little windburn on the walk here. It's a little chillier outside than I expected."

Astrid's eyebrows knitted. "You walked all the way here from your apartment?"

"Mmm-hmm." Sabrina nodded. "Harry and I enjoy walking together, don't we sweetie?"

He smiled up at her. "I l-like d-doing whatever you l-like d-doing, M-mom."

"You don't have a shift at the station later, do you?" Astrid asked Gard.

"Nope. I'm free all day and evening so, in anticipation of your suggestion," he nodded at his mother, "yes, I'd be happy to give Sabrina and Harry a ride home."

"There's no need for that," Sabrina insisted. "Really. Walking is the only way I get any exercise." She offered light laughter.

Gard's eyebrow shot up. "Are you kidding? You're on your feet running around all day at the café."

"And M-mom's always b-busy w-working around the house t-too."

"That settles it." Gard slapped his knee. "Tundra and I will be driving the two of you home."

"Yay!" Harry clapped before turning to his mom. "It r-really is a p-pretty long walk, M-mom."

"Thank you." Sabrina felt her cheeks flush again. She wished her skin wasn't so pale, giving away any hint of a blush at inopportune times.

After scooting off the bed, Harry stood at Gard's desk, looking at the books, papers and instruments gathered there. "What d-do you do in y-your office?"

"Glaciologist stuff," Gard said simply. When Harry frowned, planting his fists on his hips, both Gard and Astrid laughed.

"Aw, c-come on, G-gard," he protested with a dramatic sigh. "D-don't treat m-me like a kid. I really w-want to know what you d-do."

"Don't be rude, Harry," Sabrina scolded. Harry looked down at his feet and muttered an apology. "Sorry. I think he's had far more than his share of sugar since we got here."

"No problem." Gard waved his hand through the air. "There are enough sweets downstairs to turn the entire town into diabetics."

"I'm about ready to bounce off the walls myself," Astrid confessed.

After gazing at Harry for a long moment, Gard said, "Are you really interested in hearing about glaciology?"

"Sure!" Harry's head bobbed. "I d-don't know a-any other ice experts."

"Most kids your age," Gard told him, "would sooner plant themselves in front of a videogame than listen to some *old* guy rattle on about glaciers."

"My d-dad doesn't l-let me play v-videogames," Harry said. "He s-says I should read and s-study instead."

Sabrina swallowed hard. The real reason Stuart didn't allow Harry to play videogames was because he was too cheap. Any money spent on his son was money he couldn't spend drinking. But she wasn't about to throw a pall over their pleasant conversation by telling them that.

"Oh...okay then." Taking a seat at his desk, Gard hauled Harry onto his lap. "Aside from working in Antarctica and here at home as a firefighter, I also teach, mainly giving lectures on glaciology to students of geology and geophysics at Wisdom Harbor University."

"I didn't know you were a teacher too." Sabrina's eyebrows elevated in surprise.

"It's one of the things he enjoys most," Astrid said with pride.

"Teaching means I have to do lots of research, making sure all the information is accurate and up to date. Otherwise I won't know what I'm talking about when I give lectures to students. To help my research I make endless notes while sitting on top of glaciers and—"

"I'll b-bet you get a c-cold butt." Harry covered his mouth with his hands, giggling a mischievous laugh.

Gard shifted the boy in his lap, slanting his head so he could look into Harry's eyes. "Harry, you have no idea. Trust me, it's no fun having your backside turn into a butt popsicle." That had Harry laughing harder.

"Tell them your frozen butt story," Astrid urged.

"I don't think they want to hear about that, Mom."

"Oh yes we do," Sabrina said. Harry agreed with a hearty nod.

Groaning, Gard shifted his gaze from one to the other. "Okay, you asked for it. It was on my first trip to Antarctica. I didn't bother listening to all the boring safety lectures. I figured I was smart enough to know what I should and shouldn't do. Big mistake."

"Gard can be a bit of a know-it-all," Astrid added.

With mock annoyance, Gard said, "Do you think maybe once, just once, I can tell my story without any edification from you, Mom?"

"Sorry. You go right ahead, dear." Astrid made a motion of locking her lips and throwing away the key, which had Harry giggling again.

"As I was saying before I was so rudely interrupted," Gard shot his mother a humorous warning look, which she returned with an entirely innocent expression, "the second day on the job I was getting samples while sitting on a huge chunk of ice. I sat there too long without adequate protection. And I got frostbite on—"

"Smack dab on the middle of his butt," Astrid finished, clapping her own backside.

"You'd think I'd have learned by now just to let my mother tell my stories." Gard gave a resigned laugh.

"That didn't really happen, did it?" Sabrina asked. "You're exaggerating, right?"

"No exaggeration," Astrid chimed in. "I have a photo of his bandaged frostbitten butt that one of his coworkers took if you want to see it. As they say...one picture's worth a thousand words."

"Yeah!" Harry said without hesitation, while Sabrina merely covered her mouth trying to muffle a laugh.

"Don't you dare, Mom." With a warning expression, Gard jabbed an accusatory finger at Astrid. "Seriously. I mean it."

"Oh hush." Astrid made a raspberry sound while giving a dismissive wave. "I wasn't really going to show it."

"Yeah...right." Gard shot his mom a knowing sideways glance before returning his attention to Harry and Sabrina. "Half of Glassfloat Bay has already been treated to pictures of my naked frozen butt, thanks to my mother."

"Now you're exaggerating." With her hand curving at the side of her mouth, Astrid leaned toward Sabrina and Harry, her voice dipping to a conspiratorial whisper. "It was only a third of Glassfloat Bay at the most."

Sabrina enjoyed the easy, fun-loving give and take between mother and son. They seemed to have a wonderful relationship.

Gard sat back, folding his arms across his chest. "It was an incident I'll never forget. One brought on by my own stupidity and stubbornness. I had to get help from my coworkers to get my backside thawed out. Talk about embarrassing!" He winced.

Harry laughed harder and Sabrina couldn't help joining in.

"That certainly is quite a visual, Gard," she said, alternately giggling and apologizing for doing so.

Gard's expression twisted. "I still get teased about it. It's one mistake I'll never make again." He jostled Harry on his knee. "That's why it's always important to pay attention to safety instructions, Harry. No one wants to turn into a butt popsicle."

"Were you able to sit while you were recovering?" Sabrina asked.

"He had to use a donut pillow," Astrid said.

"Which only added to the jokes and teasing." Gard winced at the memory.

Sabrina tried in vain to curb her laughter. "I can imagine," she said, clearing her throat.

"Getting back to what I do, Harry, part of my job as a glaciologist is to study all aspects of ice, from the polar ice caps to mountain glaciers. I'm part of a network of glaciologists who share our findings with each other. We study what we've discovered and then design experiments."

"Experiments? L-like u-using ice c-cubes to s-see what happens when you p-put them in a d-drink?"

Gard's eyebrow hiked. "You've got one inquisitive boy here, Sabrina. I put most kids to sleep when I start talking glaciology."

"Well what you do *is* pretty fascinating," Sabrina said. "I've never even heard of an ice expert before."

"D-do you know e-everything in the w-world about ice?" Harry asked.

"Pretty much."

"A-about ice c-cubes too?"

"Uh...sure, I guess so."

"L-like what?" Harry gave him an earnest look.

"Well..." Gard scratched his head. "Like making ice cubes using water you've boiled first makes the cubes clear instead of cloudy. Using distilled water does the same thing."

Harry seemed suitably impressed.

"That's an old trick Gard learned back in college," Astrid said. "He and his roommates used it to impress girls."

"Yeah, we made clear ice cubes to impress girls...no wonder I'm still single." Gard chuckled to himself. "Harry, did you know glaciers store about seventy-five percent of the world's fresh water?" Harry shook his head back and forth. "And that in the United States, glaciers cover over 30,000 square miles?"

"Are there any g-glaciers h-here in O-oregon?"

"No, most are located in Alaska. How much do you think sea level would rise if all the ice on Earth suddenly melted, Harry?"

"About up t-to here?" he guessed, placing his hand about the height of his chin.

"Nope."

"Fifty feet?" Sabrina guessed.

"Nope. Two—"

"Two hundred thirty feet," Astrid finished.

Gard's eyebrows hiked in surprise. "How'd you know that, Mom?"

"I've only heard you say it a hundred times, honey." Astrid gave him a wink. "You tend to get very passionate about ice facts."

About to respond to his mother, Gard shook it off instead, turning back to Sabrina and Harry. "It amounts to about thirty-eight men who are six feet tall standing on top of each other," he told them.

"That's a l-lot! C-could that h-happen?"

"That's my question too," Sabrina said. "Is it possible the oceans could flood all over the world?"

"Not in our lifetime. Global warming's a real concern, as it should be. Since we glaciologists research all the natural phenomena on Earth that involves ice, we know the average temperature in Antarctica is minus thirty-four-point-six degrees Fahrenheit, which means that while the ice there is slowly melting, it will take a long time before the effect causes catastrophic problems throughout the world."

Harry's eyes glazed over at Gard's technospeak. After a long moment, he blinked and started fidgeting. "I w-wonder if L-lilly is here yet." Scooting from Gard's lap, he asked, "C-can I g-go downstairs and check?"

"It seems Harry's experienced a case of fascination overload," Gard teased.

"I'll take him and Tundra down to the playroom," Astrid offered, taking Harry's hand. "And then I'll take some photos of you and Lilly to add to my photo album," she told Harry. "How does that sound?"

Beaming a broad, genuine smile up at Gard's mom, Harry said, "G-good, M-m-miss Astrid. Real g-good."

Sabrina's heart swelled at the joy on her child's face. Today would be a day neither of them would soon forget.

Chapter 5

~<>~

AS SOON AS Harry and Astrid left the room and were out of earshot, Gard laughed. "Once again I've succeeded in numbing the mind of a student," he said. "I hope I didn't bore you to tears too."

"Not at all. I love listening to you talk." Sabrina's cheeks turned pink, as he noticed they did often. He found it quite endearing.

"I mean I like listening to what you have to say about global warming. It's very interesting."

Gard sat silent for a moment, gazing at Sabrina. He was glad that her soon to be ex-husband was back in Pennsylvania. He'd heard stories about Stuart Hanklen from Annalise and Hud. The guy sounded like a real piece of work; controlling, unsociable, sarcastic, and an alcoholic who took his bad temper out on his wife and kid. And it seemed Gard and Sabrina shared the experience of having an unfaithful partner.

Until he'd met her Gard had decided he was finished with women, at least when it came to lasting relationships. The thought of settling down again after what his ex-fiancée put him through when he was hospitalized soured him. He'd learned that nothing good came of putting your heart on the line for a woman.

Now? Meeting Sabrina and her son had Gard contemplating things he never thought he would again.

This afternoon she wore a nice-fitting pair of jeans, topped by a red pullover sweater that looked as soft as rabbit's fur. He was tempted to reach out and stroke her arm just to see. It was the first time he'd seen her in anything other than her waitress uniform. While she had the curves he'd suspected were hiding beneath that retro dress and apron she wore at the café, her too-thin appearance was even more evident in street clothes. She could definitely benefit from a few of Annalise's hearty meals.

"Is there something wrong?" Sabrina looked down at her sweater, brushing it with her fingers, just the way Gard wanted to do. "Please tell me I don't have sticky fruitcake crumbles embedded in my sweater."

Until she spoke Gard hadn't realized how intently he must have been staring at her while lost in thought. "No, nothing like that." His laughter sounded nervous to his own ears. "I was just absorbed in my thoughts about one of my upcoming lectures. Sorry. Sometimes I get to thinking about work and my mind wanders."

"I understand. The same thing happens to me."

"So you like fruitcake too?" When she gave him an odd look he reminded her, "You were asking if you had fruitcake crumbles on your sweater."

"Oh!" She slapped her forehead and laughed. "Mind like a steel trap," she joked, tapping her temple. "I love fruitcake, but only when it's my sister's."

"Nobody makes fruitcake like Annalise," Gard agreed. "How can you not love all that rum-soaked fruit? Especially those big juicy candied cherries."

"Tell me about it." Sabrina licked her lips. He wanted to lick them too. "She covers the cakes with cheesecloth and lets them steep for months until the rum, brandy, and orange liqueur are smooth and mellow. Annalise told me you're her biggest fruitcake fan."

"And not just during the winter holidays," Gard said. "I love it all year."

"A nice small slice with a cup of tea is good any time of the year."

"Or a big slab with a vat of coffee," Gard suggested.

"Or that too." Sabrina laughed. "My sister loves making people happy with her cooking."

"Laila is the same way with her baked goods. She works hard coming up with recipes for scones, cookies, brownies, and all sorts of things that are usually off limits for dieters. I don't know much about cooking or dieting but even I think it's amazing how my sister gets them to taste so good while being so much lower in calories."

"I know. I can't tell the difference between the regular and her reduced calorie versions. I love the name of her bakery—The Great Pretender." Sabrina spread her hands as if spanning a banner when she spoke. "That says it all; healthier foods pretending to be their fatty, decadent counterparts. Have you tasted Laila's new chai spice scones?"

"Not yet."

"Mmm, so delicious." Her eyelids fluttered shut for a moment, giving him the opportunity to study her picture-perfect profile. "Especially while sipping from a warm mug of chai latte."

They were talking as though they'd known each other for years. Light, smooth, easy give and take conversation. Gard felt at ease with her...wanted to get to know more about her.

After a short lull in their conversation he noticed Sabrina shifting in her seat and looking slightly less comfortable. She picked up an action figure toy from his desk, absently playing with it.

"I wanted to tell you that I finally did it," she said, her eyes still on the toy in her hands. "Had the talk with Harry."

"How did it go?"

"Okay." Her smile widened as she looked up at him. "Really well, actually. I think I underestimated Harry. I was afraid he'd be surprised and upset about the divorce, maybe even scared, but he wasn't." Her shoulders lifted in a shrug. "He seemed to take it in stride, as if he'd already realized what was going on with me and his dad. The part that got to me," Sabrina blinked as her eyes grew watery, "is when my little son put his arms around my neck and told me, 'Don't worry, Mommy. I'm here. It's going to be okay.'"

Placing the action figure back on his desk, she sniffled and her chin trembled. Gard could see she was trying hard not to cry after repeating Harry's touching remarks.

"You've got quite a special little guy there, Sabrina."

With a like-minded nod, she said, "I do. I'm a truly fortunate woman." She breathed deep and smiled, looking more relaxed after telling him about her talk with Harry. "Your mom mentioned you had a bad accident on one of your Antarctica expeditions that landed you in the hospital a few years ago. It sounds like being a glaciologist can be dangerous work."

Gard felt his throat tighten, his body stiffen, as scenes from the accident flashed across his mind. "Tim..." was all he said before he became engulfed in razor-sharp images from the past.

"Tim?"

He focused his gaze when he felt the light touch of her hand on his arm. Sabrina tilted her head, regarding him with a look of concern.

Mentally shaking himself out of his unsettling memories, Gard clarified, "Laila's fiancé, Tim McKevitt. He died on that trip, falling into a deep crevasse that none of us had spotted. He was my best friend."

"Oh how awful, Gard, I'm so sorry." She gave his arm a gentle squeeze then released it, resting her hand in her lap. "That must have been awful for you."

"It was." He sucked in a deep breath. The subject isn't one he liked to talk about. When asked about what happened, Gard usually changed the subject in a way that let the questioner know in no uncertain terms that he didn't want to discuss it. But for some reason he found himself opening up to Sabrina.

"If this is something you don't want to discuss, I understand completely."

He looked into her eyes, her beautiful blue eyes. They were filled with concern. "It's not something I normally like to talk about but I don't mind telling you, Sabrina." He willed himself not to follow through on the urge to take her hand in his.

"Crevasses are one of the hazards of working in Antarctica. We're trained to watch for fissures and other dangers, and we've got rescue measures at hand in the event of someone falling but..." Those damned images of Tim's broken body dangling from the rope tied around him rushed across his mind again.

"But?"

This time she placed her hand on his upper arm and he felt the warmth of her touch through his shirtsleeve. The gesture seemed natural and caring while her expression projected kindness and compassion. No wonder he found it so easy to talk to her.

"But sometimes no matter how hard we try, people lose their lives. I tried to save Tim but...I couldn't." He gazed into her eyes. "I failed."

"I don't know all the particulars but I'm sure you did everything possible to save Tim, Gard."

Her gaze was full of sympathy. When he recognized that emotion in others it usually made him retreat. But there was something about Sabrina...

"Is that how you were injured? Trying to rescue him?"

She was absently rubbing his arm now. Gard doubted Sabrina had any inkling what her innocent touch was doing to him. Here he was mired in nightmarish memories of trying to save his best friend...while thoughts of a far more intimate and pleasurable nature prodded against those memories.

Oh yeah...he was screwed up. Big time.

He placed his hand on hers, stilling it, enjoying the brief touch of skin on skin before he dropped his hand.

"Yes. That's how it happened."

"Tell me about it."

And Gard did. He told Sabrina everything. She was one of the few people he'd fully opened up to about the tragedy and he felt good doing it. There was something healing, cleansing, about revealing his feelings to her.

The woman was not only a good listener, she made him feel like every word he said was captivating.

"I'm sorry, Sabrina. I didn't mean to chew your ear off like that."

"On the contrary, I'm honored that you shared your experience with me, Gard. I can't imagine how terribly painful the ordeal must have been for you, emotionally as well as physically. You did everything humanly possible to save Tim. You're a true hero."

Huffing a humorless laugh, Gard shook his head. "I'm no hero. Heroes don't fail."

"Don't talk like that." Sitting ramrod straight in her chair, Sabrina gave him a blunt look. "Heroes are brave, courageous people who try, rather than people who stand aside, waiting for someone else to make the effort. Your rescue attempt, almost losing your life in the process, was incredible in the same way risking your life as a firefighter is amazing." She paused a moment, her expression pinching as she gazed ahead as if in deep thought.

Less than a minute later she gave him a pensive look. "Do you like Tom Hanks?"

Amused at her somewhat peculiar change of subject, Gard gave her a strange look. "Well that was a smooth segue. Yeah, he's a favorite. Why?"

"Because he said something once, something simple yet profound, that really resonated with me. I hope it'll do the same for you."

"You mean when he was playing Woody in Toy Story and he told Buzz Lightyear that Buzz was just an action figure and not a real person? Yup, I agree, that really was pretty profound." He slid

Sabrina a sideways glance, watching as she struggled but failed to maintain her serious expression.

"No, silly." She gave his arm a playful whap. "Although...I'll admit, that bit of news must have been pretty devastating for poor Buzz." She tsked.

That added observation of hers made him smile. Looks, brains, a big heart and a sense of humor. Sabrina Griffin Hanklen was the whole package.

"Okay now, Gard, put on your serious face. This is important."

"You sound just like a teacher I used to have."

Grimacing, she buried her face in her hands, talking through her fingers. "Oh Lord, I think I just used my mom voice on you."

"Well I guess it worked. I feel a serious face coming on." He wiped the air down from his forehead to his chin, revealing a stern frown.

"Whoa," Sabrina held up her hands, "too serious."

Gard made another air swipe, erasing the scowl. "Better?"

"Much. Anyway," she broke into an easy smile, "I'm talking about when Tom Hanks said, 'A hero is somebody who voluntarily walks into the unknown.'" She clasped his hand, giving a reassuring squeeze. "That's what you do, Gard, every day. And that's what you did for Tim. Now please, no more ridiculous talk of you being a failure. Promise me." Letting go of his hand, she pointed a disciplining finger. "Don't make me use my mom voice on you again, Gerhard Malone."

He stared at her, studying her sweet face. He'd never wanted to kiss a woman more than that moment.

"Okay," he said just above a whisper. "I promise."

"Good." Getting to her feet she gave a resolute nod before gifting him with a beautiful smile that had him noticing for the first time that Harry got his dimples from his mother. "That's what I like to hear. Now let's get downstairs so I can see what my little munchkin is up to."

Like an adoring puppy, Gard gladly followed.

~<>~

The first floor of Bekka House was full of people milling around. Not wanting to monopolize Gard's time, Sabrina encouraged him to visit with the group of friends who'd stopped him to chat, ensuring him she'd be fine on her own. From the bits of conversation she heard it seemed they hadn't seen Gard since he returned from Antarctica and they were eager to catch up.

Spotting Laila and Reen talking as they poured themselves glasses of eggnog, Sabrina headed in their direction.

"It's just that she's all wrong for him," Reen was saying to Laila. "I mean look at him and look at her." She tossed her hand in the direction of the couple she spoke about and Sabrina's gaze followed, landing on her brother and an attractive blonde.

"Hudson's laid back and casual and Monica's all Barbied up with her stiletto heels, skintight dress and cherry-red lips." Her arms entwined across her chest, Reen fumed. "I thought he was smart enough not to be taken in by someone like her. The woman's as fake as a three dollar bill."

It was no surprise to Sabrina that Reen had a thing for her brother. She could tell by the way Reen looked at him whenever they were in the café at the same time. Since Hud wasn't one to talk about his feelings or the women in his life, Sabrina hadn't a clue how he felt about either Reen or Monica.

Reen tapped her foot on the floor, her attention still fixed on Hud and the woman with him. Reen's nemesis exuded classic beauty and sex appeal. With her designer clothes, expensive shoes, killer body, and blonde hair slicked back into a bun at her nape, Sabrina thought Monica could easily be mistaken for an actress or model. No wonder Reen appeared to be jealous.

Maureen, on the other hand, was a wholesome girl-next-door type; pretty, with a nice shape, striking hazel eyes, and a beautiful smile. Sabrina thought she was adorable. She hadn't known Reen or Laila long but it was clear that Reen's interest in Hud ran deeper than friendship.

"I don't even know why I should care." Reen mindlessly shoved a frosted Christmas cookie in her mouth while twirling a long lock of blonde hair with a finger of the other hand. "Hud's a big boy. If he wants to make a fool of himself over some...some sexy dragon lady, that's entirely up to him." Her eyes narrowed. "Look at her clinging to him like, like, like mustard to a hotdog." She popped another cookie in her mouth.

"In case you're keeping count," Laila told Reen, "that's the fifth cookie you've scarfed down in the ten minutes we've been standing here. That one," she gestured to her sister's hand, "will make number six."

"What?" Reen gazed at her hand with a dumbfounded look before replacing the cookie on the plate. Her expression said she wasn't even aware she'd been nibbling away. "Oh...I...I guess I got carried away. They're really good. I wonder who made them."

"Thanks, I did," Sabrina said. "It's my grandmother's recipe. Butter pecan cookies with brandied frosting, a family favorite. I had to make another batch just for Hud."

"They're delicious," Reen said. "They taste like a bazillion calories."

"That's probably close. But you don't have anything to worry about in that department." Giving Reen a quick onceover, Sabrina noted she was lean and fit with curves in all the right places. She could probably teach Sabrina a thing or two about getting her body back into its former curvier shape.

"I was looking for Harry, to make sure he's not getting into any trouble—or causing any." Sabrina laughed. "Your mom said she was taking him down to the playroom."

"They're down there with Lilly and Kevin, Drake Slattery's kids, my twins, and Delaney's daughter," Laila told her, "having a ball with all the old toys. Delaney is watching them with my mom."

"Mom loves kids," Reen said. "And there she goes, rubbing up against him."

"Mom?" Laila asked, clearly knowing that's not what Reen meant. The gleam in her eye confirmed it.

"No. Monica," Reen clarified, oblivious to Laila's humor. "She's whispering in his ear now and tittering some silly, practiced little laugh. Oh brother. I never pegged Hudson Griffin for being so shallow. The big dope's just lapping it all up." She shot Sabrina a quick apologetic glance. "Oh hell. Sorry, Sabrina. I forgot you're his sister. No offense."

"None taken, Hud *can* be kind of a dope sometimes." She and Laila chuckled while a straight-faced Reen continued her surveillance.

"In case you're wondering," Laila said to Sabrina, "Monica Sharp is a high-end real estate agent who works with our cousin, Saffron. Let's just say the two of them were less than cordial when it came to my recent real estate transaction."

"Monica was a first class bitch," Reen amended.

"She *was* somewhat ill-mannered." Laila laughed. With a sheepish look, she told Sabrina, "I know we must sound terribly catty but, well...if you knew Monica you'd understand."

"It's not like your brother doesn't know how Monica treated Laila," Reen said to Sabrina. "I know Annalise told him all about it. But ever since she clapped eyes on Hud, Monica's turned from snarling mountain lion into sweet little pussycat and she's had him in her claws ever since." Sabrina didn't catch the rest because Reen was mumbling beneath her breath while biting into cookie number six.

Shoving the rest of the cookie in her mouth, Reen turned on her heel and marched off.

Sabrina had never seen Reen so riled before. "Poor thing really has it bad, doesn't she?" she said to Laila.

"I'm afraid so." Laila watched as her sister headed out of the room. "I don't suppose Hudson has ever said anything about..." Pausing, she looked at Sabrina and smiled. "No, of course he hasn't. It's like pulling teeth to get Gard or Nevan to tell me anything about how they feel or who they might be interested in."

"Hudson's definitely not a sharer," Sabrina confirmed. "Sorry but I have no clue about what he thinks of Reen."

"Unfortunately for Reen," Laila noted, "he seems pretty taken with Monica."

"It does seem that way." Deciding it might be best to change the subject, Sabrina looked around the room at the endless platters of food. "Gard was right when he told me there'd be enough food here to feed an army."

"Better too much than too little, right?" Laila broke into a bright smile. "Annalise will gather up whatever's left and bring it to the café," she said, as if sensing Sabrina's unasked question. "Each year she invites the homeless and those in need to stop by to help themselves to cookies, cakes, sandwiches and whatever else she has available. She makes a nice holiday party for them."

"I remember Annalise talking about wanting to do that before taking over the café from our parents when they retired and moved to California," Sabrina said. "She's always believed in giving back and helping those less fortunate."

"She's got a big heart," Laila agreed, biting into one of the cookies that had caught Reen's interest. "Mmm, these really are good, Sabrina. You'll have to give me the recipe."

"Only if you promise to transform it into a reduced calorie version that I can eat without guilt."

"How can I resist a challenge like that?" Laila grinned. "You know, Gard's crazy about your little boy. I can see why. Harry's a real cutie. He's going to be a heartbreaker one day. Has he been a stutterer for long?"

Sabrina was surprised that Laila asked. Not that she minded, but most people went out of their way to avoid the subject of Harry's stuttering problem, probably because they feared offending her or saying the wrong thing.

"It's been going on since he started talking. He's in speech therapy, which has helped a lot."

"Did Gard tell you he stuttered when he was a boy too?"

"No." That was something Sabrina didn't expect to hear. "I had no idea. He's been so patient and understanding with Harry's stuttering. That must be why."

"It was tough for Gard when he was little. He got teased a lot. But, with the exception of one particularly harsh teacher, he had a lot of love and support. Fortunately, he grew out of it after a few years. I'll catch him stuttering a little every so often, when he's overtired or stressed. He said the best thing he learned from speech therapy was to sing the words when he got stuck. I have no idea why it works but it does."

"It works for Harry too. I have my fingers crossed that he'll grow out of his stuttering soon. Um..." Sabrina wasn't sure if she should mention her conversation with Gard or not, but decided it wouldn't do any harm. "Gard told me what happened to Tim. I'm so sorry." She clasped Laila's arm. "That must have been so difficult for you."

An expression of sadness briefly crossed Laila's features before she offered a warm smile. "It was. It was frightening because we were all worried we might lose Gard too. Did my brother tell you his fiancée left him while he was still in the hospital fighting for his life?"

THE FIREFIGHTER'S HEARTWISH

"No!" Sabrina gasped. So Gard hadn't told her everything about that terrible incident after all. "You can't be serious?"

"Yup. Joanne Dowser. You won't see her here. My mom purposely didn't invite her."

"I can see why." It was beyond comprehension that any woman would do something so unthinkable...especially to a wonderful man like Gard.

"Joanne claimed she didn't feel strong enough to cope with all of Gard's physical and emotional wounds. We learned later that she'd been cheating on him all along during his trips to Antarctica."

The distasteful idea of a woman doing that to her fiancé curdled deep inside Sabrina's belly. "I don't even know what to say, Laila. What an awful thing for her to do."

"He didn't deserve it. Joanne's one of those women who knows how to come across as sweet, soft and vulnerable when it benefits her. She had us all fooled." Shuddering, Laila rubbed her arms. "It still makes me angry to think about it." She helped herself to another of Sabrina's cookies, murmuring her pleasure as she bit into it.

The sound of females giggling caught Sabrina's attention and she turned toward the tittering. The tall, handsome, muscled man who was the center of all the attention looked like a model for a classic Greek statue.

"Who's that guy in the midst of all those women?"

Glancing over her shoulder at the man who was circled by several flirty women, Laila huffed a laugh. "That's my husband, Zak. He's an exercise physiologist. He leads the Sumerian Fitness classes at Wisdom Harbor University. Those are some of his students."

"Ah...now I understand."

"What do you mean?" Laila asked.

"When Annalise told me your husband has a waiting list a mile long for his classes I couldn't imagine why. I mean, come on, who loves exercise *that* much?" She tossed the group another glance before returning her attention to Laila with a mischievous smile. "Now that I see Zak I understand. You married a hottie, Laila."

Laila's face lit up as she grinned. "Yup, and he knows it too. But since he's only got eyes for me I don't mind." She took another bite of the cookie. "Too much." She gave Sabrina a wink.

"And you're a beautiful woman, so you make a perfect couple."

"I knew there was a reason I liked you." Laila clapped Sabrina's back. "You're good for my ego." She polished off the last of her cookie, making a prolonged *mmmmm* sound. "Speaking about food and exercise," she gave Sabrina a head to toe appraisal, "I can't see an ounce of extra fat anywhere on you. What do you do to stay so slender? Diet or exercise?"

During her six-year marriage, Sabrina had lost more than thirty pounds. Unintentionally. She'd developed digestive problems because Stuart turned mealtimes into a battleground. It kept her stomach tied in knots.

"I don't really diet or exercise," she answered, deciding it was best to keep things simple. "I walk a lot, which probably burns off plenty of calories." One of the positives about being without a car was that a good long walk helped to clear her mind. It was meditative.

"Zak says walking's the best exercise," Laila said. "It sounds like you're naturally fit." Her eyebrows furrowed. "You didn't walk all the way here from your apartment, did you?"

"I did." She chuckled at Laila's wide-eyed gasp. "It was a good, healthy walk. I'll be getting another car soon. The one I had was old. It coughed and sputtered all the way here from Pennsylvania and I worried it wouldn't make it. But it didn't fall apart until we got here."

"I'll make sure you and Harry get a ride home," Laila assured her.

"Your mom already recruited Gard to drive us home, even though it wasn't necessary." Smoothing her sweater over her belly which had become too flat, she said, "I know I'm too skinny." She gave a self-conscious chuckle. While some women crave an emaciated look, Sabrina missed her soft curves. "You don't have to be afraid of saying it. I'd like to gain a good twenty to thirty pounds."

"I would never dream of being that rude. But since you mentioned it," Laila said with a slow smile, "if anyone should be eating these dynamite cookies, Sabrina, it's you."

"I used to eat more than my share but the past few years I..." Laila was so nice and Sabrina was so tempted to tell her what was really going on, but she couldn't. "I just don't have much of an appetite."

"You should stop into my bakery sometime. We have a series of support group meetings going on throughout the day and evening. One of them focuses on people who have trouble gaining weight. There's a small private room behind the retail space and the meetings are free."

"Really? I've never heard of a support group for people who can't gain. It's the last thing someone like me wants to complain about because—"

"Because you're afraid of being drawn and quartered by dieters who think they'd love to have your *problem*," Laila finished for her, hanging air quotes over the word.

Sabrina let out an unexpected snap of laughter. "Something like that. I understand because I used to be the same way. I was always struggling to lose those ten or fifteen pounds responsible for preventing my clothes from hanging right." Her hands molded her torso and hips. "Now they just hang." This time her hands went up and down in a straight, non-curvy line. She laughed again, feeling less awkward about the subject now.

"Clothes." Laila rolled her eyes skyward. "You don't even want to know how many different sizes I have in my closet. I used to work as a weight loss counselor at Tuned by Turner. While doing that I learned there are lots of people who can't put on weight for one reason or another. Some of the weight loss counselors had that problem. Since my personal issues," Laila touched her chest, "have always centered around losing weight, I can't effectively counsel those people...without a tiny part of me wanting to have them drawn and quartered."

Clasping Sabrina's arm, Laila slid into laughter. "No, I'm kidding. Really. Sorry, I couldn't resist."

Sabrina loved the devilish twinkle in Laila's eye. She'd expected the Malones to be more staid and reserved, like their relatives, the Devingtons, who lived up on Beauregard Hill. Colleen Malone Devington was the sister of Astrid's first husband, Sean Malone. Stuffy and pretentious, Colleen and her husband, Walter, had moved to Glassfloat Bay from Chicago when Sabrina was a child. They'd always made her and Annalise nervous. Their daughters Saffron and Lorraine, who'd gone to private schools, were snooty too, while their brother, Red, was a great, down to earth guy.

What a pleasant surprise to learn The Malones were a warm, loving family with a ready sense of humor and wonderful wit.

"Anyway," Laila went on, "the hard-to-gain group, like the others who meet at the bakery, enjoy getting together just to talk, share, and help each other."

"So there are also groups that meet there to talk about losing weight?" Curious, Sabrina wanted to carefully word her next question to avoid insulting Laila. "Isn't that kind of tough for them to do in a bakery?"

"In a regular bakery it would be murder." Laila skewed her expression. "But my baked goods are suitable for a variety of health-related issues, so there's no problem. The dieters get a nice array of reduced calorie goodies, along with the calorie count for each piece. They love being able to indulge in something seemingly forbidden."

"And the hard to gain group gets the high calorie versions," Sabrina surmised.

"Exactly. Providing a comfortable safe haven for everyone, regardless of their weight issues, was one of my goals from the beginning. And Zak..." Laila looked at her husband again and smiled, "rather than focusing on losing pounds, he's designed his fitness classes to help people build muscle and become fit. That way they benefit most everyone."

"So you and Zak probably get a lot of crossover business."

"It's a win-win situation," Laila confirmed.

"I like what you two are doing." Sabrina wouldn't mind meeting with other people like herself—people who had a difficult time putting on weight. "I'll be by to check out the group and I might even give Zak's fitness class a try."

"Stop by anytime," Laila said. "Zak offers beginner classes," she leaned forward in a conspirator's whisper, "those are the ones Reen and I take." Her face lit up with a toothy smile. "He even has classes for people in wheelchairs or who have disabilities. I keep a schedule of Zak's classes posted at the bakery, and I post a new schedule for the bakery's group meetings every week because they keep changing as we add new groups."

"You have that many different groups?" It was clear both Laila and Zak had carefully considered and implemented many out of the ordinary options for her business and his, wisely linking them together.

"Mmm-hmm. The latest group is vegan. They meet in the morning and the paleo group meets two hours later. I do my best to make sure they don't cross paths." She made an O face. "Seriously, I think you'll enjoy it, Sabrina. There's always something fun going on, and we provide a free, supervised play area for the kids too so feel free to bring Harry."

"Thanks, I will. I—"

"Ugh, I can't believe she's still got Hud cornered over there," Reen said, joining them again. "She's draped around him like plastic wrap. God, that woman is so transparent...to everyone but Hud."

Laila and Sabrina exchanged perceptive looks.

Reen sucked in a sharp breath. "Oh my God, they're coming this way." She gasped a second time. "Just act natural." She brushed off her sweater and fluffed her hair.

Act natural? Sabrina suppressed the urge to laugh. Isn't that exactly what they were doing?

"Laila, how lovely to see you again," Monica Sharp said when she reached them. "Oh...and Maureen." She flashed a saccharine smile while clutching Hud's arm and Sabrina caught Reen's eyes narrowing. "And this is?" Monica's eyebrow arched in question as she turned her attention to Sabrina, giving her a head to toe appraisal.

"Sabrina Hanklen." She extended her hand and Monica took it...grudgingly, as if fearing it might be infected. "I'm Annalise and Hud's sister. My son and I moved back from Pennsylvania recently."

"Oh!" Monica's behavior altered abruptly. She was all bright eyes and sweet smiles. "Sabrina—I've heard so many wonderful things about you and your little boy. Well welcome back to our humble little seaside town." Her voice grew soft and she took Sabrina's hand in both of hers. "I'm so sorry about your impending divorce. I hope you don't mind...Hudson told me."

"No, it's okay." She knew it had to be a big topic of conversation in a town as small as Glassfloat Bay so it wasn't like it was a surprise for someone to bring it up. "And thanks. I'll be glad when the divorce is final."

"When will that be?" Monica asked.

"I'm not sure. My attorney says it should be within the month but there could be a delay because of the holidays." She hated waiting to put this whole ugly mess behind her and get on with her life.

"Hey Reen, Laila." Hud untangled himself from Monica long enough to give his sister a hug. "Nice to see you here, Sabrina. See? I told you it would be a great party. As usual, the Malones have done a fantastic job. I'll bet I put on five pounds sampling all this food."

"I'll bet you have," Monica noted, scanning the room. "It looks like a sea of those fattening, junky party food recipes people share on social media, doesn't it?" Her smile could easily double for a sneer.

"And I've sampled all of it."

"Me too," Gard said, waving what looked like a fried chicken strip in the air as he passed by. Maybe it was her imagination but Sabrina was sure she saw him give her what she could only describe as a special look. Aware of a flush coloring her cheeks, she returned his smile. She hadn't had this kind of reaction to a man since...well since she could remember. Definitely since before she'd married Stuart. The fluttery sensation she got when she and Gard exchanged glances was weird and wonderful at the same time.

But she had to restrain her feelings until her divorce was final.

She watched him until he was out of view.

"Have you bought a house yet?"

Sabrina realized Monica was talking to her and when her question registered, a bubble of laughter caught in Sabrina's throat. She couldn't even afford to buy a rundown used car much less a house. "Not yet. I'm renting for now."

Monica opened the clasp on her small designer purse, drawing out a business card. "The market is hot right now and I've got some great properties to show you. There's a stunning Victorian that's just become available up on Beauregard Hill. Give me a call when you're ready."

Monica had just suggested the priciest area of Glassfloat Bay, the neighborhood where the town's wealthiest residents lived. "Uh...thanks. I'll be sure to do that."

"Beauregard Hill? Sabrina's a Griffin, Monica," Hud said, "not a Vanderbilt."

Laila, Reen and Sabrina laughed. Monica didn't.

"Don't wait too long," Monica said to Sabrina, ignoring Hud's comment and the resulting chuckles, except for patting his arm. "Interest rates will be going up soon."

"Thanks for the tip," Sabrina said.

"We really should mingle, Hud." Monica looped her arm through his in a way that seemed inextricable. Smiling up at him as if he were Adonis, she gave his arm a tug. "Happy holidays to all." She gave a finger wave as they moved on.

"Later," Hud called over his shoulder.

"Well," Sabrina muffled a laugh, "*that* was an interesting experience."

"Did you hear that crack she made about the food?" Reen asked. "And Hud..." she visibly bristled, "did you see the way he was drooling over her?"

"He wasn't drooling," Laila said. "But I'll admit Monica has captured his attention."

Sabrina could tell Reen was hurting. Unsure as to what to say, she decided it was best to offer only what she hoped was a sympathetic smile. While pouring herself a cup of eggnog she glanced at Laila's hand resting on Reen's shoulder. The ring she wore resembled Gard's. In the center sat a lustrous, dark-hued opalescent stone, smooth on one side and rough on the other, as though it had broken from a larger stone.

"You and Gard have similar rings. Is that some sort of special Malone family ring?"

Laila held out her hand, turning it back and forth. "No. I got this from Delaney, who received it from our Grandma Bekka. Gard's ring belonged to Delaney's husband, Varik. Legend has it they're two halves of the same stone," she fingered the rougher edge, "split in two by Odin, the Nordic god. They're heartwish rings."

"It's beautiful." Sabrina touched it. "I love the bluish color of the stone. It seems to change as you move your hand, doesn't it? When Harry saw Gard's, he announced it was a magic ring." She smiled at the memory. "Kids are so imaginative."

"Your little boy said that?" Laila asked, exchanging a meaningful look with Reen. "He said the ring was magic?"

Sabrina nodded, wondering at their curious looks. "Harry can be so convincing in his magical beliefs that I swear I almost thought I saw the ring glow when he touched it. Can you imagine?" When Laila and Reen were silent for too long, Sabrina pointed between them. "You know, Gard had that same stunned look on his face after Harry told him about the ring being magic. Is there something I'm missing?"

"You saw the ring glow when Harry touched it?" Reen asked.

"I'm sure it was just my imagination because it couldn't possibly—"

"Harry was right, Sabrina," Laila interrupted. "The rings *are* magic."

"How could Harry possibly know?" Reen asked Laila.

"Children can be very perceptive," she answered with a shrug. "They pick up on things adults don't because they haven't been conditioned yet to stop believing in magic." Laila's features relaxed. "You're probably thinking we're a little nuts right now, hmm?"

"No, I—" Sabrina stopped as the fragrance of ginger cookies she'd smelled earlier floated overhead. Shaking her finger in the air, she noted, "That's the second time I've smelled that today. And you're about to tell me it's Grandma Bekka, right?"

"Ahhh," Laila chuckled, "so you've already heard about her *pepperkaker*."

"And the friendly ghosts," Sabrina confirmed. "From your mom."

Laila sniffed the air. "It's gone now. I think she stopped by to give you confirmation that our heartwish rings really are magic."

"And that we're not completely loony." Reen laughed.

Sabrina closed her eyes in a long blink. "Forgive me but it's all been a little overwhelming. I like fairytales as much as the next person but I'm having a difficult time trying to wrap my mind around all of this supernatural stuff."

"She sounds just like Gard," Reen said, elbowing Laila.

"One day we'll sit down over a trio of chai lattes so Reen and I can tell you all about the heartwish rings," Laila promised.

"I'd love that."

"If you can believe in friendly cookie-baking ghosts it won't be too much of a stretch to believe the story about me and my genie."

Sabrina's eyes flew wide. "Genie? As in," she twirled a finger, "out of a bottle?"

Mirroring Sabrina's gesture, Laila simply said, "Yup."

Leaning close, Sabrina looked left, right, then whispered, "Do you still have the genie?"

"Oh yeah. I married him." Laila clearly enjoyed the stunned look on Sabrina's face.

"You got her with that one." Reen elbowed Laila again.

"Aw, come on, you're teasing me...aren't you?"

"Nope." Laila's grin stretched wide while she and Reen crossed their hearts.

"It's a strange and incredible story," Reen said. "You can ask Drake Slattery about it if you don't believe us. He witnessed everything too."

"Professor Slattery? Huh...and here I thought it was bizarre when I discovered my son has an angel for an imaginary friend—and that she's your great-grandmother, Helga. Now—"

"Whoa!" Laila's jaw dropped. "What?!"

"Ask your mom," Sabrina smiled at Laila's confusion, "she'll tell you all about it." Angels, friendly ghosts, magic rings and genies. Sabrina's quiet little hometown of Glassfloat Bay had turned out to be quite the fascinating little destination.

Chapter 6

One Week Before Christmas

~<>~

SABRINA AND ANNALISE waved goodbye to their brother, Hud. He and his Griffin of all Trades crew were on their way out of town to work on a major library renovation project that had to be completed before the new year. That meant they'd be gone for at least a month, but the premium pay would be excellent. Sabrina had missed him while she lived in Pennsylvania. It was so good to be back at home with her sister and brother again.

"It's good to have you back home with us again, Sabrina. Hud and I missed you."

"You must have been reading my mind," Sabrina said. "I was just thinking the same thing. I'm especially glad Harry and I will be here for Christmas. He'll be in seventh heaven."

"Just the way we felt when we were his age." Annalise gave her a hug. "There's no place like Glassfloat Bay at Christmastime." Her gaze shifted quickly to the clock. "Okay, get ready to take a break in about fifteen minutes because I'm just about to take a pan of cinnamon rolls out of the oven."

Sabrina closed her eyes and sniffed the air. "They smell amazing," she said as Annalise headed for the kitchen. Painting the fluffy pompom at the end of Santa's cap on the café's window, she smiled, thinking about the pleasant afternoon she and Harry spent at the holiday open house the day before. She enjoyed meeting lots of new people as well as reconnecting with those she hadn't seen in years.

It was a pleasure looking through Astrid's photo albums and listening to Gard talk about his glaciology experiences. Of course, she'd be happy listening to him ramble on about most anything...even how to make those clear ice cubes. The thought made her chuckle. Any excuse she had to just sit and gaze at Gard Malone made her happy.

Yesterday had been mindboggling. The evidence of Bekka's ghost in the form of the tantalizing ginger cookie aroma, plus the discovery that Harold's angel might be Bekka's mother, Helga, still had her mind reeling...not to mention Laila's seemingly preposterous revelation that her husband used to be a genie.

She felt like Dorothy in the Wizard of Oz when she told her dog, "Toto, I've a feeling we're not in Kansas anymore." Except that this was definitely still Glassfloat Bay, not Oz. Weird magical goings on or not, she was immensely grateful to be here instead of Horntik, Pennsylvania with Stuart and his controlling mother, who might be perfect for the role of Oz's wicked witch.

The wayward thought had her snickering to herself.

"I see something's tickling your funny bone this morning," Gard said, startling her.

Sabrina jumped, making her brush squiggle a paint line, which she quickly wiped away. She'd been so lost in thought she hadn't noticed him come in.

"Sorry, didn't mean to scare you. I can't believe how amazing the windows look, Sabrina. Great job."

"Thanks." She took a moment to study her artwork and smiled. "I think it's turning out pretty well."

"The other shops and eateries along Ocean Charm Boulevard have stepped up their decorations this year because the café's windows are putting theirs to shame."

"That's really nice to hear. I've always loved how our main street stores participate in the holiday festivities. My sister and brother and I had such fun when our parents would bring us to the center of town so we could see all the windows and decorations. I'm honored that I can be a part of it this year."

She'd just finished with the white paint and was switching colors when movement outside caught her attention. Her eyes widened when she spotted a man coming up the walkway, stopping for a minute in front of the painted windows.

"Oh no..." she whispered. She blinked a few times to make sure her mind wasn't playing tricks on her because her soon to be ex-husband was the last person she expected to see strolling the streets of her hometown.

"H-hey, M-mom, it's D-dad!" Harry waved and Stuart waved back.

Sabrina set her paintbrush down and froze. "What on earth is he doing here?" she muttered.

"That's your husband?" Gard asked.

"Yes." She couldn't believe he was here...had no idea what would bring Stuart all the way to Oregon from Pennsylvania, since he'd used up all of this year's vacation time from work. Everything had been going so well since she left him, filed for divorce, and moved across the country to be with her family and friends. She could breathe easy again, thinking she was finally rid of the man who'd made her and Harold miserable for years.

She honestly thought she was free.

Her shoulders sagged at the realization that might never be the case.

"I can't believe he followed me all the way to Oregon," she said, not sure if she was talking to Gard or to herself.

The door jingled, alerting Stuart's arrival. Sabrina watched as he greeted a stunned Annalise before heading straight for Sabrina. With Stuart's back turned, Annalise' expression turned into a question mark as she lifted her hands and shrugged her shoulders.

"Stuart," was all Sabrina managed to say when he stood two feet away from her.

"Glad to see me?"

"Surprised," she answered honestly. Calmly, slowly, she cleaned her brushes in the water and set them on toweling to dry, giving herself time to gather her thoughts. She rose from her seat, facing him...looking him straight in the eye. "What are you doing here?"

"I came to see my wife, of course."

He stepped toward her and she took a step back. She wasn't interested in a display of affection or possessiveness.

"Ex-wife."

"Not yet." Smiling, he angled his head, waving a teasing finger. "Divorce decree's not final, remember?"

Sabrina felt a chill zigzag up her spine. She couldn't tell for sure, it was often hard to tell with Stuart, but he appeared to be sober. It had been eons since she'd seen her husband so...smiley. It looked unnatural.

"How did you know where to find me?" She picked up a towel and wiped her hands so he wouldn't see they were shaking.

"Are you kidding?" Stuart gave her a look like he thought she was crazy. "In a town the size of a postage stamp everyone knows everyone else's business." He chuckled. Stuart never chuckled. "All I had to do was ask someone on the street. I wasn't surprised to learn you've been working here at your sister's coffee shop." He looked around the retro-themed café, nodding his approval. "She's got a nice place here."

She watched Stuart's gaze scan the paints, brushes, rags and bucket of water next.

"I can see by the throwback waitress uniform that you work here but as what? A server or an artist?"

"I'm a server. I'm just—"

"This," he cocked his head toward the painted windows, "doesn't look like an order of chicken pot pie to me." He laughed at his own lame joke. A moment later his gaze swerved to Gard who stood a few feet away.

Gard offered his open hand with a smile as Stuart appraised him. "I'm Gard Malone."

Sabrina watched Stuart give Gard a lengthy onceover before making a slow turn and giving Sabrina the eye. She briefly wished Gard looked more like a geeky nerd than a movie star. Her hands began to perspire and she wiped them on her apron while reminding herself that Stuart no longer had any claim on her.

After what seemed a small eternity, Stuart shook Gard's hand. "Stuart Hanklen. And you know my wife how?" The tone of his voice was like someone finger pointing. "You one of her old high school boyfriends?" *Chuckle, chuckle, chuckle...*

Embarrassed, Sabrina said, "Gard is one of the café's regular customers, Stuart. He's only lived in Glassfloat Bay for a few years. He's one of the town's firefighters."

"I see...good to meet you, Gard." He ended their handshake. "You're the helpful café regular and town hero who brought my wife home last night."

Sabrina stiffened. How did he know about that? She'd thought he just arrived in town this morning. Apparently that wasn't the case.

"What you saw yesterday was Gard driving us, Harold and me, home after a get-together hosted by his family," Sabrina explained, keeping her voice quiet. "Of course, what I do, where I go and who I see are no longer any of your concern, Stuart."

"We didn't want Sabrina and Harry walking all that way home in the dark," Gard offered with a less exuberant smile. "It was the neighborly thing to do."

"Of course it was," Stuart said, that practiced smile of his still firmly in place as he spoke to Gard. "And I appreciate it. Sorry, if I came across less than friendly before." Sabrina couldn't believe she actually heard her husband offering someone an apology. "I'm still recovering after that godawful long drive from the airport. Thank you for seeing to my wife and child's wellbeing, Gard."

"No problem," Gard nodded, "my pleasure."

"When did you arrive, Stuart?" Sabrina asked, trying to figure out what game he was playing with his Mr. Nice Guy routine.

"Yesterday morning. I found out where you live and took a hotel room just across the street."

She rubbed the goosebumps from her arms. "Why? So you could spy on me?"

"Don't be silly. Of course not, Sabrina." His smile was warm and charming. "It was tough finding a vacancy a week before Christmas and that was one of the only rooms available. I'm just here on a holiday visit to see you and our son. I wanted to make sure you were okay way out here all on your own."

"I'm not exactly on my own. This town is full of good people I've known all my life...people who watch out for me and Harry. Why did you wait until this morning to come see us?"

"I didn't want to intrude on your fun when I saw you and Harold were dressed up and going out yesterday. Plus I was tired from that endless flight and decided it was better if I waited until this morning when I was rested." He had eye crinkles when he smiled, something she hadn't seen in years. Sabrina felt like she'd stepped into some weird paranormal show where everything was opposite of normal.

She fought to keep her eyes from narrowing to slits. No matter how jovial and good-natured Stuart was acting, she didn't trust him.

After serving nearby customers plates of eggs benedict, Annalise walked over to her brother-in-law. "It's been a long time, Stuart. I'm glad you could be here to see Sabrina's holiday artwork on the windows. Isn't it fabulous?" Like a gameshow hostess, she waved an arm across the wide expanse of windows Sabrina had painted.

"Beautiful work." Stuart said following Annalise's motion. "My wife is very talented. I've always been proud of her artistic efforts."

Sabrina's jaw dropped. The last time he'd said anything even remotely like that was during their first year of marriage. All he'd offered was criticism since then.

"Take a look at Harry's wonderful Christmas drawing too" Annalise gestured toward the colorful paper her nephew worked on. "He's quite the little artist. Just like his mom."

"Why aren't you in school, Harold?" Stuart turned to where Annalise pointed, apparently unaware Harry was even in the room until she'd mentioned him.

"I-I-I-I-I..." Harry's eyes grew wide while his cheeks flushed beet red.

"Daycare doesn't open until seven," Annalise explained. "Harold stays here when Sabrina works before or after school."

"And I-I'm on Christmas v-vacation from k-kindergarten," Harry told his father. "Aunt Annalise m-makes m-me ch-chocolate p-pancakes. Y-you should t-try some, D-d-dad."

"Harry's a great kid. I've been dropping him off at preschool on my way to the fire station the past couple of weeks," Gard offered, and Sabrina wished he hadn't, knowing it would only fuel Stuart's outlandish suspicions.

"G-gard has a—"

"You mean *Mr.* Gard," Stuart corrected and Harry's mouth snapped shut.

"It's okay, I gave him permission to call me Gard."

Sliding a quick glance at Gard, Stuart nodded.

"He has a d-d-g too," Harry continued. "His n-name is T-tundra."

"Well isn't that nice," Stuart said, shifting his gaze to Sabrina. He picked up his son's drawing, looking at it as if it were something alien. "What's this supposed to be?"

Harry's stuttering was always worse when he was nervous, which usually coincided with being around his father. It took him a small eternity to explain that it was a Christmas drawing he was making for Gard as a thank-you for driving him to school, pointing out each character he'd drawn as he spoke.

Sabrina prayed Stuart would be kind this time. Just this once.

"Well sure..." Stuart said, "why not put the Hulk in a Christmas drawing? Nice work, Harold." He ruffled Harry's hair, surprising both Harry and Sabrina with his agreeable, mild-mannered attitude.

"Why are you here, Stuart?" Sabrina asked bluntly. It was beyond obvious that he was up to something.

Looking at Annalise, Gard, and the diners around them, Stuart suggested, "Let's go home so we can talk about it in private."

"Home? We don't live together anymore." Sabrina folded her arms across her chest,

"Sorry." Bracketing his forehead with his hand, Stuart laughed quietly. "Force of habit. I meant let's go to your apartment. We have a lot to discuss. I've heard great things about Nevan's Irish Pub in your building. Maybe the three of us can stop for lunch there."

"We've already discussed everything...with our attorneys. Besides, I have a shift to finish, Stuart."

"No problem. We can sit here and talk." Stuart slid into the booth seat opposite Harry. "I flew all the way out here from Pennsylvania just to see you, Sabrina, so we could talk. The least you can do is give me a small amount of time out of your busy schedule." He shot a glance to Annalise. "I'm sure your sister won't mind you taking a break from serving pancakes so you can talk to your husband. Right, Annalise?"

Annalise looked from Annalise to Stuart and back again. "I'm in agreement with whatever Sabrina chooses to do."

"And I'm sure Gard won't mind if I sit here and have a nice chat with my wife, will you, Gard?"

"As a matter of fact," Gard glanced at the wall clock, "I was just about to take Harry to daycare," he said without really answering Stuart's question. "Why don't you gather up your stuff, Harry."

"That won't be necessary." Stuart placed his hand over Harry's as the boy started collecting his paper and crayons. "I'm here now. I'll watch my son while Sabrina is working."

Harry looked up at his father in obvious surprise.

"Oh...okay then." Gard looked uncertain, his smile strained. "Hey, Annalise, how about a big mug of strong coffee and a plate of chocolate chip pancakes?" Before heading to a stool at the counter, he added, "Good to meet you, Stuart. Enjoy your stay in Glassfloat Bay."

"I'm sure I will." Stuart's gaze slipped to Sabrina. "Just a discussion. That's all I want." He perched his elbows on the tabletop and leaned forward. "What do you say, Harold? You think it's a good idea for your mom and me to have a talk, don't you?"

"Stuart, that's not fair. Don't pull our son into this."

"Nonsense," Stuart said with that same creepy smile he'd had plastered on his face since he arrived. "It's only fair that we include Harold. Harold thinks so too, don't you, boy?"

Contemplating, Harry absently scratched his ear before looking up at his father. "W-will it b-be a happy t-talk?" Looking down at the table, he drew invisible squiggles with his finger. "I m-mean w-without any y-yelling?"

Stuart's face lit up with an even wider smile. "You bet it will. Your mom and I are going to talk about Christmas and your birthday."

"R-really?" His face all gleeful, Harry looked at Sabrina. "That s-sounds happy, M-mom. I th-think it would b-be g-good for you and D-dad to have a t-talk l-like that."

Stuart sniffed the air. "Do I smell cinnamon rolls?" He turned his smile on Annalise who, obviously concerned, had been hovering nearby.

"I just pulled a tray out of the oven," she said. "I'll bring you a warm roll with butter and a cup of coffee. Take as much time as you need, Sabrina. Cora can cover. Anything for you?"

"Just some coffee, please." Sabrina rested her hand on Harry's arm. "Honey, why don't you go sit over there," she pointed across the aisle to a small secluded booth, "so your dad and I can have some adult talking time."

"S-sure. G-good idea. I c-can work m-more on m-my d-drawing." He scooped up his materials, stuffed them into his backpack and was about to head for the booth she'd suggested when Stuart held his arms open.

"How about a hug and kiss for your dad?" he said, much to Sabrina's shock, no doubt Harry's too.

With a tentative glance at Sabrina, Harry set down his backpack and walked into his father's embrace. Stuart kissed the boy on the cheek. It was the first time Sabrina had seen Stuart show any affection to their son for at least a couple of years.

Harry's gaze was full of wonder and his cheeks dimpled with a smile as their hug ended. That brief sign of affection meant so much to Harry it almost broke her heart.

Sabrina slid into the booth across from Stuart, folding her hands in front of her on the tabletop. "Okay, what's with all the ideal husband and father playacting after all this time? We both know that's not like you. At all. Why are you really here, Stuart?"

"I'm a different man, Sabrina. I stopped drinking after you left." He covered her folded hands with his. "I should have done it a lot sooner."

"You did...several times, in fact," Sabrina pointed out, slipping her hands from his grasp.

"I know." Stuart's head bobbed. "I'm hoping to spend this week with you and Harold...through Christmas. I want to show you and my son that I've changed. I mean really changed this time. I want you to give me another chance, Sabrina."

Sabrina sat back against the booth. "Sorry, it's too—" Sabrina stopped when Annalise arrived back at their table with two coffees and a cinnamon roll. "Thanks." She smiled, noting the look of apprehension on her sister's face.

"Yeah, thanks, Annalise," Stuart said. "Looks great." He started buttering his roll. "And I'll bet it tastes as good as it smells."

Once Annalise left, Sabrina continued, "It's too late, Stuart. I can't even begin to count all the chances I've already given you. You made a food out of me more than once for believing in you."

"Look," he raised his forefinger, "I'll make you a promise. You let me spend this week with you and our son and then," he tapped the table, "on the day after Christmas, if you still want the divorce...if you still want me out of your life, I'll fly back to Horntik." He motioned with his hand through the air. "And I'll stop contesting the divorce. You have my word. What do you say, Sabrina? One week. That's all I ask." He broke off a piece of his roll and ate it. "Mmm, your sister makes a mean cinnamon roll."

Sabrina sipped from her coffee and let out a protracted sigh. "Stuart, I'm sorry, but I've already made up my mind. You've made so may promises but never keep them. I can't do this anymore." She closed her eyes, shaking her head from side to side.

"It wasn't easy to leave," she went on, "it took me two years to get up the courage to file for divorce. Your temper, Stuart...it isn't..." she stopped herself from using the word *normal*. She'd made the mistake of suggesting he wasn't normal before and she wasn't about to do it again, risking her husband becoming unhinged in the middle of her sister's café.

"I've tried to tell you before that you could benefit from seeing a therapist but you get belligerent every time I've suggested it. You won't accept responsibility for your anger and end up blaming everything on me and Harry. I can't live like that anymore and I can't have our little boy subjected to that either."

Stuart was silent for a while, before slowly nodding his head. "You're right. Everything you've said is spot on. I started seeing a therapist over a month ago, right after you left for Oregon."

Her eyes widened in surprise. "You did?" She didn't think anything Stuart said could surprise her but this had her downright flabbergasted.

"He says I've been making good progress, Sabrina."

"You're serious? You're really seeing a therapist?" Stuart nodded. "Who?" Sabrina asked, astonished but still not ready to trust him. "Where did you find him?"

"Through work...human resources. His name is Dr. Pape. He was the one who suggested I come out here to spend this week with you and Harold. He said if you saw the improvements with your own eyes it might make a difference."

Retrieving his phone from his pocket, he brought the doctor up in his contacts and held it out to her. "Here's his number if you want to call and verify." He looked at his phone again. "We're three hours behind Pennsylvania so he should be in the office by now."

Though she was tempted, Sabrina pushed his hand away.

"Think about it, Sabrina," he slipped the phone back in his pocket, "even if you still want the divorce after the end of the week, this will give us one last opportunity to spend Christmas together as a family. I think that would make Harry happy, don't you? I think he needs this before we split up for good."

Sabrina was torn. She had no idea what to do. On the one hand, she knew without a doubt that she wanted the divorce. He'd managed to eradicate any love she had left for him and she had no interest in trying to rekindle old feelings. But she had to remember Stuart would always be Harry's father, which meant they'd always remain connected.

"What if I said I would never agree to come back to you, Stuart? Would you still want to be here this week? Still want to spend Christmas with us?"

"Absolutely. You saw how much it meant to Harold. Besides, I'm becoming an optimist, believe it or not." He laughed a little, fiddling with the sugar container on the table. "There's a small part of me that clings to the belief that you might change your mind—but if you don't, then I'll accept your decision. I promise."

The news about Stuart seeing a therapist was incredible. Maybe he'd really had an awakening of sorts and was on the way to recovery...to being the Stuart she'd known six years ago. That would be wonderful for him, and for Harry. It would benefit her as well when she had to deal with him in the future regarding child custody matters, visitation, etcetera.

Slanting her head, Sabrina asked, "How did you get another week off? I thought you already used up all your vacation this year?"

"I explained to human resources that I needed this time off for an important family matter, so they let me tap into next year's vacation time."

Cora stopped by their table, pouring them each a fresh cup of coffee. Although she no longer added cream or sugar because her stomach objected, Sabrina stirred, giving herself time to think.

"If I agree to this, you can't stay in my apartment, Stuart. You'd have to stay in your hotel room and sleep there. At the end of the evening when it's time for Harry to go to bed there wouldn't be any sex. Understand? I won't sleep with you, Stuart, so if that's what you have in mind..."

"While I'd be lying if I said I wouldn't love sleeping with you," he reached for her hand, clasping it as he gazed into her eyes, "I'll respect your wishes and won't make any overtures. You know I'd never force myself on you."

Again she extricated her hand. "You've come close when you've been drunk."

"I'm a different man when I drink. We both know that. As you've told me in the past, like Jekyll and Hyde."

Stuart didn't smile that time, as well he shouldn't. There wasn't a single damn thing funny about his abrupt shift from one persona to the other when he was drinking.

"So you plan to spend time with Harry during the day when I'm working? Do you honestly think you'll have the patience to be with him for hours each day?" The last thing she wanted was to put her son in a tense situation. He'd already been through enough of that with his father.

"I'd say it's about time my son and I get to know each other better," Stuart answered, looking over his shoulder at Harry and returning the boy's friendly wave. "I've been pretty hard on the little guy and I don't want him to be left with that impression of me. A lack of patience is one of my shortcomings, and I admit that I find his stuttering difficult to deal with, but Dr. Pape has been helping me with that so I can cope better and not take it out on Harry."

Sabrina was trying hard not to be impressed but this was huge. This is what she'd wanted for so long. This is what Harry had deserved all along. "Why now Stuart? What finally brought you to this point?"

"Losing you, the only good and decent thing I've ever had in my life. When you walked out, Sabrina, something happened to me. I had...what do you call it?" His eyebrows knitted. "An epiphany. I finally realized what an asshole I've been and how unfair that's been to you and Harry. The drinking, the anger, the other women—I'm done with it. It's like it's been burned out of me."

It sounded good but Stuart had always been a convincing actor. "I can't count the times I've bought into your stories and your many, many promises. How do I know this time will be any different?"

"You don't. I know I probably don't have a chance with you after everything I've done, but I'm asking this one last time for you to give me an opportunity to prove to you that I'm not the same man I was before you filed for divorce. I don't know what more I can say, other than please don't send me back to Pennsylvania without letting me try. At least give me the opportunity to leave Harold with some positive memories of his dad. I know I've been a rotten father, but I love the kid and I'd like to show him the Dr. Jekyll side of me for a change."

They sat there for a small eternity while the gears turned inside Sabrina's head. Should she or shouldn't she? She weighed the potential benefits against the possible detriments.

After a lengthy sigh, she looked up at her soon to be ex-husband.

"One week, Stuart."

Chapter 7

~<>~

"SON OF A BITCH." Gard slapped the countertop with his open hand. "Have you ever seen anything like that before in your life?"

"What...where?" Annalise looked left, then right before frowning at Gard. "What's got you all riled up?" She glanced up at the clock. "And what are you still doing here? I thought you said you were heading over to the fire station twenty minutes ago."

"Yeah...I was. It's okay, my shift doesn't start for another thirty minutes. Can you believe Sabrina and Harry left with Hanklen? You didn't tell me he was such a good actor. He's playing her, Annalise. Your crafty brother-in-law's got Sabrina believing him."

Planting one fist against her hip, Annalise smirked. "Well I'll be darned."

The scowl Gard had been nursing for the last hour was still in place and he wasn't ready to let it go. "What's that supposed to mean?"

"Wow, am I dense or what?"

He definitely wasn't in the mood for guessing games. "Annalise, what the hell—"

"You're hooked on my sister."

"What?" Gard's head jerked back. "No I'm not." His denial sounded doubtful even to his own ears.

"Nope, uh-uh, don't try to deny it." She was smiling and pointing at him now. "Gard Malone, you've got a thing for Sabrina. I can't believe I didn't see it before. I mean, I knew she was interested in you but—"

"Wait, what?" His posture straightened. "Did Sabrina tell you that?" He cringed at the hormonal teenager tone of his voice. It was like high school all over again.

"No but she didn't have to. Just like you don't have to tell me. Good. I'm glad." She gathered an empty coffee mug and cake plate from the counter two seats away from where Gard sat.

His eyebrows scrunching in confusion, Gard wished Annalise didn't talk in circles. "Glad that I didn't say anything to you?"

"You're a little slow on the uptake today. I think you need more coffee." Snickering quietly, she refilled his mug. "I mean I'm glad that you care. If I could cherry-pick anybody to be with my sister, Gard, it would be you. You're a good guy. You'd treat her right and take care of her."

"Hey, hold on a minute before you try to marry me off to your sister, okay?" He laughed, lifting his hands in protest. "One, she's still married. Two, I'm not interested in a relationship." Wiping down the counter, she just looked at him and smiled. "I'm serious, Annalise. Just because I might think your sister is attractive doesn't mean I'm looking to get tied down. I'm done with all that."

"Mmm-hmm." Annalise straightened a plastic-covered menu resting between a sugar dispenser and napkin holder.

He sipped from his coffee, staring off into space. "Why do you think she did it?"

"Why do I think who did what?"

He angled her a look of incredulity. "Come on, you know what I mean. She left with Stuart. She must have bought into that *I'm-all-reformed* line of crap he was feeding her. Either that or she's still in love with the guy and wants to call off the divorce."

"No, and no" Annalise slapped her hand on the counter in front of him. "I talked to Sabrina right before they left. She's only doing this for Harry, Gard. Trust me, she definitely doesn't love Stuart anymore and is still going through with the divorce. But..."

Gard watched as Annalise nibbled on her bottom lip. She was silent for so long Gard heard the irritation in his voice as he asked, "Yeah? But what?"

"But you're right about Stuart being an SOB," Annalise told him. "And as much as I believe my sister when she says she's finished with Stuart, I also know she's a bleeding heart who always looks for the good in people. Frankly, I doubt whether there's any left in him...and I want to make sure he doesn't do anything to hurt her more than he already has. Sooo..." She looked up from the clean counter she was wiping for the third time.

Again, prolonged silence.

"For chrissakes, Annalise, just spit it out, will you?" Gard shook his head and laughed. "Has anyone ever told you that trying to hold a conversation with you is like trying to work a jigsaw puzzle where all the pieces are the same color?"

"Sorry." Her shoulders hiked in a shrug. "So...I was hoping you could kind of sort of keep an eye on my sister and nephew while Stuart's here to make sure they're okay."

Looking at her like she was crazy, Gard made a raspberry sound. "What am I supposed to do? Go over to her apartment and invite myself to tea while she and her husband work on their marriage? Yeah, I don't think so, Annalise."

"You may not be ready to admit to me that you have feelings for Sabrina, but we both know you're crazy about Harry."

Gard couldn't help smiling at the thought of the cute kid.

"Stuart's been awful to him, Gard, treating my poor little nephew like he's a worthless idiot. And he hasn't treated my sister much better. Stuart's a bully, plain and simple. And...well, I can't help worrying."

There were few things Gard detested more than bullies. Being a smaller boy hadn't prevented him from protecting weaker kids from bullies like Stuart. His parents had been called by the principal more than once after Gard had administered a healthy dose of retribution in the form of a punch in the nose or gut to a deserving bully.

Today, as a firefighter and Emergency Medical Responder, he was in the business of saving lives, whether those in need of saving were bullies or not.

"Since Stuart claims to want his wife back and he seems to be intent on acting like a decent father, I doubt the guy's going to purposely mess things up for himself, Annalise. Granted, I took an instant dislike to him and don't believe or trust a damn thing he says, but I don't think there's anything to worry about."

Except, Gard's thoughts warned, for maybe losing Sabrina if Stuart succeeds in making her believe he's a transformed man. But there wasn't anything Gard could do about that...nor would he want to. Sabrina was a big girl. If that's what, or rather *who*, she chooses, then so be it.

"He's always been a jerk," Annalise said. "Hud and I saw through him almost right from the beginning but Sabrina swore she saw the good in Stuart. And then," she lifted her arms and let them slap at her sides, "he took her away from us, all the way to Pennsylvania so he wouldn't have to deal with her family. Bastard."

"Why Pennsylvania? Does he have family there?"

"Oh yeah." Annalise rolled her eyes. "I only met her once, at their wedding, but, trust me, meeting Nancy Hanklen was an experience I won't forget. Talk about the mother-in-law from Hell. Sheesh!" She shook her head back and forth. "My poor little sister, out there all alone with that controlling witch. I don't know how she lasted as long as she did before coming back home to people who really love her."

Gard watched Annalise wringing a napkin in her hands until the paper shredded, pieces fluttering like snowflakes to the café floor.

"What if he hurts Harry while Sabrina is here at work? He's never had patience with Harry...except for that ridiculous Father of the Year shtick he pulled here today. Do you think we should call the police or maybe child protective services, just in case?"

"Being a firefighter automatically makes me a mandatory reporter." In response to Annalise's quizzical expression, Gard explained, "Police, doctors, nurses, daycare providers, and teachers also fall into that category. If we suspect a child is being abused, we have to report it to the Department of Human Services or the police."

"So are you going to call?" Annalise looked encouraged.

"There aren't any grounds, Annalise. Stuart may be an SOB but he hasn't done anything wrong." Recalling the guidelines from his certification training, Gard explained, "We need to call if a child sustains a serious physical injury, or if we believe they're in imminent danger. When a report's made it's either screened out as not meeting the criteria for abuse or it's assigned for investigation. If it's verbal abuse only, DHS can't really do anything. In Stuart's case, we haven't witnessed physical or verbal abuse."

"So we just have to stand by and wait to see if he harms Harry. That seems screwy to me. I know he hit Harry hard once when he was still a baby, but I don't know if he's hit him since. Sabrina put the fear of God into him when she found out what he'd done and told him she'd leave him if ever he harmed Harry again."

It was damned difficult for Gard to understand how any man could treat his baby that way. He plowed his hand through his hair, realizing he had to be careful of what he said. He didn't want to rankle Annalise any more than she already was.

"My training taught us that if we have a gut feeling something is wrong, it's better to be safe than sorry. If I feel there's a reason for concern, I'll give Officer Hartinger at police headquarters a call to let him know what's going on. Both his kids took classes from my brother-in-law, Varik, at the university. Hartinger's a good guy and he's had experience with domestic violence cases."

"Just thinking about Stuart makes my insides clench." Annalise's eyes narrowed as she hugged herself. "I hate that he's going to be here for Christmas."

"I'm not all that tickled about it either but," Gard shrugged, "there's nothing we can do about it."

"Sabrina's changed since she married Stuart. We used to go on endless diets together, trying to get off those annoying ten pounds that didn't want to budge from our hips." Grinning, Annalise clapped hers. "Now she eats like a bird. She looks like a healthy breeze might carry her away." Her gaze narrowed again as she looked at Gard. "That big blustery clod probably made her too upset to eat."

"Your sister's just a little slip of a thing," Gard agreed, remembering how fragile Sabrina appeared when he first met her. "But as delicate as she may look, I can tell she's a strong woman."

Gard recalled how strongly she worded her warning to him when she'd heard him refer to himself as a failure in regard to his unsuccessful rescue of Tim. Thinking of how she defended him, refusing to even consider he was anything less than a hero, made him smile. Sabrina Hanklen was quite a woman, and Stuart was a jackass for not appreciating the hell out of her when he had the chance.

"You need to take care of my sister, Gard."

"Annalise, I already told you...I can't get mixed up in their marriage. It's not my place." No matter how much he cared about Sabrina he had to remember she was still a married woman...with a husband here in town who'd flown a couple thousand miles just to make sure they stayed married. Nope, uh-uh, Gard didn't want to be a third wheel...didn't want to find himself in the middle of a sticky situation that was none of his business.

"And I told you before," Annalise insisted, "I know how you feel about her—and I'm pretty damn sure she feels the same way about you too."

Just as the last time Annalise brought up the idea, Gard couldn't help that little spike in his cardiovascular activity at the notion that Sabrina might return his feelings. He eyed Annalise who'd somehow managed to look clear into Gard's soul.

"Look, I know you love your sister and you're trying to look out for her, but I don't know what you're talking about as far as my supposed feelings for her, or vice versa. Sabrina's a really nice, pretty woman but I don't—"

"Yes you do." She nodded, giving him a warm smile...one of those all-knowing smiles of hers that spoke volumes. "Yes you do."

"Come on, Annalise." Gard groaned.

"My lips are sealed if that's what you're worried about. I promise I won't tell a soul about your feelings for Sabrina. But, Gard," she gave him the softest, sweetest smile, "please don't try to deny it anymore because it's written all over your face." Annalise smoothed her hand along his arm.

"Coffee," Gard practically growled. Annalise brought the pot from the burner and gave him a refill. He sucked the burning liquid down in a few gulps, setting the empty mug hard against the counter.

"Is it really that obvious?" he asked, leaning his elbow on the counter and resting his forehead in his hand. "Am I that transparent?"

"Probably only to me and your mom and sisters."

"My...? You talked to them about this? Aw hell..." He groaned.

"No, Mr. Over Dramatic, I told you earlier that I only just figured it out for myself. But if I can tell then I'm sure the Malone women can too."

"Aw hell..." he repeated. Damn...she was right.

"Mmm-hmm." Annalise chuckled patting his cheek. "You're a good man, Gard Malone. The sort of man my sister needs and deserves."

"I guess here's where I'm supposed to say thanks," he groused. After a moment he glanced up at her, cracking a half-smile. "Thanks."

"And Sabrina's the sort of woman you deserve, especially after what that selfish ex-fiancée of yours pulled. Joanne did such a number on you, Gard, and when you were at your most vulnerable. That woman stomped on your heart and made mincemeat out of it, not only when you learned she'd been cheating on you, but again when she dumped you while you were in the hospital fighting for your life."

Closing her eyes, Annalise shuddered. "My sister would never do that to you. She's not capable of that kind of treachery."

His gut told her Annalise was right. They'd only known each other a few weeks, but Gard knew Sabrina would never have cheated on Stuart during their marriage. She was miles different from Joanne, his former fiancée. No, Sabrina wouldn't abandon her man if he truly needed her...like if he was laid up in a hospital suffering from broken bones and a grieving heart.

"Okay so you're right," Gard admitted. "I care...a lot. I don't want you worrying, Annalise. Short of meddling in their marriage, I'll do everything I can to keep Sabrina and Harry safe." He glanced at the clock, then kissed her cheek. "Now I've really got to get over to the fire station."

"Thank you, Gard. You'd make a great brother-in-law." Annalise gave a playful jiggle of her eyebrows, then started gathering up another customer's empty plates.

With one eyebrow arrowing down, he warned, "Let's not get carried away now." She winked at him in return and he laughed. "Women," he muttered.

Chapter 8

The Day Before Christmas Eve

~<>~

ANNALISE WAS GLAD to see Zak Tymon's Sumerian Fitness class packed with people of all ages. All of the proceeds of this special holiday class were going to a good cause. The wood wainscoting and crisp white walls of Zak's exercise studio were festooned with paper chains and popcorn garland made by the members' children while in the center's child care facility. In place of the usual exercise music, lively holiday instrumentals played over the sound system.

"Man, I'm ready to keel over," Reen complained.

"Me too," Delaney agreed, mopping the sweat from her forehead.

"Tell me about it," Annalise whined. "Tomorrow's Christmas Eve. I should be in my kitchen baking cookies for the café's holiday crowd tomorrow, not killing myself in your husband's brutal exercise class, Laila." Annalise hunched over, blew out a deep breath and rested her hands on her knees. "I mean it. This is ridiculous. I'm too damned old for all this exercise crap."

"Oh hush up and start pumping those chubby little legs," Laila teased, marching in place to "Jingle Bells."

"You're too damned old too, Laila." Annalise laughed.

"Oh puhleez," Astrid chimed in. "The last thing I want to hear is you whippersnappers complaining about your age. If I can do this grueling workout, so can you. Period. Case closed."

"I just mean we're at the age where we shouldn't have to worry about eating health food and getting fit," Annalise insisted. "We've earned the right to chow down on cookies, chocolate, fruitcake and—"

"I don't like fruitcake," Delaney said.

Astrid sucked in a sharp breath. "Don't ever let your brother hear that. He worships at the altar of Annalise Griffin's Holiday Fruitcake."

"Yeah, well Gard's always had quirky tastes," Delaney claimed. "I prefer to eat healthy over the holidays."

After exchanging disbelieving glances the others chorused a vociferous, "Ha!"

"I do!" Delaney insisted.

"Well excuse me, Ms. Contrary...or should I say, Ms. Chocoholic?" Annalise rolled her eyes before wiping the sweat from her forehead with her sleeve. "Don't give me that holier than thou bit. I know how you really feel about eating health food, especially at this time of year. Remember?"

"Listen to you," Astrid addressed the other four. "A teensy bit of exercise and you're sniping at each other."

"A teensy bit?" Reen's eyes bugged. "I haven't worked this hard since I was ten."

Lifting an eyebrow, Astrid teased, "You didn't work this hard then either, Maureen. You were too busy playing with my yarn."

"I was knitting," Reen objected, elevating her chin.

"You were pretending to knit, dear."

Laila barked a laugh.

"Watch it Mrs. Exercise Guru," Astrid warned with a sparkle in her eye. "You weren't any more active than Reen as a child...unless you call turning my kitchen into a disaster area a workout."

All eyes were on Delaney who held her hands up in surrender. "Uh-uh, don't look at me. I'm not saying a thing. I know I was a slug who spent most of her time daydreaming about marrying a Viking." She grinned at them. "Which I did."

"And if you hadn't found your Viking," Reen said, "Mom wouldn't have found hers."

"That's true," Astrid agreed. "Okay now, ladies, let's focus on getting through this workout. If I can do it at my age without moaning and complaining every two minutes, so can you spring chickens." She dutifully marched to the beat of the music and sound of Zak's encouraging voice. "With each step," Astrid continued, "with each beat of your heart, you're extending your life. Isn't that a wonderful feeling?" The oldest of the five women who'd come to the holiday exercise session together, she was the only one not dripping with sweat.

Annalise and Delaney shared an eye-rolling smile.

"The thing is, Mom," Delaney said, "I'm not so sure I want to extend my life if it means I have to exercise and eat nothing but cruciferous vegetables until I kick the bucket. Where's the fun in that?"

"There's always hollandaise to drown those veggies in," Reen suggested with a wicked laugh.

"Or buckets of ranch dressing," Annalise added.

"Broccoli and cauliflower are great," Laila said. "When they're breaded and fried."

"And dipped in Annalise's ranch dressing," Reen said.

Astrid offered a warm smile, continuing to march with the airy lightness and stamina of a teen rather than a sixty-something. "I want us to be healthy as we age so we can all celebrate our centennial birthdays together. Wouldn't that be wonderful?" She blinked. "Although my centennial may come a wee bit before yours." Her smile returned.

"Decrepit fun," Delaney said, snickering.

"Our centennial celebrations would have to include gobs of chocolate," Reen answered.

"Yeah but we'd be too old to appreciate it by then," Laila said, her breathing labored from marching and talking at the same time...a dilemma her mother didn't seem to have. "Our caregivers could give us kale chips and tell us it's chocolate and we probably wouldn't know the difference."

"I guess that's when ignorance is bliss." Annalise laughed.

"When you reach a hundred, Mom," Delaney said, "we'll all probably be up there," she hiked her thumb toward heaven, "feeding our faces with Snickers bars and watching while you try to gum your way through a festive birthday bowl of cream of rice."

"Now let's get those arms pumping as we march, people!" Zak instructed the large class in his rolling, accented baritone.

"Your son-in-law's trying to kill us," Annalise complained to Astrid.

Astrid followed Zak's example, moving her arms as if pulling a train whistle. Grinning, she added, "I haven't had cream of rice cereal in ages. I'll make a nice big pot for us next time we do breakfast together."

That earned her a joint round of *eeeeews!* as her daughters and Annalise looked horrified. Astrid just laughed.

Doing an abbreviated version of the arm pumping, Delaney noted, "Anyway, this fitness stuff is for women who worry about how they look—the ones trying to snag husbands. Like you, Reen and Annalise."

"Oh come on, Delaney." Annalise moved her arms somewhere in the middle of Delaney's and Astrid's examples. "Like you don't care how you look. I've never seen you without makeup and your hair done. I'll bet you don't even go out to the mailbox without lipstick and mascara."

"You're right," Astrid confirmed, "she doesn't."

"As if you're not the same way, Mom," Delaney retorted with a sniff. "And you too, Annalise."

"True," Annalise admitted.

"Shame on us." Laila glanced around the large room. "We're so busy talking that we're not keeping up with the rest of the class. Look at Millie and Grace Shunck over there, keeping up with the music. They're eighty-years-old. Come on...we can't have everybody thinking we can't keep up with the Shunck twins." She stepped up her pace and the rest followed suit. "You know, we should make a pact to exercise more often. Doing this once in a while isn't going to kill us."

"Says the wife of the exercise guru." Annalise made a raspberry sound. "I'm frickin' dying here."

"Laila's right," Astrid said. "Plus we're supporting the charities Laila's bakery and Zak's exercise studio support by working out here today," she reminded them. "Come on, doesn't it make you all feel good to participate in The Great Pretender's first annual Christmas Exercise-a-thon?"

Annalise shoved a sweaty lock of hair behind her ear. "Not nearly as good as I'd feel eating a slab of my fruitcake and drinking a mug of hot cocoa with—"

"A shot of Baileys and Kahlua," Reen offered. "Mmmm..."

"Topped with whipped cream," Delaney added.

"Is there any other way?" Laila grinned. "But seriously, we have to remember we're doing this for a good cause." She smiled at them. "Not only to get our fat butts in shape." She clapped her backside.

"Okay, okay, I know this is for charity so I guess I can try to get through this torture without complaining *too* much. But—" Annalise stopped marching and arm pumping long enough to point a finger at Laila. "Don't think you can charm your way into getting me to agree to do this more than a couple times a year."

"Keep marching and moving those arms." Reen elbowed her. "Laila plans to do these benefits for Wisdom Harbor Children's Hospital at least once a quarter. For every ten dollars we exercisers pledge, The Great Pretender will match that. Think of all those sick children we're helping."

"I don't know how you can afford that, Laila, without your company going broke," Annalise said.

"I've been truly blessed," Laila explained. "Since I've experienced so much goodness in my life, it's important to me to give back."

"I'm proud of you, honey," Astrid said, pulling Laila into a hug and touching cheek to cheek. "I'm proud of all my children." She turned to Annalise and smiled. "And I'm proud of you too, sweetie."

"Well hell," Annalise said. "I can't make a joke after that." They all chuckled together.

"Because we love Laila," Astrid said, "and because we love the idea of helping sick children get better, I know we'll happily agree to put on our exercise gear and participate in this worthwhile charity event four times a year." She gave her daughters and Annalise a meaningful look. "Minimum."

"Devil woman," Annalise muttered.

"Last twenty reps," Zak called out.

"Thank God," Annalise and Reen chorused, dropping their arms.

"Not yet, ladies, keep those arms going," Astrid encouraged.

"Don't forget, there's going to be a big, delicious lunch buffet for our reward," Laila reminded them. "Including six different flavors of my scones."

"And two of my big, special rum-soaked fruitcakes," Annalise said. Glancing at Delaney she laughed. "Good grief, you look like hell."

"You don't look like you just stepped out of the salon either," Delaney shot back. "All I have to say is that it's a darned good thing you took those photos of us *before* we started exercising, Mom."

"Don't get too complacent. I'll be taking another round of pictures once we've finished."

Grumbles and *aw hells* were evident.

"What? We need before and after shots for this year's holiday album." At the sound of further griping, Astrid offered an innocent smile.

They all turned to Astrid, who looked petal-fresh and dewy.

"Do you see that?" Annalise asked, thumbing toward Astrid. "Admit it, ladies. Your mother isn't human. Nobody looks like that after thirty minutes of agony."

Wide-eyed and pursing her lips, Astrid cocked her head to the side. Moving her arms in a chopping motion, she walked in a small circle. In stilted mechanical tones, she replied, "You have discovered my secret. I am a robot. Take me to your leader."

"You're a nut, Mom." Delaney laughed, giving Astrid a nudge. "Come on, let's go get cleaned up so we can hit that lunch buffet."

As they walked to the showers, Reen stopped in her tracks, uttering a fleeting gasp.

"What's wrong?" Laila asked.

"I didn't know Hud was going to be here with *her*," Reen said the word like it was soured milk on her tongue. All eyes turned to where Reen's narrowed gaze was locked.

"They go pretty much everywhere together lately," Annalise said, looking at Monica Sharp and her brother canoodling as they left the exercise floor. Poor Reen...she looked miserable. It was obvious she had a thing for Hud but it appeared Hud's main focus was Monica.

"Hey, Drake!" Astrid waved at Drake Slattery who was heading to the men's showers.

He looked their way and his exhausted features immediately brightened. If Reen could only get her mind off Hud, Annalise thought, maybe she'd notice a great guy who only had eyes for her—like Drake.

A moment later he had joined them and they made small talk and jokes about the killer exercise class. He and Reen were great friends but it seemed clear it went beyond mere friendship for Drake. After a brief chat he was on his way.

"What happened to Sabrina?" Delaney asked. "I thought she was coming today?"

"She'd planned to." Annalise's expression twisted. "Until Stuart talked her into spending the day with him and Harry today, tomorrow and Christmas day." The idea had Annalise steaming but she tried to hide it. Annalise imagined Stuart had succeeded in monopolizing her sister's time using some sob story.

"Have you talked to her about him?" Laila asked. "Do you think she's going back to him?"

"Please tell me she's not considering taking that crumb back," Delaney said.

"Oh hell no!" Annalise said with more gusto than she'd intended. The others gaped at her and she laughed. "Sorry, as you've probably guessed, Stuart's not one of my favorite people."

"Mmm-hmm, we may have noticed," Reen teased.

"Sabrina swears she's only doing this for Harry because she doesn't want to spoil his Christmas," Annalise explained. "She's crossing her fingers that Stuart will be on his best behavior since his goal is to win her back, so she's not overly concerned. But she said she's looking forward to the day after Christmas when he heads back to Pennsylvania. It's been a strain on her."

"I can imagine," Astrid said. "That whole situation is so sad. Really heartbreaking."

"I tried calling her a couple of times but it went to voicemail," Reen told them.

"I think she's trying to keep Stuart from getting cranky the way he used to when he thought she spent too much time with her friends," Annalise said. "She probably wants to give her full attention to the way he's treating Harry too."

"Are they still planning on coming to the nativity play at the church tomorrow night?" Laila asked.

"Yup." Annalise nodded. "Yesterday was Sabrina's last day of work until after Christmas. Before Stuart came to the café to pick her up—he avoids coming in," she added, rolling her eyes, "Sabrina told me she and Harry are doing fine and confirmed they'd be there tomorrow night for the Christmas Eve play. Harry's playing Joseph."

"He'll be adorable," Reen said. "And Drake's daughter, Lilly, will make a darling angel. I can't wait to see them all dolled up for the play."

Annalise nodded, easily picturing the kids all decked out in their holiday costumes.

"I'll be there with my Kodak, taking lots of pictures," Astrid promised.

The younger women shared good-natured smiles, with none of them at all surprised by Astrid's assurance. They'd all come to expect her clicking away to preserve memorable moments at gatherings of friends or family.

"I'm glad we'll get to see Sabrina and Harry tomorrow," Delaney said. "I haven't seen her in nearly a week. She's never been at the café when I've stopped by."

"She shortened her hours," Annalise said, "and made them earlier so she could be there to keep an eye on Stuart and Harry."

"Smart thinking," Laila said.

"Did Sabrina mention whether or not Stuart will be at the church?" Astrid asked.

"No, but I hope to hell he won't." Annalise's eyes narrowed. "Sorry, but I can't imagine trying to be civil if I see him. That's one of the reasons he stays out of Griffin's. He knows damn well how I feel about him, and I'm quite sure the feeling's mutual." Astrid reached over and gave her a hug. "Are you all going tomorrow?" Annalise asked.

"Gard's on call at the fire station tomorrow," Astrid said. "Same with today, which is why he couldn't make the exercise class. So I doubt he'll make it to the play."

"That's too bad," Laila said. "Gard told me they've got extra people at the fire and police stations standing by because the holidays seem to invite more fights, accidents and fires."

"Except for Kady," Astrid said, "who's due back from her overseas backpacking trip very soon," she crossed her fingers, "the rest of the sizeable Malone entourage will be at the church."

Annalise studied her friends as they entered the locker room. "Honestly, thinking of how you kept track of six children boggles my mind, Astrid. I could never do that."

"I'm not buying that for a minute." Delaney shrugged out of her exercise gear. "The way you look out for every staff member and all your regulars. You're like a mom to every one of them, Annalise."

"Not to mention the way you open up the café to the homeless and anyone in need of a meal on holidays," Laila added.

"Speaking of which," Reen said, "you can count on the Malone sisters and our mom being there bright and early tomorrow to pitch in. It's the least we can do."

Astrid responded by giving two thumbs up.

Annalise's mouth opened and closed. Twice. She'd always had trouble accepting compliments and was at a loss for words. It was true, she loved nurturing people as much as she loved cooking and baking. Knowing some small effort on her part might bring a smile to someone in need made it all worthwhile.

Elbowing Reen, Delaney noted, "There, see how easy that was? All we have to do is compliment Annalise and she clams right up. Ahhh...silence is golden, isn't it?"

"Very funny," Annalise said, finding her voice again and laughing along with them. "You know how much I appreciate you all volunteering on Christmas Eve morning. I don't know what I'd ever do without you. Now last one to the buffet is a rotten egg."

Chapter 9

One Day Later: Christmas Eve

~<>~

"IT'S JUST NOT like it was when I was growing up," Sabrina whispered, studying a Christmas photo of herself standing with Annalise, Hudson, and their parents when she was eight-years-old. Each Christmas their living room was adorned with holiday decorations, evergreen swags, glittery garland, a fat, tall tree full of mostly handmade ornaments and strung popcorn, platters of cookies, and more. It was downright magical. More important than the decorations was the warm, cozy feeling of love and happiness permeating the household.

The album was full of precious photographs and mementos. Most photos of Stuart showed him smiling. It was when he looked his most handsome and charming. Anyone viewing those pictures would get the impression of a happy, satisfied man. But Sabrina knew better. She'd watched him turn his salesman's smile on and off like a light switch. Appearances meant everything to Stuart Hanklen. It was important that the outside world see him as the perfect husband, father and businessman.

His carefully crafted facade only fell when he was behind closed doors, especially when he'd had too much to drink. Surprisingly he'd kept up his new improved persona all week. There were times Sabrina detected a strained expression, like when Harry was caught in a lengthy bout of stuttering and the sweat trickled down Stuart's temple to his jawline. But he kept his cool and never showed any impatience with his son. It was nothing short of amazing.

Sabrina looked up from the album, gazing at the brick wall across the room without really seeing it. Instead, she saw an album of mental images featuring happier times.

In the beginning, her relationship with Stuart seemed perfect. He wooed her with dinners, flowers, candy—and sometimes they just sat together, cuddling close while listening to music.

Now, she barely recognized the man she fell in love with. For the longest time she believed that same wonderful man was still in there somewhere and it was up to her to bring him back out. But that was before Stuart destroyed any love she had left for him. Before alcohol and other women had replaced Sabrina and Harry as the most important things in his life.

Their life together began to unravel the day Sabrina discovered Harry in his crib with an angry red handprint covering one side of his little face. Gripped by disbelief, she confronted her husband. Stuart balked, denying he'd laid a hand on the baby, but at the same time making it clear that it was Sabrina's job to keep Harry quiet. He complained that all he did was cry. How could he think with all that wailing going on?

"He's just a baby," Sabrina told him. "Babies cry. It's one of the ways they communicate. Harry's happy and smiling most of the time, Stuart. It's not like he cries an abnormal amount."

"From now on," Stuart told her in a quiet, controlled tone, "when he cries, go change his diaper or give him a damn bottle with some whiskey-spiked milk or something, *anything* to shut him the hell up." By the end of the sentence he was yelling.

He'd been drinking before their conversation began. He never spoke to her that way when he was sober. It was an alarming switch from Dr. Jekyll to Mr. Hyde.

Sabrina warned Stuart that day that if he ever hurt Harry again, she'd take the baby and leave him.

"W-what's the m-matter, M-mommy?" Climbing onto the living room couch, Harry alternately rubbed and patted Sabrina's back. "Y-you l-look s-sad."

She gave Harry a hug. "Nothing's wrong sweetie. I'm just tired."

"Th-that's b-because we worked s-so hard b-baking all those c-cookies." Harry took in a deep sniff. "They m-make it smell j-just like C-christmas in here."

"Mmmm, I love that smell." Sabrina closed her eyes and breathed in. "I had a lot of fun baking cookies with you today. You did such a good job."

"Thanks! I think s-so t-too. Dad's g-going to like the w-way they smell, and the t-taste too. He'll be h-happy." His expression stretched to an ear to ear grin. "He's b-been p-pretty happy for a while n-now. I hope he s-stays h-happy until he g-goes b-back to P-p-p-p." He took a deep breath. "B-back home," he modified with a smile.

"Are you sure you're okay with that, honey? With your dad going back to Pennsylvania to live after Christmas while you and I stay here in Glassfloat Bay?"

Harry's head bobbed up and down without hesitation. "Yeah, M-mom. I think it's a g-good idea. I l-like it here a l-lot."

They hadn't talked about it much but Sabrina was sure Harry was just as surprised by his father's vastly improved behavior as she was. And that maybe he, too, was praying they'd make it through Stuart's entire stay without him reverting to his previous ways personality and spoiling yet another holiday. Harry obviously hoped to have the first Christmas in their new home be as merry as possible.

"Before your dad gets here I'll simmer a pot of orange rind and spices so it'll smell even more like Christmas."

"I made a s-sizshun."

Sabrina thought for a moment. "A decision?"

"Right...d-decision." He gave a thought nod. "When I g-grow up I'm going to be a b-baker too. L-like you and Aunt Annalise and

M-miss L-laila. You know," he shrugged, "when I'm n-not b-busy being a fireman."

"Hmm..." she tilted her head, smiling at him, "sounds like a good career plan to me."

Glancing at the album in his mom's lap, Harry said, "Look at m-me! T-that's when I w-was still l-little."

His words made her chuckle. "Right," she mussed his hair, "you were just a little kid of four-and-a-half there."

"Yup and t-tomorrow I'll b-be five," he held up spread fingers, "j-just like one of the b-big k-kids."

"Indeed you will, sweetie." He put his arms around her neck and she turned to kiss his cheek. Sabrina's gaze slid to the large teak and brass atomic starburst wall clock across the room. It belonged to her grandmother and she remembered admiring it as a child. It definitely helped to brighten the living room of their small, two-bedroom apartment. She imagined the clock acting as the star atop the Christmas tree once they placed it there.

Closing the album, she gave Harry another hug. "Why don't you go put your costume for tonight's pageant on over your clothes so I can see how you look? I'll bet you're excited, hmm?"

Harry's head bobbed enthusiastically. "Is Aunt Annalise g-going to b-be there? I m-miss her a lot."

"She will. She'll be happy to see you too."

"How about G-gard? I m-miss him and T-tundra too."

"Um, I don't know if he'll be there or not, Harry. Call me if you need help getting into your costume, okay?" she said as he scooted off to his bedroom.

Thank goodness she'd briefed Harry on certain taboo topics to bring up in his father's presence...topics like Gard. She could imagine Stuart's eyeballs bugging if he heard Harry say he missed Gard.

While Stuart had tried to finagle his way out of their agreement, Sabrina insisted that he sleep at his hotel. No way was she about to share a bed with him. She'd reminded him several times that the only reason she'd agreed to his request to spend time during the week before Christmas with them was for Harry's sake. It would be the last time they would be all together as a family for any holiday.

While Stuart was on his best behavior, doing everything short of somersaults to win Sabrina over and keep her from going through with the divorce, there wasn't a chance in hell that she'd change her mind. She couldn't wait to be rid of him. After everything Stuart had done to belittle, bully, and humiliate her and Harry the past few years, nothing he said or did now could conceivably convince her that he'd made any lasting transformation.

Fool me once, she thought.

She and Harry had Stuart over for Christmas Eve breakfast this morning. Harry poured the orange juice and buttered the toast, gobbling up his father's show of praise. Tonight the three of them planned to put up all the decorations together.

Before Harry headed for his bedroom to get into his costume, he asked, "D-daddy s-seemed p-pretty happy at b-breakfast this m-morning, didn't he?"

"Yes he did, Harry."

"He was real n-nice to m-me." He gave a dimpled smile. "M-maybe he won't b-be sick anymore." He skipped out of the room.

Sick. That was the word she'd used in the past to explain Stuart's drunkenness.

"All I care about," Sabrina muttered to herself, "is that he avoids being *sick* through Christmas...then gets the hell out of my life." She hated how hard and jaded she'd become but she was done with him. And he had no one to blame but himself.

After breakfast, Sabrina made a big bowl of popcorn and she and Harry had fun stringing it into long, fluffy garlands. Stuart left to shop for Harry's presents and the big, fat, fragrant evergreen tree they'd talked about, with Harry drawing an example to show Stuart.

Smiling, he'd pocketed his son's picture, telling Harry it would help him pick out the best tree for them.

Glancing again at the photo album, she tucked it into her black and white zebra-striped canvas tote bag, snapping it closed. It held her most prized possessions; family photos, Harry's artwork, some of her own drawings, and several other small *treasures* as she liked to think of them.

Sentimental claptrap, Stuart called it.

She remembered the time in Pennsylvania when he'd come home from work and was drinking too much. He grabbed the tote bag from Sabrina, making a show of going outside and shoving it into the garbage dumpster. It was the same dumpster used by the tavern in their apartment building. That night after Stuart passed out on the couch, Sabrina donned an old sweat suit and sneakers, tiptoed out of the apartment, and became a dumpster diver.

She'd cleaned her tote bag and hid it in the far back corner of Harry's closet on the floor beneath his shoes, where Stuart wouldn't have any reason to look.

Harry found the bag one day and asked her about it. Sabrina told him it was her special bag of treasures and she knew it would be safe in Harry's closet. He was a perceptive boy. Even at his young age she knew he understood she wanted to keep the location of the bag a secret from Stuart, and that she could trust Harry not to reveal its hiding place. But neither spoke of it. While she hated engaging her son in deception, it was the only way Sabrina could keep her mementos secure.

Now, out of habit, she and Harry still kept the tote in his closet.

She wouldn't have to hide her tote from Gard. He'd understand.

Her features skewing, Sabrina wondered at the random, out of nowhere thought that had popped into her head.

Since meeting Gard she realized she'd been counting the minutes until her divorce decree became final. The tall, dark blond, nicely muscled glaciologist and firefighter was intelligent, witty, and kind. Harry had definitely benefitted from his time with Gard, who'd been patient and encouraging, never making her son feel like he was a bother. And with Gard it was genuine, rather than playacting as she suspected Stuart was doing since his arrival in Glassfloat Bay.

When Sabrina spoke, Gard showed interest, asking questions and offering his thoughts, making it a true give and take conversation. It had been so long since a man treated her with respect; treated her like an intelligent woman with more than half a brain. During their discussions she never felt foolish. Awkward, maybe, but that was because of the fluttering going on in her stomach when he was nearby.

She'd tried to hold meaningful conversations with Stuart countless times in the past but he had little interest. He claimed once Sabrina became a mother, talking to her was a snoozefest because she was so dull. Of course this last week he acted as if the sun rose and set solely because of Sabrina.

"Look, M-m-mommy." Harry came bounding into the kitchen, twirling around. "The only thing I c-can't get r-right is the b-beard."

"Oh Harry!" Sabrina smiled at the beaming little boy before her. "You look like a little angel."

"Aw, Mom. I'm n-not an a-angel, I'm s-supposed to be Joseph, r-r-remember?"

Sabrina laughed. "Yes. And a fine Joseph you make. But you'll always be my little angel." She gathered her son in a hug and pinched his cheek affectionately.

"Aw Mom," he protested again.

"Go get the rest of your things together. I'll help with the beard and whatever else you need as soon as I finish tidying up the apartment. I want everything ready for our Christmas tree decorating party with your father. If you want to, you can leave your costume on so your dad can see it."

"S-sure, Mom." Harry looked at Sabrina, then at the coffee table. "M-maybe I should t-take your treasure b-bag and p-put it away before D-d-daddy gets here."

Sabrina followed her son's gaze, her teeth sinking into her bottom lip. She'd forgotten about the tote bag. As far as Stuart knew, it was still at the bottom of that dumpster back in Horntik.

"Thank you, Harry. I'd appreciate that."

Sizeable tote bag securely in his grip, Harry pointed to the folded sheet of yellow construction paper on the kitchen counter. "D-don't forget to p-put the card I made for Lilly in your p-purse so I can g-give it to her at church. I can't w-wait to see her in her angel c-costume." His grin was ear to ear as he left the kitchen.

"I won't forget." Sabrina smoothed her fingers across Harry's handmade Christmas card with its bold crayon depictions of a Christmas tree with an angel topper, Santa, a snowman, and a grinning boy and girl holding a big red heart between them.

Pressing the card to her chest, she leaned her head back against the wall and smiled. "He's so excited," she whispered, elated that Harry was so happy about the pageant. As he told her many times, playing Joseph is a *very* important role. He was so proud that his Sunday school teacher chose him for the part. Sabrina chuckled softly. It felt so good to laugh and forget about the stress and pressures that weighed so heavily lately.

Sabrina placed the card Harry made for Lilly in her purse.

"M-mom?" Harry had popped back into the kitchen, surprising her.

"What is it, honey?"

"You d-don't think G-gard is a b-bad man, d-do you?"

Sabrina's eyebrows scrunched in confusion. "Gard? No. In fact I think he's a very g—" She stopped abruptly when Harry's question set off alarm bells in her head. Dear God, was it possible she'd misjudged Gard the same way she'd misjudged Stuart? She couldn't believe he'd hurt Harry but...

"Why, honey?" she asked, working to maintain her calm while anxious about her son's answer. "Has Gard ever said or done anything mean to you—anything to hurt you?"

"No." Harry shook his head. "G-gard's always n-nice to m-me and he d-doesn't r-roll his eyes or anything when I s-stutter. It's j-just that D-daddy said G-gard was a b-bad man."

Sabrina stiffened. Doing her best to remain composed when she wanted to growl instead, she asked, "When did he say that?"

"A few d-days ago when y-you were working at the c-café. I was in the l-living room watching TV with D-dad and he said G-gard was t-trying to k-keep us from b-being a family."

Sabrina saw red. *That paranoid son of a bitch.*

"Then D-dad asked m-me some q-questions."

"Like what, honey?" She deserved a gold star for maintaining her cool. Sitting on a kitchen chair, she pulled Harry onto her lap.

"Oh...stuff l-like if I thought y-you l-liked G-gard a lot and if I ever s-saw you and G-gard k-kissing. I was p-pretty sure I knew w-what was h-happening." He gave her a knowing look.

"What do you mean?"

"Well, it s-sounded l-like D-dad felt the s-same way I feel when Jordan Schroeder b-butts in and t-talks to Lilly when I'm t-talking to her and I g-get j-jealous. I t-told D-dad I d-didn't know anything about that s-stuff." He gazed up at her with a devilish smile. "D-did you and G-gard ever k-kiss? It's okay...I won't t-tell if you d-did." He giggled.

"No, Harold." His giggling was infectious and she smiled. "I haven't kissed Gard or any other man since I married your father. But since we're getting divorced, that will probably change. Is that okay with you?"

"Sure." Harry gave a nonchalant shrug. "I c-can t-tell by the way G-gard looks at you that he p-probably wants to k-kiss you, but d-don't worry," he held both hands up, "I didn't s-say that to D-dad."

Sabrina smiled. "Good decision, Harry. That definitely wouldn't make your dad happy"

"D-dad asks m-me lots of other questions t-too. Like if you ever s-say b-bad things about him to m-me...or if you t-talk about him with Aunt Annalise or any of your f-friends. I t-told him n-no b-because I wanted to m-make sure D-dad stayed happy and d-didn't s-start d-drinking again."

She wondered when her little boy had become so insightful.

"I l-love D-dad," he continued, "but I'm n-not s-sad that he's n-not going to live with us."

She hugged him. "Such a large burden for a five-year-old to carry. Listen, sweetie," she held him at arm's length, "even though your dad isn't going to be with us anymore after Christmas, you can visit each other. No matter what, he'll always be your dad and I know he loves you." That last part was a lie. She knew no such thing. She only knew he was a conniving manipulator.

"Okay." He looked down at his Joseph robe, smoothing it. "S-sometimes I think b-bad thoughts that I shouldn't b-be thinking."

"You do? Like what?" She couldn't imagine where this was leading.

"Well," his hands fidgeted with the material, "s-sometimes I wish G-gard was my d-dad." His eyes grew wide. "P-please don't ever t-tell Dad b-because he'd b-be sooo mad at m-me and feel real b-bad and get...*sick* again." He scrunched his face.

"I won't say a word, Harry. We'll just keep that to ourselves." So she wasn't the only one who'd been thinking about how good Harry and Gard were together. "And, Harry..."

He looked up into his mom's eyes. "Yeah?"

"Thinking that about Gard doesn't make you a bad boy. Now go get the rest of your things together for tonight."

A quick glance at the clock told her Stuart should be arriving soon. After they put the decorations on the tree, they'd have cookies and eggnog before they hopped into Stuart's rental car and he drove her and Harry to the church. Stuart had never been a churchgoer so she didn't make much of an effort to convince him to attend. She did explain that Good Samaritan Community Church was nondenominational and welcomed everyone, regardless of faith, or lack thereof, so he shouldn't feel uncomfortable. But she was immensely glad when he said he wouldn't go.

Twenty minutes later, Harry came into the living room. "How long b-before D-daddy's here with our Christmas t-tree?"

"Any minute, probably. He said he had some shopping to do too." Sabrina normally shopped for Harry's presents herself but Stuart insisted on taking over the task this year, saying he wanted to do everything he could to make this Christmas perfect for them.

"Ooh," a gleeful Harry rubbed his hands together briskly, "you m-mean like m-maybe some birthday p-present shopping for m-me?" He giggled.

"Harry, I have no idea what you're talking about." Sabrina winked.

She and Stuart decided on a train set for Harry's joint birthday and Christmas gift. Stuart had seen one in a toy store window at Glassfloat Bay Mall and raved about it. He took pictures with his phone and showed Sabrina. It was perfect. It had a steam locomotive, six cars, and even came with a little train station and some workers. Harry loved trains and would be so excited.

"I w-wonder what S-santa's going to b-bring me this year," Harry said as if tapping into Sabrina's thoughts.

"Hmm...I don't know."

"I b-bet it's s-something for a b-big five-year-old k-kid like m-me." Harry's grin spread across his face.

He was so excited about turning five. Less than a year from now he'd be in first grade. Sabrina hoped he'd still be as enthused about school once he finished kindergarten. It was likely he'd run into difficulties trying to keep up with his schoolwork and the other students.

Referencing her son's medical records, Harry's new pediatrician explained that Harry would have to go through a battery of tests to determine whether or not he could attend regular classes, or would need to be placed in special classes instead.

Developmentally delayed. That was the pediatrician specialist's diagnosis after examining two-year-old Harry back in Horntik. Harry's stuttering and stammering began as soon as he started to talk, growing worse when Stuart was angry. Harry was slower than other kids his age, sometimes taking longer to comprehend things. The doctors said the extent of his disabilities couldn't fully be determined until he was older.

Once they advised Sabrina that the condition could have been caused by head trauma, she got a sick feeling deep in the pit of her stomach. Her initial suspicion about Stuart hitting the baby must have been right after all. The monstrous notion made her shudder.

This developmental delay was why she and Harry regularly practiced reading and math problems, with Sabrina doing her best to make a fun game out of it rather than a chore. Harry loved to read and to have her read to him. With Harry's enjoyment in their educational games, Sabrina felt confident he'd soon catch up to other children his age.

Maybe he'd even ace those class placement tests, surprising the doctors.

All Harry needed, she thought as she plumped the pillows on the sofa, was plenty of love and positive attention. And she had that to give in abundance.

Chapter 10

~<>~

"I THOUGHT YOU said you had to be out of here thirty minutes ago," Nevan Malone said to the man who'd been drinking like prohibition was just around the corner. "Maybe you've had enough, huh?"

Eyeing Nevan with disdain, Stuart Hanklen said, "I thought you were a bartender. If I wanted a babysitter I'd park my ass at a daycare center instead of a pub." He slapped the bar twice. "Now pour me another."

Nevan watched Hanklen toss back the double shot of whiskey before attempting to focus on the time on his phone. The guy sat there for a minute, soundlessly snickering at some private joke.

Looking up at Nevan, crooked smile still in place, Hanklen said, "Shhh...I'm not here. I'm out shopping for a tree and presents for our kid. At least that's what my wife thinks. Gotta make a good impression, you know? Gotta live up to expectations. Be the perfect husband and father."

Nevan opened his mouth and snapped it shut, the uncharacteristically prying questions dying on his lips. He generally avoided getting involved in his customers' personal business but he knew Hanklen had a nice wife and kid waiting for him upstairs and Nevan couldn't help feeling sorry for them.

His brother, Gard, told him about Hanklen's unexpected arrival in town and the guy's bargain with Sabrina to stay in town until the day after Christmas. Gard made it clear he didn't trust Hanklen as far as he could throw him. Since Hanklen had apparently made a big deal about having stopped drinking and being reformed, it seemed to Nevan that Gard had the guy pegged.

"It's not like I'm driving. I just have to walk two flights up to my wife's apartment." He hiked his thumb. "So give me one more for the road, or should I say one more for the stairs?" Hanklen laughed at his own perceived hilarity. "Then I'll be on my way...upstairs to my loving wife."

"Last shot, Stuart," Nevan informed him, pouring a single, reaching that uncomfortable point all bartenders had to deal with on a regular basis. He had a responsibility to cut patrons off when they were trashed, to keep them from posing a danger to themselves or others. "I'll be glad to make you a cup of coffee and a sandwich. On the house."

"What...is that a joke?" Hanklen looked like he'd just been offered cockroach on a stick. "I'm not here to eat. Jesus, you make it sound like I'm drunk," he pointed a wavy, accusatory finger, "and we both know damn well I'm not." His words were slurred, his eyes glassy. Hanklen was already way past being half in the bag.

"Sure, whatever you say, Stuart. But that's your last drink." Nevan nodded toward the whiskey he'd just poured before tending to the other patrons.

"Maybe I'll let you make me an Irish dinner," Stuart suggested, and Nevan knew damn well what was coming next. "A potato and a six-pack," Hanklen said using what he must have decided was an Irish brogue. "Hold the potato." He enjoyed a solitary laugh.

Nevan thought the guy was about as funny as that potato he was talking about.

"Told Sabrina I took a vacation from my job back in Pennsylvania. Didn't want to tell her I got canned," Stuart went on as Nevan worked. "Coldhearted son of a bitch fired me two weeks before Christmas. Can you believe that? What the hell am I supposed to tell Sabrina? Nothing, that's what." He started that silent snickering again. "What she doesn't know won't hurt her, right? Right? Gotta make her believe I'm upstanding husband material, you know?"

"It's tough losing your job right before Christmas," Nevan said in reply, wondering what the hell Hanklen had done to get axed so close to a holiday. He could imagine Stuart doing any number of asinine stunts serious enough to get him fired.

"The world is full of assholes ready to rain on my parade." Stuart engaged in quiet laughter as his finger poked through the small bowl of peanuts.

While Nevan didn't respond, he did give Stuart his attention as he wiped the bar. Being Father Confessor wasn't high on his list of job requirements, but it was a necessary evil. What he couldn't understand is why a fine woman like Sabrina would ever marry a jerk like Hanklen in the first place,

"So what if I kept a couple bottles in my desk at work?" Stuart reasoned with a righteous expression. "They were mine. I paid for them." Wagging an outstretched finger at Nevan, he added, "And I was careful. Very careful."

Wishing he could be anyplace but here, listening to Hanklen blather on, confirming his hard-earned status of First Degree Asshole, Nevan offered a half smile and nodded.

"I only drank at lunch, which was my own personal time." Stuart clapped his hand against his chest. "Or, you know, maybe on a slow day. Or one of those days when the weather was too damn shitty to go out and beg for new business." He waved his glass through the air. And you know why I'm drinking today? Huh? Do you?"

"Nope. But I'm sure you'll tell me."

"Hell yeah, I will. Because, jingle-fucking-bells, it's Christmas Eve, that's why. I mean, come on, what's wrong with a grown adult man enjoying a few drinks the day before a holiday?" He banged the bottom of his glass against the bar, sloshing the small amount of whiskey that remained.

"Told Sabrina I stopped drinking. She bought it...actually believed I gave it up because she filed for divorce." He gave a gravely chuckle. "But I outsmarted her...I keep it to vodka and—"

"That's whiskey," Nevan pointed out.

"Yeah, 'cause like I said, it's Christmas Eve and there's no reason a guy can't drink a little whiskey on Christmas. Anyway, guess what I eat to make my breath smell okay. Go ahead, guess."

"Candy canes," Nevan guessed.

"Nope, that just makes you have minty alcohol breath. If you eat a handful of peanuts, that takes the smell away." Winking, he popped some peanuts into his mouth. "You know my wife, Sabrina?"

"I've met her. Nice lady."

"Got you fooled too, huh?" Stuart snarled. "This morning, after I spent the whole week being a textbook perfect husband and father, we had our talk—the one about if she'd come back to me or not. Know what she told me?" Nevan shook his head and Stuart continued. "She said no. Said she's still getting the divorce." His expression darkened into an overall scowl. "How about that? All I get after all I've done for her and that kid is an *adios motherfucker*."

After a moment of welcome silence, Hanklen mumbled something unintelligible before poking Nevan in the arm.

"I'm going to tell you something else. That little secretary at my office," he formed a curvy woman's shape with his hands, "loved it when I pulled her onto my lap. Sure, she acted all high and mighty in front of my boss when he came in but I could tell she wanted it." His head bobbed up and down. "A man can always tell."

"Is that right?" Nevan commented, his tone nonchalant while his gut roiled at Stuart's absurd admission. It looked like Sabrina and Harry were in for one hell of a rocky Christmas. Nice. Real nice.

"She was hot for me." Hanklen nodded with confidence. "Horny. Always eyeballing me like I was prime rib. Then she made a big deal when I grabbed her. Go figure." He shook his head. "What a psycho."

Sick to death of listening to Hanklen's drunken, irrational ramblings, Nevan groaned.

"You know that punk sales manager who fired me?" Hanklen's voice rose while his eyes narrowed to slits. "Didn't like me right from the start. Had a bug up his ass to get rid of me cuz he was jealous of me. Afraid I'd take over his job, know what I mean?"

Biting his tongue to keep from telling Hanklen exactly what he thought of him, Nevan nodded and continued wiping the counter. If he wiped any harder he'd take the finish off.

"He was right," Hanklen slapped the bar, "I would have." He held up his pinky finger, gazing at it. "I've got more brains in my little finger than the starchy little prick does in his whole damn three-piece-suited body." Stuart glanced at his phone again, winced, then tossed back the rest of his whiskey. "Time to go. Gotta head upstairs to the little woman." His expression grew somber. "And that damn retard kid. Jesus," he clapped his hands over his ears, "I'm sick to death of his endless stuttering."

Nevan Malone's hands curled into fists. It was all he could do not to haul off and sock Stuart Hanklen. The man was nothing but a stinking drunk, a braggart, a bully full of misplaced righteous outrage who made the lives of everyone around him a living hell. Not being able to administer a well-deserved fist to the jaw of this asinine jerk was one of the downsides to tending bar at his own establishment.

Grinning at Nevan as he rose from the barstool, Hanklen tossed twenty bucks on the bar, saying, "Merry fucking Christmas, pal," before heading out the door...and up the stairs to deliver all that was needed to ruin the Christmas of a kind, unsuspecting woman and her unlucky little boy.

The bar was still full of customers, none even remotely close to being as plastered as Hanklen. Nevan glanced up at the clock on the wall. When his shift ended he'd head over to the fire station where Gard was on duty to fill him in about his encounter with Sabrina's husband.

Chapter 11

~<>~

SABRINA PACED across the kitchen, into the living room and back, wringing her hands. "He should have been here by now," she mumbled as her thoughts galloped with unsavory possibilities—a car accident at the forefront of her worries. If he didn't get there soon, they wouldn't have enough time to decorate the tree before she and Harry had to leave for the play.

Before she had any more time to conjure bleak what-ifs in her head, she heard a knock at the door.

"Stuart, thank goodness," she said, opening the door. "I was afraid you might have been in an accident." He took a step toward her, his arm snaking around her waist and yanking her close before he slobbered a kiss on her mouth.

Wide-eyed, Sabrina recoiled.

She tasted it, smelled it, saw it in his eyes.

"You've been drinking." She backed away, feeling foolish for stating the obvious. Freezing in place, her mind raced. What the hell was she going to do now? While she expected his ideal husband and father persona to crack and fall apart after the holidays, she was so sure Stuart would be on his best behavior for Christmas. It had seemed so important to him to get her and Harry back.

"You're wrong," he said, weaving in place. "I told you, I gave up drinking. What you smell is peanuts." The crack of Stuart's sardonic laughter stung her ears. She had no idea what he found so funny. He mumbled something unintelligible beneath his breath.

"D-d-daddy!" Racing into the room, Harry hugged his father's leg. "Look, I have m-my costume on for the p-play. How d-do I l-look?" He spun around and giggled.

Curling his lip as he assessed his son, Stuart spat, "Like a fucking fairy."

His tone, his offensive words, the look in his eye, sent a chill down Sabrina's spine. *Dear God...not tonight of all nights.*

Unaware, Harry laughed. "No, D-daddy, I'm s-supposed to b-be J-joseph, not a f-fairy."

Shrugging the child from his leg, Stuart pushed past Sabrina and staggered into the kitchen, throwing open one cupboard after another. "Where's my scotch?"

"You don't live here, Stuart, remember? I don't keep scotch in my apartment."

She peeked out into the hall before closing the door, only to be greeted by emptiness. "Where's the Christmas tree?" she asked absently, half expecting to see it if she looked harder. "Is it still on your car?"

Her eyes widened when she realized the tree wasn't all that was missing.

She went to him, grabbing him by his shirt collar, searching his reddened, unfocused gaze. "Harold's present," she whispered. "Please tell me you got the train set."

"He's got enough goddamned toys." He stared back at her, his face a sneering mask. "Harold had *me*," Stuart thumbed his own chest, "playing with him here all week. That's all he needed. It sure as hell was a lot more than what I needed, pretending for days on end that the little shit didn't annoy the hell out of me."

Sabrina's heart sank.

"Vodka's gone, too." He checked the cabinet beneath the sink. "What did you do with it?"

"There is no vodka here, Stuart. There never was. You need to leave. Go back to your hotel room and sleep it off."

"I'm not going anywhere." On his hands and knees, he rifled through the cabinet with her baking pans. "No gin either...Jesus Christ!" He slammed the cabinet door so hard, she and Harry flinched. "You got rid of everything. What the hell am I supposed to drink?" He clanked around through the rest of the cabinets until he found the small pint bottles of brandy and rum with Sabrina's baking ingredients in an upper cupboard.

Offering an accusatory look, he said, "Cute. Thought you'd be real clever and hide them with your cooking shit." He glared at her in a soulless way that sent a shudder through her.

"Those are for the fruitcake, cookies and eggnog," Sabrina explained.

Looking at his wife as if she had two heads, Stuart dissolved into maniacal laughter. "*Fruitcake*? The only fruitcake around here is you, Sabrina, if you think I'm going to spend Christmas Eve sipping eggnog," he mimicked drinking with his pinky finger extended, "eating those damn Christmas cookies you've got strewn all over the place, and letting you pour good booze over that inedible brick you and your asshole sister call a fruitcake."

"M-m-mommy?" Harry whispered, tugging at his mother's dress.

Cupping the back of her son's head and gazing down at his troubled expression, Sabrina placed her finger to her lips in a shushing motion. "Shh, it's okay, sweetie. Why don't you go to your room for a while?"

"You stay here until I give you permission to leave, Harold." Stuart pointed a threatening finger at his son before grabbing the brandy and rum, turning on the television, and plopping on the couch.

Harold stood rigid in place.

She had to get Stuart out of here...away from Harry. Or maybe she could just grab Harry and run out of the apartment. As her thoughts reeled, Stuart turned to her, waving an outstretched finger.

"Don't even think about getting on my case about the damn tree. It's Christmas-fucking-eve. Everyplace was sold out." He twisted the cap off the brandy and took a slug.

"W-we're not g-going to have a Christmas t-t-tree this year?" Harry asked softly, staying close to Sabrina.

"Right. No t-t-t-t-tree," Stuart said, mocking his son. "Why don't you get your crayons, draw a big green t-t-t-t-tree," he gestured, his arms wide, "and we'll tape it to the w-w-w-w-wall. How's that? You like drawing so much, so draw us a Christmas tree."

"I think I might know of a place that still has trees," Sabrina suggested, hating to see the hurt in her son's eyes due to Stuart's cruel mimicking. "Harry and I will just run over and—"

"I said there were no trees left anywhere." Lurching from the sofa, Stuart loomed over her, narrowing his eyes. "Are you calling me a liar?" The look he gave her was lethal and she noticed he'd balled his hands into fists.

Stiffening, Sabrina felt sure her face went ashen. "No." She'd never seen Stuart this bad and it scared her. Swallowing hard, she said, "Of course not, Stuart. I just meant—"

"Don't you *ever* call me a liar," he warned, stepping toward her and jabbing a threatening finger that connected with the soft tissue just beneath her collarbone three times. "You hear me?"

"Yes." Sabrina took a step back, keeping Harry behind her. "Yes, Stuart, I hear you."

"This apartment's too damn small for a tree anyway." He looked down at Harry who was peeking from behind Sabrina's skirt. "And that spoiled rotten kid of ours doesn't need any presents for Christmas or his birthday. All he cares about are his crayons and paper anyway."

Resting his hands on his knees, Stuart specifically addressed his son, a forbidding smile across his face. Sabrina imagined it was the sort of humorless smile a sadistic kid has just before pulling the wings off a fly.

"Santa and I are good friends. Did you know that, Harold?"

He shook his head back and forth. "N-n-no s-sir."

"Oh yeah." Stuart's head bobbed. "I called him and told him you're spoiled. Told him to permanently cross your address off his list. So he won't be coming here again. Ever. Got that?"

Clearly frightened, Harry remained silent.

"Answer me when I speak to you," Stuart roared.

"Y-y-y-yes s-s-sir."

Sabrina looked down at her son. His face was sheet white and his chin trembled.

"Oh, Stuart..." Those two simple words held a heartbreaking mixture of sorrow, disappointment and fear.

Cocking his head in her direction, Stuart turned his wrath on his wife. "Don't give me that *oh Stuart* crap. This is all your fault. You turned my life upside down when you filed for divorce, Sabrina. You may as well have stabbed me in the heart. And after all I've done for you and that stuttering little shit." He motioned to Harry.

He took another swig of brandy and focused on her. "I'm talking to you, Sabrina. Didn't you hear me?"

"Yes, I heard you." She wanted to ask how she could possibly miss hearing him when he was bellowing at her. "I-I'm sorry you feel that way but please..." she patted the air with her hands, "please try to keep your voice down. My neighbors will hear."

Nearly bug-eyed, Stuart craned his neck, jutting his face toward her. If the situation was different, the cartoonish gesture would have made her laugh. Now it had her trembling with fear. "*Your* neighbors. *Your* apartment. You just can't wait to cut me out of your life, can you?"

Oh dear God.

Sabrina's eyes closed in a long blink as her mind raced with options. Whatever she said could be misconstrued and cause for attack. She had to find some way to communicate without further triggering his anger.

"Not at all, Stuart." She gave him her best smile. "It's just that this is Christmas Eve and tomorrow is Harold's fifth birthday. It's our first holiday here in Glassfloat Bay."

Sabrina picked up a platter of cookies from the coffee table in front of the TV. "Harold and I baked these for you this morning. They're your favorites. Bonbons with candied cherries inside and brandied frosting." Unlike the cookies she'd brought to the holiday open house, she'd used flavoring instead of actual brandy in these.

With one quick flick of his wrist, Stuart knocked the full platter of cookies to the wood floor where it broke into several pieces. Thankfully it didn't shatter near Harry.

"I don't want cookies," he thundered as Sabrina bent to pick up the cookies and plate fragments. "I don't want fruitcake. I don't want eggnog. All I want is for you to call off the divorce and come back to me. All I want is for us to be a family again. I came here to take you back home to Horntik where you belong. And I'm not leaving without you."

Sabrina sidestepped to kitchen where she'd left her phone on the counter. She'd call Annalise, or maybe Gard, to come pick her and Harry up.

Stuart watched her as she reached for the phone. It was extraordinary how fast a drunken man could move when he wanted to. Before she knew it he was at her side, grabbing her phone.

"Who you planning to call, your boyfriend, Gard?"

"He's not my boyfriend. He's just a customer at the café. I'm going to call my attorney, Stuart, to tell him to stop the divorce proceedings." The preposterous lie nearly caught in her throat. She held her hand out for the phone but Stuart hurled it across the room where it hit the brick wall of the industrial-style apartment.

Sabrina felt cold panic course through her veins.

"You know what? I don't believe you," Stuart said. "No more than you believed me when I said you could call my therapist, Dr. Pape."

"But I did believe you, Stuart. In fact, that sounds like an excellent idea. Why don't you call Dr. Pape right now and talk to him."

"Well if you believed me then you're an idiot, Sabrina. There is no Dr. Pape. The guy on the other end of that line would have been by buddy Artie Pape, pretending to be my doctor. Now *that*," he tapped his temple, "takes some brains to set up. And you bought it, hook line and sinker. You always were gullible, Sabrina."

He was right. Like an idiot she'd believed Stuart when he told her he'd started seeing a therapist. And here she'd been convinced that Stuart couldn't fool her anymore.

"Clever, huh?" he asked.

"Very clever," Sabrina agreed.

"You don't honestly think I'd ever agree to see a shrink when there's no reason, do you?" His twisted frown showed how ridiculous he found the notion.

"No, Stuart."

After she'd finished cleaning the cookie mess, Sabrina stood behind Stuart, who'd been watching her every move. She let her fingers tiptoe up his back to his neck where she massaged it and his shoulders the way he liked. "How does that feel...honey?" Verbalizing the endearment brought a sick taste to her mouth.

"It always feels good when you touch me."

"Mmm-hmm...nice and relaxing, right? I'm going to work out all the knots and tension. That way we can calm down and enjoy the holiday together...as a family...just the way you want."

If she could get him quiet and relaxed maybe he'd go to sleep and she and Harry could leave.

Turning to face her, his lip curled. "By *we*, I assume you mean me. That *I* should calm down. Is that right?"

The faint sound of Harry sniffling snagged her attention. Her patience was running out.

"I just want you to feel happy and comfortable, Stuart, so you can enjoy the holiday and your well-deserved vacation."

"See? There's another thing." He shook a finger at her. "You're too trusting, Sabrina." He muttered something she couldn't make out, something about some punk in a three-piece suit deserving something or other. "I'm not on vacation. I was fired...and for no damn good reason."

"I'm sorry, Stuart. You know what? You deserve a nice evening of stress-free relaxation. Come on." She led him by the elbow. "Why don't you sit back on the couch and watch one of your football games. You can just stay here and relax while Harry and I go to the church for his play."

Once she and Harry left the apartment she wasn't coming back unless it was with the police.

"Church?" He gave an incredulous look. "You're not going to church." Standing in place, Stuart glared down at her. The vile way he looked at her, like she was nothing more than a moldy slice of bread, cut her to her core.

A feeling of dread seeped through her. "But Harold is in the play, Stuart, remember? He's so thrilled about playing Joseph."

Stepping closer to her husband, she spoke in a whisper so Harry wouldn't hear her. The boy looked miserable...petrified. "Please, Stuart, try to calm down. Look," Sabrina motioned toward their son who stood in a corner of the kitchen now, crying silent tears, "you're frightening Harry, and I know you don't want to do that. I know how much you love him. You've been so great with Harold all week long."

After keeping his gaze locked on his wife's face for a small eternity, Stuart shifted his attention to Harry, walked over to him and peered down. Sabrina prayed it was regret she spotted in her husband's expression as he watched his son. She hoped he'd pull him into a hug, holding him close while whispering kind, loving words Harry longed to hear.

That would be better than a Christmas tree. Better than any train set.

Sabrina let out a horrified yelp when, instead, Stuart slapped the boy hard across the face, knocking him against the oven door. Harry gasped, his face a mask of terror.

"Quit your namby-pamby sniveling, Harold!" His eyes wide as saucers, Harry silently stared up at his father. Scowling at his son as he shook the boy by the shoulders, Stuart said, "I'm speaking to you."

"Y-y-yes s-s-sir."

"You make me sick, you know that?"

"Stuart!" Sabrina's mind spun. This couldn't be happening. She didn't know what to do. "My God, Stuart, stop!"

Nodding in reply to his father, Harry's words were nearly inaudible. "Y-yes...I know." One fat tear rolled down his cheek. "I'm s-s-sorry, D-daddy."

"Look at you," Stuart spat, "standing there dressed like a girl and whimpering like one. I won't have my son acting like a pussy, especially when you're turning six or seven or whatever the hell age it is."

"F-five, D-daddy." Harry held up his spread fingers. "I-I'm g-going to be f-five."

"Well whoop-de-fuckin'-doo." Stuart gripped Harry's face and pushed him to the ceramic tile floor where he hit his head.

Panic stricken, Sabrina ran across the living room to retrieve her phone, praying it still worked. She let out a strangled cry when it didn't. Hurrying back to the kitchen she grabbed a couple of paper towels, went to Harry and got down on one knee, wiping his nose and eyes as she whispered words of comfort to the frightened little boy.

"You're nothing but a retard, Harold." Yanking his son into a sitting position, Stuart squatted, getting eye to eye with him.

Getting to his feet, Harry looked like he wanted to melt into the wall and disappear. His mouth opened and closed a few times. Nothing came out. The child was clearly petrified.

"Stop it, Stuart!" Sabrina stepped between her husband and Harry, shielding the boy. "That's enough! Don't speak to your son that way." Growling, Stuart pushed her aside with such force he knocked her to the floor. Determined, for Harry's sake, not to cry, Sabrina merely groaned at the painful shock to her hip.

Harry stood at attention, his little face beet-red, partly from crying and partly from fear. He bit his lower lip to keep it from trembling. "P-please, D-daddy, d-d-don't hurt M-mommy again."

A sob caught in Sabrina's throat at the sound of her brave little boy trying to protect his mother. Getting to her hands and knees, she crawled to Harry, encircling him with her arms as he buried his face in the crook of her shoulder. "It's okay, sweetie. Mommy's fine. Don't worry."

"Are you trying to tell me what I can and can't do? Let me tell you something, Harold. If you want to keep your mommy from getting hurt you won't open your mouth about any of this," his finger twirled around them, "you hear? Because if you do, I'll know. I'll find out. If you ever tell anyone I hurt you or your mother I'll deny it. I'll say you're a liar. Then you know what I'll do after that?"

Harry's head moved slowly from side to side.

"I'll find your mother, wherever she is, and I'll hurt her...real bad."

"Stuart, stop...please," Sabrina pleaded.

Ignoring her, he went on, "And you know whose fault it'll be if that happens, don't you? Yours. Your fault, Harold."

"I-I-I w-won't ever t-tell. I-I p-promise."

"If anyone asks, you tell them you love your daddy. You tell them I'm the best dad ever, got that?"

"Y-y-yes s-sir."

"You tell them you got bruised from falling...or from walking into a doorknob because you're clumsy." His tone was eerily subdued now as he leaned down, inches away from Harry's face. "Because if you ever tell anybody I hit you, I'll hurt your mother. Remember that." He poked Harry's shoulder hard.

"I-I'll r-remember, D-daddy."

From her position on the floor Sabrina could see the outline of Stuart's phone in his pants pocket. As stealthily as she could, she reached for it, hoping Stuart wouldn't catch her.

"If I want to hurt you or your mother that's my right," Stuart said, his voice growing louder again. "She's my wife. My property, just like you're my property." Giving Harry's chest a shove, Stuart knocked the back of the boys head hard against the wall. All the while he sported a heartless smile as if having the time of his life.

An instant later his hand grabbed Sabrina's as she was inching the phone from his pocket. "So you're really itching to make that call to your attorney, huh?" His eyebrows arrowed down. "How stupid do you think I am? You think you're going to call your firefighter boyfriend and he'll come to your rescue, hmm?"

"No, Stuart, I—" Sabrina tried to stop him when Stuart's fingers dug into her shoulders but he effortlessly tossed her aside like a sack of onions. She landed with a sharp crack on her elbow and saw stars, briefly surprised that it didn't happen only in cartoons.

"Well he's not coming." He grabbed Sabrina's forearm, wrenching her to her feet, squeezing so hard she feared he'd snap her bone. Finally he let up the pressure, hurling her hard against the wall.

"He doesn't care about you like I do, Sabrina. Nobody loves you like I do. Don't you want us to be happy again? Don't you want us to go back to Horntik together? It could be just like it used to be." He slobbered another wet kiss on her, almost causing her to vomit.

"Yes, Stuart. Yes, I want that too," she lied as convincingly as humanly possible. "I want us to be together, happy, just like when we first got married."

"Then why do you keep pissing me off? Don't give me that wide-eyed innocent look of yours, Sabrina. This is all your fault, not mine. You always have to push me." He shoved her. "Push, push, push," he shoved her again, making her head jerk back, "until you make me so damn angry. Why do you always have to do that? Huh? Why?"

How the hell was she supposed to answer that? It was like he'd gone off the deep end. A brief recollection of the conversation she'd had with Stuart's mother years ago popped into her head—the one where she'd told Sabrina he'd been diagnosed as bipolar...with manic highs and lows. Is that what this was? She had no clue. It was petrifying not to have any inkling how to deal with Stuart when he was like this. It seemed anything she said or did made him worse.

"I-I don't know, Stuart. I'm sorry. I'll try very hard not to make you angry anymore."

Giving his wife a onceover, he sneered. "Look at you, all gussied up in your fancy red Christmas dress. You must think you're going someplace." His laughter sounded as callous as he looked. "I've got news for you, Sabrina, you're not going anywhere tonight." His gaze swept her hair and makeup. "Except the bedroom." His smile was oily and she struggled not to visibly shudder. "It's about time you invite me in there. Hell, I don't need an invitation. I'm still your husband. It's my right."

Oh God...oh God...

She had to get herself and Harry out of the apartment...had to escape Stuart's deranged behavior before he severely injured Harry, or hit Sabrina so hard he'd knock her out and she wouldn't be able to protect him.

She wanted to cry, dear God how she wanted to wail. But she had to keep her head.

"I'm glad you're still my husband, Stuart. And I look forward to us enjoying each other tonight." She forced a seductive smile. "But first, it's the church's Christmas Eve pageant tonight. Remember? Harry's playing Joseph," she reminded him. She glanced at the wall clock. "We're already late."

"So?" He gave a dramatic shrug. "You really want to sit in the back of some church with a bunch of holy roller hypocrites watching a boring religious fairytale...when you could be here with me?" His eyebrows jiggled in a suggestive manor.

Sabrina shook her head, as if to knock some sense into it. She had no idea what had happened to push her husband to this point. Maybe it was the divorce? Or him being fired. Perhaps it wasn't anything in particular. Maybe he just snapped for no reason. He'd been a problem drinker for years but this was disturbingly different. It went beyond simple drunkenness. She wasn't sure how to cope...how to keep herself and Harry safe, especially without a phone to reach out for help.

She prayed for strength and stamina. She was no match for her husband physically but, by God, through sheer will, determination, or adrenaline alone she'd pick the bastard up and hurl him across the room before she allowed him to hurt Harry again.

She glanced at her quivering little boy. He looked so lost, so confused and frightened. It was Christmas Eve. They were supposed to be decorating the tree, singing Christmas carols. He was supposed to be excited about Santa's visit, and be full of anticipation about playing Joseph. There's no way she'd have that joy taken away from him today. One way or another she'd get Harry away from his father and to the church.

"You're right, Stuart," Sabrina said, giving an Oscar-worthy performance of a loving, caring wife. "I want nothing more than to spend Christmas Eve night in your arms, my darling. You just stay here and rest. I'll drop Harold off at my sister's and then I will be back so the two of us can spend the entire night alone. We'll have a special, private, intimate celebration...in the bedroom." She'd forced herself to smile, saying the last part with an inviting lilt to her voice.

"Yeah...that's good." Stuart gave a slow nod. "I like that. That's what a man wants in a wife."

Hating the lascivious manner in which Stuart eyed her, Sabrina went to the table where he'd tossed the car keys, grabbing them.

"What do you think you're doing with my car keys?"

She glanced at the keys she'd fisted. "Annalise's place is a good mile away. It's only thirty-some degrees outside."

"A mile-long walk won't hurt that pussy kid of mine." Stuart yanked Harry up until he dangled from the floor by his arm. "You need to toughen up, Harold. Be a man." Stuart pitched his son against the wall and Harry crumpled into a heap on the floor.

Be a man. Sabrina choked on the irony of it all. Stuart Hanklen was the farthest thing from a real man that she could imagine.

She closed her eyes, counting to ten before she spoke, measuring her words. "Good idea, Stuart. We'll walk." Sabrina didn't care if they walked, ran, drove or flew. She just wanted them out of there. Turning to Harry, whose cheeks were a shade of crimson no mother should ever see on her child's face, she smiled. "Come on, honey. Let's get you bundled up for our walk."

"You're just dying to get out of here, aren't you?" Stuart asked and, oh brother, how she wanted to let him know how spot on he was. How she wanted to scream her revulsion for the cruel, hostile drunken sot of a man he'd become. More than anything, she was dying to let him know of her abhorrence of the way he treated his own flesh and blood; how he'd abused his infant son nearly five years before, and now ridiculed little Harry for the boy's resulting limitations.

But now wasn't the time to open her mouth and risk being pummeled. Once they reached the church she'd explain everything to Annalise and ask if she and Harry could stay at her place for a while. She knew her sister would welcome them with open arms.

"What I'm dying for, Stuart, is to hurry and get back to you. In the meantime, all I want is for you to rest and feel better," she assured her husband, smiling sweetly. Patting Harry's head, she said, "Let's go get our coats and hats on," already experiencing a sense of buoyancy.

Once in Harry's bedroom she drew her son into a gentle hug. "Are you all right, honey?" There was swelling and she knew he'd be bruised, but a quick check didn't detect any blood or signs of sprains or breaks. "I know it hurts but are you okay to walk to the church?"

"I think s-so." He nodded. "Are you?" His fingers skimmed her face. "You l-look l-like you were in a f-fight, M-mommy. I'm s-sorry D-daddy hurt you." His chin trembled.

"I'm okay. We'll both be okay now. Let me help you take off your Joseph costume so it won't get dirty on our walk to the church." Folding it, she placed it on top of several other items of clothing she'd placed in Harry's backpack.

"We're going to have to be fast, Harry. We need to hurry and get out of this apartment before your father—"

"I know, M-mom." He touched her cheek, giving her a sad smile. "I know."

Fighting back tears, Sabrina went to her closet to get the largest purse she could find. The one she chose used to be her mother's. She'd given it to Sabrina before she and her dad moved to California, sure that Sabrina would put it to good use. The memory made her smile. She used to tease her mom for carrying around an old lady purse because the thing was ridiculously big. Now she was elated to have it. It was plenty big enough for Sabrina to stuff her treasured tote bag inside, along with a few items of clothing and the essentials she'd need while staying at Annalise's.

Back in Harry's room, Sabrina dug the tote from the back of his closet, stuffing it in her purse, just to be on the safe side. She doubted Stuart would find it but on the off chance he went rifling through their closets, she didn't want him getting further enraged, realizing she'd fished the tote out of the garbage back in Pennsylvania. He'd make sure to permanently destroy her mementos for sure.

"I was s-so scared. I d-don't ever w-want D-daddy to h-hurt you again, M-mommy." Harry pulled his mother into a fierce hug, bringing tears to her eyes.

"I love you, honey. Everything's going to be all right. I promise."

As soon as Harry's pageant was over she'd call child protective services to report what Stuart had done. Then she'd get a restraining order and get the damned divorce finalized once and for all.

Just let Stuart try to come after us. Just let him try to lay a hand on my precious little boy again.

After adding the last items to the backpack, Sabrina and Harry returned to the living room. A quick scan of her surroundings told her there was little of any importance that she'd be leaving behind...nothing she couldn't replace if Stuart tore through the apartment before Sabrina and Harry were able to return. Right now all she cared about was getting herself and her son away from Stuart before he went ballistic again.

"Aren't you going to give your husband a kiss before you go?" Stuart asked, his eyes half-lidded with passion.

The unsavory idea curdled in her gut. "Of course, darling." She leaned over the sofa, giving him a kiss on the cheek. He grabbed her, turning it into a sloppy tongue dance. Tempted to wipe the liquored taste of him from her lips with the back of her hand, she smiled lovingly. She'd do whatever it took to avoid another belligerent confrontation.

"You c-can put it on m-me," Harry said, patting his backpack. "I'll c-carry it for us."

Bending, Sabrina cautioned in a whisper, "It's pretty heavy, honey. I've got a lot in there."

Giving his mom a reassuring smile, Harry assured her, "That's okay. I'm a b-big b-boy. I can m-manage."

Smiling at her son's resolve, Sabrina slipped the weighty canvas pack onto his shoulders. "Okay?" she asked. He gave a thumbs-up in response.

As they walked to the front door, Harry turned back to look at his father. Stuart was sprawled on the sofa, the capped pint bottles of rum and brandy resting on his belly. Harry opened and closed his mouth without saying anything.

Sabrina gazed down at her pint-sized child, a tear trickling down his cheek while he managed his heavy backpack without complaint as they walked down the hallway.

Once they opened the building's vestibule door and hit the sidewalk, she breathed an audible sigh.

"Free," she whispered beneath her breath, nearly giddy with a newfound sense of relief. "Oh Harry, we're free."

Chapter 12

~<>~

IN THE MIDST of performing a routine maintenance check at the fire station, testing apparatus and equipment, Gard looked up when he heard the door open and slam shut. "Hey, Nevan. What are you doing here?"

"Taking care of my pals at the fire station," he said. Nevan hefted the large package he carried under one arm, while raising a smaller container with his other hand. That snagged not only Gard's attention, but brought the other four guys on call to the front of the station.

"Figured you guys might enjoy one of my Irish pork pies with baked garlic potato wedges on the side."

"A whole pie?" Gard salivated as he held out his hands to take the package. "Now that's what I call real hospitality! What did you bring for the other guys?"

Jeff, another firefighter elbowed Gard out of the way, taking the container from Nevan. "Yeah, right, like we're going to let Nevan's brother take charge of the pie. I don't think so." The men, including Gard, shared a laugh, well aware of his reputation for glomming down inordinate amounts of Nevan's pork pie in one sitting.

Gard took the smaller bag, holding it high and studying it. "I don't imagine this is Guinness." He grinned, knowing Nevan wouldn't be delivering anything alcoholic when they were on duty.

"It's a couple thermoses of my famous Irish coffee." He looked from one man to another with a waggish grin as he watched their reactions. "Minus the Irish, of course."

Gard and the other firefighters thanked Nevan, who told them it was the least he could do, since they were giving up their holiday to protect the people of Glassfloat Bay.

"It's already cut into big slabs," Nevan said of the pork pie. "Mustard and mayo are in those small cups. The larger one has garlic dip for the potatoes. I remembered that you have plates and silverware here at the station so I didn't bring any."

"You just saved us from chowing down on another one of Jeff's bean surprises." Gard elbowed Steven as they enjoyed a mutual snicker.

"You'll be missing out on my special Christmas edition of bean surprise but I guess I can save it for the next time we're on call together."

"Yay," one of the other men said without enthusiasm.

"What makes the dish Christmas?" Nevan asked.

"It's all red and green. Cherry tomatoes and kidney beans for the red, and bell peppers and broccoli for the green." Jeff shrugged as the rest of them sneered. "Okay, okay...I'd rather have the pork pie too." He laughed and they all helped themselves to the dinner Nevan provided.

"Got a minute?" Nevan asked Gard as they sat off to the side, away from the others. "I've got something to tell you."

"Yeah, sure. Everything okay?"

"With me, yeah, fine." Nevan gave an indifferent wave. "This is about Sabrina's husband."

"Hanklen?" Gard felt himself tense up at the subject. "What happened? Did he make trouble for you at the pub?"

"No," Nevan shook his head, "nothing like that. I had to cut him off today and he wasn't happy about it."

"You must be mistaken," Gard said, his voice dripping with sarcasm. "That's impossible because he swore to Sabrina that he'd stopped drinking." He followed that with cynical laughter, not at all surprised at Neven's revelation. Gard had Hanklen pegged as a liar all along.

"Yeah, right. The guy was trashed. And really talkative." Nevan told Gard the details about Stuart's visit to the pub.

Gard was incredulous. Any doubt he'd had about Hanklen having a few screws loose was gone now. "How could he do this to Sabrina and Harry?"

"He's a drunk," Nevan said, "who only cares about his next drink. Trust me, I've met and talked to enough of them to know what I'm talking about."

"You don't have to convince me," Gard said. Looking off into the distance, trying to digest everything his brother had told him, he absently shook his head back and forth. "It tears me up to hear the way he referred to his son when he spoke to you. Son of a bitch." Gard fought the urge to find Hanklen, grab him up by the collar, and knock the crap out of him.

"That family's in for a stormy holiday. Poor little kid." Nevan tsked. "Hanklen looked like he was ready to spit nails when he left the pub. Why the hell he seemed pissed with his wife and kid I don't know."

Gard's eyes narrowed. "Because she wants him gone...wants out of that marriage and Hanklen's obviously not about to let her go without causing problems."

"I figured you'd want to know what's going on, seeing as how you're sweet on Sabrina and all."

"What do you mean?" Gard's eyebrows pinched. "Who told you that?"

"You did."

"What? I never said anything."

Nevan offered a slow smile. "You didn't have to. It's pretty obvious."

Groaning, Gard scratched the back of his head. "Why do people keep telling me that?"

"Maybe it's the way your cute little ears perk up whenever her name is mentioned," Nevan teased, pulling at the top of his brother's ears while Gard swatted him away. "I've got to head out, Gard. Last minute shopping. See you and the family tomorrow at Bekka House for Christmas dinner. I've got another pork pie stashed away just for you, bro."

Gard gave him a thumbs up. "Thanks for the food and drink...and for telling me about Hanklen. Much appreciated."

As soon as Nevan left, Gard picked up his phone and called Annalise to fill her in.

~<>~

"Hey, kiddo." Sabrina ruffled Harry's knit cap as they walked. It was a teddy bear hat Reen had knitted for him. "You still doing okay?" She examined his face, seeing purple-red evidence of Stuart's hard slaps across his cheek. Her stomach lurched at the sight. How could he do that to his own son? And for no reason. Sabrina was angry with herself for not anticipating Stuart's actions. She should have known. *She should have known!* She'd failed to protect her innocent son from her husband's drunken, unwarranted abuse.

"I'm f-fine." Squeezing his mother's hand through his puffy mitten, Harry smiled up at her. "I was s-scared f-for you and m-me. D-daddy got r-really m-mad. What d-did we d-do wrong?"

"Nothing, sweetie. Your father had too much to drink and he lost his temper." After what had happened tonight, she was past the point of trying to make Stuart look like a hero in his son's eyes.

Within a matter of minutes their lives had been turned upside down. One thing she was sure of—they'd survive. Together. She was determined she and her son would come out of this mess intact.

Sabrina pulled the thick knitted scarf up over Harry's nose to shield him from the cold air. At thirty-some degrees, with little wind and no snow, the temperature wasn't too uncomfortable. But since Harry was prone to catching colds, she wanted to make sure he stayed toasty. The worst part was the hilly, rain-soaked streets getting icy.

"I'm g-glad D-daddy's n-not coming to the p-play. He n-needs to just s-stay b-by himself when he's s-sick from d-drinking so he d-doesn't hurt anybody."

"You're right, Harry." She wasn't going to make any more excuses for her husband. How foolish she was for agreeing to let him stay this week, thinking it would benefit Harry. What was she thinking?

Harry was quiet for a long moment. "Mom?"

"Hmm?"

"I was real m-mad at D-daddy when he hurt you. I had b-bad thoughts, like I wanted t-to hit him real hard." Harry punched the air.

"Oh, you poor thing..." Sabrina didn't even know how to respond to his confession. She hated that Stuart had put him in that position.

"I d-don't think D-dad meant to b-be so m-mean. He was r-real n-nice the other d-days." Shaking his head from side to side, he added, "I think he was j-just feeling real b-bad from all the d-drinking."

Choosing not to respond to Harry's assumption, Sabrina told him instead, "We're going to have a wonderful Christmas, Harry. You'll see. We'll have a pajama party sleepover at Aunt Annalise's house tonight. Doesn't that sound like fun?"

Boasting a big smile, Harry clapped his mittened hands together. Sabrina watched his expressive face shift from delight to concern. "J-just you and me...not D-daddy, right? He's g-going to s-stay at

home so he c-can get b-better, right? So he d-doesn't hurt you again."
He wrapped his hands around Sabrina's arm, pressing his face close.

"Right. Harry, honey, I don't want you to worry. I'm not going
to let your father hurt you—or me—again, okay?"

"Okay. G-good." Harry nodded silently. "I-I'm going to s-send
a p-prayer to heaven," he gestured toward the sky, "to m-make
D-daddy feel better so he c-can be happy. D-do you think that will
h-help?"

Surprised by the sudden rush of tears rising to the surface,
Sabrina blinked them back. Cupping her son's face, she gave an
affirmative nod.

"I'm sure it will." She bent down to hug him. "I'm going to be so
proud of you up there at the front of the church tonight."

"I-I'm going to do a g-good job. I've b-been p-p-practicing a lot."

"You'll be the best Joseph ever."

"D-don't feel bad, M-mommy." Harry patted his mother's arm.
"I don't care about not g-getting presents from S-santa. Honest. All I
c-care about is that I have you."

Choked with emotion, Sabrina wasn't able to respond for a
moment, other than to curl her arm around his shoulder and give
him a squeeze. If she tried to speak, she'd start bawling and would
have a devil of a time pulling herself together.

Sabrina felt infused with a new sense of hope and optimism. She
breathed in the cool evening air, which now seemed permeated with
an abundance of Christmas spirit. The sky grew dark as they headed
to the church and mother and son had fun pointing out the festive
displays of plastic snowmen, angels and Santas, as well as colorful
lights draped over houses and storefronts.

When they came upon a group of carolers a block and a half
from the church, Sabrina felt especially merry. "It's like they're giving
a special Christmas concert just for us, Harry. Isn't it wonderful?"

"Wonderful," Harry readily agreed.

The carolers' rendition of Silent Night ended and the next carol immediately grabbed Harry's attention.

"Hark! the herald angels sing, glory to the newborn King! Peace on earth, and mercy mild, God and sinners reconciled. Joyful, all ye nations rise..."

Tugging on the sleeve of Sabrina's coat, Harry excitedly asked, "Mommy! Did you hear that? They're singing my Harold song!" He punctuated his question by jumping up and down.

Sabrina noted the absence of stuttering or stammering in Harry's speech. It was one of the few times she'd heard him speak without faltering. The sound of her son's happy, unimpeded voice made her heart glad.

They stood still for a moment, listening to the carolers. Harry quietly sang along, the way he heard the words to the carol, "Hark, the *Harold* angel sings..."

"Is Hark the angel for every Harold, or just me?"

"Oh, well..." She looked into her son's innocent, hopeful eyes and saw an enchanted spark of Christmas magic flickering there—the same magic that should be in every child's eyes this time of year.

Her child would be five tomorrow. There'd be no visit from Santa. No Christmas tree. No presents, and he wouldn't be seeing his father for a long time. What harm could it do to embellish a little about his angel if it meant an extra dose of joy? Why not give her deserving little boy some Christmas magic he'd always remember?

Sabrina took her son's hand and they continued toward the church as the carolers finished the last verse of the song.

"Just you, Harold." She smoothed her hand across his cheek as they walked. "Hark is your very own Christmas angel," she said, loving the expression of pure delight greeting her. "Your guardian angel."

"That's what I thought." Harry gave a matter-of-fact nod. "I felt it, inside." He clapped his hand over his heart, tapping it.

"That Christmas carol has always been my favorite," Sabrina told him, making the story up as she went along. "It's why I decided to name you Harold. Hark whispered the name into my ear the moment you were born. And then she sang that carol."

"Really?" Harry's eyes widened.

If there was indeed a God up in heaven, Sabrina prayed he'd excuse her grandiose fib.

"Absolutely." She blinked back happy tears. It gave her immense pleasure seeing her son's face light up with unbridled joy. This couldn't be a bad thing...it couldn't. If Harold's angel was real, Sabrina felt sure she'd understand about the tall tale spun straight from a mother's heart.

"Wow." Harry looked skyward.

Patting her son's head, Sabrina said, "We need to hurry, sweetie, or we'll be late for your play. We wouldn't want that to happen, would we?"

"No!" Taking his mother's outstretched hand, Harry walked at her side, picking up the pace. "Mommy?"

"What, sweetie pie?"

"I think Hark is really pretty—almost as pretty as you." The little charmer beamed a sunny grin at his mother.

Sabrina bent to plant a kiss on Harry's nose. "Promise you won't ever lose that wonderful way you have with women when you grow up."

"I won't," he said with an air of confidence, though Sabrina doubted he had an inkling about what she meant.

The lack of stuttering in his speech was wonderful. Apparently a big dose of happiness was the best medicine for Harry's speech impediment.

"One day, many years from now, we'll spend Christmas with Hark when we're all together up in heaven. We'll sit at a sparkly golden table on a fluffy white cloud drinking eggnog from shining crystal goblets. And we'll munch on hand-sized Christmas butter cookies," she spread her fingers wide, "with rainbow-colored sugar sprinkles as we celebrate your Christmas birthday with Hark."

"Do you think we can have a real Christmas tree too? Do they allow those in heaven?"

"Are you kidding?" Sabrina waved her hand through the air. "You bet they do. We'll have the biggest tree you could imagine, covered with sparkling ornaments, twinkling stars, and garlands of spun gold and silver. Right smack in the middle of all that gold and silver will be our very own handmade ornaments, the ones you and I made together, along with the ones Grandma and Grandpa, and Aunt Annalise and Uncle Hud helped us make. It'll be just magical."

"That really *does* sound like heaven! If I close my eyes I can see it." Harry giggled. "That would be the best birthday Christmas ever." He stopped walking and looked up at Sabrina. "How about you, Mommy?"

"How about me what?" Captivated by Harry's stutter-free voice, she doubted he was aware of the change himself, and didn't want to bring it to his attention to make him self-conscious. It filled her with renewed hope that one day he'd be free of any speech impediment or other disabilities caused by the abuse he'd suffered at the hand of his father.

"Do you have an angel, too?" he asked.

"I already told you, sweetheart. You're my little angel, and you always will be."

"Come on, Mommy." She could tell Harry was trying not to smile. "For real."

"Yes, I have an angel too." Sabrina laughed softly. Her spirits hadn't been this light in ages. "Everyone has a guardian angel, Harry, but not everyone has a special Christmas angel too."

"Look, we're almost at the church," Harry said, pointing.

"We are. Listen, honey...isn't that beautiful?" Sabrina cupped her hand to her ear. "The church bells are ringing. That's a special secret sign to you from Hark. Want to know a secret?"

"Uh-huh."

"Sometimes, because we both love you so much, Hark and I talk about you." Sabrina put her finger to her lips. "But that's just our little secret, okay?"

"Okay." Harry mimed his mother's gesture.

"Come on, Harry, let's hurry so we're not late. We still need to get you into your costume before the play starts." They ran together.

"Okay. Mommy, do you *see* Hark when you talk to her or do you just hear her voice?"

"That's a good question." Having reached the curb, just across the street from the church, Sabrina paused, hoping they'd made it with a little time to spare. "Sometimes, if I concentrate really hard and think happy, positive thoughts, I can see her." Sabrina looked skyward, lifting the arm Stuart hadn't injured. "I just look up toward heaven like this and—"

In the blink of an eye, a skidding car jumped the curb, just missing Harry and slamming into Sabrina, propelling her with such velocity she was hurled against the windshield of a parked car.

"M-m-mommy!"

Chapter 13

~<>~

"WE'VE GOT A 911 dispatch call," the firefighter manning the station's computer center said. "Accident involving a motor vehicle and at least one pedestrian at the corner of Shellvine and Windsand, across from Good Samaritan Community Church. Possible fatality."

"Jeff and Steven, you two suit up and come with me," Gard, the most senior firefighter and EMR on duty instructed. Turning off the instructional video they'd been watching, and grabbing his gear, he closed his eyes in a long blink and let out a deep breath. Like the rest of the men, Gard hated thinking of anyone being hurt or killed at any time, but it was especially difficult for family and loved ones when it happened during a holiday.

"We'll take the fire and rescue truck and leave the engine here," Gard continued. "Bob, you and Chuck stay here in case there's another call. Contact the ambulance service and have them meet us there. Shouldn't take us long. It's only about a mile from here."

Chaos met them when they arrived at the scene. The church steps overflowed with onlookers. People, including children in costume for the nativity play, spilled into the street. A large group hovered at the center of the action. As he got out of the vehicle Gard spotted his mother and sisters, as well as Annalise...who had Harry in her arms, comforting him as he struggled to get down.

Gard felt his stomach pitch.

While his crew checked for downed electrical wires, gasoline spills, or unstable vehicles, Gard rushed to the center of the crowd where he was met by the unreal spectacle of Sabrina Hanklen's lifeless body draped, face-up, across the dented hood and cracked

176

windshield of a parked car. In the stillness of that instant he thought she almost looked like a painting...a tragic yet tranquil canvas of a young woman on the cusp of life, in the process of crossing over to eternal sleep.

Gard's dramatic interpretation of the scene was a sure sign his emotions had come into play. He couldn't allow that to happen. Blinking quickly, once, twice, had him surveying the accident scene with a more rational perspective.

A strangled cry from Harry had Gard shifting his attention in that direction. The boy was visibly and audibly close to hysteria.

Gard's gaze met Annalise's and Astrid's as they held on to the boy's arms and legs, trying to ease him away from the scene. Their faces were sheet-white and their eyes saucer-wide, while Harry's face was beet-red as he screamed and cried, reaching out for his mother. It was impossible not to be moved.

Only a matter of seconds had passed since Gard exited his vehicle, though it seemed like time stood still as the rat-a-tat of his racing heart pounded through his pulse points, momentarily obliterating all coherent thought.

Focus. Focus and get a grip. Do what you were trained to do...

"G-g-gard!" Harry cried, reaching an arm out to him, fingers stretched and curling in entreaty.

"You hang tight, Harry," Gard called, doing his best to offer the boy a reassuring smile, "while I check on your mom." Reaching the parked car, he got a close-up look. The contents of her purse spilled across the car's hood and sprawled on the pavement. There was a significant amount of blood, most of which seemed to come from Sabrina's head, indicating head trauma from the impact with the windshield. Simple observation of twisted body parts told him one of her wrists, an elbow, and one of her ankles appeared to be broken.

Due to the damage of the vehicle she'd landed on, he suspected additional injuries would be found.

"Stay with your Aunt Annalise," he told Harry, sucking in a deep breath as he scanned Sabrina's body for additional visible injuries. "I'll be there soon."

Steven joined Gard. Together they checked Sabrina's vital signs. She wasn't breathing and they were unable to detect a heartbeat. Sending up a silent prayer, Gard began cardiopulmonary resuscitation while Steven performed a head to toe exam, checking her skin, head, eyes, ears, nose, throat, abdomen, extremities and spine.

While they worked, Jeff arrived at their side, advising Gard that the driver of the car that hit Sabrina was dazed and bruised but otherwise in good condition. There was no indication he'd been drinking. He was apologetic and concerned, explaining his car had careened out of control when it hit a patch of black ice. After plowing into Sabrina, his car smashed into the right front fender of the vehicle she'd landed on.

Curious bystanders closed in, asking questions and talking among themselves.

"Everybody please keep back so we can do our jobs," Gard said. "The ambulance will be here soon and we need the area clear." A quick glimpse revealed the wide-eyed faces of frightened children, some of them crying. They shouldn't be witnessing something like this. "Please, take the kids back inside."

Between mouth to mouth ventilation, Gard said, "Come on, breathe, Sabrina, breathe." Nothing. No change. He was losing her...just the way he'd lost Tim to that crevasse...that damned icy chasm that became Tim's eternal tomb.

Despite the cold, rivulets of sweat trickled from Gard's forehead to his jaw, dripping onto his shirt collar. Seconds later, listening to the heart-twisting sound of Harry crying out for his mother, Gard was imbued with a new sense of drive, determination not to fail Harry or his mom. One way or another he'd wrench Sabrina

Hanklen back from the greedy claws of death, returning her to life. To her son. To him.

"Breathe! Get that heart pumping, Sabrina," he commanded. "You've got a little boy who needs his mom." Still no change. God, he'd give his right arm to see any sign of life in her. "Come back, Sabrina. Fight. You've *got* to fight. Harry needs you."

Gard knew the longer she went without oxygen or a heartbeat, the less her chances of survival, and if she did live, neurologically she'd never be the same. He followed procedure, did everything by the book. Getting emotionally involved was not only unprofessional, it was distracting. Watching the frail woman as he performed chest compressions and artificial ventilation, he felt the technique was missing something, missing that X-factor. Yes, he was maintaining circulatory flow and oxygenation until the ambulance arrived but it wasn't enough. She needed more.

Gazing down at her motionless porcelain-like features he made the decision to allow his visceral emotions to lead. To hell with by the book rules.

Drawing from the depths of his soul, he leaned over Sabrina and whispered directly into her ear, "Harry needs you, Sabrina." He caught himself before adding, *I need you.* "You've got to breathe. Dammit, Sabrina, if anything happens to you, you'll be leaving your son alone with Stuart. You don't want Stuart to raise Harry without you, do you? Breathe! For Harry's sake, breathe!"

And she did.

Gard found himself fighting back a sudden threat of tears, which surprised the hell out of him. He wasn't a man who cried. The last time he had was three years ago when he'd lost Tim. The sting behind his eyes this time was for an entirely different reason. Sabrina Hanklen was alive. She was alive!

She showed some slight motion as they checked her pulse, blood pressure and temperature. Sabrina was finally stable but still unconscious. Gard's medical training told him her chances for survival were slim.

By this time the ambulance and the police had arrived. The ambulance attendants took over for Gard and his crew, transferring Sabrina onto a stretcher and into the vehicle. At the same time, the police interviewed the driver of the car and managed crowd control.

"P-p-please can I g-g-o with M-mommy?" Harry begged Gard.

For safety and liability reasons, neither the ambulance attendants nor Gard and his crew could transport Harry to the hospital in their vehicles. "I'm sorry, Harry, they're not allowed to take you." Gard smoothed his fingers through the boy's hair.

"I'll take him," Annalise said, and Astrid said she'd accompany them. Gard nodded.

"Is M-mommy g-going to be o-okay?" Harry had his arms wrapped tight around Annalise's neck as she held him, clutching her like a life preserver.

Gard wanted more than anything to tell the kid, *yes*, to assure him he had nothing to worry about, that Sabrina would be absolutely fine, good as new. But he wouldn't lie to the boy. He had no idea if she'd make it...and if she did, what the extent of her injuries might be.

"The ambulance is taking your mom to the hospital," he told Harry. "The doctors and nurses will do their very best to make her better." He slid his thumb across Harry's cheek, wiping away a fat tear. "I need you to be brave, Harry." He hoped his smile and calm tone would assuage some of Harry's fears. "Can you do that for me?"

His chin trembling, Harry gazed up into Gard's eyes. After a long moment he nodded.

"You go with your Aunt Annalise and my mom now," Gard said, "and I'll see you later, okay?"

"O-okay...okay." His head bobbed slowly. "C-can you c-call my d-dad to t-tell him about M-mommy?"

Gard's insides twisted into a knot at Harry's innocent request. He didn't want that son of a bitch anywhere near Sabrina, or Harry.

"He's at h-home. He's s-sick," Harry explained, his eyebrows furrowing. "He'll b-be worried about M-mommy," he added softly.

Yeah, *sick*, Gard thought with contempt, careful to keep his true feelings about Hanklen from reaching his expression.

Astrid and Annalise turned their attention to Gard, their gazes questioning and full of concern. Regardless of how he felt, Gard knew he had to follow the law and inform Stuart about the accident. SOB or not, he was still Sabrina's husband and Harry's legal guardian. He had a right to know. Besides, Harry wanted to be with his father.

"Of course I will," Gard answered, unable to bring the smile back to his face as the muscle in his jaw twitched. "Don't worry, Harry, I'll make sure your dad knows what happened and where your mom is. I'll tell him you're at the hospital waiting for him."

"Maybe I should I take Harry home with me instead," Annalise suggested. "I can look after him until we know more. I think that might be better than—"

"P-please," Harry tugged on his aunt's sleeve, "I w-want t-to go to the h-h-hospital to b-be with M-mommy."

Annalise's heartfelt expression as she turned her attention to Harry told Gard she understood the child's need to be close to his mother. "Yes...yes, of course, honey." She smoothed hair from his tear-dampened cheeks. It was then that Gard first noticed the angry red-purple mark on the boy's face. "We'll get you right over to the hospital."

"They'll allow Harry in the emergency waiting room as long as he's supervised," Gard said, lightly running his fingers across the swelling redness on Harry's face that crept close to his eye. "But since he's under twelve he won't be allowed to see Sabrina."

Annalise and Astrid nodded. "What about Stuart?" Astrid asked, also noticing the mark on Harry's face. She elbowed Annalise who studied Harry's cheek and nodded. It didn't take a mind reader to figure out they were both deeply concerned for Sabrina's son, and feeling apprehensive about turning him over to his father.

Gard sucked in a deep breath. "I'll personally see to it that the boy's father gets to the hospital."

"But Gard..." Annalise's troubled expression mirrored Astrid's.

"I know," Gard replied. "But it's what we have to do." At this point they had no way of knowing whether Harry's injury had something to do with the car accident, or with his father.

Gard wished he knew exactly what had transpired between Sabrina and Stuart after he went up to her apartment from Nevan's pub. He couldn't ask the boy about what happened. The kid was already stressed enough as it was.

"We'll make sure the doctor takes a look," Annalise said, motioning to Harry's face.

"I h-have to g-get M-mommy's special b-bag." Harry pointed to the items spread across the pavement.

"Don't worry, honey," Annalise said, "we'll make sure everything is gathered up and brought to the hospital. Then we'll give it to your dad for safekeeping."

"No!" Harry's eyes grew wider still. "M-mommy t-trusts m-me to p-protect her special bag."

"You mean her purse?" Astrid asked, taking a tissue from her purse and drying Harry's tears.

The little boy shook his head back and forth. "Her b-black and white t-tote bag."

Before Annalise could stop him, Harry scrambled out of her arms, running toward the car where Sabrina had been moments before. He scooped up two items, one a wet piece of yellow construction paper, the other, a black and white zebra-striped canvas tote bag nearly half his size. He clutched the bag to his chest as if it held rare, priceless treasure.

"C-could you give this t-to Lilly?" Harry asked, handing the damp folded paper to Astrid. "I m-made it for h-her. But..." he glanced from the card to Astrid's eyes, his chin trembling, "...but it g-got all w-wet and d-doesn't look too good anymore."

Looking down at the handmade Christmas card as she accepted it from Harry, Astrid offered a loving smile. Gard noticed his mother's eyes glistening with tears that she quickly blinked back.

"Your card is beautiful, Harry," she said. "I can see you put a lot of time and thought into making it."

Harry nodded. "And lots of g-glitter. Lilly l-likes g-glitter."

"Well then she'll really love it. I'll make sure she gets it," Astrid assured. She walked to the parked car and spoke to a police officer. After he nodded, Astrid gathered up the spilled contents of Sabrina's purse from the car's hood and the street, bringing the purse back with her. "I've got the rest of your mom's things here, Harry." She patted the purse. "I'll hang on to this until I see your father at the hospital. Is that okay with you?"

"Yes, I think i-it's okay f-for him to have M-mommy's regular purse stuff."

Holding the big zebra tote by the straps, Harry hefted it a few inches off the ground. "Please," he thrust the tote bag at Annalise, "can you keep this in a s-safe p-place until M-mommy's b-better? It's her most important t-treasures." It was clear from the surprised expression on Annalise's face as she lifted it that the bag was unexpectedly heavy. "Don't b-bring it t-to the h-hospital though, o-okay? D-dad can't see it."

"I won't." Annalise clutched the bag close as she squeezed Harry's hand. "Her treasure bag is a special a secret just between you and your mom, right?"

Harry's head bobbed up and down. "R-right. But," he sucked in a weighty breath, letting it out with a whoosh, "I can't hide it anymore now w-without my d-dad knowing."

"I promise to keep it safe," Annalise assured. "What about your backpack, honey? It's awfully heavy for you to carry around. Can I take care of that for you too?"

"Okay, thanks." He unclasped the backpack's tie from around his waist and shrugged the bag from his shoulders. When Gard picked it up, he gave Annalise an incredulous look. The backpack weighed a ton. She'd been holding its weight along with Harry's without saying a word about her discomfort.

"I'll keep all your stuff and your mom's in a safe hiding place," Annalise promised. "And we won't say a word about any of it to your dad, will we, Astrid?"

Astrid made a locking motion over her lips, throwing away the key. "Not a word."

Gard had no clue what all that was about but relief was evident across the boy's features.

"I'm heading back to the station with Jeff and Steven," he told them, pulling his phone from his pocket to check the time. "My shift's over in fifteen minutes. I'll pick up Stuart then. Harry, is your dad at his hotel or at your apartment?"

"At the ap-p-partment."

"Pick him up?" Astrid's eyebrows knitted as she folded her arms across her chest. "Why? Just call him and give him the particulars. Let him get over there himself."

"I'm with Astrid." Annalise gave a resolute nod.

"I have a hunch, that since Stuart is *sick*," Gard gave them a meaningful look, "he may not be in any condition to drive to the hospital, much less see his son, Sabrina, or anyone else. I'll make sure he's feeling less *sick* before we go."

"Gotcha," Annalise said, understanding dawning in both her and Astrid's expressions.

Astrid grabbed Gard into a spontaneous hug, smacking his cheek with a kiss.

He gave an embarrassed chuckle. "What was that for?" He wiped at the smudge of lipstick past experience told him was there.

"Because I love you," Astrid said. "You're a good man, Gard."

Harry gave a nod of agreement. "That's w-what M-mommy said too."

~<>~

Twenty minutes later, Gard was back in his street clothes, knocking on the door of Sabrina's apartment. When there was no answer, he knocked harder. Finally, he rang the bell. He could tell the guy was inside because he heard groaning and muttering.

"It's Gard Malone. Open the door, Hanklen," Gard said loud enough for Stuart to hear but monitoring his voice to keep from disturbing the other tenants on the floor, especially since it was Christmas Eve. "It's important."

"Get outta here and lee-mee alone," Hanklen called back in a voice that didn't sound at all sober.

With his mouth close to the door, Gard said, "Stuart, let me in. It's Sabrina. Something's happened."

"What? You see her makin' a mistake while paintin' a store window or somethin'?" He followed that with laughter.

"Come on, man...your wife's been in an accident. She's in the hospital."

"You're a stinkin' liar, Malone." Gard heard a jingling sound. "She wasn't in an accident. I got my car keys right here." More laughter. "Wouldn't let her take my car."

Gritting his teeth, Gard growled out, "Open the goddamned door, Hanklen!"

Gard heard more movement and what sounded like shuffling. A moment later Stuart opened the door a couple of inches, peering out at Gard. The smell of his breath told Gard all he needed to know.

"My wife dropped the kid at his aunt's before she comes back here to me, and our bed. Now get lost."

Gard pushed the door open as Stuart started closing it, catching Stuart off guard. Hanklen stumbled backward, falling over the arm of the sofa and onto his back on the cushions. Too bad. Gard much rather would have seen the jerk falling hard on his ass on the wood floor...and maybe cracking his skull while he was at it.

"Sabrina was hit by a car across the street from the church," Gard told him as Stuart stared up at him with rheumy eyes. "It's serious. You need to get to the hospital. Annalise has Harry there waiting for you. He wants you there with him."

"Annalise...ah yes, my loving holier than thou sister-in-law." Stuart laughed again. "Good. She's his aunt. Let her babysit the little shit."

His patience worn thin, Gard took the few steps to the sofa, bent to grab Hanklen by his shirt collar and dragged him to his feet. "Listen to me you asshole," he shouted a few inches from the guy's face. "Your wife is in bad shape. She may not make it. Your wife, Hanklen. Sabrina. For chrissakes, man, pull yourself together. She needs you. Harry needs you."

"Yeah, well I had enough of Harry. None of this would have happened if Sabrina had listened to me when I told her not to take the kid to church." His lip curled into a sneer. "How come you know all this about Sabrina, huh?" Stuart's eyes narrowed. "Were you with her? I saw the way she looked at you. Were you fucking my wife? Is that how you know what happened."

"Look, you worthless piece of shit," Gard spat. "I know you don't like me and I sure as hell don't like you either. In fact I wish it were you in the hospital instead of your wife." Gard sucked in a deep breath, counting silently to ten. "I'm a firefighter, that's how I know. My team got the 911 call about the accident." He tossed Hanklen back onto the sofa, then looked around the sparse apartment.

"Where's the coffee?" he barked.

"Thirsty? Well, Mr. Firefighter, where do you think it'd be? Maybe in the bedroom, huh? Or maybe the coffee's in the bathroom. Yeah," he started to move off the couch, "let's look in there."

Ignoring him, Gard went into the small kitchen and started opening cabinets. Locating the package of coffee from Griffin's café, he put it on the counter. Once he found the coffee filters and the coffeemaker, he put on a full twelve cups to brew, adding extra grounds to make it stronger.

"You stink, Hanklen. I can smell it all the way over here. What did you do, clean all the alcohol out of Nevan's pub?" Gard took the largest mug he could find and set it on the counter.

"I didn't invite you for coffee, Malone. You want coffee, go over to my sister-in-law's place."

"The coffee's not for me, it's for you."

Stuart's entire expression puckered. "Bullshit. I'm not drinking any coffee." He dug a couple of empty pint bottles from the sofa cushions, bringing them to the kitchen counter and setting them down hard. Gard glanced at the rum and brandy. "Don't have any room after my dinner." He banged the bottles against each other, chuckling. "Just go away, will ya? I wanna take a nap. I'm tired after working hard playing perfect husband and daddy all week."

Twirling on his heel, he headed for the couch but Gard stopped him, grabbing his shirt again.

"You're not taking a nap, Hanklen, you're going to drink coffee until it's coming out of your ears. Then I'm carting your sorry, sober ass over to the hospital so you can be the father your son needs. Do you have any idea how frightened Harry is? That little boy is scared to death he's going to lose his mother. He needs his father, Hanklen. You need to step up for him, you hear me?"

Sneering, Hanklen huffed a humorless laugh. "Little retard is always pissing and moaning about something or other," Stuart complained. "He's nothing but a whiny crybaby who can't string two damn words together without stuh-stuh-stuh-stuttering." He made a drop-jawed, big-eyed dopey look as he mocked his son.

At the grating sound of Stuart's repulsive words, Gard's spine stiffened. It was hard for him to believe what he'd just heard. Furious, he fought to maintain control.

Knowing full well he shouldn't...knowing without a doubt it was wrong, immature, uncivilized, Gard grabbed Hanklen by his shirt, slapping him fast across one cheek and backhanding him across the other. It took everything he had not to drive his fist into the imaginary bull's eye at the center of the man's face.

Hanklen's eyes flew wide and he staggered back, the back of his hand spread over one red cheek. A moment later he tried to retaliate but was too damn drunk to even do that.

Gard slammed Hanklen's butt onto one of the kitchen chairs.

"You lousy, rotten son of a bitch," Gard raged. "If I ever hear you refer to your son in that way again I'll make sure the only way you can have another drink is through a feeding tube because, trust me, I'll rip out your throat, you miserable, selfish, sorry excuse for a man."

Returning to the coffeepot, he poured a black stream into the large mug, thrusting it at Hanklen.

"Drink."

"I don't want any." Pushing the ceramic mug away, Hanklen started to snivel. "I could sue you for laying your hands on me. I should." He sniveled again.

"Go right ahead, be my guest." Gard watched the man sniffling and whimpering. "So who's the whiny crybaby now, huh, Hanklen?" He gave a disgusted tsk. "Harry is one of the finest boys I've known. And you know what? He loves you. God knows why, but the kid loves his drunken sot of an old man." Gard shook his head back and forth in disbelief. "And he's worried about you. Says you need him because you're *sick*." He made air quotes around the word and laughed.

Gard wiped the spittle from his chin, unable to recall the last time he'd been this angry.

"Pick up that mug and start drinking unless you want me to force your jaws open and pour it down your throat. And don't think I won't." He jabbed a threatening finger into Hanklen's shoulder.

Grabbing the mug in both hands, Stuart drank.

Gard's gaze landed on the atomic starburst wall clock across the large open space. "We're leaving here in thirty minutes, Hanklen. Come hell or high water, you're going to be all tidied up, nice and clean and sober, you got that? Drink faster." He refilled the mug.

"I-I can't. I'll make myself sick."

Gard grabbed the plastic trash container from a kitchen corner, slamming it on the floor next to Stuart. "No problem, you can puke your guts out right here, pal. It'll probably get you sober faster. Drink!"

Back to sniveling, Stuart downed the second mug of coffee and Gard gave him another refill.

"That's enough," Stuart said. "I'm better now...I'm sober."

"Like hell you are. I told you, you're going to suck up every last drop of that coffee."

It wasn't long before Stuart drained the third deep mug. Gard watched as he turned two shades of green before grabbing the trash container and retching.

While Stuart was busy heaving, Gard called Annalise to check on Sabrina. The doctors told her Sabrina was in bad shape, having suffered a number of broken bones, including two broken ribs, which Gard wondered if he may have caused during CPR.

Annalise said Harry was being brave, eager for his father and Gard to get to the hospital.

"What sort of state is Stuart in?" Annalise asked.

"He was stinking drunk when I got here." Gard moved to a far corner of the living room, keeping his voice soft. "After a slight...disagreement...I've got him sucking down a pot of double strength coffee. He just finished puking, which is a good sign. Let Harry know I'll have his dad at the hospital in half an hour."

"Are you doing okay?" Annalise asked.

"No," Gard said honestly. "It's taking an inner strength I never knew I possessed not to beat your brother-in-law to a pulp."

"Oh Gard, I'm sorry you got stuck with this."

Letting out a sigh, Gard shoved his fingers through his hair. "Don't mind me. I'm fine. Just bitching. Sabrina and Harry are the ones we need to worry about."

By the time he ended the call, Gard watched Stuart pour the last mug of coffee, drinking it down. He could see in his eyes that Hanklen was sobering up. Once Stuart drained the cup, sounds of him throwing up filled the apartment. After a bout of dry heaves, he went to the kitchen sink, scooping handfuls of water and rinsing his mouth.

"That's better," Gard said. "Your shirt's got vomit on it. Get yourself cleaned up and change your clothes so we can get out of here and over to the hospital."

"Can't. All my clothes are at my hotel room."

"Fine, that's where we're headed." With a tight grip on Stuart's wrist, Gard dragged him out of the apartment and across the street to his hotel room.

Once there, silently, without giving Gard any guff, Stuart did as he was told, getting cleaned up and changed and coming back into the room a few minutes later, looking almost human.

"What happened to my wife?" Stuart asked, his voice and demeanor subdued as he tucked his shirt into his pants. "Is she going to be all right?"

"Sabrina was hit by a car that had skidded out of control on the ice. She was thrown onto a parked car. Several broken bones and internal bleeding. It...doesn't look good."

"Shit."

"You can learn more when you talk to the doctors."

"The kid okay?"

Gard nodded. "Harry's fine, just scared and rattled as far as I know...except for a red, badly swollen cheek." He gave Stuart a pointed look.

Stuart shrugged. "He's a clumsy kid, probably walked into a doorknob or something." Shoving his hands in his pockets and looking down at his feet, he said, "Look, Malone, I'm sorry about—"

"Save it, Hanklen. I didn't come here to help you, I came here to help your wife and son. They need you. I don't. If you've got an apology or something nice, something decent to say for a change, say it to your kid when you see him—and to your wife, if she makes it."

Chapter 14

~<>~

AFTER FILLING OUT the necessary paperwork at the desk, Stuart and Gard headed for the emergency waiting room.

"D-d-daddy!" Harry ran to his father as soon as he spotted Stuart, wrapping his arms around Stuart's legs and squeezing.

Gard gave Hanklen a hard look when it seemed apparent that he was about to shrug out of Harry's grasp. "Why don't you let your son know how glad you are to see him?" Gard suggested.

Nervously licking his lips, Stuart looked left then right at all the people waiting with Harry before patting the boy's head and saying "How's it going, Harold?"

Besides Annalise and Astrid, Gard's sisters, Delaney, Reen and Laila, were there. Drake's daughter, Lilly, sat with Harry, playing with a wooden puzzle while Drake talked with Zak and Varik. A handful of the café's regulars were there too.

"I'm w-worried about M-mommy. Are you f-feeling better, D-dad? Y-you're n-not sick anymore, r-right?"

"I'm fine," was Stuart's reply. "Where's the doctor," he asked no one in particular. "Who can I talk to about my wife?"

"That's Doctor Shadrik." Annalise gestured toward the physician walking their way. "He's one of the doctors taking care of Sabrina."

When the doctor reached them he looked up from his clipboard. "Gard," he said, keeping his voice soft. His surprise was obvious as he extended his hand. "It's good to see you again." His gaze skimmed Gard from head to toe. "I'm glad to see you looking well."

"Thanks to you, Doc." Dr. Shadrik was the senior physician in charge of Gard's medical care when he'd been admitted with multiple injuries three years earlier. Gesturing, Gard told him, "This is Stuart Hanklen, Sabrina's husband."

"How's my wife?"

Dr. Shadrik glanced from Stuart to Harry and back to Stuart, who stood staring at the doctor.

"Oh..." Annalise stepped in, seeming to understand the doctor didn't want to speak in front of Harry. Taking Harry and Lilly by the hand, she walked them to Delaney, asking, "Would you mind taking the kids to the cafeteria for a scoop of ice cream or a cookie or something?"

"Absolutely. Text me when it's time to come back."

"Well?" Hanklen said to Dr. Shadrik, crossing his arms over his chest, making no bones about his impatience.

Being in the midst of a group of people was the only thing that prevented Gard from hauling off and smacking Hanklen in the back of his head.

Once the children had left the area, the doctor focused his attention on Stuart.

"Mr. Hanklen, why don't we step into a more private area where we can discuss your wife's condition?"

With the doctor's suggestion, Gard knew they wouldn't be getting good news. He looked at Astrid, who knew the doctor well from Gard's ordeal, and they exchanged knowing glances. From Annalise's edgy stance, he could tell she also wasn't expecting positive news.

Before the doctor turned on his heel, Annalise quickly touched the sleeve of his jacket. "I'm her sister and these are family friends." She motioned to herself, Astrid and Gard. "Is it all right if we come along?"

"Mr. Hanklen?" Dr. Shadrik's eyebrows rose in question and Gard turned to Hanklen, daring him with a steely gaze to suggest that he and the women weren't welcome.

"Fine," Hanklen said, though it was obvious he wasn't happy about it.

The doctor led them to a small room, closing the door once everyone was inside. Gard noticed the sparse room was painted yellow, pale, like butter, unlike the muddier light gray-green of the emergency room's general waiting area. There was a table in the room with a small vase holding artificial flowers. One wall held a painting of a field of flowers. He imagined all of it was somehow meant to soothe people as they were given bad news.

It didn't make a damn bit of difference to Gard if the walls were black, white, blood red or papered with daisies. No can of paint could make what they were no doubt about to hear any less traumatic.

While Dr. Shadrik remained standing, he gestured toward the chairs lined around the table. "I'm afraid the news isn't good," he said once they were seated, with Stuart on one side of the table and Gard, Annalise and Astrid on the other. "We're doing all we can for your wife, Mr. Hanklen, but her condition is deteriorating. Her prognosis is poor. It doesn't look promising. Sabrina has sustained significant injury. In addition to fractures of," he read from a printed paper, "the ribs, arms, hip, pelvis, tibia, fibula and femur, there are scalp lacerations, contusions and supplementary lacerations and abrasions."

Muttering in disbelief, Gard, Annalise and Astrid winced at the unsavory laundry list of injuries. Sitting between his mother and Annalise, Gard put his arms around their shoulders, tugging them close. Frustrated beyond belief, it was all he could do not to yell out in anger at the incredible injustice of it all.

"It sounds bad," Stuart said, keeping his gaze on the table. Glancing up at the doctor, he said, "Once you put a cast on her, give her crutches, pain meds, shoot her up with drugs, she should be better within a week or two, right? Ready for a plane trip back home to Pennsylvania. My mother's a nurse. She'll take good care of Sabrina."

"Pennsylvania?" Annalise gasped. "My sister's not going back there with you."

"She is," Stuart said. "Before she left for the church tonight, Sabrina told me she was calling off the divorce."

Rising halfway out of the chair, Annalise said, "Why you lying—"

Grabbing Annalise's arm, Gard pulled her back down into her chair, giving her a meaningful look and shaking his head from side to side. He knew damn well how angry she was, because he felt the same way. But this wasn't the time or place to start a scuffle with Hanklen.

"Travel wouldn't be possible," Dr. Shadrik told Stuart. "We're still uncertain as to spinal cord injuries. She's also sustained a skull fracture, which means her brain may have been jostled inside the skull due to the force of impact causing bruising, bleeding and swelling of the brain. I'm sorry to say Mrs. Hanklen may not regain consciousness."

"Oh dear God..." Annalise turned into Gard's shoulder, weeping.

"She's so young," Astrid said through her tears, clutching her son's hand tight.

"We'll know more once she's out of surgery," Dr. Shadrik glanced at the clock, "in another hour, maybe two. If she makes it through the night, which seems unlikely, there's a slim chance she may recover...at least to some degree. Acute brain damage is likely."

Gard had a difficult time processing Dr. Shadrik's prognosis. How could something like this happen to such a sweet, vibrant young woman—a woman so undeserving of such a cruel fate? How could a life be altered so drastically in the blink of an eye?

"How long before she can leave the hospital?" Stuart asked. "She needs to be at home to take care of Harold. Are we talking more than a week? A month?"

All eyes were on Stuart.

To avoid conveying a hateful stare, Gard closed his eyes in a long blink. He wasn't sure if Hanklen was in shock at hearing the tragic news, or if his brain was scrambled from all the booze, or if the guy was simply a moron. He decided to give him the benefit of the doubt.

The doctor was silent for a long moment as he studied Hanklen. "I suggest that you stay close by, Mr. Hanklen, because your wife may not live through the night." When Stuart simply sat there, across the table from Gard and the women, looking at the doctor with no discernable change in expression, Dr. Shadrik distinctly clarified, "I'm saying that Mrs. Hanklen may die tonight."

"What about our son?" Stuart asked, giving no indication that the doctor's grim words had registered.

"How old is the boy?" the doctor asked.

"Six or seven." Stuart shrugged.

"Harold will be five tomorrow." Annalise gave Stuart a disgusted look. "Christmas day."

"Give your son all the love and support you can," the doctor replied. "He'll need it. If we're unable to save his mother we can refer you to a grief counselor here at the hospital. Losing his mom when he's so young would be very hard on him."

"I mean what do I do with him if anything happens to Sabrina?"

Dr. Shadrik circled around the table, placing his hand on Stuart's shoulder. "The two of you will have each other, Mr. Hanklen. This town is full of loving, supportive people who'll be there to help you. There are other single parents here too. You can find out about support groups through the hospital."

"You don't understand." Stuart fidgeted in his chair, leaning his elbows on the table. "Harold's not normal. He's slow." Stuart tapped his temple. "Not right in the head. The doctors call it developmentally delayed. His mother takes care of him. I can't."

Gard groaned at Stuart's words. "Selfish sorry son of a bitch," he muttered beneath his breath, soft enough so no one else heard.

Dr. Shadrik's eyebrows shot up in surprise at Stuart's response. Maintaining his professional calm, he said, "Hospital personnel can help you in matters regarding child care for special needs children. If you'll excuse me," he walked to the door, partially opening it, "I need to get back to the operating room to see how things are progressing."

The room was silent while everyone digested what they'd just heard from the doctor...and from Stuart.

"I can take care of Harry." Annalise looked at her folded hands instead of Stuart. "He can stay with me until Sabrina gets better. Or until..."

"I'll help," Astrid told Annalise, "when you're working at the café. I'm at home most of the day, so I can watch him while you're there."

Hanklen remained silent, examining his fingernails.

Gard knew both women were determined not to let Stuart take Harry home with him after what they'd heard. He sure as hell didn't blame them.

"You taking him home with you is a good idea," Stuart said, staring at his hands and twiddling his thumbs. "I can't babysit Harold. I-I've got a job to get back to in Horntik. I can't take any more time off or they'll let me go."

At the sound of Hanklen's lie, Gard's head snapped in Stuart's direction. Annalise shot Gard a look too. She knew from their phone conversation earlier that Stuart had lost his job.

"There's no reason for me to stay here anyway," Stuart said. "There's nothing I can do for her. You heard the doctor. She might already be dead for all we know. And if she pulls through she'll probably be a vegetable." He looked around the room and shuddered. "I can't be here. I hate hospitals. They smell of illness, disease and death." He rose, sliding his chair back. "I need to get out of here."

Gard, Annalise and Astrid exchanged astonished expressions.

"Stuart...wait." Astrid jumped up from her chair, running to him before he could leave the room. Clutching his shirtsleeve, she said, "I know this isn't easy for you. I know you must be in shock. Let us help you through this, Stuart. Don't leave yet, please."

Stuart looked at Astrid's hand on his sleeve and back up at her. Astrid let her hand slip to her side. He resembled a caged animal, desperate to escape his confines. "I already told you, I can't stay here. And who's going to be paying for all this? I don't have good insurance. I can't afford a whopping hospital bill."

"You don't have to worry about that, Stuart, the bill's already been taken care of," Astrid said.

"By who?"

"George Thomas, the man who caused the accident. He insisted that Sabrina be well cared for and he'd foot the bill. Mr. Thomas's family helped to found Glassfloat Bay. He's one of the town's wealthiest residents and he's on the hospital board. He's a good man and he feels just terrible about what happened."

"I'll just bet he does." Hanklen snickered. "He's probably shitting bricks, worried I'll sue his rich ass."

"But I told you already," Astrid said, "he's paying for all of Sabrina's care. There's no need to sue."

Stuart huffed a humorless laugh. "I mean for *my* pain and suffering." His fingers tapped against his chest. "Sabrina's got doctors hovering around her, keeping her comfortable. What about me, huh? No one's doing anything to try to make me more comfortable."

The room went dead silent. Gard had every reason to believe he, his mom and Annalise all had the same mindset regarding poor put upon Stuart Hanklen.

"What about tomorrow?" Annalise asked, breaking the silence and getting to her feet. "It's Christmas and Harry's birthday. I'm sure you'll want to spend some time with your son. You're welcome to come to my place."

She spoke with the same calmness Astrid had earlier. Gard had to give them both a world of credit, and special kudos to Annalise for her kindness. There's no way he'd be able to maintain his cool trying to talk to Hanklen. It was apparent the women were determined not to tick the guy off so he'd storm out, taking Harry with him—maybe back to Pennsylvania and his mother.

"That won't work. I've got things to do tomorrow. For my job. I'll be on the phone and my laptop all day."

"On Christmas day?" Gard asked, one eyebrow arched high as disbelief tinged his voice.

"Yes, on Christmas day," Stuart retorted, snapping his head in Gard's direction and challenging him with narrowed, bloodshot eyes to question him further.

The only one still seated, Gard struggled to keep his mouth shut. Being so pissed off he could spit nails, he suspected nothing he said would be of any help and he didn't want to be responsible for having Hanklen take off while Annalise and Astrid were trying to talk some sense into him.

"We understand, Stuart, Astrid said. "We'll stay with Sabrina and monitor her progress...until you feel up to doing it yourself. That way she won't be alone. If you give me your phone number I'll keep you posted. How does that sound?"

Stuart stood in thought for a moment. "I love my wife, you know. Don't try to make it sound like I don't give a damn." He stabbed the air with his finger. "None of you know all I've been through in my life. So don't try making me out to be the bad guy here."

"Of course you love her," Astrid said. Gard watched his mother reach out her hand, most likely to pat his arm, but then pull back, thinking better of it. He was amazed at how she maintained such a cool, pleasant attitude in the presence of this insufferable jerk.

"We all know how important Sabrina is to you," Astrid continued. "You're just having a difficult time. And you're busy with your job. That's why we want to help you...and Harry."

"It would be different if Sabrina just broke an arm or leg." Stuart ran his fingers through his hair. "But what am I supposed to do when she's all broken up in there on her deathbed? Nothing. Why stick around just sitting on my ass passing time until the last drop of life oozes out of her?"

It was beyond difficult for Gard to sit there listening to Hanklen make excuses for himself—his whiny, spineless self. He couldn't fathom a man leaving his wife, the woman he loved, the mother of his child, to die alone in a strange hospital room surrounded by machines and medical personnel. Stuart had asked what he could do. How about holding Sabrina, whispering to her, assuring her that Harry would be fine? He could just be there, dammit, not even saying a word...just letting her know he cared.

"Here." Annalise dug in her purse, drawing out a pen and a slip of paper and writing. "This is my phone number at the café and at home." She wrote more. "And here's my home address so you can come and see Harry."

"Here's mine too." Astrid jotted her number at the bottom of the paper. "Call either of us anytime for an update on Sabrina or to see how Harry is doing, okay?"

"All right. Thanks." Stuart took the paper.

"Why don't you give us your number too?" Annalise suggested, taking her phone from her purse. "I can add you to my contacts right now."

"Not necessary. I've got your numbers. I'll call you. Besides, the hospital has my number. They'll call if anything changes."

"That's fine," Astrid said. Gard noticed she kept her voice soothing, as if speaking to a child of ten. She placed her hand on Stuart's back, patting it before leading him out of the room. "You need to relax and take care of yourself. You've had a difficult day."

"Right...right," Stuart agreed with a repetitive nod. "My car...I don't have my car. I came here with him." Stuart's hand flitted in Gard's direction, as though Gard was nothing but a mere annoyance in the room.

All eyes were on Gard as he contemplated what to do. He was afraid if he was alone with Stuart for the drive back to his hotel he'd end up beating the shit out of him.

"I'll drive you back to your hotel," Astrid offered, knowing her son well enough to pick up on what Gard was thinking. She turned her attention to Gard and Annalise. "I'll meet you two back here at the hospital after I drop Stuart off."

Closing his eyes, Gard nodded. "Thanks." He glanced up at his mother who gave him a reassuring smile.

Stuart's final words as they exited the room were, "Jesus, I need a drink."

~<>~

After Stuart and Astrid left, Annalise looped arms with Gard as they walked back to the emergency room's general waiting area.

"You did a fine job in there, Gard," Annalise told him

Gard gave her an odd look. "Are you kidding? I didn't do a damn thing."

"Exactly." Annalise leaned her head against his shoulder. "I know how much you wanted to rip Stuart's throat out when you heard everything he said. But you kept composed. I'm proud of you."

"Thanks. It was murder. I'm sure it wasn't any picnic for you or my mom either. I'm so, so sorry about your sister, Annalise. I'm still having trouble believing this is all real."

"I know. Me too." She patted his arm. "I'll admit I had a lot of prayer going on while we were in there. Some for Sabrina, some for Harry, and a powerful chunk devoted to me asking God to let me keep it together before I gave in to the urge to use Stuart's face like a punching bag."

"I'm relieved that he agreed to let you and my mom take care of Harry."

"It would have been nice if he'd given us a tougher time," Annalise said. "But his son obviously isn't high on his list of concerns."

"Neither is his wife." Gard still couldn't believe Stuart's indifference. "I'm trying like hell to give him the benefit of the doubt, Annalise. Hoping he was just shocked and disoriented because of the news."

Annalise's gaze slid sideways as she looked up at Gard. "My brother-in-law's disorientation had more to do with drinking than it did hearing the news about his wife. And that crap he tried to give us about Sabrina agreeing to stop the divorce? Bullshit. Plain and simple. I spoke to her this morning and she told me she made it clear to him after breakfast that she was going through with the divorce."

"That's probably why he ended up in my brother's pub getting stinking drunk," Gard surmised.

They reached the waiting area to find it had thinned out quite a bit while they'd been in the private consultation room. Harry and Lilly were asleep, their heads resting on Laila's and Reen's laps, respectively.

"Any news?" Gard asked Delaney who rose to talk to them.

"She's out of surgery." Delaney took in a deep breath. "It's still touch and go," she whispered so she wouldn't wake Harry. "We saw Harry's father leaving with Mom. What's going on?"

Gard looked down at Harry, his little brow furrowed as he slept. "I'll fill you in later. Annalise and Mom are going to watch Harry for a while. He'll be staying at Annalise's place."

"That's good." Delaney yawned. "Sorry, it's been a long day."

Gard looked at the wall clock. "Nearly ten-thirty already. You should all head home," he told his three sisters. "You too, Annalise. You look beat. Let me take care of Harry until you've had a chance to rest. I'll stay here at the hospital and I promise to call immediately if there's any change."

"I can't leave my sister, Gard. I can't." She shook her head. "But I'd truly appreciate it if you stayed with me. Hud's still working out of town and I'm afraid to call my parents in California with the news. They both have weak hearts. I don't know if I can do this alone."

"I'll be right here with you," Gard promised. "Whatever happens."

Annalise mouthed her thanks through silent tears.

Laila finger-combed Harry's hair as Gard slipped his hands beneath the boy to pick him up. "Poor thing has been an angel," she said.

"He really fought going to sleep," Reen said. "He wanted to be awake so he could hear news about his mom. God I hope she'll be okay."

Gard wanted nothing more than to believe Sabrina would survive, but he doubted all the positive thinking in the world would make much difference.

"Lilly insisted on staying here with her boyfriend, Harry," Reen whispered with a chuckle. "Sweet, sweet kids." Her yawn matched Laila's.

"Nevan arrived just as Mom and Stuart were leaving the hospital," Laila said. "We filled him in on the basics. Drake, Zak and Varik went down to the cafeteria with him to get some coffee and give him the rest of the details." She grabbed her phone from her purse. "I'll let them know we're ready to go. Oh Gard, poor Nevan...he's blaming himself for not cutting Stuart off earlier."

"I figured he would," Gard said, shaking his head. "Stuart's drunken state was nobody's fault but his own. Thanks for letting me know. I'll talk to Nevan about it later."

Before Laila could call, Dr. Shadrik returned. Everyone in the area was silent, waiting for his all-important words.

He looked at the group, then at Gard. "Is Mr. Hanklen still here?"

"No, he left," Gard said simply, biting his tongue before adding, *because he doesn't like being around sick people and hospitals...or his son or his wife.*

Since she was Sabrina's next of kin, Dr. Shadrik spoke to Annalise. "She's in the recovery room. In critical condition. The injuries are extensive. She's holding on by a thread. It's clear she's fighting to stay alive but...we don't expect her to live through the night. I'm truly sorry the news couldn't be more positive."

The women cried softly and Gard swallowed back the huge lump in his throat.

"Where is she?" Annalise asked. "I want to see my sister. Harry needs to see her too...before he loses her."

Gard cradled the sleeping child close to his chest, his heart breaking for the little boy who might soon be motherless. Motherless and all but fatherless.

"I'd like for Gard to accompany us," Annalise added, clutching Gard's shirtsleeve.

"I understand. We do make visiting exceptions for children in these cases. Mrs. Hanklen is in SICU."

"What's that?" Annalise asked.

"The Surgical Intensive Care Unit," the doctor clarified. "She's comatose. In the unlikely event that she regains consciousness, she's intubated to assist her in breathing and won't be able to speak. Harry needs to be prepared so he's not overly traumatized by his mother's appearance and all the tubes, IVs, etcetera. Seeing a parent like that can be frightening for a child."

"Can Annalise and I stay in Sabrina's room overnight?" Gard asked and Annalise nodded. "We don't want Sabrina to be alone. Nobody should be alone when..." He couldn't bring himself to say *when they die* because as long as she was alive, there was still hope.

"Of course. There's a large reclining chair in the room."

"How about my nephew?" Annalise gazed down at the boy asleep in Gard's arms.

"Hospital policy states overnight visitors must be at least eighteen." Dr. Shadrik, who looked exhausted, glanced down at the chart in his hands, then glanced at Harry. "But this is one of those times when I believe rules can be broken." He held Annalise and Gard's gaze for a moment.

"Thank you," Gard said, relieved they wouldn't have to put up a fight. "I appreciate it."

"I'll have one of the nurses come by to take you to Sabrina's room." Dr. Shadrik clapped them gently on their shoulders. "It might take a while. They're still connecting her to monitors and such."

"Thank you, Doctor." Annalise dabbed her eyes with a tissue.

Gazing down at Harry, Gard closed his eyes, breathing a sigh. "I need to wake Harry up so I can prepare him. Delaney, do me a favor, okay?"

"Sure, whatever you need."

"Text Mom to let her know what's happening with Sabrina." He watched Delaney's eyes close in a long, sorrowful blink. "Tell her Annalise and I are staying here until..." His chest expanded with a sigh. "Tell her we'll head to Bekka House with Harry afterwards. Mom should go straight home instead of coming back to the hospital."

"I'll tell her. Are you sure you two are going to be all right here? I'd be glad to stay with you." Reen and Laila joined their sister, chorusing, "Same here."

"We'll be all right. Thanks," Annalise said, kissing the top of Harry's head. "We'll call you."

Nevan, Drake, Varik and Zak had returned from the coffee shop, gathering everyone to go home. "Gard?" Delaney said, and he lifted an eyebrow in response. "Call...no matter how late it is...okay?"

"I will." Gard's head bobbed.

Once they'd all said their goodbyes and left the hospital, Gard sat down next to Annalise, holding Harry in his arms. The kid was so exhausted he never opened an eye during all the talking. Gard was glad. He didn't want Harry learning about his mom by overhearing people talk. He wanted the boy to hear it directly from him and his aunt.

"Harry. Harry, wake up." Gard nudged and wiggled the boy's cheek with his knuckle. "We need to have a talk...about your mom." Harry's eyes flew open and he gazed at Gard, blinking a few times to help him come fully awake. Before speaking, Harry looked around. Seeing Annalise, he clasped her hand, giving it a squeeze.

"Where is everyone else?"

"They left a few minutes ago. But you and Aunt Annalise and I are going to stay here so we can be close to your mom, okay?"

"Okay." A fat tear escaped the corner of his eye. "I think I know what you want to talk about." He struggled to sit up in Gard's lap and placed an arm around Gard's neck while still holding Annalise's hand with his other hand. "I had a dream. Mommy was holding Hark's hand. They were on a cloud going to heaven together. It made me very sad but happy at the same time."

Gard was acutely aware of Harry's lack of stuttering. "It sounds like it was a beautiful dream, Harry. Like your mom wasn't in any pain."

"And like your angel was taking good care of her," Annalise said.

"Yes." Harry gave a slow nod. "It was like that." He looked in their eyes. "Is Mommy there now? In heaven?"

"No, not yet," Annalise told him. "She just had a long operation where the doctors worked very hard trying to save her. But they don't know yet if it worked."

Gard watched as Harry's eyes pooled with unshed tears. "We'll go to your mom's hospital room so you can be close to her but I have to prepare you a little bit first," he said.

"What do you mean?"

"It might look kind of scary," Annalise said. "Your mom has a lot of bruises and swelling so she might look different."

"She'll have tubes and needles sticking out of her," Gard explained, "and there will be lots of wires hooking her up to machines that are helping her breathe and monitoring her heart and blood pressure. The machines will be beeping and sometimes they might sound like an alarm." He watched the boy's eyes go wide.

"Does it all hurt her a lot?"

"No, she's in a coma," Annalise said. "That means she's in a very deep sleep."

"She'll have a tube in her mouth so she won't be able to talk if she wakes up," Gard said. "But if you talk to her she'll be able to hear you. The doctor said you and your aunt and I can stay in your mom's room together overnight."

"Or until..." Harry's chin trembled, "until it's time for Mommy to go to heaven?" With his blink, the tears freely ran down his cheeks.

A quick glance at Annalise confirmed that she'd followed suit.

Near tears himself, Gard swallowed the lump in his throat. "Right...until then. You'll need to be very brave when you see her

with all those tubes and needles. Don't worry, you won't be alone."
Gard smoothed the tear-dampened curls back from Harry's face.
"We'll be right there with you, Harry."

Harry nodded. "Thank you. I promise I'll do my best to be brave.
Aunt Annalise?"

"Yes, sweetie?"

"Where's my dad?"

"Oh...oh he's, uh, well..."

As genuinely tongue-tied as Annalise, Gard gathered his
thoughts. Neither of them were about to let on that Harry's old man
cared more about himself than his wife or son. The boy didn't need
to deal with any of that now with his mother close to death just down
the hall.

"Your dad had to go home because he was so worried about your
mom that it made him feel sick here." Gard patted Harry's belly.

Harry nodded. "Maybe he wanted to be by himself so he could
cry when nobody was watching. I do that sometimes."

Gard took in a deep breath. "Yes," he agreed for the boy's sake,
"that's probably it. We told your dad we'll take good care of you until
he's feeling better...and that might be a few days."

Expressionless, Harry looked into Gard's eyes, holding his gaze.
Then he rested his head on Gard's chest. "I understand," was all he
said.

And Gard was afraid that he did.

The side of Harry's face that wasn't against Gard's shirt was
swollen, red, blue and purple. The bruising had crept closer toward
the boy's eye area from when Gard had first spotted it earlier. With
everything happening, he hadn't had a chance to ask Harry about it.

Annalise told him that when they arrived at the hospital she and
Astrid asked one of the nurses to check out the oversized bruise. She
told them Harry would probably have a black eye before morning.

She'd asked the boy what happened and Harry claimed he fell into a doorknob because he was clumsy.

Funny...that was almost the same explanation Stuart had suggested.

Gard needed to find out for himself. "Hey, Harry, what happened to your face? That's a pretty nasty bruise you've got there." Gard touched Harry's cheek lightly and felt heat generating from the injury. Gut instinct told him the mark had nothing to do with the car accident or tripping and falling, and everything to do with Hanklen's big paw.

"Oh..." Harry's hand flew to his cheek. "Nothing. I just fell. I'm always clumsy and I walk into doorknobs a lot. Nobody hit me or anything like that."

Gard and Annalise exchanged knowing glances. It was obvious he was protecting his father for some reason.

The nurse arrived to take them to Sabrina's room.

"Ready, Harry?" Gard asked as Harry slipped off his lap to stand. Gard stood up, bending to pick him up but Harry took a step back.

"I'm ready, but don't carry me in there like I'm a baby, okay? I want to walk in there...like a man." Harry held one hand out to Gard who clasped it, giving it a gentle squeeze, then Harry took Annalise's hand.

Gard heard the catch in the nurse's throat and felt a similar catch of his own.

"Sure thing, Harry." At five years old the kid was already more of a man than his father could ever hope to be.

Chapter 15

~<>~

THE SICU WAS just as intimidating as Gard knew it would be. He'd been in several of them and knew what to expect. But none of those rooms had Sabrina Hanklen on the bed, tied to all those machines and looking so frail and helpless it made Gard's stomach lurch.

But he had to keep it together for Harry's sake. If this was difficult for Gard to see it must be terrifying for the boy to see his mother this way. His gaze slipped to Annalise who, sheet white now, looked just as frightened as her nephew.

As they stood together at the foot of Sabrina's bed, Harry squeezed Gard's hand tighter than the boy probably realized.

"You doing okay, Harry?"

"I'm a little scared."

"That's okay...me too," Annalise said.

"That makes three of us," Gard said. "The doctors and nurses are doing everything possible to take care of your mom and keep her comfortable."

"Can I touch her arm?"

Annalise looked to Gard. "Is that okay? You're more familiar with hospitals and ERs than I am."

"Yes, you can touch her, Harry," Gard said. "You too, Annalise. Just keep away from any of the needles and you'll be fine."

Harry stepped closer to the bed. Tears streamed silently down his cheeks as he gently rubbed Sabrina's arm. "I'm here, Mommy. Me and Aunt Annalise and Gard. We're going to stay with you. It's going to be okay. Everything's going to be okay. I love you, Mommy. I love you so, so much." Ever so gently, he rested his head on her arm.

As Annalise wrapped her hands around his arm for support, Gard heard Sabrina's faint moan. "Your mom hears you, Harry." He put his hand on Harry's shoulder. "She knows you're here with her and you're making her feel better."

"Nobody ever had a better mommy," Harry told them.

"I know." Gard heard his voice break and he cleared his throat. "She's the best, Harry."

"The best," Annalise agreed standing close to the bed and smoothing her fingers over Sabrina's arm. "The best sister too." She choked on a sob, clearly doing her best not to fall apart for Harry's sake.

Gazing at his mom, Harry said, "It's just like in the song you always sing to me, Mommy. You are my sunshine," he sang softly, slowly, "my only sunshine. You make me happy when skies are gray. You'll never know dear, how much I love you..." He lightly caressed her arm. "Please don't take my sunshine away."

At that last line Harry's chin trembled. He began to cry hard, but silently, as if he didn't want his weeping to disturb his mother. Annalise grabbed a tissue for herself and one for Harry, wiping his eyes and nose, doing her best to comfort the boy. Before he spoke, Gard gathered his composure, afraid he'd choke up. Watching Harry sing so lovingly to his dying mother was one of the most heart wrenching things he'd ever witnessed, and he'd seen a lot through the years.

"I know how much you love your mom, Harry," Gard assured him. "Believe me, she knows how much you love her too. The last thing in the world she wants to do is to leave you. If she could stay with you, she would, you know that, right?"

Harry's head bobbed slowly. "I know."

Gard lifted Sabrina's hand, slipping his beneath it. She felt cold and so delicate, like holding a robin's wing in his palm. "I don't want you to worry, Sabrina," he told her, leaning close to her ear. "All the people who love and care about you are praying for you and sending love and healing wishes. If anything happens...we'll take good care of Harry. You have my word."

Sabrina moaned again.

The three of them stayed at Sabrina's bedside a while longer. Nurses entered the room periodically to check on tubes, needles and machines, with Gard, Annalise and Harry staying out of their way. Each nurse took a moment to speak kindly to Harry, answering any of his questions about his mother and asking if they could do anything for him.

Gard was used to the kindness of nurses, from his own hospital stay, to his many encounters with them in his line of duty as a firefighter and EMR. He was also accustomed to seeing them act with the utmost professionalism, which included a certain sense of detachment. Tonight, however, he saw a group of men and women who were understandably touched by witnessing the love of a five-year-old boy for the precious mother he was about to lose.

Although Gard realized this could be the end, he still had trouble wrapping his mind around losing Sabrina forever. He had hoped for a last minute miracle...for the doctor to tell them that Sabrina had inexplicably made a remarkable recovery, against insurmountable odds.

In all likelihood, that wasn't going to happen. Before morning, Sabrina would be gone.

"I want you to stay here with me, Mommy," Gard heard Harry telling his mother as a nurse tiptoed out. "Forever. But if you can't, don't worry because Hark will take care of you. She promised me she would. You don't have to be scared because she'll be waiting for you when...when you're ready to...to go." He swiped at his tears with his sleeve. "And then, just like you said, Mommy, one day we'll be together again...up in heaven."

That undid Gard. Tears freely ran down his cheeks unlike any other time in his life. When Harry saw that he ran to him, wrapping his arms around Gard's legs and hugging him. Gard clutched him close, smoothing his hand along Harry's back as they quietly wept together. Standing at Sabrina's side, Annalise reached her hand out to Gard, clasping his hand in support as she cried into her tissue.

They'd been in the room for an hour when Gard saw Harry's knees buckle. Until then, the boy had insisted on standing near his mother's bed. Clasping Harry by the shoulders to steady him, Gard bent to talk to him.

"We should let your mom rest for a while. Did you see the recliner chair they have for us?" He pointed to the sleep chair which was wide enough for an adult and a child. "You can get a little sleep and still be right here, real close to your mom. Okay?"

"Okay. I know Mommy needs to rest."

"Annalise." Gard beckoned with his hand. "Come on, we all need to get some rest. There's plenty of room for you and Harry on the recliner. I'll take the chair." He motioned to the arm chair a few feet away.

Without protesting, Annalise got on the recliner first, then had Harry climb up next to her. She put an arm around him, tucking him close. Opening a couple of the white cotton knit blankets from a nearby shelf, Gard spread them over Harry and Annalise.

He smiled down at Harry. The little trooper had to be thoroughly exhausted. He looked ready to collapse, but he never complained once, not even a peep.

In less than a minute Gard heard the sound of Harry's gentle snoring. The kid really needed to sleep. Tomorrow could be a long, tough, emotionally exhausting day for him. Gard yawned as he kept his attention on Sabrina. There hadn't been any change. She was still clinging to life by a thread. It seemed she was fighting to hang on for Harry's sake.

A moment later he heard soft buzzing coming from Annalise. It's no wonder, she was exhausted.

As Gard settled in the armchair with another blanket, his eyes were on Sabrina. Even bruised and battered, she was still lovely. So young. Far too young to die. It was so hard to imagine the world without her beautiful smile. In such a short time she'd enriched Gard's life, the same way she'd enhanced the lives of all who knew her. Glassfloat Bay would be a town in mourning if she didn't make it.

Gard felt himself blinking, on the verge of sleep, when he spotted the glass door to the room sliding open and the sound of muttering followed by shushing. He'd expected to see nurses walking in but, instead, watched his mother, Delaney, Laila and Reen creeping into the room, crouching and tiptoeing like a quartet of thieves at a break-in.

They went to Sabrina's side, whispering to her, kissing her on the cheek. When they turned around after a few minutes, they realized Gard was awake, and they looked guilty as hell.

"What are you four doing here?" Gard whispered so he wouldn't wake Harry. "I thought you were supposed to go home?"

"I decided not to text Mom about going home after dropping Stuart off," Delaney admitted, kneeling next to Gard's chair. "We wanted to stay here because..." she bit her bottom lip and shifted her gaze to their mother.

"Because we didn't want you three to be here alone." Astrid bent to give Gard a kiss on the forehead, smoothing his hair back with her fingers, just the way she'd done since he was a boy. "Not after what you went through with Tim, sweetheart. Besides, we love Sabrina and Harry and wouldn't feel right unless we were here too." She sat on the floor cross-legged next to Delaney, followed by Laila and

Reen. Spread out between his chair and the recliner, it looked like they were having a powwow.

"This is the best and most productive place for all of us to be right now, Gard." Laila slanted her head, studying him for a moment, then smiled. "See there? You're already looking more relaxed since we arrived."

Gard had to admit that, under the circumstances, he felt better with his mom and sisters close by. These four wonderful women had always had his back...had always been there when he needed them most. Sure, sometimes they could be exasperating, butting their well-meaning noses in his business when it was the last thing he wanted, but they were aces as far as he was concerned. Sheer gold. He was lucky to have them in his life.

"You're not angry we came are you?" Astrid used her best wide-eyed innocent expression, craftily designed to thaw his heart, just in case.

It worked.

"No, of course not, Mom," Gard assured. "I love you guys and really appreciate you being here with me. It's just that...I can't believe you did this. You should all be at home sleeping." He glanced through the room's large window, into the corridor. "Did the nursing staff see you come in here?"

"I promised the two women and the cute guy at the desk free scones every day for a month if they stretched the rules a little," Laila said, putting a finger to her lips.

"How's Sabrina doing?" Reen asked. "They told us there hasn't been any change since she came out of surgery."

"They expect her to be gone by morning." Gard's gaze fell to the boy in Annalise's arms. "You should have seen Harry singing to her, it would break your heart...just the way it broke mine."

"Poor sweet lamb." Laila's sympathetic smile warmed Gard's heart.

Astrid took her son's hand, squeezing it. "Are you doing okay, honey? I mean," she gestured around the hospital room with her hand, "with all this around you? It can't be easy for you."

"It's hard," Gard admitted. "But when I start feeling uncomfortable, I think about how brave Harry's been. The kid is amazing."

Astrid rested her hands on Gard's knees. "Poor Harry's is out like a light. He hasn't moved a muscle since we got here. He must be emotionally spent."

"Such a difficult ordeal for a child to be worrying about the fate of his mother," Reen said, biting her bottom lip.

Gard rose from the chair, mentally chastising himself for not doing so sooner. "Mom, sit here. I'll go ask at the nurse's station of there's another recliner we can bring in here." Astrid took the abandoned chair, bringing her knees to her chest and snuggling under the blanket.

"Don't worry, Gard," Delaney told him, grabbing on to his leg. "Laila, Reen and I have ample padding to camp out here on the floor with you for a while. If you could just grab a couple more of those blankets from the shelf that'll make it perfect."

"Seriously, you guys are too old to—" Gard wisely shut his mouth as soon as his trio of sisters gave him The Look.

"We'll just pretend you didn't say that," Delaney told him, passing blankets and small pillows to her sisters and keeping one for herself. "Now let's all close our eyes so we can get some rest. We're going to need it."

Gard settled in on the floor next to them.

~ ~ ~

"I'm going to anchor and rappel down, Tim," Gard called down the chasm.

"No!" Tim hollered. "Too dangerous. Listen, Gard, I'm—"

The horrific sound of Tim shouting out as he slid further down the icy crevasse, along with the snapping sound of cracking ice, chilled Gard to his marrow. Tim's deep cry of anguish grew more distant as he fell.

"Tim?" Dead silence. "Tim! Don't give up, man, I'm not going to let you die, you hear me? I'm going to get you out of there."

"It's no use. I'm done, Gard," Tim called from what seemed like miles away. "But you can save her...you can save Sabrina. You're the only one who can save her, Gard. Save Sabrina!"

"What? Tim, what are you talking about? How can I save her? She's dying. I can't save her...just like I couldn't save you."

"The ring, Gard," Tim called, his voice closer this time. Gard watched as Tim's ghostly presence, all radiant, rose from the chasm. He was smiling at Gard, nodding his head up and down. "Your heartwish ring, Gard."

Gard gazed hard at his ring, watching it glow with blue light.

"You can save her," Tim assured. "You can save her...you can save her..."

~ ~ ~

"I can save her! My God, Sabrina, I can save you!" Gard shouted, snapping himself out of his dream and bolting up, vaulting over his sisters and waking everyone up in the process.

The metal band had grown warm around his finger and the stone gave off a gentle, pulsing glow with the same blue light he'd seen in his dream.

"What happened?" Harry cried. "Is Mommy—"

"No, Harry, it's okay," Gard said, turning to the boy and clasping his shoulders. "She's still alive."

"Gard," Annalise said, "what's going on?" She blinked a few times. "When did you guys all get here?" She sat up, pulling Harry onto her lap and rocking him. "Did we lose her? Is my sister gone?" She rubbed the sleep from her eyes.

"No, shush," Gard said excitedly. "Please, everyone just keep quiet while I think about how I'm going to do this."

"Do what?" Astrid asked. "Honey, what are you talking about? You're scaring Harry. Did you have one of those awful nightmares again?"

"No...on the contrary. The ring, Mom...the heartwish ring!" He held his hand aloft, displaying the glimmering stone. "I can't believe I didn't think of it before now. Tim came to me in my dream...he reminded me." Gard burst into a grin so wide he thought his face might split.

"The ring!" Astrid gasped, bolting to her feet.

"Oh my God, the ring!" Delaney said, bounding up from the floor. "Of course!"

"You mean like the one Laila used to save her husband?" Annalise asked with obvious confusion.

"That's the one," Reen said excitedly.

"Okay," Gard said, making a shushing motion with his hands, "keep quiet and let me think. I need to do this right...need to make sure this wish comes straight from my heart." He looked at Harry, whose cheeks were flushed pink, and eyes saucer-wide. "Harry." Gard held out his hand, smiling as he summoned the boy with his fingers. "Come on, son. Come over here with me. Remember when your angel told you my ring was magic?"

"Yes." His nod was enthusiastic. "That's what Hark said."

"Well she was right. I want you to be a part of this. I want this wish to come from your heart as well as mine."

Harry stood at Gard's side, looking up at him. It seemed clear he had little idea what was going on.

Astrid sat on the fully opened and flat reclining chair, patting the seat on either side of her as she looked at her daughters and Annalise.

Annalise sat on one side, Delaney sat on the other, and Laila and Reen sat at their feet on the floor, huddled together.

"Harry, you and I are going to make a wish using this ring right now," Gard told him.

"Really?" His expression was a shining beacon of hope. "A magic wish for Mommy?"

Gard smiled. "Exactly."

Harry placed his hand over Gard's, letting out a surprised gasp. "The ring is warm...and it has light."

"As I say my wish, Harry," Gard instructed, "I want you to make a wish that comes straight from here," he tapped Harry's chest, "your heart. A wish for your mom to be all better. That'll be my wish too. Are you ready?"

"Yes. Yes!" He beamed a bright smile.

Gard knelt in front of Harry so their hearts would be about the same height. "I'm going to hold the ring next to my heart, Harry. You move in real close and wrap your fingers around mine so that the ring is over your heart too. Got that?"

"Yup." He got into position. "I can feel the ring getting warmer."

"Me too. The wish we make now," Gard began, looking into Harry's eyes, "comes from the depths of my heart and soul and Harry's too. We wish that—"

The hospital room's door slid open and the last person any of them expected to see barged into the room.

Chapter 16

~<>~

"STUART!" Astrid gasped. "What are you doing here?"

Scrunching his features into a mask of disbelief, Stuart Hanklen looked at Astrid and the others. "What am *I* doing here?" He clapped his chest. "This is my wife's hospital room. I got a call from the hospital that Sabrina's out of surgery and still alive." His eyes narrowed to slits as he glared at them. "The question is, what are all of *you* doing here? It looks like Grand Central station."

His gaze landed on Gard, kneeling on the floor, still holding Harry close. "And what the hell is he doing with my son?" Hanklen barked. "What's going on?"

"Shhh!" Annalise patted the air with her hands. "For heaven's sake, Stuart, can't you see my sister there on the bed? You're going to upset her."

"Who the hell do you think you are?" Pointing at Annalise, Stuart snarled, "Don't you dare shush me. And yeah, I see my wife." He glanced at Sabrina, giving her a quick head to toe scan before turning away. "She looks like hell. I don't know why they bothered calling me when she's still in a coma. Keyword, *coma*," he placed air quotes around the word, "which means nothing I say or do is going to upset her because she can't hear me." He rolled his eyes. "Now why don't you go fry up a stack of flapjacks, waitress lady, and mind your own business?"

Folding her arms across her chest, Annalise mumbled something unintelligible.

"Even though they can't respond," Gard explained, remaining *relatively* calm when he longed to pounce on the jerk, "comatose

220

patients can often hear what's going on around them. Look," he gestured toward one of the machines, "her heart monitor and blood pressure are both going higher. If you care about Sabrina, if you want her to survive, keep it down, okay?"

"Hmm...let's see..." Tongue firmly planted in cheek, Stuart stood there bobbing his head. "You chop up glaciers," he counted on his fingers, "you fight fires, you're a first responder, and now you're a doctor too, huh? Jack of all trades, master of none, that's what you are. Keep your nose out of my business, Malone, and keep away from my boy...and my wife."

"I know you're only lashing out in an unkind manner because this is an upsetting time for you, Stuart," Astrid said kindly. "Try closing your eyes and focusing on your breath for a few minutes...in and out...in and out..." she demonstrated with deep, slow breaths. "It will help relax you."

Stuart stared at Astrid, dumbfounded. "Kook," he muttered. Without further acknowledgement of her he whistled and snapped his fingers twice at his side, as if calling a dog. "Get over here, Harold."

"B-b-but D-daddy," Harry protested, still clutching Gard. "I c-can't. I have to—"

"Oh yes you can and you will. I'm your father and what I say goes, you got that?"

"Y-y-yes s-s-sir."

"Why are you in here anyway, Harold? A dying woman's hospital room is no place for a kid. Whose bright idea was it to bring—"

"Mine," Gard offered, struggling not to raise his voice to Stuart's level. "My idea. For God's sake, Hanklen, it may be the boy's last opportunity to say goodbye to his mother. Have some heart."

"You." Stuart huffed a laugh. "I should have known. From the looks of it," he glanced at Sabrina again, "he may not have a mother for long, but the kid still has a father, and that's me, not you. Come on, Harold." Stuart held out his hand, snapping his fingers once this time. "You're coming home with me."

"P-p-please, D-d-daddy...I c-c-can't yet."

Listening to the boy, Gard winced. It was sorely evident that Harry's stuttering was back in full force.

"Stuart, please." Annalise's eyes were wide and she was wringing her hands. "You agreed to let us take care of Harry until...until his mother is out of the hospital, remember?"

"All we want to do is help," Astrid added, looking every bit as apprehensive as Annalise.

"Please, Stuart," Delaney said.

Stuart looked again at Harry and Gard. "I changed my mind. I don't want you nut jobs poisoning my son's mind against me."

"We would never dream of doing that, Stuart," Astrid assured.

With Stuart Hanklen in the driver's seat, Gard feared it was a no-win situation. Legally, Hanklen was free to take his son whenever and wherever he pleased. Gard looked at Harry's face. Aside from being bruised, it was flushed. He'd give anything so he never had to see that look of panic on Harry's face again.

His eyes still on Gard, Stuart shook his head back and forth. "No, I can see what's happening. I know what's really going on here. This guy," he gestured toward Gard with a nod, "wants to take my place, wants to play house with my wife and kid. Well he's out of luck because Harold's my son and Sabrina's my wife, and that's the way it's going to stay."

"That's not true Hanklen," Gard protested, knowing he was lying through his teeth because this was one thing Hanklen was right about. Gard would move heaven and earth to take his place, to have the opportunity to provide Harry and Sabrina with the love and care they deserved. To make sure neither of them were ever in fear of Stuart's bullying again. "We're just concerned for Harry's welfare."

"Right." Stuart's lip curled into another sneer. "You've got your mother and sisters straight from the loony bin along with my busybody waitress sister-in-law over there helping you to plot against me. You think I don't see that? Really? Come on, Malone, give me more credit than that."

"Loony bin?" Delaney sputtered, disbelief obvious across her features. "Does he mean us?"

Waving a dismissive hand, Annalise pulled Delaney close for a supportive hug. "Just ignore him, sweetie," she whispered.

Giving Harry a hard look, Stuart asked, "Didn't I tell you to get over here? When I give you an order I expect you to obey it." He pointed to the floor at his side. "Now."

Harry took a step then hesitated. "G-gard and I w-were g-going to m-make a wish t-to s-s-save M-mommy."

"Make a wish?" Stuart gurgled a chuckle. "You think this is the land of Oz or something? You think you're living in a fairytale? I got news for you, Harold, this is real life and real life sucks. If you think you can wish your mother well you're even stupider than I thought."

"I wish you wouldn't speak to Harry that way," Astrid said. "Please, Stuart..."

"You can wish all you want, lady, but wishing won't even get you a cup of coffee. He's my son and I'll speak to him any way I damn well please."

A distinct, prolonged moan came from Sabrina.

"There, see? See what you've done?" Annalise accused. "My sister can hear you. You're making her distressed."

"Harry, listen to me carefully," Gard said. "If you're afraid to go with your father, tell me. If you're afraid he'll hurt you we won't let him take you with him, understand? We'll protect you."

Harry seemed frozen in place. He didn't speak...didn't move a muscle.

"Harold wants to be with me," Stuart claimed. "He thinks I'm a great dad, don't you, Harold?" When Harry still didn't move, didn't answer, Stuart gave him a pointed look. "Remember our talk, Harold? Remember what I told you would happen." He looked from his son to his wife in the bed and back again, arrowing one eyebrow down as he glared at Harry.

Harry left Gard's side and walked to his father as instructed.

"I-I-I l-l-love my d-d-dad," Harry said as Stuart elevated his chin displaying a pompous grin. "He's a g-great d-d-dad. I-I-I want t-to b-be with him."

Gard didn't believe Harry for a minute and he imagined the women didn't either. But there wasn't anything he could do about it at this point.

"Listen, Stuart," Astrid said, "you don't understand. Gard can save Sabrina. I know it sounds incredible, completely implausible, but if you'll just calm down and give him a chance to—"

Competing with the beeping machines, the grating sound of Stuart's laughter filled the room. "Holy shit, you're all nuts." He twirled a finger at his temple. "Certifiable. The bunch of you. Fucking lunatics."

Before Gard could respond, the door opened.

"What's all this commotion? I'm Dr. Kang," the man said, frowning as he entered the room. "Your voices are carrying all the way down the hall and disturbing the other patients. Don't you people know this is a hospital?" He gazed around the room. "Why are you all in here?" He took Sabrina's chart, studying it for a moment before looking up at them again. "We've got a patient in critical condition here. Get out, all of you."

"I'm her husband." Stuart's chin jutted high again. "I have a right to be here."

"Your name?"

"Stuart P. Hanklen."

"You can stay. Everyone else out. Now. Including the child."

"I'm Sabrina's sister," Annalise said.

"And she's responsible for upsetting my wife," Stuart accused, pointing a finger. "I only wanted to be here with my son to give him a chance to say goodbye to his mother," he asserted, placing his hands on Harry's shoulders, kissing the top of his head, and doing a perfect imitation of a caring father.

Gard watched as Harry looked up at his father with an incredulous expression.

"What a piece of work," Gard muttered.

"I understand, Mr. Hanklen," Dr. Kang said. "Your son may stay for a short while longer."

"Ms. Griffin and I have permission to be in here, doctor," Gard said. "Dr. Shadrik knows all about it."

"He's off duty. I'm on duty now and I say you need to leave—everyone but Mr. Hanklen and his son. I won't have you people causing a ruckus and disturbing this patient or any of the others in ICU any further."

"Thank you, doctor," Stuart said. "Except for her difficult sister, my wife and I barely even know these people."

"You lying sack of—"

"Gard..." Astrid warned as her son rose from his kneeling position.

"They're troublemakers, doctor," Stuart insisted. "All of them, sticking their noses into my personal business. I don't want any of them allowed near my wife." He waved a finger toward Sabrina's chart. "Put that in there. No visitors allowed except for me, her husband."

"Please don't do this, Stuart," Annalise said. "I understand you're upset but—"

"Out," Stuart said, gesturing to the door.

"Please, Dr. Kang," Astrid said. "I'm sure you can see that Mr. Hanklen is agitated and not thinking clearly. We were just trying to help calm him, that's all. We're close friends with Sabrina and care deeply about her and her son. We just want to—"

"She's lying, doc," Stuart said. "They're all lying. You can tell they've been upsetting my wife. People in comas can still hear stuff, right?"

The doctor gave an affirmative nod while Gard and the women looked at Stuart, aghast.

"Oftentimes, yes," Dr. Kang replied.

"That's what I've been trying to tell them," Stuart claimed. "Before you came in here, Doctor, I was begging them to stop yelling because they were making Sabrina stressed. Those machines she's hooked up to," Stuart motioned in their direction, "were going crazy and my wife started to moan."

"You son of a bitch," Gard said under his breath.

"Oh D-d-daddy..." Harry looked up at his father, shaking his head from side to side. The child's expression was a heartbreaking combination of sadness, disappointment and worry.

"Remember our talk, Harold," Stuart reminded him. "Remember what I told you."

"Y-yes s-s-sir."

"What about Harry?" Annalise said. "You were going to let us watch him while Sabrina is in the hospital. Who's going to take care of him now? You said you'd be too busy with work—that you needed to get back to Pennsylvania, remember?"

"What?" Stuart gave her a clueless look. "I never said that. I don't know what you're talking about. I'm perfectly capable of caring for my own son without your interference. In fact I've made arrangements to take some additional time off from work so I can be with him during this upsetting time."

"We know all about your job, Hanklen," Gard said. "Or should I say, the lack of it? You spilled your guts to Nevan when you were stinking drunk at my brother's bar earlier this evening." Gard's eyebrow shot up. "Sound familiar?"

"You see, doc?" Looking as innocent as a lamb, Stuart gestured toward Gard with his hand. "This is the disrespect, the craziness I've had to put up with while I've been here at the hospital worried sick about my poor wife."

Seething inside, Gard did a slow clap. "Somebody give this guy the Academy Award for best actor," he said through gritted teeth.

"That's enough," Dr. Kang warned. "Please leave. Your visiting privileges for Mrs. Hanklen have been revoked."

Before he could usher Gard and the five women out the door, the machines Sabrina was hooked up to began beeping and making alarm noises. Almost instantly, two nurses entered the room, rushing to Sabrina's side, checking what was going on. Dr. Kang joined them.

Gard heard one of them say the patient was deteriorating fast.

"What's happening?" Stuart asked, panic-stricken.

"We're losing her, doctor," another nurse said.

"I don't want to be in here if that's happening. I don't want to see it." Stuart backed up to the wall, leaving Harry standing at the center of the room alone, obviously confused and afraid. "I'm getting out of here." Hanklen's voice reached a fevered pitch. "I've got to get out of here!"

"Please calm down, Mr. Hanklen," Dr. Kang said, looking over his shoulder. "You're getting hysterical. You'll frighten the child." Turning to one of the nurses, he said, "Get all of those people out of here, stat."

"Let us take Harry for you, Stuart," Astrid implored, reaching for the boy's hand. "Please."

"No, we're getting out of here." Stuart took two giant steps to the center of the room, grabbed his son's elbow and, looking deranged, sped out the door.

Gard and the women were shooed out immediately after that. He believed they felt as lost and helpless as he did as they stood in the corridor several feet from Sabrina's room, peering through the glass door and large windows, watching the doctor and nurses tending to Sabrina.

"Nooooo!" Harry yelled as Stuart hustled him down the hall. "Let me stay! I want to stay with Mommy! She needs me!"

"Shut up...shut up!" Stuart spat, attracting attention as he flew toward the exit.

"Harry," Gard called after them, certain Stuart wasn't about to listen to his son. He watched the little boy turn his head toward him as he ran, trying to keep up with his father. Tears streamed down Harry's face and he looked terribly frightened. "Don't worry," Gard assured him. "I'll make that wish for the both of us, Harry. I promise."

That got a small, hopeful smile from Harry, who lifted his hand to wave, before his father yanked the boy's arm hard and turned the corner.

Gard and the women stood helpless, watching as more medical personnel rushed into Sabrina's room.

"They're losing her, Gard," Annalise whispered, a catch evident in her voice. "My little sister's not going to make it."

"Gard," he felt his mother's hand clutching his arm as she spoke, "you need to hurry. The ring will only work if Sabrina is still alive."

"I know." The pressure was crushing as an overwhelming terror of failing to save Sabrina clawed at him. His breathing erratic, Gard struggled to ignore the agitation, the fear, the flashbacks, and the other familiar symptoms of PTSD threatening to engulf him.

"I've got to hurry!" he urged himself, watching all the movement in Sabrina's room. "We don't have a moment to lose." He was speaking more to himself than anyone else, doing his damnedest to stay composed, and distressed that it wasn't working.

"Gard, honey, are you all right?" Astrid asked, alarm in her voice. "You're ghost-white and dripping with sweat." Taking a tissue from her purse, she smoothed it across his forehead. "It's the PTSD again, isn't it? Is there something I can do?"

Gard grimaced, working to shove the unsavory emotions from his head...his body. There was no time for him to languish in unwanted thoughts and fears. He'd live. He'd be fine. But if he didn't get his shit together—fast—Sabrina would die.

"Fine, I'm fine," he insisted, doing his best to convince his mother as much as himself. Beneath his breath, Gard muttered the mantra designed to help keep him in the here and now. "Home...Glassfloat Bay. I'm here...I'm here..." He gazed at the hospital room across the corridor. "This is a good spot. We're close enough to Sabrina's room to see what happens after I make the wish." He lifted his ring hand, watching it shudder.

"You need to sit down." Laila clasped Gard's hand between hers to still the shakiness. "It'll be easier for you."

Annalise and Astrid looked around them. The only chairs were behind the nurses' desk several yards away, and those were already occupied.

"Where?" Astrid asked.

"Right here." Laila plopped down on the floor. After digging in her large tote, she fiddled with her phone until, a moment later, the calming sounds of an instrumental filled the space around them.

Annalise angled her head while listening. "Is that...do I hear dolphins?"

"And ocean waves?" Astrid added.

"It's the ocean Zen music Zak likes to use for meditation. Now sit." Laila patted the floor next to her and they all joined her. "Gard, you sit in the middle. We'll make a circle around you." She held out her hands and the women all clasped each other's. "We need to hurry...Sabrina is fading fast." Laila turned to Gard. "Just take a few deep breaths," she instructed, demonstrating.

Too filled with angst and pressed for time to think about deep breathing exercises, Gard shook his head back and forth. "I don't have time for this, Laila. I just need to make this wish before we lose Sabrina."

"Breathe!" Laila ordered in a no-nonsense manner. And Gard did. It took just a few deep breaths and a matter of seconds before he felt better and more in control.

Resting his elbows on his crossed knees, he raised his ring hand. It still trembled. He gripped his wrist, trying to steady his hand. In a moment he felt the five women wrapping him in their arms, holding him close as the sounds of dolphins and ocean waves soothed them.

He looked at each of them and nodded. "Good. That's good. Thanks...I can do this now...with your help." They remained clustered together on the floor, ignoring the curious looks of passersby. Gard engaged in a long blink and silent prayer before speaking the most important words he'd ever utter.

"The wish I make now," he began, his voice as shaky as his hand was a moment ago, "comes from the depths of my heart and soul. This is Harry's wish too." Gard felt himself growing stronger, more confident as he spoke. "I wish that vibrant life be restored to Harry's mother, Sabrina Hanklen, so that she is alive, completely and entirely healthy, and that she will live a long and happy life surrounded by those she loves, and who love her."

The six of them watched, stunned, as a blue-white light originated from the heartwish ring like a streak of electricity, zooming into Sabrina's hospital room. In an instant, her hospital bed was aglow with the same light. They chorused a gasp and could clearly hear the unmistakable sound of raised, astonished voices coming from medical personnel scurrying around Sabrina's room as it illuminated and the machines next to her bed went crazy, beeping and ringing, with chart lines zigzagging like mad.

People outside the room, both hospital staff and visitors, mingled and muttered, wondering what had just happened. "Must be an electrical malfunction," one nurse told another, exiting Sabrina's room.

The hospital room was soon filled with more medical personnel who rushed by the six still seated on the floor, leaving the door to Sabrina's room open.

"This can't be right," they heard one of the nurse's say, her voice coming out a near screech.

"It's not possible," another said.

"Incredible...the patient was no more than a blink away from death." The last comment came from an astonished sounding Dr. Kang.

Gard and the women got to their feet, watching the flurry of activity as Sabrina was thoroughly checked from head to toe and back again.

"Her heartbeat is strong and regular," a nurse said, her tone agitated. "I don't understand. What just happened here?"

One by one her vital signs checked out as normal with staff in her room stating their confusion and amazement.

"Sabrina's eyes are still closed. She still seems to be comatose," Gard noted as they peeked into the room. "Do you think it worked?"

"Definitely." Astrid's smile was bright and confident. "Sabrina was so close to death that it may take a while for her body to fully recover, but recover she will. Absolutely. Positively. If she just got better like that," she snapped her fingers, "it would create too much of a commotion, too many questions that can't be answered. Don't worry, Gard. It worked. It worked!"

Gard glanced up at the wall clock. It was five minutes past midnight, Christmas day. He closed his eyes and let the joyful laughter bubble up from his chest, spilling forth from his mouth. "Merry Christmas," he said, then looked at the women. "If only Harry could have been here to see it for himself."

"He would have witnessed a Christmas miracle," Astrid said, tears in her eyes as she added, "just like we all did. I'll never forget this day for as long as I live."

"You can say that again," Annalise agreed. "Oh my God, I have my sister back!" She wrapped her arms tight around Gard. "Thank you, Gard. Thank you so much. I was so afraid I was going to have to make those awful calls to my parents and my brother."

"Incredible," Reen whispered, clasping Laila's hand. "Just as amazing as when it happened to you and Zak."

Weeping happy tears, Laila nodded.

"Merry Christmas and happy birthday, Harry!" Gard said, mentally reaching out to the heart of the frightened little boy, hoping that somehow Harry would instinctively know his mom was okay. "We did it, kid. Your mom's going to be just fine. How's *that* for the best Christmas-birthday gift ever?"

"I'm so damn happy I could cry...and laugh...and sing." Annalise twirled in place.

"You did it, son," Astrid said, clasping his arms and shaking him. "You saved Sabrina."

"It wasn't me," he protested, "it was the ring's healing magic."

"The ring's magic," Laila said, "combined with the power of your wish and Harry's." She cupped the side of Gard's face. "Wishes created with two hearts full of love."

"Seven hearts full of love," Gard amended. "Harry's and mine along with all of yours. I couldn't have done it if the five of you hadn't been here with me, sending me positive vibes and love." He offered Laila a grateful smile. "I swear I'll never make fun of Zak's meditation stuff again. The dolphin ocean Zen music really helped." He gave each of them a kiss on the cheek.

"No doubt about it," he said. "This heartwish was definitely a joint endeavor."

Happily smothering each other in a group hug, the four of them laughed and cried together.

Chapter 17

~<>~

"YOU CAN GO ahead and say it now, honey," Astrid told Gard, patting his back as the group of six walked out of the hospital. "You have my permission."

Gard furrowed his eyebrows. "Say what, Mom?"

She turned to her son as they reached the parking lot. "That Stuart Hanklen is a lying sack of shit." She gave a sweet smile.

Gard couldn't help the rush of surprised laughter that escaped after hearing his mother so eloquently express her feelings. It was rare for her to say anything so off color.

Annalise grumbled, kicking at a stone on the pavement. "Ooh what I wouldn't give for five minutes alone with that jerk."

"Tell me about it," Gard agreed. "I have never wanted to break every bone in someone's body until today."

"You know the huge new dough mixer I told you about," Laila said, "that was delivered to my bakery this morning?"

"The one with the gargantuan dough hook?" Reen grinned.

"You mean that big-ass mixer that's large enough to hold a grown man?" Annalise asked.

Delaney rubbed her hands together briskly. "I like where this is headed."

"That would be the one," Laila confirmed. "I've just thought of the most creative use for that piece of machinery." She gave them all a shrewd look.

"Gard," Astrid said matter-of-factly, "after you break all of Stuart's bones, you can help me and Annalise stuff that son of a bitch head first into the dough mixer so we can take him for a little spin. All right son?"

"Anything you say, Mom."

The laughter washing over them was the stress breaker they sorely needed after the tension of some mighty serious heartwish making.

"Should we go to Stuart's hotel to let him and Harry know about Sabrina?" Annalise asked.

"It might be best if we steer clear of Stuart for a while." Gard fished his phone from his pocket, checking the time. "It's nearly one a.m. Probably best if we wait until morning."

"I'm sure the hospital will contact him to let him know Sabrina's stable," Astrid said. "God only knows what might set him off and I don't want it to be us."

Once they'd reached Astrid's car, they stopped.

"I just wish we could visit my sister to see firsthand how she's doing," Annalise said

"And to let her know we love her," Laila added.

"I'll be doing that in the morning," Gard assured them.

"You can't," Delaney reminded him. "We're been removed from the approved visitors list, remember?"

"Yup," Gard met her gaze, "I remember." With a secretive wink he waited for them to get into Astrid's car, then twirled his keys around his finger, whistling as he walked to his vehicle.

~<>~

"I remember Annalise saying Sabrina always had a book with her and spent her breaks at the café reading," Gard said to Tundra as they ran along the sand early Christmas morning. He barely got any sleep after getting home from the hospital. Although dead tired and emotionally drained, he suddenly found himself infused with

Christmas spirit, staying up most of the night stringing colored lights around Bekka House. The couple hours of sleep he got were restful and free of nightmares. When he awoke it was with a renewed sense of vigor...and hope.

"So I thought I'd bring a book and read to her," Gard advised Tundra. The tongue-lolling dog looked up at Gard as if he understood. "How does that sound, Tundra?"

With his dog's amiable bark of agreement, the two of them concluded their run, heading home so Gard could grab a cup of strong coffee and prepare for his hospital visit.

Last night he dragged out boxes of family decorations, doing his best to make the house look Christmassy. While design wasn't his strong point, he thought he did okay, mimicking some of the things he remembered his mother and sisters doing in previous years.

Since Bekka House was the meeting place for family, friends and neighbors on holidays, Gard wanted the place to look inviting. He figured his mom and sisters would probably be over early to decorate, assuming Gard had let the chore go. Thinking of the surprise they'd find made him smile.

Thirty minutes later he entered the hospital wearing an old paint-stained jacket, oversized sunglasses and a ball cap with the bill pulled low to help disguise his identity from staff members he knew. Walking toward Sabrina's room he felt his heart stutter when he saw the room was empty. At the nurses' station he asked where they'd moved Sabrina.

"She was moved from SICU," the nurse said. "Let me see what room she's in now." A moment later she looked up at Gard, her smile gone. "Are you a family member?"

"Yes." He kept his head down. "I'm Stuart Hanklen. Her husband," Gard lied without blinking an eye.

The nurse's smile returned. "I needed to ask because Mrs. Hanklen's visitors are restricted, as per your request, Mr. Hanklen. I see that we called you several times this morning, trying to reach you. We left you a message with your wife's new room number, explaining she no longer needs to be in SICU. She's still in a coma but doing much better."

"I'm very glad to hear that. You probably have my work number there instead of my personal number," Gard said. "What number do you have listed for me?" The nurse read it and Gard made a mental note to remember it. "Right, just as I thought. Here, let me give you my regular cell number." Gard proceeded to give the woman his own phone number.

Once he was a few feet from the nurses' station, he put Hanklen's phone number in his phone before he forgot it.

He was able to enter Sabrina's new hospital room without any trouble, simply telling the people at the desk that he was Stuart Hanklen. Gard felt certain he wouldn't have any problem executing his devious but well-intentioned plan. One look at Stuart's face and the speed with which the guy had bolted at the first sign of any medical trouble last night convinced Gard that Hanklen wouldn't be around to visit his wife anytime soon.

Sabrina looked peaceful and serene. Some color had returned to her cheeks. The atmosphere in the room was different, more positive somehow.

While still too thin, she no longer looked so frail.

Pulling a chair close to her bed, he sat. "Good morning, Sabrina, it's Gard. Merry Christmas." He heard what sounded like a sigh. "You can probably feel it deep inside but just in case there's any question, I want you to know you're going to be fine soon. You're going to live a long, happy, healthy life, Sabrina." He slipped his hand over hers, clasping it gently. "I promise."

Gard could no longer deny his feelings for Sabrina. He loved her. When making his heartwish he wished for her to enjoy a long, happy life surrounded by those who love her...and those she loves. He hoped that might include him.

He didn't believe Stuart's claim that Sabrina was calling off their divorce. Although she'd told Annalise she was following through with it, he needed to hear it directly from Sabrina, and she wouldn't be able confirm his suspicion until she was out of the coma. Because that drip she was married to didn't like hospitals, Gard would make sure she wasn't alone, with nothing but medical people popping in and out of her room.

"I haven't seen Harry yet this morning," Gard told her, "but I think he knows you're going to be okay." He shook his head back and forth, chuckling at the ludicrous statement about to come out of his mouth. "You see, Sabrina, Harry and I made a wish. A wish for you to be well."

He gazed at the heartwish ring still snugly affixed to his finger as he held Sabrina's hand. The stone glowed like soft candlelight. No matter how many times he saw the ring glimmer, it was still unsettling.

"I made it using my magic heartwish ring." Just hearing himself say it made him wince. "I know how crazy it sounds, but it's true." He sat silently, watching her. If angels came to earth they'd look like Sabrina, he thought.

He couldn't help wondering, for the umpteenth time, what she'd ever seen in Stuart Hanklen. The guy must have been vastly different when they first met. A charmer. Maybe even a good guy. Maybe Hanklen was okay until his son came along and stole some of Sabrina's attention. Gard felt his eye twitch at the thought.

Or maybe Hanklen had always been a conniving son of a bitch who put on a great front, persuading Sabrina he was quality husband material—just like the eye-popping show he put on for the doctor in Sabrina's room last night.

He groaned aloud at his unsavory thoughts, only to hear a soft moan coming from Sabrina. Her eyes remained closed. She could hear him, most likely. He wondered if she could also sense what he was thinking or feeling.

That was enough to snap him out of his melancholy thoughts. He was here to keep Sabrina in good spirits, not depress her.

"Annalise said you like to read so I brought my Kindle. I've got a copy of one of my sister's *Delaney's Diary* books on here. It's collections of humorous stories from her newspaper column and website."

Gard could swear he caught the slightest hint of a smile across her lips as he spoke.

"We Malones think laughter's the best medicine," he went on. "No matter how bad I feel, if I can laugh, it always helps."

Not one for small talk, Gard was surprised at how the words kept flowing. Maybe it was because he could talk to her without fearing he'd put her to sleep...since she already was. He was tempted to groan aloud again, this time at his seriously bad pun.

"Anything mildly amusing that my sisters, brother, or my mom do ends up in Delaney's column, exaggerated for laughs. Same for her husband. Poor Varik." Gard laughed. "Delaney has a knack for turning our family's most embarrassing moments into comedy sketches."

Gard sat forward in the chair. Resting his elbows on his knees, he just kept talking. The more his jaws flapped, the easier it got.

A quick glance at the clock surprised him. He'd been jabbering away for close to an hour. Talking to the lovely Sabrina came so easy, whether she was asleep or awake.

"Remember at the open house when you asked about the vintage aluminum Christmas tree in the family room? I told you there was a long story behind it. Delaney's first husband was a stodgy English professor who didn't like Christmas, Delaney's favorite holiday. He wouldn't allow a Christmas tree in the house. As soon as they got divorced my sister found the silver tree discarded by a neighbor at the curb. She dragged it into the house, fixed it up, and adopted it as her own. She hasn't taken it down since, and refuses to let anyone else take it down either."

The memory made Gard chuckle.

"Delaney and Varik insist there's something magical about the tree. It has something to do with their heartwish ring experience. You know...I've actually grown to like the metal monster. It's kind of hypnotizing when the fireplace is ablaze and I'm enjoying a beer while I watch the flames crackle and the silver tree glisten."

Gard brought her hand to his lips, kissing it tenderly. He couldn't help himself. Then he leaned over her and kissed her cheek, her forehead, her chin, and the tip of her nose.

Sitting again, he told her, "I'll bring you and Harry over to Bekka House after you're out of the hospital, Sabrina, so you can get a better look at the tree and its eccentric collection of ornaments. We'll plug the rotating color wheel in and watch the metal branches change from blue to red, green, yellow and back again. Harry should get a kick out of that."

Gard's gaze shifted again to the wall clock and his eyebrows shot up. He'd turned into a regular windbag.

"Anyway, Sleeping Beauty," he said, unable to keep himself from uttering the appropriate analogy, "believe it or not, I didn't come here to talk your ear off. I came to help put a smile in your day, and to make sure you know everything's going to be okay."

He made no mention about Harry being with his father because, as far as Gard was concerned, that was the furthest thing from being okay. The last thing he wanted to do was upset Sabrina as she was healing.

Gard opened his Kindle and read to Sabrina for the next hour, looking up every so often and watching the restful breathing of the slumbering woman who'd captured his heart.

Chapter 18

Christmas Night

~<>~

HIS FACE CONTORTING as he let out an anguished howl, Stuart Hanklen clapped his hands over his ears and shut his eyes. Fisting his beer can, he stormed into his son's bedroom.

Harry's father had thundered around the apartment all day and the sounds had become a sort of white background noise, which Harry did his best to ignore. Oblivious at first to his father's arrival in his room, Harry continued to play, absently singing his favorite Christmas carol as he lined up the miniature hard plastic cowboys, Indians and soldiers, deciding to have them come together for a peace treaty because, after all, it was Christmas.

The old toys had belonged to his grandfather when he was a boy. Along with the miniature figures, Harry kept an old pipe cleaner with his toys that served as a variety of necessary tools and implements. Tonight he twisted it into the shape of a peace pipe.

After humming the parts at the end of the song where he didn't know the words, he returned to the beginning again, happily singing out, "*Hark, the Harold angel sings, glory to the newborn king. Peace on earth and—*"

With an assist from his father's fist, the bedroom door banged open, hitting the wall and seizing Harry's attention.

He gazed, wide-eyed, as his father glared down at him. His father looked particularly fearsome this time. He'd been drinking since he woke up this morning.

"What the hell are you doing in here? What's all that racket?"

"N-nothing, D-daddy." Harry scooped the toys into a pile near his feet. "I was just p-playing and s-singing m-my Harold angel s-song." He nervously smoothed his fingers over the carpet.

He watched his father's expression screw into one of incomprehension. "Your what?" he bellowed, making Harry flinch. "Nothing you say ever makes any sense. Stop all this talk about angels. You sound like a damned sissy." He kicked at Harry's toys, sending some of them across the room. "Boys don't play with dolls."

With his eyes locked on the toppled and strewn plastic figures, Harry said absently, "It's the s-song about Hark, the Harold angel. M-mommy said Hark is m-my guardian angel."

Stuart drained the beer from the can, crushed it, and whipped it at Harry's head. It bounced off his forehead, making Stuart laugh, but Harry didn't move a muscle.

"Don't talk about your mother." He slammed his fist against the doorjamb and Harry recoiled. Bending low so his face was inches away, Stuart went on, "You have no right to talk about her. Every bit of pain and misery she suffered is because of you. Don't you ever forget it."

He was so close Harry had no trouble smelling the dense fog of whiskey and beer on his father's breath.

"No s-sir."

"And what did I tell you about singing Christmas carols?" He scowled at Harry, who sat stone still. "Because of you, we will never celebrate Christmas with your mother again." Stuart advanced on his son, who was too terrified to move. Yanking Harry's arm, he hiked him high off the floor until Harry dangled like a ragdoll.

Sheer dread raced through the boy. "D-daddy! P-please. D-daddy, no, d-don't."

"D-d-d-d-daddy," Stuart mocked in a whiny voice. "Spit it out, Harold. For once in your worthless life I want to hear you say Daddy without butchering it. Say it!"

Harry stammered, so panicked he was unable even to get the initial D sound out. He tried again, feeling his cheeks burn from fear and frustration.

"You make me sick." The palm of Stuart's hand cracked across Harry's face as the back of the boy's head slammed into his bedroom door.

Still hanging from one arm, virtually helpless, Harry whimpered softly, but didn't cry. He'd learned it only made things worse if his father spotted tears on Harry's cheeks.

With one mighty swing of his arm, Stuart hurled Harry against the wall opposite his bedroom door, where, after a crushing impact, the boy fell to the floor, cowering in a shuddering heap.

Variations on the same theme occurred since they'd arrived home from the hospital. Harry doubted there was a single spot anywhere on his body that didn't hurt.

"If my beautiful wife hadn't been dropping you off at church so you could be in that stupid play, she'd still be alive."

"B-but, D-daddy, I k-keep t-trying to tell you...M-mommy *is* s-still alive. I-I know she is. G-gard and I m-made a wish so she would b-be okay."

"Don't you say that son of a bitch's name in this house."

"O-okay."

Harry knew he wasn't getting through to his father, who was convinced Sabrina was dead. And Harry was to blame.

"You may as well have put a gun to your mother's head and pulled the trigger," Stuart said. "And there you are singing Christmas carols when your mother is dead. Maybe you'll want to dance on her grave too once she's buried."

Mumbling incoherently, Stuart staggered out of the room, returning to the kitchen where he sat with his whiskey, beer, cigarettes, and overflowing ashtray. As Harry watched, Stuart mixed whiskey and beer together in a tall glass, downing one drink after another. As soon as he was done with one cigarette, he'd light another one.

"You were supposed to be here with me, Sabrina," Stuart wailed, holding the glass and staring at it. "Getting ready for us to go back home to Horntik tomorrow." He stared at the glass in his hand again. Harry wasn't sure what his father was looking for in it. After draining the contents, he pitched the glass at the refrigerator where it shattered, resting with the other shards of glass from previous glasses he'd thrown.

Harry sat motionless for what seemed an eternity, watching his father through the hinged crack of the door. Before long, Stuart sat hunched over at the table, his head resting on one of his hands. Reasoning that his father must have passed out, Harry allowed himself to indulge in a lengthy sigh.

Gazing out the window he could see the reflection of the colored Christmas lights from Nevan's Irish Pub two floors down, flickering in the glass-front shop windows of the hotel across the street where his father had stayed. He could hear laughter and singing in the distance.

"Hello, Hark," Harry whispered, gazing up at the inky, starlit sky. "It's m-me again, Harold. I n-need to t-talk to you for a l-little while if that's okay." He paused to listen, just like he always did, in case Hark replied.

"D-dad really n-needs help. He thinks M-mommy d-died b-but I'm p-pretty sure she d-didn't." He frowned, feeling the familiar sting of tears behind his eyes. "I d-don't know what to do. I hate that Mommy was hurt so b-bad because of me." His chin quivered and he took a deep breath. "Now D-daddy is sad and m-madder than ever."

Harry paused remembering the wretched sound of his father's anguished cries all day and the way he called out for Sabrina to come back to him.

"P-please help D-daddy feel b-better."

Aware that tears streamed down his cheeks for the first time all day, Harry swiped at them with the sleeve of his sweatshirt. He had to make sure his father didn't notice.

"Sabrina...Sabrinaaaa!"

Harry winced at the sound of his father's drunken howl. He remained silent for a moment, listening, before he dared continue.

Taking in a deep breath, he threaded his fingers together and clasped his folded hands tight. "I want t-two things, Hark. I want to s-see m-mommy again and h-hug her and t-tell her I l-love her and I'm s-sorry she g-got hurt. And I want D-daddy to b-be happy and forgive m-me and love m-me again." Harry's chin trembled again. "Please, Hark."

A moment later, Stuart's towering figure filled the doorway. His T-shirt was spotted with beer and the stinky cheese he ate with it. Harry hadn't eaten all day. He was so hungry he'd even eat some of that cheese right now. There was a plate of cookies in the kitchen but when Harry reached for one earlier, his father snatched the platter away, throwing it against the wall, then stomping on the cookies. He said Harry didn't deserve to eat cookies his mother baked.

"You praying?" Stuart spat before taking a deep drag from his cigarette.

Looking down at his folded hands, Harry flattened them against the mattress.

"For what, a miracle?" His father sneered at him as curls of smoke exited his nostrils. Harry thought his father looked like a dragon when he did that.

More than anything, Harry wanted the next moment to be like it would be in the old movies with the happy endings that he and his mom watched on TV together. He longed for his father to suddenly understand things...to grab him into his arms and kiss him all over his face, whispering words of love and forgiveness as they hugged.

Then Harry would live happily ever after in a house filled with joy and love and his happy mom and dad.

But movies weren't real life.

"Miracles don't exist. There is no God, no angels, no heaven, and your mother's dead and gone forever. Because you killed her."

Harry hated listening to the scary, ugly things his dad said. He believed with all his heart that Gard's magic ring worked. But what if it hadn't? What if his dad was right?

"M-maybe you should ch-check your phone," he suggested, "to see if the hospital c-called t-to t-tell you Mommy's okay."

"I turned my phone off last night. I don't need confirmation from the hospital that your mother is dead and I sure as hell don't want to get phony sympathy calls from your aunt or any of your mother's friends...bunch of hypocrites." His father's face changed, his eyebrows bunching, his jaw muscle twitching. "And who do you think you are telling me what to do, huh?"

Before Harry knew what was happening, Stuart picked him up and threw him against the large oak chest of drawers. The jolt rocked the dresser, knocking the lamp from the top. It fell. Hanging from its electrical cord, the lamp's marble base swung into Harry's head.

As Harry lay crumpled and whimpering, Stuart kicked him in the stomach.

Harry didn't cry. The pain was so bad, so deep, it was worse than the sort of aching that made him cry. He curled into a ball, trying to protect himself.

Stuart stood over him, eyeing his son with disgust. Before staggering back to the kitchen, he gave Harry a final kick, then tossed his still glowing cigarette butt at him.

Harry glimpsed a portion of his bed sheet pooling onto the floor, alarmed when it began to smolder from the lit cigarette. He attempted to get up so he could run from his room, but he couldn't move. He tried calling out to his father but his voice seemed to be trapped deep inside, coming out in nothing more than a gurgle.

Something wet and coppery tasting collected in his mouth. He recognized the taste from when he'd sucked a trickle of blood from his cut finger.

He'd only turned five today but Harry didn't have to be any older to realize he was probably going to die. Strangely enough, he wasn't afraid...at least not too much. Maybe he was meant to trade his life for his mom's so she could be alive and happy and healthy.

The last thing Harry remembered before he could no longer keep his eyes open was watching the small glowing orange line of flame crawl up the edge of the sheet. He thought of his mother, hoping that after she got out of the hospital she'd be able to spend the rest of her life with someone who would be nice to her, like Gard.

As Harry's eyes closed, he smiled, telling himself that one day, many years from now, he'd be reunited with his mother up in heaven where they'd celebrate Christmas together at the base of a giant Christmas tree, sitting at a sparkly golden table on a fluffy white cloud drinking eggnog from shining crystal goblets, and munching on hand-sized Christmas butter cookies with rainbow-colored sugar sprinkles.

Chapter 19

~<>~

IT WAS CLOSE to eleven when Gard plopped down on the couch in the family room after a long day of celebration. With Sabrina still comatose and a captive audience, he'd talked her ear off before reading a few chapters from his sister's books. She'd made little hums and murmurs, which were the best sounds Gard could have heard. After leaving the hospital, he spent the rest of the day at Bekka House with family and friends, with all of them talking about Sabrina and Harry.

Harry...God how Gard wanted to see the little guy, to know he was okay. With Hanklen being so unstable, Harry's welfare was the one worry everyone had at the Christmas gathering. The boy wasn't going to enjoy Christmas or his birthday unless Stuart had some sort of epiphany, transforming himself from a drunken asshole into some semblance of a loving father.

"Like that's ever going to happen," Gard muttered as he watched the color wheel turn, shining jeweled hues on the silver tree in the corner.

He had the TV remote in his hand, but was too tired to bother turning the set on. He needed to close his eyes and get a little sleep...just a short nap. Gard slipped into sleep as soon as the thought crossed his mind.

"Gard...Gard!"

"Nice," Gard mumbled at the sound of Sabrina's voice. "Good dream." He snuggled against one of the throw pillows. "Sabrina..." he muttered against it.

"Gard, wake up. You have to save him. You have to save my son."

Gard's eyes flew open. Not six feet away from him stood—no, *floated*—Sabrina's transparent form. He blinked hard. She hovered there, wearing her hospital gown.

"Sabrina?" he asked, sure he must still be dreaming. He *had* to be dreaming.

Tundra, who'd been sawing logs at his side, perked up out of a sound sleep. Gazing straight at the apparition, he offered a brief woof. He didn't bark his fool head off as if he'd spotted an intruder...it was more of an acknowledgement.

"You see her too, huh, boy?"

With a quick glance at Gard and then returning his attention to Sabrina, Tundra woofed again.

"Save Harry. Please, Gard. Save my little boy!"

Gard had no idea what was happening. He hadn't been drinking in case an emergency call came in from the fire house, so he knew he wasn't drunk. "Sabrina?" he said again, rubbing his eyes. And then the thought hit him...had she died after all? Was he seeing her ghost?

"I'm not dead," she said, seeming to read his thoughts. "I'm still in a coma at the hospital. My baby...my little boy is going to die, Gard. Save him...please save him."

"What? Where?" Gard's heart hammered in his chest as he leapt from the couch, still unsure whether or not he was hallucinating. "What happened? Sabrina...what's going on?"

"At the apartment...fire...fire...fire..." With each word Sabrina spoke, her voice and image faded until she was no longer there.

"My God...my God..."

After making a call to the crew at the fire station, Gard grabbed his keys and was out the door.

~<>~

"Harold."

Harry heard his name, as if the sound came from a long way off. He tried to open his eyes, but couldn't and assumed it was only a dream. One last dream before he died.

"Harold. Open your eyes."

This time, the voice was closer. Harry was able to open his eyes and, through the thick blanket of smoke, saw the bright orange glow of flames surrounding him. Normally he'd be terrified but he didn't feel much of anything. He was also vaguely aware of the whine of fire engine sirens in the distance.

"Harry."

Now the voice was right there in the room with him. Harry tried to sit up but he couldn't move. In an instant his room filled with glowing rays of white and pastel colored light, the most beautiful colors he'd even seen. He heard music...harps and brass horns. It was the Christmas carol he loved so much.

Harry tried to move again, but still couldn't budge. There was so much pain it even hurt to breathe.

The next time he heard his name, he saw her. With white-blonde wavy hair flowing down her back, and kind pale blue eyes that twinkled, she was beautiful beyond words. Her cheeks were rosy and there was something magnetic about her smile. She looked exactly like the photo of young Helga in Miss Astrid's album.

She extended her hand and spread her magnificent wings. That's when Harry noticed she was wearing the patchwork coat.

"Hark! It's you!"

The angel placed her hand on Harry's forehead, smiling down at him. "*Ja*, my dear, it is Hark, your Christmas angel...your guardian angel."

"I never saw you so clear before." Harry studied her lovely face.

"I've never been so close before. Come into my arms, little one."

Using every bit of strength he possessed, Harry still couldn't move, which broke his heart. "I want to but I can't move."

"Take my hand and arise, Harold."

Looking into the angel's kind, loving eyes, he tried to reach for her hand but still couldn't move. "I'm trying, but I can't, Hark. I hurt all over."

Nodding with understanding, Hark assured him, "Yes, you can. But first you must let go of your fears, your worries, and your pain, Harold. Leave them behind and come to me." Tilting her head, Hark smiled, telling him, "I hear your thoughts and know you're very worried about your father. Everything is all right now, Harry. Soon your papa will be at peace and suffer no more."

"He won't be sick or sad anymore?"

"He'll never be sick, angry or sad again. And he'll never hurt you or your mother again." Hark kissed his forehead, then combed her fingers through his hair and he felt more deeply comforted than ever before.

"Is Mommy okay? Did Gard's wish on the magic ring work?"

"The heartwish ring. *Ja*, your mama is fine. She will wake from the coma soon. Now take my hand."

Harry's chin quivered and the tears he'd held in all day finally spilled. "But I've been very bad. I made Mommy get hurt in the accident."

"That's not true," Hark assured him gently, still stroking his hair. "You're a very good boy, Harold. None of this was your fault."

"Am I going to die? Are you going to take me up to heaven?"

"No, dear, it's not your time. You still have much to accomplish on Earth. You're destined to do many wonderful things in your life, Harold."

She held out her hand once more. This time Harry reached for it, grasping it tight. He felt a surge of loving energy course through his entire being. The most wonderful sense of peace and contentment cloaked him and he basked in the glow of unconditional love.

Harry sat up and moved his head from side to side. Then he opened and closed his fingers, bent his arm, and finally, felt his ribcage. "I don't hurt anymore!" He took a good look at Hark and grinned. "You're beautiful, just like the pictures Gard's mom showed me." He placed his arms around the angel's neck and hugged her as she enveloped him in her wings.

"*Ja*...yes...my sweet granddaughter, Astrid," Hark said, her smile even more radiant. "Harold, you must never forget that you're a good boy with a good heart. And you'll be a good man when you grow up." She touched his forehead and whispered, "*Always remember*."

Furrowing his eyebrows, Harry touched his head. "My thoughts feel better now. Not so mixed up. Did you do something magical to me?"

Giving an affirmative nod, she told him, "I restored your thoughts to where they should be. You'll never think of yourself as a bad boy again, because you're not. You never were."

"Thank you." Harry felt so good in Hark's arms. Safe. Hopeful. Protected. And there was no pain anymore.

"The fire department will be here soon. Gard is coming to save you. I'll protect both of you until you're safe. You can always trust Gard, Harry. He's a good man. He will never hurt you."

"I like Gard very much." Harry nodded. "Am I going to feel the pain again?"

"Yes...some of it. Soon. So you'll need to be a brave boy. You'll be slipping in and out of consciousness at first, so you won't feel it too much. When you're awake in the hospital doctors and nurses will take good care of you. They'll give you medicine to make the pain less, and they'll help your broken bones mend perfectly. You'll be good as new before your next birthday, Harold. I promise."

"I'll be brave. I can do it, Hark."

"I'll be watching over you, keeping you safe...always, Harold...always. Now be brave, son...be brave..."

In the next instant, Harry became more aware of the angry flames engulfing his bedroom as he tried to breathe through the smoke. The pain was returning fast and hard, but knowing his mother was alive and well, and that his father wouldn't suffer anymore, was worth any discomfort he had to endure.

A sensation of calm and relief washed over him as he realized Hark was still in the room, spreading her wings over him to protect him from the flames. He wanted to thank her but the pooling blood in his mouth and the pain in his chest prevented him from speaking.

~<>~

"Looks like the fire started on the third floor," one of the firefighters told Gard as they unloaded hoses from the engine and watched raging flames consume the building's top floor.

People came out of their homes, and the hotel across the street, milling around outside, talking to each other and to residents of the building as firefighters directed them to move back a safe distance.

"Is everyone accounted for?" a firefighter asked.

"I think everyone got out," someone else said.

"They're all out," another said. "Building's empty."

"Okay then, let's get the hoses directed on the flames," one of the firefighters said.

"No," Gard said, "there's a little boy and his father still in there. Apartment 309. I'm going in."

"Don't be crazy, Gard," one of his crew said, grabbing Gard by the arm. "You can't go in there, man. It's suicide. They're either already out of there, or dead."

Before he could move, a woman touched Gard's arm. He turned to look at her and blinked a few times. It was Sabrina's visage again. A quick glance at the fireman standing beside him told Gard he wasn't aware of the transparent woman.

"Harry is in the bedroom off the kitchen," Sabrina told him, "curled up in a heap on the floor." She looked at him with a mixture of kindness and concern. "Save my son, Gard. Save Harold." Just as before, she faded away to nothing.

"Harry, Sabrina's son, in there. I've got to save him," Gard yelled, grabbing his equipment and running toward the burning building.

The smoke in the stairwell thickened as he reached the third floor. He found the apartment and broke the door down. Black smoke infused the space. He couldn't see. It was the worst fire he'd been in and Gard was terrified...for himself and for Harry.

He got down on all fours and crawled, making sure to keep in contact with the wall so he wouldn't lose his sense of direction. He knew it was easy to get swallowed up by the smoke, just as a drowning man often can't find his way back to the water's surface.

"Harold," Gard cried out. "Harry, answer if you can hear me." Feeling along the floor he realized he was crawling along ceramic tile. The first thing he encountered was a door, but it was the refrigerator. As he crawled along he felt what must be broken glass beneath his knees. The protective material of his turnout pants helped to keep most of it from cutting him but some got through, tearing up his kneecaps.

With one hand still against the wall, Gard connected with something slim, tall and angular, like a table leg. Following it up he felt along the tabletop and found the unresponsive body of a man. Using his flashlight, Gard saw it was Stuart Hanklen. He couldn't tell if he was dead or alive. Aside from a filled ashtray, there were beer cans and a liquor bottle near his head, which had obviously fueled the fire.

He'd get back to Stuart after finding Harry.

Sabrina said Harry's room was off the kitchen. Back on his hands and knees, Gard felt his way along the wall and floor, coming to an open door. Furniture in the bedroom was on fire, flames licking the ceiling.

"Harold," Gard called out again. "Harry, answer me!" He needed to find the boy fast because he wouldn't last long in the inferno. He couldn't imagine the kid surviving it. Once again, terror seized Gard.

In that moment Gard sent up a silent prayer, asking for God's protection, for his help in rescuing the little boy and guiding them both to safety.

Looking up from the floor where he'd been searching, Gard was startled. His gaze locked on what had to be a hallucination. At the base of the burning chest of drawers knelt what looked for all the world like an angel with her wings spread, protecting the prone form of a little boy. Harry. The angel glowed with white light.

Gard recognized the angel from Harry's drawings, and from his mother's photo album. She wore the same multi-colored coat as the one his mother showed them at the open house. The only difference is that the angel's garment seemed to be lit from within.

"My God..." Gard muttered, utterly astonished and still not believing his own eyes. "Great-grandma Helga?"

"*Ja.*" The angel made eye contact with him, smiling warmly. "Also known as Hark." Instantly Gard knew his prayer had been answered.

Near impenetrable smoke and heat were so pervasive in the small room that it was next to impossible for Harry to still be alive, but there he was, still breathing and nestled in a bubble of light, sheltered from the horror around him.

"Handle him with care, Gard," the angel instructed. "He has internal injuries and several broken bones."

"From his father?" Gard asked, incredulous. "Stuart did this to him?" The angel nodded. A flood of revulsion churned in his gut. Gently gathering the boy in his arms and nearly powerless to take his eyes from the heavenly vision, he looked down at Harry, whose eyes had opened.

"It's okay, Harry, I've got you," Gard assured him. "You're going to be okay."

The little boy moved his mouth. Gard leaned down close to hear him. Harry offered his thanks.

"Touch my garment, Gard," the angel said. "I'll lead you to safety."

Cradling the limp boy against his chest, Gard hurried out of the apartment, making sure to keep one hand on the angel's gown. It was remarkable how her presence acted like a beacon for him in the thick smoke, allowing him to see a good two feet in front of him despite the smoke's density.

Gard hit the street to the sound of cheers but didn't linger long enough to listen. As soon as he handed Harry off to one of his crew, letting him know the boy was in bad shape, Gard ran back into the burning building as they all tried to stop him.

"Leave, Gard," the angel told him, blocking his way. "There's no time. The floor up there is about to collapse."

"Thanks, Helga," he said skirting her and running up the steps, "but I wouldn't be able to live with myself if I just left Hanklen there to burn...even though part of me wants nothing more. Like it or not, it's my job to save the bas—" He caught himself before uttering an expletive. "To save the man," he altered.

"You've always been a stubborn boy," the angel noted.

With a sense of renewed energy Gard rushed headlong into the fiery hell of the apartment, heading straight for the kitchen table he'd located earlier.

He quickly assessed the situation. Carrying Hanklen over his shoulders wouldn't be safe because smoke and heat are greater higher up and could be fatal. Gard pulled the still unresponsive Hanklen from the chair, getting him down on the floor in a supine position so he could drag him along the floor by his shoulders.

As he dragged Hanklen he heard him mumble *it's Harold's fault.* So the guy was alive. Gard wasn't sure if he was happy or mad as hell about the revelation.

When he reached a certain point in the apartment, an overhead beam crashed down, barely missing Gard and his charge. The flames shot higher and the smoke was blacker and denser, making Gard disoriented. He couldn't see a damn thing. His flashlight was worthless in this smoke. He couldn't find his way out and was struggling not to panic.

Conserving his breath in the acrid smoke, Gard didn't speak but sent out a silent plea for help.

Hark, if you're still there, help me. Please. The last thing I want to do today is check out of this world with Stuart Hanklen in my arms.

He would have laughed at the irony if he wasn't so short of breath and close to passing out.

"I'm right here, Gard," she said, lighting the way. "Hurry...you must hurry."

How she could possibly illuminate a distinct path through such impenetrable black smoke was beyond him...but then, she *was* an angel. Gard didn't want to think about how flat-out insane that sounded. He'd have plenty of time to sit and analyze all this craziness after it was over. Right now he had to keep his head on straight and get him and Hanklen out of there...alive.

Gard felt the floor bow beneath him. There was no sound, no warning, just his awareness that the floor had buckled. It was collapsing. Using every ounce of strength he could muster, he yanked Hanklen along, knowing every second mattered.

In the next moment, Gard hauled Hanklen out onto the street. He had no idea, no recollection, how he'd gotten down the stairs. He wanted to thank the angel but she was gone. He'd never be able to tell any of the other firefighters what happened because they'd think he was crazy.

On the other hand...he wondered if perhaps other firemen had encountered heavenly visions under similar circumstances.

"A miracle," Gard whispered, bringing Hanklen to the ambulance where he was immediately worked on.

"You could have killed yourself going back into that building, Malone," one of his crew said as Gard's knees buckled and he grabbed onto the footplate of the ambulance for support. The other firefighter grabbed Gard's shoulder. "Let the EMTs check you out, then get your ass to the hospital to get treated for smoke inhalation before you keel over."

"I will..." Gard removed his breathing apparatus and attempted to smile. "Did they get Harry, the little boy, to the hospital?"

"No, he's being tended to but the kid refused to leave until you were out of the building."

"Sure." Gard nodded, removing his helmet and mask. "Poor kid was worried about his father."

"No." The other firefighter turned toward the gurney that held Harry, gesturing toward it. "He was worried about you."

Going to Harry's side, Gard glanced down at the boy. He looked so small, so weak and helpless. Taking a better look at Harry's injuries made him wince. He looked like he'd been in the ring for three rounds with the heavyweight champion.

"You're safe," Harry said, opening his eyes and smiling up at Gard. He reached up and Gard leaned close, letting Harry wrap his arms around his neck. Cautious of his injuries, Gard gingerly returned the boy's embrace.

"Yeah, I'm safe, Harry. And so are you." Gard glanced left and right, then whispered, "Thanks to Hark."

"She told me she's your guardian angel too," Harry said.

His great-grandmother's voice became crystal clear inside Gard's head. *As you suspected, dear Gard, it was me that you saw when your*

*father rescued you during the school fire many years ago. I was indeed
your guardian angel...then and now.*

As soon as she spoke the words, the memories flooded back with
clarity. Gard remembered that she'd been there shielding him and his
father, Sean, as Sean gathered Gard into his arms, bringing his son
out of the smoke and flames to safety before running back into the
burning school to save more children.

*It was your father's time that day...but it wasn't yours. And it isn't
today either. You have many years left, son. Blessings upon you and little
Harold.*

Harry's gaze shifted to the side and he waved his fingers.
"Goodbye, Hark." Blood trickled from his mouth as he spoke.
"Thank you." He returned his attention to Gard. "She has to go back
to heaven now."

"Yes," Gard looked skyward, "thank you, Hark." Gard realized
that all the time they'd been speaking, Harry had never stuttered.
Gard smiled down at him.

"Gard?"

"Hmm?"

"Thanks for going back to get my dad. That was really dangerous.
You could have got killed."

"Sure, Harry." Gard was amazed he could speak of his father with
such caring after what the monster had done to him.

"Hark told me Daddy's going to heaven soon."

Gard's eyes flew wide at the boy's statement. He'd delivered it
calmly, without any angst. "I'm sorry, Harry."

"It's okay. She said he won't be sad or hurting or sick anymore.
I'm glad about that." Harry yawned. "I'm sleepy now." He wrapped
his small hands around Gard's neck, yawned again and closed his
eyes. A smile was on his lips as he said, "I love you, Gard."

With a sharp intake of breath, Gard gazed at the innocent, badly beaten little boy who'd nearly lost his life. Harry's admission was unexpected.

Gard had been involved in countless rescues. As a firefighter and first responder he was frequently faced with a steady onslaught of harrowing events, trauma and intense emotion. The peril of flames and dense, pungent smoke were customary hazards. Then there were explosions, collapsing buildings, the torment of burn victims, and serious injuries such as dismemberment. He'd responded to car accidents and suicide attempts. There was always the imminent threat of death—his as well as those he was committed to rescue.

Already being treated for PTSD, Gard knew if he allowed his emotions to get the best of him he'd be in danger of making mistakes, putting himself, his crew, and the victims at risk. Controlling his emotions was a learned skill that he'd mastered over time. But today...

Today was different.

Today he'd experienced a torrent of emotion that had his head reeling. Today, he'd been warned about a little boy in danger by the boy's comatose mother who appeared to him as a ghostly visage.

And today Gard Malone came face to face with a bona fide angel. Not just any angel, but his great-grandmother, who guided him out of a menacing inferno twice.

Gard wondered what his therapist, Dr. Svenningsen, might have to say about those particular events.

As wildly peculiar and unnerving as this day had been, it was a day of miracles. And Gard had never been more in awe or more thankful.

Harry's words, his honest expression of love, caused an unexpected rush of emotion to target Gard's heart in the most gratifying way.

"I love you too, Harry." Tears stung behind his eyes as he kissed Harry's cheek and smoothed the hair from the sleeping boy's forehead. "I'll see you and your mom at the hospital."

Watching as the ambulance crew wheeled Harry into the waiting vehicle, Gard found himself at a loss for words, other than muttering *My God* repeatedly beneath his breath as he gazed at the heavens, as if seeing the vast star-filled sky for the first time.

Chapter 20

~<>~

"MY SON." Sabrina's voice came out in a gravelly whisper as the nurse leaned over her, checking her vital signs. "I need to see my son."

Her eyes widening in surprise, the nurse let out a gasp. "You're awake," she said absently, before stepping out of Sabrina's room to notify the desk that the comatose patient was alert. A moment later she was back, monitoring Sabrina and the machines she was connected to.

Bracing her elbows to lift herself from her pillow was more difficult than Sabrina had anticipated. She felt weak as a baby. "My little boy, Harold. Please..."

"We'll call and inform your husband that you're awake, Mrs. Hanklen. He can bring your son to see you, but for now you need to stay here in bed and rest." The nurse did her best to press Sabrina down against the mattress while Sabrina struggled to get up, gaining more strength with each attempt.

"You don't understand. Harry's here...in the hospital," Sabrina said. "In the emergency room. He's hurt. I have to see him." She tried to swing her legs over the side of the bed while the nurse restrained her.

"I can't let you do that, Sabrina." After pressing the call button, the nurse shouted into the corridor, "I need some help in here." Making eye contact, she said, "I'm Nurse Meyer, Sabrina. I'm here to take care of you. You need to relax. You were severely injured. You've got several broken bones and a skull fracture."

Focusing on her body, Sabrina was aware everything ached, as if she'd been dipped in a deep vat of hurt. Bewildered as foggy wisps of memories fought for her attention, she looked around, almost surprised to find herself in a hospital bed.

"Injured? What happened?"

"You were hit by a car. You're very weak. You've been in a coma. You must have had a bad dream, that's all. I'm sure your little boy is just fine." She glanced at the wall clock. "He's probably sound asleep right now."

A vague recollection of a car hitting her flitted across Sabrina's mind. She remembered little other than the sudden impact and the flash of blinding pain that followed. Her next memory was the sound of voices, loving, soothing, nurturing. Harry and Gard...Annalise, Astrid, Delaney, Laila and Reen.

That was followed by Stuart's harsh voice, causing a commotion of some sort.

While memories of what had happened blurred her thoughts, Sabrina was crystal clear about her son. He was hurt. He needed her. And he was here in the hospital.

"We fully expected we'd lose you," Nurse Meyer said. "You're our miracle patient, Sabrina." Her smile was warm and genuine.

While in the coma Sabrina was mostly aware of what went on around her, but unable to speak or move as she teetered close to the brink of life and death. She recalled the voices in the hospital room fading into the background as her deceased grandparents came to greet her, arms outstretched in invitation. It was wonderful. Immensely comforting. Just as she was about to follow them into the light, leaving her pain behind, Sabrina felt herself whisked back.

"There was...I think there was an angel," Sabrina said, more to herself than the nurse.

"Being that close to the other side, I wouldn't be surprised," the nurse said, gently smoothing Sabrina's hair back with her fingers. "I've heard that many times from people who nearly died."

Gard...it was something Gard had done. He'd saved her somehow...returned her to the living. Later, she was aware of Gard visiting her, talking to her, offering comfort and assurance.

"She's got a lot of strength for someone who just came out of a coma," the aide who'd responded to the nurse's request for assistance said as they strived to keep Sabrina in the bed.

"Sabrina, please, you need to remain in bed," Nurse Meyer insisted. "You have breaks in your leg and hip. You can't walk."

Her recollections were clearer now. Sabrina definitely remembered being visited by an angel, the same angel Harry had drawn wearing that colorful patchwork coat. Hark...Helga...she'd guided Sabrina back to the living, warned her Harry was in danger. The angel did something magical, helping Sabrina leave her earthly body and travel to Gard in spirit form so she could tell him about Harry.

And Gard, bless him, came through. He saved her little boy.

Focusing on Nurse Meyer and the aide, Sabrina clutched their arms. "Please, you have to listen to me. My baby is badly injured," she cried, her voice growing frantic. "I need to be with him. He needs me. He needs his mother."

"All right, you really need to calm down, Sabrina," Nurse Meyer urged. "If you agree to remain still for a moment, I'll have Tiffany check about your son, okay?" After Sabrina offered a nod of agreement, the nurse told the aide, "Tiff, will you check with ER to see if Mrs. Hanklen's son was brought in?"

As frazzled as Sabrina was, she recognized the skeptical look of disbelief the aide gave the nurse. Sabrina wasn't sure how she knew Harry was there, but she did. Her encounter with the angel was too real to be merely a dream.

"But—" Tiffany objected.

"Just do it, Tiff," the nurse said, "so we can assure Sabrina that her son is safe at home and she can relax again."

Glancing from Nurse Meyer to Sabrina and back again, the aide shrugged and was on her way.

Though her thoughts were still fuzzy, Sabrina remembered more about the angel's warning. Stuart had hurt Harry. And there was a fire.

"Fire!" Sabrina yelled as the recollection sped across her mind, once again scrambling to get out of the bed. "My son was in a fire!" She felt her heartbeat skip at the terrifying memory.

"Shhh, please, Mrs. Hanklen," Nurse Meyer admonished, "you'll frighten the other patients. You can't just jump out of bed like that. You'll collapse and make your injuries worse. Plus you're all full of tubes and wires. The doctor needs to check you over and unhook you before you can get up." Her grip around Sabrina's arms became firm. "If you don't stop I'll need to call in reinforcements."

Tiffany returned, looking sheet-white. "He's here," she said simply.

Still holding Sabrina down the nurse asked, "What are you talking about?"

"Mrs. Hanklen's son, Harold, is in ER. So is her husband. There was a fire..."

Stunned, Nurse Meyer's mouth dropped open. "But how...?" She focused on Sabrina. "How could you possibly know?"

"Mother's intuition." Sabrina unfastened herself from attached tubes and wires. "Help me, Nurse Meyer," she pleaded, frustrated with herself for feeling so weak. "You don't need to worry. I'm fine. My broken bones have all mended."

"That's not possible. Please, Mrs. Hanklen..."

Sabrina all but exhausted herself fighting to get out of the hospital bed, and she worried she wouldn't be able to put her full weight on her feet to get to Harry.

"Do you have any children?" Sabrina asked the nurse.

"Two. Both in high school."

"Then you understand." Sabrina squeezed her hand. "From one mother to another, I'm asking you, Nurse Meyer, begging you. Help me get to the ER so I can be with my little boy. Please."

Her eyes scanning the equipment Sabrina was hooked up to, the nurse hesitated. "But I can't just—"

"Yes...you can." Smiling warmly, Sabrina reached for the nurse's other hand, clasping both of the woman's hands in her own as they locked gazes. Somehow she knew the energy she felt sparking between them was fueled by the same angel that came to warn Sabrina earlier. She could tell Nurse Meyer felt it too. At that moment Sabrina received a strong inner knowing, telling her the nurse wouldn't face adverse consequences for helping her.

"You can," Sabrina assured with a nod. "It's going to be all right. I'll be fine and I promise you won't be reprimanded. You have to trust me, Cynthia...*please.*"

Dumbstruck at the sound of her first name, which she hadn't revealed, the nurse stood stock still for a long moment before snapping to attention. "Yes...yes." Nurse Cynthia Meyer turned to the aide. "Tiffany, contact the doctor on call to let him know Mrs. Hanklen is awake and that I'm taking her to the ER in a wheelchair to see her son."

~<>~

The sight of Harry's broken body as the nurse drew back the blue-green curtain around his bed was almost more than Sabrina could bear. He looked so small, so helpless and weak. And yet, his expression was tranquil. There was even a faint smile on his lips. Sabrina wondered if they'd given him something for the pain which, by the look of the sizeable bruises all over his body, must be considerable.

His back to Sabrina, Gard was still in his firefighter gear at Harry's side, bending over him as he held his hand and spoke to him.

"Don't you worry, buddy, I'm not going anywhere. I'm staying right here with you until they come to take you in to surgery," she heard Gard assure Harry. "You know, being a fireman, I've brought lots of people to the hospital over the years, so I know the doctors and nurses are all very good at helping people, Harry. They're going to make sure you're feeling much better soon. Believe me?"

"Yes." Harry nodded, doing his best to smile. "Thanks, Gard." His voice was no more than a weak whisper. "Hark promised I'd be all better by my next birthday."

"I know...she told me too."

Sabrina smiled. The man had such a wonderful way with her son. As exhausted and battered as Gard must be after battling the smoke and fire, he still took the time to make sure Harry wasn't alone or afraid in the hospital.

Maybe it was due to the blur of tears gathering in her eyes, but for a second, Sabrina could have sworn Gard Malone was a knight in shining armor.

Harry's eyes widened as he caught sight of Sabrina. "Mommy!" he cried, reaching out to her.

"I'm here, sweetheart," Sabrina assured, wiping her eyes as Nurse Meyer wheeled her next to his bed. "Mommy's here." She took her son's hand gingerly, without giving it the hearty squeeze she longed to give him. She was so thankful to see Harold alive she had to keep from laughing and crying at the same time.

"Sabrina..." Gard's expression was full of surprise. "You're awake." He coughed as he spoke, a coarse, raspy sound. His face was black with soot and his eyes were bloodshot.

"Thanks to you," she told him. "I don't know what in the world you did to bring me back, Gard, but..."

"I promise to tell you all about it one day."

Sabrina nodded in agreement. "Thanks to you, my son is alive too." She bent over Harry, giving him a tender kiss on the forehead. His face was discolored from bruises and lumps, there was a trail of dried blood from his mouth down his neck, and one eye was swollen almost shut. With a sideways glance up to Gard, Sabrina told him, "I'll never be able to thank you enough for saving Harry."

"Gard was really brave," Harry murmured. "He saved me, then went back into the fire to save Dad."

"Hey, too much talking, Harry," Gard said gently, seeming uncomfortable about the praise. "You need to relax now."

Like Harry, Gard's voice was strained and he coughed often as he spoke. Sabrina was amazed her own voice was so strong after just awakening from a coma. She felt weak but lucid, and exhilarated to see both her son and Gard alive.

"The other firemen yelled at Gard not to go," Harry struggled on, "because it was so dangerous." He spoke with obvious difficulty, but was clearly determined to have his say.

Unable to imagine the sheer terror of the situation, Sabrina shuddered. "Gard's a very brave man," she agreed, looking at Gard. "A hero." His mouth opening and closing, Gard shook his head while absently making invisible crosshatch marks on Harry's mattress with his thumb.

She looked at him thoughtfully, noticed the gash across his forehead, the cuts and bruises on his face. She also noticed blood on his jacket and pants. Yes, he was a hero all right. All he was missing was the cape.

"Mom?"

"Yes, sweetie?"

"I'm sorry to make you feel bad but..." Harry's bottom lip trembled.

He'd already been through so much. She wondered what he struggled with now. "It's okay. Go ahead and tell me."

"Hark told me it was Daddy's time to go to heaven."

"It's all right." Closing her eyes, Sabrina breathed deep. "I know. I had a talk with Dr. Kobandor about you and your dad after Nurse Meyer brought me to the emergency room. They told me he died from smoke inhalation." Another look at her battered son nearly had her sobbing. Stuart was in heaven? Her eyes narrowed. She doubted it.

"The doctors did all they could to revive him," Gard explained, "but he succumbed shortly after arriving at the hospital. I'm sorry. I did everything I could to—"

"Sorry?" Sabrina whipped her head in Gard's direction. "My God, Gard, you have nothing to be sorry for. You went above and beyond the call of duty, rushing back into that inferno to save the man who—" She caught herself before spewing the ugly thoughts thrashing inside her head. "To save Stuart," she amended after taking a deep breath.

She extended her other hand to Gard, who took it gently. "God bless you, Gard. I don't know what I would have done if..." Her eyes welled with tears as she looked at Harry, her gaze taking stock of the myriad wounds over her child's body. "Oh my sweet baby, I'm so sorry your father hurt you." She choked on those last words.

God forgive her, but she was glad Stuart was dead. Glad! Not only did she feel no grief, all she could think of was how she could have killed him herself if he was still alive. What kind of a monster does this to his own child?

"It was bad," Harry whispered. "I was pretty scared. But I know Dad didn't mean to do it." He patted his mother's hand, taking on the role of comforter. "Hark told me Daddy had a bad sickness inside his head. He was scared and angry because he thought you died, and he thought it was my fault." Harry's lip trembled again and he swiped at a tear.

"None of what happened was your fault, Harry," Sabrina whispered. "None of it."

"I know that now. Hark told me. I told Daddy in a prayer that I forgive him for what he did."

Sabrina and Gard exchanged glances.

"I've gotta tell you, Harry," Gard said, shaking his head in obvious disbelief. "You really set the bar high."

"I don't know what that means but it sounds good." Harry's lips curved into a smile.

"It means you're a real superstar, and I'm proud to have you for a friend."

"Thanks. I feel the same about you, Gard."

After speaking to Dr. Kobandor before coming in to see Harry, Sabrina had a soul shuddering idea of what her son had been through at the hands of his drunken father. Harry's injuries were so extensive they needed to transport him to Wisdom Harbor Children's Hospital in the next town after tending to his initial emergency care.

The doctors assured her he'd be fine but his healing would take many months.

"I don't remember a lot of it," Harry admitted, his weedy voice faltering. Sabrina could tell he was pushing himself. "Hark said she'd help me forget some of what happened. She promised I'd get better and not have more pain than I can handle. So it's okay, Mom. I'll be fine. I promise I'm not going to die or anything." He reached out his hand to her. "Please don't cry anymore."

Sabrina was unaware she'd been sobbing. Nurse Meyer tucked a box of tissues into her hands and Sabrina wiped her eyes and nose. Then the nurse plucked a tissue for herself, tending to her own sniffles. Turning his back to them, Gard seemed to be wiping tears as well.

Although Harry's voice was strained due to his injuries and the smoke, it dawned on Sabrina that he hadn't stuttered or stammered since she'd arrived at his side in the emergency room. It was odd. She would have thought the fear and stress of all he'd been through would have had him nearly tongue-tied.

"I'll let you three have some privacy," Nurse Meyer said. "I'll be just outside if you need me." She pointed to the corridor. "They'll be here to take Harry into surgery soon."

"I saw her," Gard told Sabrina once the nurse left the room. "Harold's angel. Without her I wouldn't have found him with all the smoke and flames. I couldn't have gotten him out of the building without her guidance."

"I saw her too," Sabrina told him. "She warned me...helped me to get to you so I could tell you about the fire."

"I couldn't believe it when I saw you there in the house," Gard said. "At first I thought..." He stopped, his eyebrows furrowing as he swallowed hard and seemed to be examining the floor. "You looked like a ghost. I was afraid you'd died." With his caring gaze locked on hers, Gard absently finger-combed her hair. "I'm awfully glad you didn't."

"Me too." Sabrina smiled up at him. "I don't understand any of it. I don't know how it happened. I'm just glad it did. I feel so blessed...and so thankful."

"I know what happened to us." Harry held his hands out to both of them.

"What, sweetie?" Sabrina stroked his soot-covered blond hair, carefully taking his hand.

"A miracle," Harry claimed. "A Christmas miracle."

The three of them exchanged looks filled with something that felt a lot like love.

"You won't get any argument from me, Harry." Gard took Harry's other hand.

"Me either." Sabrina locked eyes with Gard.

Two technicians entered the room, interrupting the moment.

"We need to take your son into surgery," one of them said. "Come on, Harry," he smiled at the boy, "ready for a ride down the hall? We've got an expert team ready to help you get better."

"I'm ready." Turning to Sabrina, Harry whispered, "Don't worry, Mom, Hark said she'll be in there with the doctors to make sure they do a good job."

"Well," Sabrina offered a reassuring smile, "with an angel in surgery watching over things I don't have anything to worry about." She kissed the tip of his nose. "And neither do you. I'll see you when the operation is done. I love you, sweetheart."

"Love you too, Mom."

"I'll keep your mom company, Harry. We'll wait for you together." Gard turned to Sabrina. "If it's okay with you."

"I'd like that." She knew she was being selfish, considering how utterly exhausted Gard must be, but it just seemed right.

"Not so fast, Gard." Dr. Kobandor had entered the room. "I told you when you came in here that you need to get checked out. The EMTs said you're pretty banged up. Now that Harry's heading to surgery, no more stalling or excuses."

"Hey, come on, Terry, I'm fine," Gard replied, clearly on a first name basis with the doctor. "I don't need you practicing on me." He laughed, giving a dismissive wave followed by another round of hoarse coughing. "So take your little stethoscope and knee hammer and go play doctor with someone else."

Terry Kobandor's eyebrow hiked in amusement. "Look at you. You're a mess for chrissakes." He gestured from Gard's head to his feet. "You're full of dirt, grime and blood. You're coming with me so I can take care of those knees and treat you for smoke inhalation." He jabbed a pointed finger at Gard, giving him a straightforward look. "You know damn well how important that is. It'll only take ten to fifteen minutes."

As Gard opened his mouth to protest, Sabrina said, "He's right, Gard. You don't want Harry to think you're afraid of the doctor, do you?"

"Afraid?" Gard puffed himself up. "Of him?" He hiked a thumb at Terry. "Trust me, I am *not* afraid."

"Good," Sabrina said. "You'll find me in the waiting area when you're all fixed up."

"Nope," Nurse Meyer said, popping back into the room and taking Sabrina's wheelchair by the handles. "You'll be waiting back in your own hospital room where you're supposed to be. Doctor's orders."

"But I don't need to—" Sabrina started to object.

"But nothing." The nurse wagged a finger. "For heaven's sake, you just woke up from a coma. Stop making a fuss. I'm taking you back to your room so the doctor can check you over."

"Looks like I'm not the only one who'll be getting a checkup." Gard folded his arms over his chest. If that playful smirk had been across anyone else's face, Sabrina would be full of indignation but on Gard it looked adorable.

"Hey, Gard?" Harry muttered as he was being wheeled out the doors. He curved his fingers, motioning for Gard to come close.

"Yeah, Harry?"

"Mom and Doctor Kobandor are right. You need to listen to them."

As he gazed down at Harry, cautiously holding the boy's hand, Gard lifted his shoulders in a shrug. "Looks like I'm outnumbered. Okay, Harry, I'll be getting fixed up while they fix you and your mom up, and we'll both see you later."

"Okay." Harry gave a thumbs-up sign. "Thanks again for saving me, Gard. I love you."

Sabrina saw Gard's eyes glisten with unexpected tears. "I love you too, Harry."

The exchange touched Sabrina's heart.

Close to an hour later, Sabrina had been thoroughly checked and given the good news that she was doing remarkably well. Something in the magical wishing mechanism Gard used to heal her must have addressed the inevitable questions the medical staff would have about the sheer impossibility of her broken bones mending so fast, because no one even mentioned it. The doctors seemed to have forgotten she'd been in a coma too.

Tiffany, the aide, helped bring Sabrina's bed up into a near sitting position, placing a couple of pillows behind her back, plumping them while making cheerful chatter and making sure the blood pressure monitor was connected.

After Tiffany left, Sabrina spotted Gard walking toward her room. Except for his boots, he was in street clothes, dressed all in black from the turtleneck to the black jeans, which were torn at the knees. His face and hands were clean and he'd been bandaged on both knees as well as on the forehead over his left eye. The man looked seriously, devastatingly handsome.

Sabrina fought to switch off her inappropriate feelings...her deep attraction to Gard Malone. Her husband had just died. Yes, she'd left him and they were getting a divorce, but the last thing she should have on her mind right now is how appealing another man looked, or how her heart skipped at the thought of him coming closer and sitting next to her.

Her heart beat faster as Gard approached. Her palms grew sweaty and she felt warm all over.

"Hey," Gard said, snapping her back to the present as he set his bulky firefighter gear on one chair and pulled up another so he could sit next to her bed.

"Hey." It was all Sabrina was capable of saying at the moment.

"Terry lied," Gard complained, covering his mouth as he coughed.

"The doctor?" Sabrina frowned. "What do you mean? Is...is something wrong?" She worried about smoke inhalation from the fire and what it might have done to Gard's lungs. One of the firefighters he worked with recently lost his life due to breathing toxic smoke.

"No," Gard swatted the air, "I'm fine, just a few stiches here and there. Terry lied about me being out of there in fifteen minutes." He glanced at the clock. "He and his nurse poked and prodded me for nearly an hour."

Sabrina breathed a sigh of relief. "You never would have gone if he'd said it would take that long."

"You're right," Gard admitted, offering a tired shrug. "How about you? What did the doc say? You okay?"

"It's weird," she whispered, motioning him closer. "Apparently I had all these broken bones and because of whatever you did, they're not broken anymore. The doctors seem totally clueless about it. I mean, as if they never even knew I had any broken bones."

"I won't even pretend to understand the magic of the heartwish ring," Gard said examining his finger. "All I know is I'm glad it worked and you're alive and healthy."

"Me too." Sabrina breathed a sigh of relief. "They said I'm good enough to go home tomorrow. They want to keep me overnight just to make sure everything's okay."

"That's great news. Amazing after all you went through." Gard's gaze roved her face. "You look good but you look exhausted. It's been a long, stressful day for you, Sabrina."

"I could say the same about you," she said, plainly seeing the fatigue across his features.

"Yeah but I'm not the one who just woke up from a coma a few hours ago." He gave her a pointed look. "And then you went right into having to deal with the trauma of Harry and Stuart."

Looking into the distance, Sabrina engaged in a long, slow nod. "It's been a strange day. First there was fear and dread, worrying about my little boy. That was followed by elation that I'm awake and that Harry is safe and sound," she gazed at Gard, "thanks to you." Looking at his bandaged forehead, she reached out to touch it.

"And then," Sabrina continued, looking away with another sigh, "there's Stuart." Never prone to getting headaches, she was surprised to feel the mother of all headaches commencing. "My head is swimming with a jumble of thoughts and feelings. I'm very confused."

"It's no wonder." Gard took her hand in his, smoothing his thumb across her knuckles. "You almost lost your son and you're grieving the loss of your husband."

"My husband..." She squeezed her eyes closed. "I don't feel anything except for soul-deep anger for what he did to Harold, and relief that he's gone and can't hurt us anymore. The man nearly killed his own son. I'm sure I should be feeling some grief, a sense of loss. But..."

"You've been through a lot, Sabrina. It makes sense that you're going through a whirlwind of emotions. In a day or two the grief of Stuart's loss will set in and you can deal with it then." He gave her one of his charismatic smiles. "I learned that from my therapist. That's how I know it works."

"You see someone for the PTSD?" She thought that was so wise.

"Dr. Rikard Svenningsen. Wish I would have started seeing him long before I did."

"I'm glad you reached out for help. If only Stuart had agreed to see someone, maybe he could have conquered his inner demons."

Her gaze settled on the mattress. Absently smoothing her hands across the light woven cotton blanket, she told him, "Before the car accident, Stuart came home drunk. It got ugly...pretty brutal. He hurt me and Harry. I was frightened and angry."

"He hit you?" Sabrina nodded. Gard muttered something unintelligible beneath his breath.

Thinking about Harry, she felt a wistful smile take hold. "You should have seen Harry, Gard. He must have been scared to death when he saw Stuart throwing me around but he stood up to his father, trying to protect me. What did I ever do to deserve such a wonderful child?"

"Plenty. Harry's mighty lucky to have you for his mom."

"Thank you. I feel so bad that you risked your life trying to save Stuart. He didn't deserve it...doesn't deserve me spending even an instant grieving for him after what he did."

Tilting her chin up, Gard smoothed his fingers through Sabrina's hair. "What Stuart did was terrible. I hate that he hurt you and Harry. I get that you're mad as hell. You have every right to be. But you loved Stuart once and I'm sure you must have shared some happy times together." Gard's hand slid to her cheek. His expression was kind and supportive. "When the grief sets in, and it will, you shouldn't feel guilty about it. It's okay to experience grief along with anger. It doesn't make you a bad person."

Sabrina's eyebrow arched and she smiled at him. "More wise words from your therapist?"

"Bingo." His expression was jovial. "When it comes to anger and grief getting muddled together inside, trust me, I speak from firsthand experience."

Sabrina thought for a long moment. "Once I'm out of here and Harry is healing, I think I'd like to talk to Doctor Svenningsen."

"Sounds like a smart more to me," Gard agreed.

Studying his face, Sabrina skimmed her hand down his cheek. "You're a good man, Gard. Thank you for being here for me and Harry."

The loving look he gave her spoke volumes without Gard needing to utter a word as he brushed a kiss across her knuckles.

Chapter 21

Six Months Later

~<>~

"MY FIRST SUMMER at the ocean in nearly six years." Sabrina hugged herself. "This is wonderful. So nice after all those months of fog and rain." She leaned her head back on a thick, bleached driftwood log, closed her eyes and sighed. "I haven't been on a picnic in far too long. Great idea, Gard." She tugged her cardigan close over her chest.

"Cold?"

"Just right. I'd rather be a little chilly and cover up than be too hot."

"Yeah, I learned quick after moving here that Oregon's coastline isn't like California's. Summers in Glassfloat Bay often mean chilly breezes and cloudy skies. But I love it. It keeps away the hordes of tourists looking for a hot, sunny beach experience." He threw a stick across the sand and they watched Tundra chase after it.

Tundra retrieved it and plopped down, resting his head on Sabrina's crossed ankles.

"Good boy, Tundra," Sabrina praised.

Gard's gaze locked on her. He'd never seen anything more beautiful than Sabrina leisurely reclining on a blanket in the sand. He studied her profile; the creamy skin, deep red hair and serene smile. He remembered first spotting her in the café and thinking she looked like one of the delicate antique dolls his mother collected. Being so waiflike, Sabrina gave the impression of porcelain fragility.

She still looked like a doll, his very own beautiful life-size version, but she no longer looked breakable. He liked taking Sabrina out to eat, watching her enjoy her food. She admitted suffering with a nervous stomach for years because of Stuart's intimidating nature, often subsisting on little more than coffee, toast and salad. She told him the hard-to-gain support group at Laila's bakery had helped her a lot. Now with the addition of twenty pounds, Sabrina looked strong, healthy, and vibrant.

And so damn beautiful it made him ache with want.

"Harry's really doing well in summer school," she told him, shielding her eyes from the sun as she looked up. "He's excited about the spelling bee next week. I've been helping him practice."

"I'll be there to show my support."

"He'll love that."

After rescuing Harry from the fire, Gard had one final nightmare...with a twist. By the middle of the dream it had morphed from the usual deeply disturbing scenario where he'd failed to save Tim, to ending on a positive note. The last image in that dream was Tim, smiling and waving as he stood in a cloudy mist, accompanied by Helga, aka Hark, Harold's angel.

After that night, Gard's dreams took on a happier, upbeat nature, including intimate encounters with the woman he loved.

Sabrina cocked one eye open, gazing at Gard. "I feel so guilty."

After what he'd been thinking, Sabrina's words caught him by surprise. Carefully shifting his mindset, he said, "Because you're taking one Friday off? Everybody deserves some downtime, Sabrina. Especially someone who works as hard as you, picking up all those extra shifts at the café. Annalise said she can't understand how anyone can keep up that pace."

One of her shoulders lifted in a shrug, allowing the strap of her sundress to slip down, capturing his attention and lustful thoughts.

"Those extra shifts are necessary if I want to get all those medical bills for Harry paid before I'm too old to totter across the café floor balancing three plates of pancakes on one arm while holding two plates of eggs benedict with the other hand." Her laughter was genuine and bubbly as she demonstrated.

A flock of raucous seagulls flew overhead, snagging Tundra's interest. In an instant he'd bolted, barking and dashing after the feathered congregation.

"Annalise insisted you need a little R & R. And I," Gard spread his fingers on his chest, "just happened to be available to take you on a picnic. She told me she's paying you for the hours you'll miss so—"

"Which only adds to my guilt." She flipped the hair from her eyes as she propped up on her elbow. "My sister shouldn't do that."

"Come on, Sabrina, you should know Annalise lives to make other people happy. It gives her pleasure to do something for her little sister, who also happens to be her hardest working server, so no more arguments. Okay?"

"Okay," she answered softly, offering an impish smile. "So...can we open the picnic basket yet? My stomach's growling and I'm sure whatever Annalise packed for us must be delicious. Maybe a couple of her strawberry-rhubarb tarts? Or her fabulous curried chicken-apple salad with the candied ginger and pistachios?" She sat up, fumbling with the latch on the wicker basket.

"Hey, no peeking." Giving her hand a playful swat, he dragged the basket close. Sabrina's surprised expression had him laughing. He didn't want her seeing the basket's contents until the time was right. "Didn't you have anything for breakfast?"

"Bacon, eggs, toast and potatoes at the café...oh, and one of the chocolate chip pancakes Harry couldn't finish." When she caught him snickering, she added, "Hey, a girl's gotta eat." Her smile lit her whole face. "Don't look at me like that, Gard. It's your fault I've become such a foodie. Until you came along, dragging me out for one meal after another," she shot him a sideways glance while trying to hide a smile, "I hardly ever thought about eating. Besides, breakfast was early, right before I dropped Harry off at summer school."

"I can't believe he's already well enough to go back to school."

"I know! I'm so proud of him." She paused as Tundra returned, depositing a sizeable seashell next to her and wagging his tail, waiting for her approval. "Well thank you, Tundra. What a nice gift." Laughing, she mussed the fur behind his ears as he leaned into her.

Gard could have sworn his dog smiled. No doubt about it. Tundra was just as smitten with Sabrina as he was.

"I've learned my son is a determined boy. He wants to get caught up with his classes so he isn't held back a year, which is why he insisted on attending summer school." Shaking her head, Sabrina sighed. "The doctors are astounded. They didn't think he'd be doing this well so soon."

As usual, Gard found himself filled with emotion thinking of Harry's brave fight back from his life-threatening injuries at Christmas. He'd amazed not only his doctors, but everyone else who knew him with his positive, strongminded attitude.

"I've known a lot of people suffering severe injuries who gave up hope or surrendered in the battle to regain their health," Gard told her. "Harry's a shining example for them. And for me. The kid is a true inspiration." The look of motherly pride in Sabrina's eyes told him she felt the same way.

As Harry recovered in the hospital during his long stay and later during his follow-up visits with doctors and physical therapists, he graduated from a wheelchair, to crutches, and now, a cane. Gard had no doubt that before long the boy would be walking without any support.

Sabrina sat up, reaching into her purse, drawing out a tissue and dabbing her eyes.

"Hey, why the tears?" He reached over, wiping a single tear from her cheek with his thumb, caressing her face. Watching Sabrina, Tundra's head inclined to one side and he moaned.

"Because I'm so happy." Sabrina's eyes glistened as she looked up at him. "Six months ago my world was in shambles. I was filled with anger and sadness. I was so worried about Harry's recovery from that brutal beating."

While Gard still harbored intensely negative feelings for Stuart for what he'd put both Harry and Sabrina through, he kept reminding himself that Hanklen paid for his heinous deeds with his life. Each time he saw Harry limping because of the multiple bone breaks in one of his legs, Gard broke into a cold sweat, warring with himself as he struggled to gain control of his anger and vengeful thoughts.

In the past he would have been consumed by the animosity he felt toward Stuart, hoping the guy was burning in hell for his deeds. Now Gard had two excellent reasons to keep his emotions on an even keel—his love and respect for the amazing woman sitting at his side, and the wonderful little boy who had stolen his heart.

"I wouldn't be here to enjoy all this happiness if it weren't for you." She snuggled close to Gard and he breathed in her fresh, flowery scent. "The handsome glaciologist-slash-firefighter who saved me with his magical heartwish ring."

"For a guy who never believed in anything even remotely supernatural," Gard said, "I'm still astounded by it all. Nobody would ever believe it."

"I still have trouble myself," Sabrina admitted.

He took her hand in his and the heartwish stone glimmered with a soft, radiant glow.

"Have you noticed that happens each time I hold your hand?"

"Have I noticed?" Sabrina cocked her head, looking at him like he was crazy. "Are you kidding? Seriously, how could I not notice a stone that emits light each time it touches me?"

"I'll never get used to that." Gard covered the stone.

"Me neither," Sabrina agreed. "Do you know who gets the ring next?"

One night over dinner Gard had told Sabrina the entire backstory of his and Laila's rings.

"Not a clue, but Delaney, whose ring went to Laila, assured me and Laila that we'll know without a doubt when the time comes to give our rings to the next person in line."

"Does it go to another family member?"

"Not necessarily. The rings are meant for whoever needs their magic most at the time. Ultimately, they always return to the families Odin gave the stones to."

"Odin..." A smile teased at Sabrina's lips. "Sometimes I feel like I'm living in a fairytale."

"Yeah, I know. Viking gods, cookie-baking ghosts, angels and, lest we forget," he rolled his eyes, "a former genie for a brother-in-law." He held up their intertwined hands, scrutinizing the heartwish stone ring. "I used to be the world's biggest skeptic. But I'm a believer now."

Gard's lips curved in a half smile as he absently patted the picnic basket. If the day progressed as he hoped, Sabrina wouldn't be the only one who felt like she was living in a fairytale.

"This all feels so right to me." Sabrina leaned her head on Gard's shoulder. "You, me, a picnic at the beach. The two of us talking about everything under the sun." Tundra interjected a soft bark. "Yes, and you too, Tundra." She massaged behind his ears. "It's all so...normal. The way life is supposed to be."

"I feel the same way." He couldn't help wonder how many normal days Sabrina had experienced with Stuart. From what little he knew about the tense, hard-drinking guy, Gard suspected Stuart spending a relaxed, enjoyable afternoon with his wife was a rarity.

Just as he'd expected, Sabrina eventually allowed herself to experience some grief over Stuart's passing. She'd fought the feelings at first, worried any inkling of sorrow over losing him was a betrayal to Harry. Regular sessions with Dr. Svenningsen helped her iron out her emotions, get closure and some peace.

"Um, Gard?"

"Hmm?" He ran his fingers through Sabrina's hair, loving the soft, silky feel of those wavy red locks.

"Do you think we can eat now?"

That caught him off guard and had him laughing. "Boy, you've sure got a one track mind. There's something I need to say first."

Sabrina's head slanted and she looked wary. "Okay."

"Six months ago when I returned home from my expedition in Antarctica I was cranky, negative and generally miserable. While everyone else was busy making merry plans for the holidays, all I wanted was to be left alone."

"You make yourself sound like an old curmudgeon." A smile teased at Sabrina's lips. "That's very different from the Gard Malone I first met."

"It's true. I even made up a nickname for myself. The Scrinch."

"The what?" Giving a dubious look, Sabrina laughed.

"It's a hybrid name, part Scrooge, part Grinch. The Scrinch. Get it?"

"Oh, Gard, you really do know how to make me laugh. That's one of the things I love best about you."

"Anyway, all that changed the day I met a cute towheaded kid with an infectious dimpled smile and a resolute belief in angels. Things only got better when I met his mom, a woman as beautiful inside as she is outside."

He watched her expression shift from fun-loving to sentimental.

"That's one of the sweetest things I've ever heard." She clasped his hand, squeezing it. The glow from the heartwish stone shone through the slim space between their hands.

"I wonder how long it will be before I stop thinking about kissing you every time I look at you." He leaned close until his mouth was inches from hers.

"A long, long time, I hope," she whispered, her smile so sweet, her lips so inviting.

Gard took her in his arms, capturing her lips with his. He kept the kiss gentle until he heard sweet little murmurs in the back of Sabrina's throat and felt the way she clung to him as he kissed her. That was all the encouragement he needed. Gard allowed all the passion he felt pour into that kiss.

When their lips parted, Sabrina smiled, their gazes locked.

"I've wanted this for so long," she muttered against his mouth. "This...us." She sat up, gazing at him, her cheeks flushed, her lips swollen, her glistening eyes losing him in their beautiful depths. "I'm so happy when I'm with you, Gard."

"I'm awfully glad to hear you say that." Gard opened the picnic basket and drew out a small, velvet-covered ring box, opening it to display the vintage diamond ring that once belonged to his great-grandmother, Helga.

Her hands flying to her cheeks, Sabrina gasped.

"I love you, Sabrina. I want you to be my wife, to be mine forever...and for me to be Harry's dad. Sabrina, will you marry me?"

"Yes! Oh, Gard, yes!"

He slipped the ring on her finger. Perhaps there was a touch of magic at work because it was a perfect fit.

"It's stunning." She turned her hand back and forth, admiring the ring. "So unique."

"It was Helga's."

"Your great-grandmother...Hark." Happy tears sparkled in her eyes. "That makes it all the more special." Clutching the ring to her chest, she said, "I've loved you since the first time I ever saw you." She took his face in her hands, kissing him softly. "You were my secret romantic fantasy, Gard, my very own Prince Charming." Suddenly her eyes went wide. "Oh my gosh! Harry's going to be thrilled!"

"I hope so." Gard held her tight. "I'm not the world's most romantic guy, but holding my beautiful fiancée in my arms like this makes me the happiest man in the world."

They embraced for a kiss full of love, passion, and the promise of what was to come.

Sniiiiffff...

Awwww...

Shhhhh...

Click...click...click...

At the quartet of noises, Gard's and Sabrina's eyes shot open. Wide-eyed and lips still locked, they stared at each other.

"I don't believe this," Gard said, breaking their kiss. "For God's sake, please tell me that's not you, Mother."

"Not just me." Camera in hand, Astrid peeked from behind the sizeable cluster of nearby bushes. "Your sisters and Annalise are here too." The others peeked out and waved.

"Great," Gard said sarcastically, "that's just great."

"But you two just go ahead and don't pay any attention to us," Astrid urged before snapping another few photos.

Gazing up at Gard, Sabrina covered her mouth and giggled.

"Annalise," Gard looked at her, his eyes narrowed, "I told you this was supposed to be a secret."

"It is," Sabrina's sister protested. "The only people I told are your mom and Delaney...and, well, she may have mentioned it to Laila and Reen."

"That's like telling the entire Pacific shoreline," Gard grumbled.

"Oh hush, Gard," Astrid said. "After all you two have been through, there's no way we were going to miss witnessing the first tender moments of your happily ever after."

"How could you do this to me, Mom? I was—"

Click...click...

Gard tsked at his mom. "As I was saying..." Doing his best to keep his muttering free of the expletive-laden language on the tip of his tongue, he continued, "I was in the middle of proposing. A man likes a little privacy at a time like this."

"Don't exaggerate, Gard," Delaney said. "You were all done proposing."

"And it was beautiful." Reen sighed. "We got the whole thing on video." She waved her phone.

"No..." Gard dropped his head into his hand.

"This is going to be the best album," Astrid said, patting her Kodak. "I can't wait to get these developed."

"And I got some great still shots to post," Laila said.

"Do *not* put any of those online," Gard warned. "I mean it. You hear?"

"Too late," Laila said, looking at her phone. "Oh boy, you should see the comments already pouring in!"

"Let me see, let me see!" Delaney moved in close to get a look.

"Whoa, look at all those congratulatory comments," Annalise said. "And that lip-lock picture of you two is the cutest damn thing ever."

Gard uttered something beneath his breath. "You may as well know it now, Sabrina, this is what you're marrying into. Along with your sister, they," he gestured to his mother and sisters, "come as sort of a package deal. You've been forewarned."

"I wouldn't have it any other way," Sabrina said. "I love them almost as much as I love you." Tundra wedged himself between them, tongue lolling. "That goes for you too, Tundra." Wrapping one arm around Gard's neck and the other around Tundra's, she brushed a kiss across Gard's lips, then kissed Tundra above his nose, getting a lavish lick in return.

Astrid clicked away with their every motion.

"So sweet. Sabrina's the yin to his yang," Laila said on a sigh.

"The hot fudge to his ice cream." Delaney nodded.

"The cheese to his macaroni," Reen added, and the women engaged in a tuneful, collective sigh.

"The cheese to my macaroni?" Gard nearly squawked. "Seriously? You know what you guys are?" Gard pointed at them. "You're the nuts in my fruitcake." He couldn't hide his laughter. The occasion was too joyous, too special, for him to be irritated with some of the people he loved most in this world.

"Just so you know," Astrid said, a playful gleam in her eye, "I'm picking Harry up from summer school and taking him back to the condo. He's staying with me and Tore overnight." Astrid's eyebrows jiggled playfully. "If you get my drift." She followed that with an overstated wink.

"Subtle, Mom...real subtle," Gard said, failing to keep the levity from his voice.

"You'd better open that picnic basket before Sabrina keels over from hunger and the champagne gets warm," Annalise told Gard.

He did. The basket revealed cold champagne in an insulated bag and a pair of fluted glasses, caviar with toast points, crème fraîche, sieved eggs, and all the standard fixings. There was also soft brie cheese and sesame crackers, smoked salmon, some of Laila's mini cherry-almond scones, Annalise's strawberry-rhubarb tarts, and another insulated bag containing Belgian chocolate truffles.

"Wow..." Sabrina eyed the basket's contents. "Look at all this. It's a feast! I've never had caviar. And that's real French champagne. Gard, this is fabulous."

"Only the best for the future Mrs. Malone." He leaned over to give his new fiancée a quick kiss. "As much as I'd like to take credit for all this," he spread his hands over the stuffed basket, "this was all Annalise's doing. She wanted to make something extra special bec—"

"Because I knew without any doubt that you'd say yes when he *finally*," popped the question," Annalise hurried, briskly rubbing her hands together. "It's from the five of us, actually. We all chipped in."

"We placed the order for the caviar a couple months ago," Delaney said. "We knew—at least we *hoped*," she snickered, "it was only a matter of time before Gard *finally* got around to proposing."

"Sheesh." Gard laughed. "You guys make it sound like I was purposely procrastinating."

The women exchanged knowing looks. "Well..." Laila said with a shrug.

"Hey," he protested, "I was waiting bec—"

"Gard was just trying to be considerate because of everything that happened," Sabrina advised them. "Including Stuart," she added in a softer voice.

"Right." Nodding, Gard gave Sabrina a satisfied smile. "Thank you, sweetheart."

"Although I'm sure glad he *finally* got around to it," she appended with a mischievous little laugh while wrapping her hands around Gard's arm and leaning into him.

Resolved to defend himself from female bombardment, Gard opened his mouth, then closed it, realizing he was outnumbered and wasn't about to get anywhere in the midst of all the womanly comradery. So he joined them in laughter instead.

"Now why don't you two lovebirds take your basket of aphrodisiacs," Astrid offered an impish look, "and head over to Bekka House where you can enjoy this in private, without us hovering."

"Excellent idea." Gard started to get up.

"But," Astrid held up her hand, "how about a shot of the two of you toasting with your champagne glasses first?"

Gard groaned but, unwilling to rob his mom of her picture-taking joy...or another of her special Kodak moments, he agreed. He and Sabrina posed...and re-posed while Astrid took a series of photos from different angles, as well as a bunch of pics with his sisters and Annalise posing with them too.

After a small eternity, Astrid gave them a satisfied grin, announcing, "Perfect!"

"I'm sure there's more than enough here for all of us to enjoy together," Sabrina offered, gesturing to the group, then the chock-full basket. "Why don't you all sit with us and—"

"Nope." Gard hastily rose from the blanket. "I agree with my mother. There's just enough for us two lovebirds to enjoy. *In private*," he emphasized, giving the women a no-nonsense expression. Extending his hand, he pulled Sabrina to her feet. In the blink of an eye he had everything packed and they were on their way.

~<>~

"I love it here," Sabrina said as she and Gard clinked glasses and sipped champagne in the family room of Bekka House. After eating the last of her caviar-embellished toast points, she added, "I think it's the perfect place for us to..." Her gaze dropped and she cleared her throat. "Um..."

"To make love together for the first time." Gard placed their glasses on the coffee table, taking her face in his hands and kissing her tenderly. "I absolutely agree." He could hardly wait to bring Sabrina to his bed. Gard held his hand out for hers. "Let's head on upstairs and—"

"Oh..."

Oh? Oh didn't sound good.

"Have you changed your mind?" He prayed she'd say no. He'd waited six long months for this and he was ready to implode. "If you have it's okay, Sabrina. I'll understand." Gard prided himself in his patience, doing his best to do the right thing...to be proper, waiting until enough time had passed after the whole ugly incident with Stuart before making love to Sabrina. Acting like a monk was getting harder all the time but the last thing he wanted was to make her uncomfortable.

In the midst of his deep, complex, soul-wrenching inner angst, Sabrina laughed. She *laughed*!

"Changed my mind?" Surprising the hell out of him, she repositioned herself, sitting on his lap. She dragged his shirt up from his waistband and slid her hands up his chest, skin on skin. The little purring sounds in her throat as her cool hands roved his chest drove him wild.

It was the first time she'd touched him in an intimate way. It felt damn good. Her sultry sigh as her fingers explored his pecs had him hardening in an instant.

"Not on your life," she assured him, planting a kiss on his jaw, then trailing kisses down his neck. "Mr. Malone, I've thought a lot about us making love, wondering what it would be like. Wondering..." Her gaze dropped to his crotch and, clearly aware of what was there, she blushed.

She was a grown, experienced woman but that innocent blush of Sabrina's never failed to get to him. Though he wouldn't have thought it possible, he grew harder still.

When she looked up again, into his eyes, she said, "What I mean is, I've daydreamed and night-dreamed and cooked up all sorts of fantasies in my head about what it would be like to..." Gard watched her pale cheeks burnish to an even deeper pink. "Well, you know." She shrugged.

"Oh yeah...I know." He pulled off his shirt to let her see what her fingers were so busy exploring.

"Mmm-hmm, I knew it," she said with a throaty laugh.

"Knew what?"

"That you'd have the body of a superhero. Look at all those muscles."

He drew her close, the cotton lace on her neckline abrading his chest. One by one, he unbuttoned the tiny pearl buttons down her front, opening her dress and nearly passing out with lust when he caught his first glimpse of her breasts, cradled in a silky pale-pink bra. The partially naked flesh and blood Sabrina was even sexier than the fully naked version in his fantasies. His fingers, and every other part of him, itched to get her naked and beneath him.

"It's just," she breathed into his ear, "that when you said we should go upstairs, well, I thought it might be kind of nice to enjoy our first time together here in the family room."

"Here? On the couch?" His thumb circled her breast, where his gaze was transfixed. "Like a couple of horny teenagers?"

"Exactly like that." Her head dropped back and he watched her eyebrows wiggle with mischief. "This is my favorite room in the house. But we have to set the scene first." She jumped off his lap, leaving him feeling empty and alone.

"We do?" As far as he was concerned, two naked, willing bodies was all the scene setting he needed.

"Mmm-hmm. First we'll close the vertical blinds, just—"

"Just in case our favorite group of five decides to come nosing around," Gard guessed.

"Better safe than sorry." Exchanging a knowing glance with Gard, Sabrina walked to one corner of the room where she bent to pick up an electrical cord. "For ambience, I'll plug in the light wheel so it spins its colored lights on the aluminum Christmas tree." She stood back, admiring her work. "Isn't that pretty?"

Gard wondered what it was about women and that old metal Christmas tree. But, heck, if it turned Sabrina on, he was totally on board.

"Very," he answered, barely seeing the tree as he watched her instead. "But I see something a lot prettier."

"Thank you." She did a mock curtsey. "I remember you talking to me when I was in the coma, telling me the story behind this tree."

"You do?" He'd sat in her hospital room talking incessantly about whatever popped into his head. He didn't even remember telling her about the tree.

"I loved hearing about it." She stood still, gazing at him. "I loved hearing your voice." She did a slow twirl and her dress swished around her knees. "Know what I'd like you to do?"

"Whatever it is, I'm at your service." He salivated at the sensual notions flitting through his head. "What is it you want me to do, pretty lady?"

"I want you to come over here..." Sabrina crooked her finger in invitation, "and build a roaring fire in the fireplace."

Gard's anticipatory expression deflated.

"When you're done," she continued with a seductive smile, "we'll finish the last of our champagne, get naked, and then..." Her beckoning expression said it all.

"You want a roaring fire just a few days before July?" Gard asked, dumfounded. As soon as the words left his mouth he knew he was an idiot.

"I-I thought it would be romantic." Sabrina's sexy smile vanished. "Silly idea?"

Hell. Now he'd gone and made her feel stupid and uncomfortable.

Transforming from kittenish vixen to insecure female in the blink of an eye, she gazed up at him, waiting for his response. In that instant he decided that if his fiancée thought it would be romantic to have sex on the couch in front of a decades-old Christmas tree and a raging fire at the end of June, then that's what they'd damn well do.

"On the contrary, I think it's a wonderful idea. I should have thought of it myself. There's nothing more romantic than a blazing fire." *In the middle of summer.*

Sabrina's eyes lit up again.

As soon as he finished building the fire, he turned, just in time to see Sabrina shimmying out of her dress until it pooled at her feet on the floor. Smiling as she stood before him in nothing but her matching pink bra and panties, she looked like a confection begging to be licked, nibbled and savored. Bending at the waist to pick up her dress, she posed to give him the best shot of her cleavage.

Gard swallowed hard. How could he have gotten this lucky? The woman was exquisite. She exuded charm, intelligence, wittiness and a heaping helping of sex appeal. The fact that she was kind and sweet was the icing on the cake.

The perfect woman. *His* perfect woman.

God how he loved her.

Sabrina's smile was ear to ear as she eyed him. She issued an unmistakable invitation with her eyes and like an obedient puppy, Gard closed the distance between them.

In a nanosecond they both stood naked, their hands traveling each other's bodies, exploring, loving, learning, enjoying.

Gard carried Sabrina to the couch, depositing her there. Lifting their champagne flutes, he quickly gazed around the room, agreeing her ideas had indeed made their first time together more romantic.

"A toast." He handed Sabrina her glass. "To the power of love and magic."

"And to heartwish stones and angels," she added, tears of happiness glistening in her eyes.

"To everlasting love with the woman of my heart...my soul."

"And the man of mine."

Linking arms, they finished their champagne, before engaging in the first of many loving, passion-filled joinings to come.

Chapter 22

Six Months Later: Christmas Eve

~<>~

STANDING ROOM ONLY was something rare to see at Good Samaritan Community Church, even at holiday time. But this evening, as the Sunday school cast of the Christmas Eve play took their bows, parishioners, townspeople, and local media had packed the church's small main room.

With the sermon and the nativity play completed, Annalise's thoughts wandered to a more troubling time as the pastor droned on with announcements of milestone birthdays, special events and other newsy happenings before the congregation was dismissed and invited for refreshments in the meeting room.

Remembering the frightening car accident just outside the church a year ago pained her. Like everyone else, she feared they'd lose Sabrina. And they would have if it hadn't been for that wonderful bit of hocus pocus Gard pulled off with his heartwish ring. She didn't know how it all worked, only that it most assuredly had—and she'd been blessed to be a part of it.

She looked up at the front of the contemporary-style church, seeing the proud grin on little Harold Malone's face as the children sat on the floor of the manger scene, waiting for Pastor Bengston to finish.

They'd almost lost Harry too...until two honest to goodness angels intervened—one in the guise of a brave human firefighter, and the other a bona fide heavenly creature, complete with wings and a colorful crocheted coat.

Magic. The very idea was preposterous. Never one to believe in such *nonsense*, as she used to call it, Annalise had received a crash course in its existence and miraculous power firsthand.

While last year wreaked havoc with everyone's emotions, leaving those who knew Sabrina and her son doubtful either of them could hope for a happy outcome, this Christmas was the polar opposite. There was a clear sense of love, laughter, and joyous celebration in the air—even more than the usual abundant merriment of the holiday season.

Amid last year's turmoil Griffin's Café had won first prize for best holiday window display because of Sabrina's wonderfully whimsical and detailed artwork. This year the café won the prize for the second time. Everything about the imaginative painted windows was striking but those in the know were especially captivated by the painted image of the smiling angel in the patchwork coat watching over the town of Glassfloat Bay.

"Look at those adorable little munchkins," Annalise said just above a whisper, elbowing Astrid on one side and Delaney on the other. "Harry and Lilly were perfect as Joseph and the angel, weren't they? I'm so happy he finally got his chance to play Joseph."

"He's come so far in a year," Delaney said. "I can't wait until he sees the big surprise birthday party we're throwing for him tomorrow. He may have missed celebrating turning five, but we'll make sure his sixth birthday makes up for that."

"I've never seen Gard look so happy." Laila gazed at her brother and Sabrina sitting together across the aisle. Leaning forward in the pew, she told Astrid, "Look how he's beaming, Mom."

Glancing over at them, Astrid radiated delight. "He's deeply in love."

"They both are," Reen noted. "It looks like Sabrina has stars in her eyes."

Exchanging happy, teary-eyed smiles, the five women clasped hands together and sighed.

~<>~

"Look at him, Gard." Sabrina looped her arm through his as she leaned close. "Harry looks so proud, doesn't he?"

"He should be." Gard gazed at the cute costumed kids and gave Harry a thumbs-up, earning an ear-to-ear grin in return. "Harry waited a whole year to play Joseph and he did one heck of a job." Covering his wife's hand with his, Gard inclined his head to deposit a kiss at her temple. "Our boy's come a long way this past year. He barely ever stutters and his limp is nearly gone."

"Harry's braver than I could ever hope to be," Sabrina said. "I'm so proud of him I could shout."

"Better wait until we get outside, or at least until Pastor Bengston is finished with his endless news updates," Gard teased. "Then we'll shout together, because I feel the same way. In fact..." he gazed around the filled church, taking in all the smiles and happy tears, "I bet we're not the only ones bursting with pride for that incredible young man. Harry's endeared himself to the entire community."

Returning his attention to the front of the church, Gard looked over the wide, colorful backdrop designed for the nativity play. Sabrina had painted a striking scene, complete with Hark spreading her wings above the infant's manger.

By now, most of Glassfloat Bay, including local media, were familiar with the miraculous story of Harold and his angel. Gard knew people had doubts about what happened, but they kept their misgivings to themselves, focusing instead on celebrating Harry and Sabrina's remarkable recoveries.

"All the work you put into the backdrop really paid off," Gard told Sabrina. "It's lively and colorful. The wood looks like wood, the straw looks like straw, and the barnyard animals look like something straight out of a children's picture book."

She'd done a lot of painting in the past year, returning to the use of SabrinArt as her artist name. Gard was glad, believing a creative gift like hers needed to be seen and shared. That's obviously what Hugo Calloway, owner of Glimmer Hope Art Gallery, thought after viewing Sabrina's portfolio. Her first SabrinArt gallery showing was scheduled for February. Gard knew it would be a great success. She was well on her way to a lucrative career doing what she loved most.

"Thank you, Gard." She squeezed his arm. "I enjoyed doing the backdrop so much, especially knowing Harry would be playing Joseph in front of that scene."

"I'm sure you know my favorite element."

Smiling at Gard, Sabrina patted his knee. "Hark's my favorite too. Never," her chin trembled and a tear trickled down her cheek, "could I have imagined that one year after such despair this...*us*...could ever happen. Not only am I lucky enough to be married to the most wonderful man I've ever known, but my son...*our* son," a bright smile took hold, "is blessed with the kind of father he deserves."

"Trust me, Sabrina, the lucky one is me." Gard lifted her chin, brushing a kiss across her lips. They were married on the first day of autumn in the family room of Bekka House, next to the aluminum Christmas tree. Sabrina's parents traveled to Oregon from San Diego for the ceremony and her dad gave the bride away. Nevan was Gard's best man, and Harry was the ring bearer.

The Malone clan was especially glad when the youngest sister, Kady, finally made it home from her overseas backpacking trip in time for her brother's wedding.

"We're so fortunate, Gard. Harry is so excited about you being his dad he's practically bouncing off the walls."

"Remember on our wedding day when Harry asked me if it's okay to call me Dad? Here I was worried he wouldn't be comfortable because...well, I was afraid he'd think I was trying to take Stuart's place."

"Harry's crazy about you, Gard. He has been since he first met you. His talks with Hark helped him put things in perspective about Stuart. She helped him understand that he wasn't being disloyal to his father's memory by loving you and calling you Dad."

"That angel really knows her stuff." Gard breathed an audible sigh as Pastor Bengston concluded his prolonged list of announcements. "Finally. I thought he'd never finish."

"Shhh. You sound like a naughty schoolboy," Sabrina accused.

"You make me feel like that lots of times." Gard's eyebrows jiggled playfully.

"Shame on you, Gerhard. You're not supposed to say things like that in church."

"It's your fault. I can't help how you make me feel." His gaze swept over her. "Think of all the fun we'll have when Harry goes to Annalise's for his birthday pajama party tonight." Lowering his voice into a near growl, Gard promised, "I'll show you just how much of a bad boy I can really be." He squeezed Sabrina close. "I love you, sweetheart."

"I love you too. More than you'll ever know." People were rising from their pews. "Looks like we need to get downstairs to the meeting room for coffee and cookies." Sabrina got to her feet, pulling Gard up along with her, standing out of the way so people could get by.

"Right. Harry's going to be center stage getting all the attention," Gard said. "That's something I definitely don't want to miss."

~<>~

"Mom, Dad! Did I do a good job?" Harry asked, running up to his parents as soon as he spotted them.

"Harry, buddy, you nailed it. You were the best Joseph in the history of all Josephs," Gard assured, bending to give him a hug. "Your mom and I are so proud of you." Looking at Harry's elated face, Gard felt his heart expand, bursting with love and happiness.

"You were wonderful, sweetie." Sabrina wrapped Harry in a big hug. "I've never seen a better Joseph performance."

"Thanks! I know you two have to say that because you're my parents." Harry offered a playful smile. "But I think I did a pretty good job." He gave Sabrina and Gard kisses on their cheeks. "I'm glad we became a regal family. I love you both so much. And Tundra too!"

"I think you mean legal," Sabrina corrected with a chuckle. "And we love you too."

"Oh I don't know," Gard said. "I think Harry was spot on when he called us regal. When we got married we were the king, queen, royal prince, and imperial pooch of Glassfloat Bay—at least for a day."

"You'll never know, not even in a million, bazillion years," Harry said, grabbing Gard and squeezing tight, "how happy I am that you're my dad. I'm so happy I don't even mind too much about not seeing Hark anymore."

Gard and Sabrina exchanged glances.

"What do you mean, honey?" Sabrina asked.

"Hark told me she'll always watch over us, and I can still talk to her, but I won't see or hear her anymore. She said I'm part of a happy, loving family now, which is even better than having an angel for a friend. She promised that one day, many years from now, I'll see her again up in heaven."

With both Gard and Sabrina still bending low, Harry gathered them in his arms. "I think our life together is wonderful," he said.

"Almost like heaven, except for us not having wings or harps. I'm the luckiest boy in the world. I love you Mommy and Daddy."

With the fragrance of *pepperkaker* perfuming the air, and the sounds of the church choir singing "Hark! The Herald Angels Sing," the heartwish stone ring on Gard's finger glowed bright, enveloping the Malone family in the light and warmth of forever love.

~<>~

Turn the page for a sneak peek of **THE KNITTER'S HEARTWISH**, book 4 in the Heartwishes series, featuring Gard's sister, Maureen (Reen), a woman with a heart of gold and a craft closet bursting with more yarn anyone could ever use in one lifetime.

ABOUT THE KNITTER'S HEARTWISH

Maureen Malone loves creating quirky handknitted character hats for the kids at the hospital where she volunteers. When delivering hats to the children's ward, Reen's usually wearing one with long yarn braids herself. The kids giggle, the nurses grin, and some people pretend not to see her. If she can provide a healing dose of laughter, looking silly doesn't bother Reen. She's convinced humor is as important as being proficient in calculus, well-read in Shakespeare, or appreciative of operas that leave her clueless.

Slipping on an icy step, Reen breaks her ankle and tailbone. Witnessing her fall, friend and neighbor, Professor Drake Slattery, takes her to the hospital. With dark, wavy hair and blue-gray eyes, the handsome single dad is brilliant, organized, and a lover of classic literature and opera. Reen's polar opposite.

Her lack of common sense and irrational habit of acting before thinking drive Drake mad. A bona fide packrat, Reen fills her house with secondhand finds and countless skeins of yarn. He sometimes wonders if she has yarn for brains.

That said, Drake wouldn't change a thing about her. He's watched the beautiful blonde knit until her fingers bleed, completing a new batch of imaginative hats for the ailing kids. There's no finer, funnier, kinder person than Maureen Malone. His twins love her. And so does he.

Of course, none of that matters because, the one time he tried to kiss her, Reen made it crystal clear she thinks of Drake like a brother.

Heartwishes, Book 4: Friends-to-lovers, tender-hearted befuddled heroine, irresistible hottie professor, meddlesome friends and family, abundant humor, and a magical miraculous wish. This guaranteed

HEA romcom can be read as a standalone but is better appreciated when read in order.

~<>~

Turn the page to read Chapter 1 of The Knitter's Heartwish...

The Knitter's Heartwish: Chapter 1

Early January: Glassfloat Bay, Oregon

~<>~

"AFTER SPENDING a few days with him, I've decided he looks like a Mortimer." Maureen Malone texted a photo to her sister as they spoke. "Morty for short. What do you think, Laila?"

A moment later, gentle laughter came over the phone. "Oh my gosh, Reen, he's darling. And look at those soulful eyes! You're right, that's the perfect name for him."

"Good, then Mortimer the Dragon it is."

"Which kid requested a dragon hat with orange hair?"

"Lucas Carmody. He's got pale skin with a flock of freckles, and had thick orangey-red hair before he lost it. I think the green and orange yarn will look good on him." Reen gave a satisfied smile as she affixed a small cellophane-wrapped piece of marzipan candy to the hat she'd knitted. The tiny marzipan dragon with a replica of the little boy's freckled face that she and Laila had created complemented the hat's whimsical visage.

"Instead of using safety pins I'm tying the packets of candy with ribbon, looping it through the knitted fabric. I thought that would be safer for children's fingers." Reen packed the hat and matching candy in the box along with the other knitted and crocheted hats and corresponding molded marzipan treats.

"Good thinking. With all the needle pokes those poor kids must get, I'm sure the last thing they'd want is to prick a finger on a pin."

Among her yarn creations keeping the dragon company in the shirt-size box was a baby blue aviator cap with pink knitted goggles on top; a purple Viking hat with a curly, crocheted red beard attached; a happy, tongue-lolling Dalmatian hat; a lion mane cap;

a teddy bear hat; and some Valentine-themed hats for next month's holiday.

Reen smiled as she looped tiny marzipan princess likenesses through the yarn on a pair of bejeweled princess crown hats. One child's face was tinted a light beige color, while the other was tinted the same soft copper shade as the little girl who'd receive it.

"I'm proud of the job I did on these hats," she said, snapping a side-by-side photo of the identical princess hats and sending it to Laila. "It's my first attempt at creating coily hair. What do you think?"

"Look at those adorable halos of corkscrew curls!" Laila said. "They match the pink squiggles we made on the marzipan princesses. How did you manage to get yarn to hold a tight spiral like that?"

Gently bouncing the springy hair, Reen said, "Ruthie Brone from the yarn shop gave me instructions. I wrapped yarn around skinny wood dowel rods, tying the ends so they wouldn't unravel. I soaked them in water, put them on a cookie sheet, and baked them in a 200-degree oven until dry, about fifteen minutes. Once everything was cool, I carefully unwrapped the yarn from the dowels to keep the coils nice and tight and, *voila*! It was time consuming but really easy. I'm very happy with the results."

"They're perfect. So who requested the pink coily hair?"

"Cute story," Reen told her, smiling at the memory. "The light colored marzipan princess is for Ava Mitchell, whose hair was blonde before it fell out, and the darker toned princess is for Shannon Brone, whose hair was dark auburn. The last—"

"Brone? Any relation to Ruthie?"

"Her great-granddaughter. Poor thing's been ill a long time. The last time I volunteered, Ava told me she and Shannie want to be twins, and asked if I could make them matching hats with super curly pink hair so they could look the same. Isn't that sweet?"

"It really is. They're going to love the hats, Reen."

"I hope so. I'm getting excited imagining the smiles on the faces of the kids when I deliver all of these," she told Laila. "Your idea to include matching candies with their likenesses was pure genius. The miniature candy versions turned out adorable. I know how busy you've been at the bakery, so I really appreciate you taking the time to do this with me."

"You've already thanked me seven billion times," Laila teased. "Believe me, helping you with this project was my pleasure. Whatever we can do for those precious kids at the hospital is a top priority as far as I'm concerned. Honestly, your talent with yarn still amazes me, Reen. Those character hats you make are incredible...like cartoons come to life. It's no wonder the kids are crazy about them. I wish I wasn't such a giant dork when it comes to knitting."

"Don't be silly, Laila, you're not a giant dork. You're just...um..."

With Reen's phone on speakerphone, Laila's laughter rang through the room.

"See? You can't even come up with a semi-plausible compliment about my sorry knitting attempts. I can almost hear the gears grinding in your head as you try like hell to come up with a synonym for *knitting challenged*."

"No, I was about to say that your...your crocheting is really coming along nicely," Reen hurried, as images of her sister's atrocious knitting and crocheting efforts flitted across her mind. "Anyway, your special set of skills are baking-related. We both know I'm as much a dork in the kitchen as you are with a pair of knitting needles."

"No you're not." Laila's tone was unconvincing.

"Ha! Without your magical kitchen wizardry I never would have been able to create a batch of marzipan. Heck, I didn't even know what the stuff was before, and now it's one of my favorite things to eat! And then coloring the individual portions with the all-natural food colorings you came up with? Sheesh, Laila, I mean, I was right there in the kitchen making them with you and I still can't quite figure out how we did it," Reen admitted.

"It was fun. I enjoyed it. Don't forget the nut-free cookie versions and the sugar-free marzipan versions."

"I've got them labeled with the children's names to keep them separate." Reen nodded to herself as she spoke. "I'm so glad you suggested checking with the nurses to see if any of the kids have food allergies, sensitivities, or possible food interactions with their medication before passing out the marzipan. It never even crossed my mind."

"That's why I'm the older, smarter sister," Laila quipped.

"Nope, forget about it, Hazelnut," Reen addressed her dog with a tsk. "I already told you marzipan isn't healthy for you. Hazel's been exceedingly attentive and affectionate," she told Laila, chuckling as she tousled the dog's fur. "That nose of hers has been going a mile a minute since we made the marzipan."

"I can imagine. Your little rescue dog certainly is a charmer."

"Little?" Eyeing Hazelnut, Reen laughed. "She's grown into more of a rescue pony. But I love my cutie pie." Wrapping an arm around Hazelnut, Reen drew her in for a hug, speaking to her in baby talk. "She's my baby, aren't you, Hazel?" The dog's tail twirled like a whirlwind. "That's why I have to take care of you and make sure you don't eat foods that are bad for you."

"So which hat are you wearing now?"

"My responsible dog owner hat, of course."

"Ha! Good one." Laila chirped a laugh. "You know what I mean."

Reen's smile stretched wide. "What makes you think I'm even wearing one?" she asked, tugging on the pair of thick, long, buttery-yellow yarn braids framing her cheeks.

"Because I know you, Maureen."

"Hmm, too well, it seems. Okay, smarty pants, I'm wearing the knitted pink Viking hat with two ivory-colored horns stuffed with pillow filling," she patted one as she spoke, "and yellow braids hanging down. It turned out cute. I look just like that woman in the opera."

"What opera?"

"Oh...you know..." Folding two layers of tissue paper over the hats in the box, Reen struggled to recall the opera or character's name.

"Nope. I don't"

"Remember the Bugs Bunny cartoon where Elmer Fudd sings 'Kill da wabbit, kill da wabbit!' in a loud opera voice and there's this rotund Viking diva wearing a horned helmet?" Reen motioned to her knitted cap. "That opera."

Laughing, Laila replied, "Yeah, I think I know the one you mean."

A diehard knitter, Reen loved creating themed hats for the kids at the children's hospital in Wisdom Harbor, just down the coast from Glassfloat Bay. She volunteered there and had a shift this morning. After seeing those brave children who'd lost their hair from chemotherapy and other treatments she was determined to do whatever she could to help make them smile.

"I heard the kids loved the hand puppets you made them for Christmas," Laila said.

"I'm so glad. When I delivered them I asked what else they'd like me to create. Honest to God, Laila, my heart nearly broke when one sweet little girl smiled shyly while patting her bald head, asking, 'Maybe you could knit me some hair?'

"Aw...poor little thing." Laila offered a sympathetic sigh.

"Several of the kids made similar requests. One asked if I could make her a bunch of purple braids, and one of the boys wanted to know if I could make him a hat that looks like a skunk." Reen chuckled at the memory. "One by one they offered their creative suggestions and I was delighted to take on the challenge."

"Just how many hats and caps have you made over the past few months?"

With an inadvertent shrug, Reen answered, "Probably more than a hundred."

"Yikes, you're a veritable knitting machine!"

On her last volunteer shift Reen encouraged the children to draw colorful crayon pictures of the hats they'd like to have, promising she'd do her best to bring their artwork to life. This morning she'd be picking up the drawings and couldn't wait to see what their youthful imaginations had conjured.

Today's delivery included her most creative attempts so far. Seeing her wear one of the hats when she arrived at the children's ward made the kids giggle and the nurses grin, so Reen happily donned a different one each time she made the trip. Not surprisingly the quirky hats made other drivers laugh or give her curious looks on the road, which is why she chose to wear a hat in the car as well.

She believed everyone could benefit from a dose of unexpected laughter now and then, and was happy to provide it. While some people boasted college degrees and were academics, Reen thought making people smile was every bit as important as being proficient in calculus, or being well read in Shakespeare.

The one element her hats had in common was attached yarn hair that had been braided, knitted, crocheted, or left flowing in colorful strings, even if it was just a small amount peeking out the bottom of the caps.

"Hold on a minute while I pick up these boxes," Reen told her sister. After tucking her blonde curls behind her ears, she wedged the phone between her ear and shoulder, then lifted a stack of the boxes from the living room coffee table with an *ooph*.

"I really should make two trips instead," she muttered.

"That would be too easy," Laila chided.

Discarding her own chastising inner wisdom, Reen struggled, adding the last sizeable box to the pile. The large, rectangular, shallow boxes weren't heavy, just awkward.

Peeking around the lidded boxes in her arms, she spotted the look Hazelnut gave her. "Hazel's giving me her typical forlorn, guilt-inducing *You're just going to go out and leave me here all alone again, aren't you?* expression."

"She must have learned it from Friday," Laila said. "He does that to me every time I pick up my purse."

"Be a good girl, Hazel. I'll be back later...I promise." Still looking mopey, Hazelnut gave a soft, reciprocating bark. Reen couldn't imagine what she'd do without her friendly, often goofy, oversized mutt.

Opening the front door, Reen was greeted with a brisk chill. "Whoa, it's cold outside."

"Yup, we've got one of those unusually cold Pacific Northwest winters," Laila agreed. "If you'd let me help you organize your garage like I keep offering, you could park your car in there instead of outside."

"I know, I know." Reen wished she'd listened to her sister. The garage was stacked with clear plastic storage bins holding countless skeins of yarn, assorted knitting needles, crochet hooks, and endless projects in various stages of completion.

To make matters worse, she was a card-carrying packrat, evidenced by her factual *Warning: I brake for garage sales* bumper sticker.

"One day I'll get everything neat and organized," she vowed to Laila as well as herself as she stepped outside. "I'll actually be able to use the garage for the purpose it was intended." At least that's what she kept promising herself. It was an ambitious goal for a woman who'd saved every scrap of artistically crayoned paper any child had ever given her.

Laila mumbled something inaudible in response.

"What was that? You're not making fun of your poor packrat sister again, are you?"

"Nope, just snickering because we're like two peas in a pod...messy, overpacked pods."

Reen's pie in the sky dream list also included owning her own yarn shop one day. Two things stood in her way—finances, and the fact that String Me Along, the long-established store where she got most of her knitting and crochet supplies, had been a treasured fixture in Glassfloat Bay for decades. Ruthie Brone opened the shop fifty years ago.

After Reen's mom, Astrid, failed in her attempts to teach Reen to knit and crochet, Astrid suggested she take a class at String Me Along. It was in sweet old Ruthie Brone's classes just a few years ago where Reen became almost as addicted to knitting as she was to chocolate.

Ruthie had the patience of a saint. The Brones were good people and Reen couldn't imagine opening a competing shop in the same town. Since moving away from Glassfloat Bay and people she'd grown to love since relocating from Chicago wasn't an option, bye-bye yarn shop ownership.

"After I deliver the hats to the kids I'll come to the bakery to work on those Valentine's Day flyers. You've come up with a mouthwatering assortment of sugar-free and gluten-free treats this year, Laila. So far the scones with the hazelnut paste in the center are my favorite."

"I knew they would be. Drive carefully. It's icy out there and we're not used to driving on icy roads like we were when we lived in Chicago."

"Okay, Mom," Reen teased. "Seriously, Laila, sometimes I think you worry about me almost as much as you worry about the twins." She laughed. "I'm a big girl now who can take care of herself."

Making sure her phone was securely lodged in place before pulling the front door closed behind her, Reen smiled over her shoulder at her mopey dog. "Quit your sulking, Hazelnut. You know I always come ba—"

In the blink of an eye, Reen slipped on the icy concrete step, going down with a mighty thud, and startled yelp. Her arms flailed while her phone and the boxes she carried flew into the air before sprawling around her.

Stunned, she sat there with one leg folded beneath her in an awkward position. It all happened so fast she wasn't sure if she was injured or merely surprised.

"Reen? Maureen? What happened? Are you all right?" Laila's alarmed voice sounded far away.

"Yeah...I think so." Reen was surprised to see the phone was no longer at her shoulder. She had no idea where it was. "I fell on the step. Practically knocked myself out."

"Maureen, I can't hear you. Reenie, what's happening?"

"I'm all right, Laila, don't worry," she called out. "I guess the phone fell when I did."

"What?"

"Aw, I'm okay, Hazel," Reen assured the concerned dog who'd come outside, whimpering while nuzzling and licking her. But as soon as she tried moving, both her tailbone and her ankle told her she hadn't come away from her fall unscathed. From the amount of pain, she suspected a bad sprain.

"Maureen!"

Reen blinked in confusion. That was odd...Laila's voice had lowered a few octaves.

Still dazed, she turned to see Drake Slattery bolting out of his car and running toward her. "Drake?"

"You're bleeding," he noted.

"Bleeding?" Laila yelled. "Reen is bleeding? Drake is that you? What the hell happened? Drake? Reen...? Will somebody please talk to me?"

When she looked down at her legs Reen was surprised to see so much blood coming through the thin, torn slacks of her pink volunteer uniform.

"I didn't realize," she said.

Drake looked left and right. "Where's your phone?"

"I have no idea."

"It's okay, Laila," Drake said after retrieving Reen's phone, which had slid across the icy lawn, landing almost at the sidewalk. "Reen slipped and fell hard. I saw it happen. It might be a sprain or a break. I'm taking her to the ER. I'll call you from there."

Reen grabbed her phone from Drake. "I'm fine, Laila, just a little banged up, that's all. I don't need a doctor. I just..." she took in a deep breath as a wave of pain hit, "...I just need to relax for a minute before I get up."

"I'm taking you," Drake said.

"No, you're not."

"Maureen Malone," Laila all but screamed in her sister's ear, "either you let Drake take you to the hospital or I swear, I'm calling an ambulance."

"Okay, okay! Sheesh, Laila, tone down that mom voice of yours, okay?" Reen managed a sickly little laugh. "I'm fine. I'll see you later, after I go to the doctor and get the hats delivered." She ended the call.

Her fingers ran across the edge of the step she sat on. It was rough as well as icy. "That damned stone step has jagged edges. I should have had it fixed long ago." Those were the things her late fiancé, Bob Brechler, used to do for her before he was killed falling from the slick, moss-covered roof trying to repair loose shingles of the fixer-upper house they'd bought together.

"I should have noticed that and fixed it myself," Drake said. "I'll get to that this weekend."

Reen winced. Not from pain but because, as book-smart as Drake was, his comically bad handyman projects were almost legendary.

"There's really no need, Drake. You're busy enough as it is and I don't want to impose on you."

"You're not—"

"I'll give Hudson a call to come over and take care of it." Noting his slightly dejected expression as she smiled up at him, Reen quickly added, "You already do more than enough for me. You're a great friend." The last thing she wanted to do was make him feel bad.

For some reason he looked even more disappointed and she wasn't sure why.

Both professors at Wisdom Harbor University, her late fiancé, Bob, and Drake had been close friends. The same year Bob died, Drake's wife, Janet, walked out on him and their two children, leaving Drake for another man. Reen adored his kids, watching them often for Drake when he had a scheduling conflict. The guy was a great dad.

Returning his attention to her injury, Drake frowned. "You need to get this looked at right away."

"No need. I'm fine, Drake."

"Should I call your sister back?" he threatened.

That had Reen laughing. "Oh my God, no!" Smoothing her fingers over Hazelnut's fur, she leaned in to hug her angsty dog. "Shhh, don't cry, Hazel, sweetie, I'm okay."

"I saw it happen as I was pulling out of my garage." He nodded a few doors down. Drake was the one who'd suggested the house for sale to Reen and Bob when they got engaged, making the two friendly couples neighbors.

"What's happening, Dad?" his son, Kevin, called from the car. "Is Miss Reen okay?" He opened the car door and he and his sister, Lilly, got out.

"Hey, remember I told you that I need you two to stay in the car," Drake told his six-year-old twins. "Miss Reen is going to be fine." He returned his attention to her while the curious and concerned kids ignored his instructions and came to Reen's side. Drake tsked at them but didn't press the matter.

"Maureen, you fell hard. Your legs are all cut up, and I don't like the look of the way that leg is bent. Can you move it?"

"Sure..."

Hearing her moan at the attempt, Drake gently helped untangle her leg from beneath her.

His hands were all over her legs, examining them as he rolled her pant legs up to her knees. "Look at that ankle," he said, his eyebrows arrowing down as he removed her shoe and sock. His touch was warm, gentle, tender. If she wasn't in agony, she'd enjoy all the attention.

As Drake's fingers gingerly explored her flesh, he frowned. "It's swelling fast. I'm getting you to the emergency room."

"No, really, Drake," she rested her hand on his shoulder, "I'm just a little stunned and scuffed up. I'll be fine in a minute." She tried to be cavalier but when she shifted position her attempted laugh came out sounding more like a sick moose. "I fell on my tailbone," she said, wincing. "If you could just help me get to my feet, I can—" Clinging to the arm of his tweed sport coat with the suede elbow patches, she tried pulling herself up, giving up quickly as pain and dizziness took hold.

"Huh..." she blinked fast, "looks like I did a number on myself."

"I think your ankle might be broken."

"How is that possible? All I did is fall off a step. I haven't had a single broken bone in all my life. I'm sure it's just a bad twist."

"Kevin, Lilly," Drake said, "you two get in the front seat of the car. I'm going to put Miss Reen in the back so she can stretch out her leg." Looking around him he asked, "What are all these boxes?"

"Hats I made for the kids in the hospital," Reen explained. Amazingly none of the box lids had come off. It would have been a shame for the hats to get soiled, or the marzipan candies smashed, before delivering them to the children. "Like this one," she flipped her yarn braids.

When Drake looked at Reen, she could swear his eyes twinkled as he smiled and happy crinkles bracketed his blue-gray eyes. "Well you make a spectacular Brynhildr. All you're missing is the spear."

"Bryn who?" Reen asked, her eyebrows scrunching.

"In Germanic mythology," Drake explained, "Brynhildr, more commonly known as Brunhilde, was a shieldmaiden and a Valkyrie. Have you ever heard the expression, *It's not over until the fat lady sings?*"

Lilly gave a thoughtful frown. "Are you saying Miss Reen looks fat, Daddy?"

He stopped in the midst of planting one box on top of another, a minor look of alarm crossing his features and he gave his lips a nervous lick. "Oh...no, no, of course not, Lilly. It's a reference to Brunhilde's famous scene of sacrifice in *Götterdämmerung*."

Her head tilted, birdlike, Lilly looked up at her dad. "Gotter..."

While Reen imagined the average man was clueless about Brunhilde, who she guessed must have been the Viking diva in the Bugs Bunny cartoon, Drake, a professor of ancient history and classical archaeology, was most definitely not your average man. He was like a walking, talking encyclopedia. He could probably rival Google.

They'd become good friends since Bob died and Janet left. During that time Reen learned Drake was as fanatical about opera, classic literature and Masterpiece Theater as most guys were about football or baseball. Once locked onto a subject of interest, he could go on at length about things that were usually way over Reen's head...and often fairly boring, at least to her. But she liked hearing him talk anyway, and was getting better all the time at suppressing her natural yawn response.

In this case, his operatic facts were happily distracting her from focusing too much on her pain.

"It's *Der Ring des Nibelungen*, the last in Richard Wagner's cycle of four music dramas," he explained to Lilly, who looked like she was suppressing a yawn herself. "When Brunhilde learns of Siegfried's death she's overcome with grief and commits suicide by throwing herself on his funeral pyre so she could join him in death."

His daughter's previously bored expression morphed as her eyes flew wide, her bottom lip trembled, and tears sprouted.

"Don't cry, sweetie, it's just a scary old made-up story," Reen assured Lilly, drawing the girl into a hug. "It never happened." Patting Lilly's head, she glanced at Drake and rolled her eyes. Although brainy as hell, sometimes the facts and figures professor could be a real dope when it came to suitable dialogue with children.

Reen would never forget the conversation one evening when she and Laila ran into Drake and his kids at Larker's Fish and Seafood for Thursday night fish and chips. They sat at a communal table where the kids were watching a funny Dracula cartoon on the large flat-screen TV. When Lilly and Kevin debated each other about whether or not Dracula was real, Drake helpfully supplied historical details about the grisly, gory deeds of Vlad the Impaler.

The complimentary-for-kids dessert of vanilla ice cream with thick, red strawberry sauce went untouched. Reen imagined there were plenty of nightmares that night.

Taking in Reen's comforting words to Lilly now, after his daughter's reaction to his tidbit of opera enlightenment, Drake looked unsettled. "Too much information again?"

"Mmm-hmm. Don't forget, Lilly thinks what happened to Sleeping Beauty is traumatic, Drake." The poor guy was so clueless and apologetic Reen had to keep herself from laughing.

"Sorry, Lilly," he told his daughter. "Sometimes Daddy gets a little carried away."

"I know." Lilly sighed, patting her father with patient understanding that belied her years. "It's okay, Daddy. I'm used to it." She fingered the yellow braids on Reen's hat. "I really like your hat, Miss Reen. Could you make one for me? I could pay you from my allowance."

"It's not polite to ask, Lilly," Drake chastised.

"I'd be happy to Lilly," Reen told her. "And it would be my gift to you for Valentine's Day, How about that?"

Her face lit up with excitement, then she turned to Drake. "Is it okay, Daddy?"

"As if you're not busy enough already," he muttered to Reen before giving a shrug. "Yes, okay, but I want you to make sure to do some chores for Miss Reen in exchange for her generosity."

"I will. I promise. I can take care of her and make her hot cocoa after school when she comes home from the doctor."

"That sounds fair to me," Reen said with a smile. "Do you like to draw, Lilly?" The girl nodded. "Good, then I want you to draw a picture of the hat you'd like me to create for you and I'll try to make one just like it."

Lilly's grin was ear to ear. "You could do that?" Reen offered a confirming nod. "Yay!" Lilly clapped. "Thank you, Miss Reen." She bent to give her a hug.

Drake glanced at the gold watch on his wrist. Rather than relying on his phone for time checks, he'd worn his dad's prized retirement watch since his father died the year before. With Drake being somewhat old school, it was fitting.

"We still have time to get you kids to school before you're late."

"I don't want to leave Miss Reen," Lilly said. "I want to go to the doctor too."

"You don't have to worry, honey, I'll be fine. After the doctor gives me a quick checkup I'll deliver the hats and then maybe I'll call Laila to tell her I need to take the afternoon off at the bakery. Then I'll just plop in front of the TV and relax until it's time to go to bed."

"You're not delivering any hats today," Drake informed her, gathering the boxes into a neat stack.

"Yes I am. I'm volunteering at the children's hospital this morning and bringing the hats. The kids are expecting me, Drake. I'm not going to disappoint them. You know what a letdown it can be right after the holidays and I thought the cute hats would brighten their—"

"Sorry, there's no way you're volunteering, making hat deliveries, or doing anything else today, Reen. The hats are going back inside your house. You can deliver them when you're better. In fact, I'll help you deliver them...but not today Ms. Brunhilde." He tugged on one of her yarn braids, making the hat sit crooked on Reen's head.

After righting her hat, she gestured toward the strewn boxes. "But—"

"But nothing," Drake insisted. "I think we'll leave this here," he told her, plucking the Viking cap from her head."

"Hey! I need that," Reen protested, unsuccessfully reaching for her hat. "I probably have hat hair now. My hair's a mess." She finger-combed it.

"Well I guess that means your messy hair will match the rest of you this morning, Ms. Malone," Drake kidded. Picking up the boxes, he opened Reen's front door and Hazelnut followed him inside. "The only activity you'll have today is me driving you to the hospital."

"Oh my gosh...I can't drive." The realization hadn't really hit Reen until that moment. Craning her neck to look up at him, she said, "I feel terrible imposing on you like this, Drake. You have an early morning class today, don't you?"

"It's no imposition, besides," he called from the living room where he set down the boxes, "I'm sure my students won't miss their crusty old professor. I'll call and have a sub cover for me." Before Reen knew what was happening, Drake was outside again, scooping her up into his arms.

She uttered an audible gasp. "Oh my God, Drake, what are you doing?"

Giving her a curious look, he laughed. "Well, definitely not the tango."

"I'm too heavy for you to carry. You'll hurt your back."

He offered a probing look that had her squirming. "Maybe you're right. I can just drop you in the mud and drag you along the icy sidewalk by your hair. Would that make you feel more comfortable?"

Caught off guard, she didn't know if she should laugh or hit him. "No, this is fine. Thank you."

"That's better." A self-satisfied smile turned up the corners of his mouth.

A hopeless romantic, Maureen Malone had been waiting her entire life for a handsome man to gather her up into his arms, gazing lovingly—or she'd take lustfully—into her hazel eyes before whisking her off for a romantic rendezvous. Lord knows she'd daydreamed about it often enough. In those scenarios she was often Lois Lane and the man was Superman.

With his dark, wavy hair and black, horn rimmed glasses—which he alternated with contacts—Drake Slattery could easily pass for Clark Kent...maybe even Superman. But it didn't matter. They were nothing more than good friends. Besides, Reen had never imagined the long-awaited romantic scene with Lois Lane having messy hat-hair, or blood-spattered legs peeking through a torn hospital volunteer uniform—or nursing an aching ankle and butt as Superman transported her to his Fortress of Solitude for a romance-saturated rendezvous.

Her ears perked. Did she just hear Drake grunt?

It made her self-conscious as hell. In her fantasies, she was effortlessly thin and beautiful. While she'd never be truly slender, not with her penchant for chocolate, at least she *usually* managed to stay within the normal weight spectrum.

Or at least she thought so until she heard that grunt.

"Jeez, Maureen, look at you. You're a real mess."

Reen sighed at his decidedly un-Superman-ish statement.

"You say something?" Drake asked with a somewhat pained expression.

"No, no...just sighing a little about the pain."

"Don't worry, we'll get you fixed up soon."

~<>~

After dropping Lilly and Kevin at school for their first grade class, Drake drove Reen to the hospital where, under her blatantly ignored protests, he carried her into the emergency room.

A thorough checkup and series of x-rays verified her injuries. She couldn't believe it. She'd gone thirty-some years without breaking any bones and now, with one abrupt slip on the ice, she'd managed to break both her left ankle and her tailbone. And, holy mackerel, it hurt like hell.

"Why am I not surprised?" Drake said, eyeing the cast on her leg as Reen struggled to find a semi-comfortable position.

Her head cocked. "You mean that it's broken?"

"Nope, I figured it was. I mean that your cast is purple."

"Oh that." Her fingers smoothed along the nearly knee-high cast. "They gave me a choice."

"And purple's your favorite color," he stated rather than asked. He'd probably heard her say it a thousand times.

"It's much more chic and less boring than white, don't you think?" She lifted her leg a few inches off the hospital gurney, showing off her stylish cast. "A white one would get gray and dirty-looking over time. Purple makes me feel cheerful, and I'll feel even better after I get one of my sisters to paint my toenails to match." She beamed a smile at him.

"Purple toenails?" His lip curling in distaste, Drake looked uncertain.

"Lighter." She studied her toes. "Just the right shade of lavender."

"The doc said you can go home as soon as they bring you the donut pillow...you know, for your *broken butt.*" A big old grin split his face as he emphasized those words.

Her eyebrows knitting, Reen mirrored his earlier question. "Why am I not surprised?"

"You mean about you having to use a donut pillow for your *broken butt*?"

"No, that you wouldn't be able to resist overusing that particular term once you learned I'd fractured my cossack." She folded her arms across her chest, wincing as the slight movement jostled her enough to make her bottom ache even worse.

"You mean coccyx," Drake corrected. "Which is your tailbone." He gave a mischievous smile. "Which, in layman's terms, means you broke your butt."

"Whatever, Professor Know-it-all." She gave a dismissive wave. "You know, if you acted this un-professor-ish at the university they'd have you disbarred. Speaking of the university, why don't you go? You don't have to stay here and babysit me." Elevating her chin, she looked away.

"Attorneys are disbarred. Professors are fired or can have their tenure stripped but they can't be disbarred. And I'm not leaving you here all by yourself, Maureen. I already told you, they've got an assistant subbing for me so—"

Engaging in a dramatic faux yawn, Reen made a chattering motion with her fingers. "Blah, blah, blah..." After rolling her eyes, she looked up at Drake, immediately regretting her uncommonly cranky attitude when she saw his taken aback expression. The man had gone out of his way to help her this morning, bringing her to the hospital and staying with her through the long battery of tests. She should be thanking him instead of grousing at him.

"I'm sorry, Drake. You didn't deserve that. I'm just," her hands flew up, "I don't know...out of sorts and cranky for some reason." Involved in her apology and forgetting to watch the way she sat, Reen put too much pressure on her tailbone, and the punch of pain had her feeling dizzy again.

Wrapping an arm around her back and shoulders, Drake smiled. "The reason you're giving a stellar Ms. Cranky-Butt performance is because you're in a lot of pain. I can see it etched all across your face." His fingers traced from her temple to her jaw. "As soon as that injection the nurse gave you takes effect you'll feel a lot better."

"Thanks." She leaned her head against his arm. "And thanks for staying with me. Thanks especially for calling Laila back and convincing her she doesn't have to worry about me. The last thing I want is my mom and sisters dropping everything to rush over here and baby me." Treated to a duo throbbing effect at both points of injury, Reen moaned. "You know, I had no idea broken bones could hurt so much."

"The doctor said a fractured coccyx is one of the most painful breaks, and it takes a long time to heal. You're dealing not only with a broken tailbone but a broken ankle too, Reen. Plus the older we get, the tougher it is to deal with fractures. At your advanced age it's no wonder you're feeling a tad on the grouchy side." He winked at her and Reen laughed out loud.

"Oh, Drake, you do know how to make me feel better...or maybe the shot's starting to work. I'm feeling kind of nice and..." she closed her eyes and sighed, "floaty."

"Probably the meds since I doubt I have a floaty effect on you." The deep sound of his laughter was rich and masculine.

Studying his chiseled Clark Kent features, Reen smiled up at him. Little did Professor Slattery know that he was having more of a floaty effect on her than he could imagine. The lusty way he looked at her made her feel like grabbing him into a lip-lock. Maybe breaking a couple of bones wasn't so bad. After all, it gave her Drake's full attention for hours. It had been eons since the two of them spent this much time together alone.

Whoa! Reen blinked. What in the world was she thinking? She and Drake were friends, pals, buddies. Nothing more. The only reason she was having these mushy thoughts about him was because of the drugs they'd given her.

Sure, her mom and sisters were convinced Drake had a thing for her but they didn't understand that a man and a woman could be good platonic friends. Just because they're the opposite sex doesn't mean they have to get all gooey-eyed with each other or hop in the sack together.

Not that the thought had never crossed Reen's mind. But aside from the fact that Drake and her late fiancé were both professors and close friends, he and Reen had little in common, other than a good sense of humor. Drake was a cat person, she was a dog person. The multi-degreed professor was just this side of being a genius while college dropout Reen was more captivated by binging on Netflix comedy shows and rom-coms than being intrigued by the academic documentaries he found so fascinating.

Drake relished doing challenging crossword puzzles. For fun. His favorite games were word or trivia-based. He enjoyed sitting through endless lectures as much as Reen loved digging through other people's junk at garage sales.

Then there was Reen's unfortunate habit of tangling words or common idioms, and forgetting to think before she spoke, which frequently resulted in something dopey popping out of her mouth...like blurting out *cossack* when she knew damn well the word was coccyx. It was frustrating because, while she might not be the brainiest girl on the block, she certainly wasn't an idiot...even if she gave a good impression of a birdbrain when flustered.

"Anything I can do to help make you more comfortable?" Drake asked. "Hungry? You haven't had anything to eat. I can get you something from the cafeteria. Something...chocolate?" His eyebrows jiggled playfully. "You've always said that's the best medicine."

Normally it was but, as shocking as it was to Reen, she had no desire for chocolate. All she wanted was her good buddy Drake, her tall, dark and handsome pal, there at her side, looking at her the way he was now, all caring and concerned...as if she was the most important woman in the world to him.

Catching the melodious sigh about to escape her lips, she shook her head, trying to clear the ridiculous drug-induced thoughts. No, the man who made her heart do flipflops, Reen reminded herself, wasn't Drake, it was Hudson Griffin, Glassfloat Bay's resident contractor and handyman. How could she possibly forget that? She was crazy about Hud. Adored him.

She frowned. Stupid drugs were addling her brain.

"Something wrong?"

"Hmm?" She blinked a couple times. "Oh...no, I'm fine. Everything's hunky-dorky. Thanks." She caught Drake trying to conceal a chuckle. "What's so funny?"

"You said hunky-dorky instead of hunky-dory, that's all. The medication must be blurring your thoughts."

Startled that she'd said that aloud, Reen sucked in a breath. "Oops, you're probably right. Slip of the tongue." She gave him a casual smile. *Hunky-dory* was a phrase her mother often used. With Drake in mind, Reen had altered the saying to *hunky-dorky* because it so perfectly described the tall, dark and handsome bookworm. Trouble was, no one else was supposed to hear her private coined phrase.

"Oddly enough," Reen continued, "I'm not hungry for chocolate, or anything else. But go ahead and get something for yourself."

Sitting on the chair beside her, Drake took her hand and squeezed it. "Naw, I'm good."

Yes indeed...every woman should have a hunky-dorky pal like Professor Drake Slattery.

Drake's phone rang. Looking up from the display he said, "Sorry, Reen, I've got to take this."

She thought her ears were playing tricks on her when she heard him say *Saffron* into the phone. She couldn't imagine why her snooty Realtor cousin was calling Drake.

As he strode out of the room she caught herself thinking he had a great looking butt.

Squeezing her eyes closed, Reen was determined to deflate her pain-killer-induced bubble of Drake-related fantasies.

And So, Dear Reader,

You've finished reading The Firefighter's Heartwish, a Daisy Dexter Dobbs book that (*fingers crossed and hopeful sigh*) you were sorry to see end. Meanwhile I, author DDD, am gleefully clacking away at my keyboard, writing yet another sensational, utterly phenomenal (*please don't burst my bubble*) book. I'd like to conclude our time together with a heartfelt THANK YOU for choosing to read this book, the 3rd in my Heartwishes series.

I especially loved writing the last couple chapters of this book. It brought me such joy to give Gard, Sabrina, and Harry their much-deserved happy ending. I got emotional (I'm talking messy, ugly crying) multiple times while writing the poignant scenes involving child abuse.

Having grown up in a physically and emotionally abusive environment myself (prior to Child Protective Services), writing this tale of love, hope, fear and miracles really touched me. I strived to maintain the right balance of lightness and humor with the heavier topics to keep the story from being too emotionally weighty or melodramatic. Hopefully I succeeded.

I took a lot of breaks from the manuscript when I found myself getting too mired in emotions and memories, reminding myself that my own personal journey, as well as little Harold's, have wonderfully happy endings. Unlike far too many abused children, I survived and thrived, which fills me with abundant gratitude.

On a more upbeat personal note—I'm an artist and craftsperson as well as a writer. I had fun telling about Sabrina's reverse glass painting since it's a technique unfamiliar to many. I've been doing it for years, selling my creations (mostly decorative glass jars of all sizes) at juried art fairs.

~<>~

If you enjoyed The Firefighter's Heartwish I'd be delighted if you left a positive review or rating on the site where you purchased it. (Not that I check daily for new reviews, or ever Google myself, or do anything else indicating I'm an insecure creative person craving validation. Nope, nothing like that.) Your review can be long, short, or just a star rating. Reviews help other readers find my books, and keep my stories from getting lost in a site's complicated algorithms. Plus, it gives me encouragement to keep on writing!

Speaking of other readers, you can help them find this book by recommending it to your friends, neighbors, relatives, coworkers, your dentist, doctor, mail carrier, all the strangers you meet in the grocery store, at the mall, the neighborhood pub, your favorite coffee shop, and, of course, everyone you know online. (I'm ready with additional suggestions if needed.)

Thanks again! Wishing you love, laughter, romance and happy reading!

—*Daisy Dexter Dobbs*

~<>~

DAISY DEXTER DOBBS BOOK LIST

Bold, opinionated Greek men, the Drakos brothers star in this hot, hot, HOT laugh out loud romantic comedy series featuring lots of hunky, delicious Greek men and the women who capture their alpha male hearts. (Can be read as standalones but better appreciated when read in order so you can get to know all the characters.)

Trained by the Greek (Book 1: Jordan and Riley)
Vexed by the Greek (Book 2: Dino and Sophie)
Bossed by the Greek (Book 3: Sebastian and Ardine)
Conned by the Greek (Book 4: Benedict and Angel)
(additional stories for more brothers coming)

~<>~

STANDALONES
Don't Even Think About It (Mindy and Archer)
Laugh-out-loud Romantic Comedy (spice level: scorching-hot and hilarious)
Avowed chocoholic Mindy handles her upside-down life with as much grace and aplomb as possible—by attempting chocolatcide. This steamy, spicy, laugh-out-loud, award-winning romantic comedy novel is brimming with love, snappy banter, sexy inventive scenes that sizzle, and numerous naughty words.

~<>~

MORE SERIES AND STANDALONES COMING SOON FROM DAISY
Daisy has written close to 100 novels and numerous novellas and short stories over the last few decades. She certainly can't have novels full of pay phones, answering machines, landlines, no email, or the internet, or social media now, can she? Nope, nope, nope. Of course not. So now that she has the rights back to all of her books and stories from her previous publishers, she's been hard at work

rewriting and updating her books for release as an indie author. Revisiting umpteen stories featuring gorgeous, handsome, oh-so-sexy hunks is a tough job, but somebody's gotta do it. So here's a sneak peek at just some of the dozens of titles Daisy's been maniacally, um, I mean, *diligently*, working on (check her website and newsletter for updates!).

~<>~

Visit DaisyDexterDobbs.com[1] for a full, up-to-date listing of Daisy's books. Sign up for Daisy's newsletter and mailing list to get notifications for new book releases, contests, and more.

~<>~

---

1. https://www.daisydexterdobbs.com

About the Author

A born storyteller, Daisy Dexter Dobbs started writing stories at five, satisfying her inner ham by reading them aloud, using a toilet plunger as a microphone. Today, Daisy creates written voyages of the imagination, infused with love, laugh-out-loud comedy, friendships, family and guaranteed happy endings. Some of her books include paranormal and fantasy elements. And some books are scorching HOT on the spice scale.

Having worked at more than 40 different jobs provides Daisy with a ridiculous amount of questionable experience to draw on for her characters. She's been: a ghostwriter for politicians; a library art director; a weight loss counselor; mayor's executive secretary; a Realtor; travel agent; editor; and a butcher's meat wrapper, quitting after she spotted a big eyeball coming toward her on the conveyor.

A Chicago native, Daisy and her husband, now live in the Pacific Northwest. Happily, Daisy no longer feels the need to use a bathroom plunger as a microphone when entertaining.

You can find Daisy here:

Facebook: DaisyDexterDobbs

Instagram: DaisyDexterDobbs

TikTok: @daisydexterdobbs

Amazon: Daisy Dexter Dobbs

Goodreads: daisydexterdobbs

BookBub: Daisy-Dexter-Dobbs

Twitter/X: DaisyDDobbs

Threads: @DaisyDexterDobbs

Pinterest: DaisyDDobbs

Email: DaisyDexterDobbs@gmail.com

Read more at www.DaisyDexterDobbs.com.